The MASTER'S BRIDE

"Perhaps the memory of your tight little bottom in those boy's trousers is more than I can resist."

"Let me go." Her voice was a hoarse whisper.

He smiled slowly, his gaze lazy with speculation. "You've wondered, too, haven't you, Connie? What it would feel like to have you naked beneath me. Hell, it's a wonder we haven't both gone up in flames before now."

"You're wrong. Imagining things. I feel nothing but loathing for you, Lock McKin. And you— you're so caught up in vengeance and hate you've forgotten how to feel."

He glared at her, his blue eyes hot and dangerous. "I feel plenty."

Dragging her into his arms, he caught her small panicky cry with his mouth and consumed it voraciously, devouring her resistance in a sense-stealing kiss . . .

"A fast-paced read that blends all the right ingredients—revenge, deception, and a sizzling passion"

Sandra Canfield, author of *The Loving*

If You've Enjoyed This Book,
Be Sure to Read These Other
AVON ROMANTIC TREASURES

FIRE AT MIDNIGHT *by Barbara Dawson Smith*
MIDNIGHT AND MAGNOLIAS *by Rebecca Paisley*
MY WILD ROSE *by Deborah Camp*
ONLY BY YOUR TOUCH *by Stella Cameron*
ONLY WITH YOUR LOVE *by Lisa Kleypas*

Coming Soon

A ROSE AT MIDNIGHT *by Anne Stuart*

The MASTER'S BRIDE

SUZANNAH DAVIS

An Avon Romantic Treasure

AVON BOOKS ◆ NEW YORK

THE MASTER'S BRIDE is an original publication of Avon Books. This work has never before appeared in book form. This work is a novel. Any similarity to actual persons or events is purely coincidental.

AVON BOOKS
A division of
The Hearst Corporation
1350 Avenue of the Americas
New York, New York 10019

Copyright © 1993 by Suzannah Davis
Inside cover author photograph by Terry Atwood
Published by arrangement with the author
Library of Congress Catalog Card Number: 92-90429
ISBN: 0-380-76821-6

First Avon Books Printing: January 1993

AVON TRADEMARK REG. U.S. PAT. OFF. AND IN OTHER COUNTRIES, MARCA REGISTRADA, HECHO EN U.S.A.

Printed in the U.S.A.

RA   10 9 8 7 6 5 4 3 2 1

To the Gang of Four
on the Tenth Anniversary of
an Evening with Friends

Chapter 1

Boston, 1850

The door of the Mermaid Tavern burst open in a rush of snow-laden January gale. A man paused on the threshold, his tall frame filling the opening from lintel to casement. Spar-straight and solid, feet planted wide from years spent on a rolling deck, he ignored the flakes icing the pea coat stretched over his broad shoulders, unaffected by the frigid blast. His Arctic-blue eyes raked the motley seagoing crowd. One by one, the teak-skinned sailors, shipyard laborers, and burly stevedores quaffing dark Jamaican rum and tucking into the Mermaid's excellent fare fell silent.

"He's come, then?" Lauchlan "Lock" McKin's voice rumbled from deep within his massive chest.

"Aye." The grizzled proprietor jerked his chin toward the private dining room at the rear. "In there."

With a curt nod of his dark head, Lock kicked shut the heavy oak door and strode impatiently through the tavern. Eyes followed his broad back, some curious, some envious, some downright hostile. Fully two-thirds of the tavern's occupants were "up for California," crews headed around the Horn with a load of gold-mad passengers, shipwrights building ships for the lucrative San Francisco trade, landlubbers eager to try their own luck at finding El Dorado. Everyone on the waterfront knew Lauchlan McKin. Iron Man McKin, they called him. A square-dealer, it was said, but not a man to cross on a whim. A loner whose business was no man's but his own.

The buzz of speculation resumed as Lock passed, but he schooled his expression to give nothing away. After all, a man didn't grow up under a cloud of disgrace without developing a thick hide, and everyone would know soon enough the rewards he intended to reap out of this profitable frenzy.

Only the scrape and clatter of cutlery broke the contrasting quiet of the private dining chamber. The peculiar watery light of a snowy afternoon fell through the thick, wavy glass of a mullioned window, illuminating a pair of figures bent over a meal, one slight and boyish in a cap and baggy sweater, the other bewhiskered, honed, and mahogany-hard from a lifetime at sea. The latter rose from the littered table at Lock's entrance, and the two men shook hands.

"Welcome, Captain Jenkins. Praise God the *Eliza's* safely home again under your capable hands." Lock had to raise his voice to be heard over the sound of enthusiastic slurping coming from the slight figure hunkered over a bowl of clam chowder. With a certain dubious amazement, Lock eyed the assortment of empty plates, platters, and tankards strewn across the table's scarred and age-blackened surface.

"Your ship is a grand sailor, sir." Jenkins's even reply recaptured Lock's attention. "Her holds are full of whalebone and oil straight from the fleets at Lahaina Harbor in the Sandwich Islands. You stand to make a tidy sum."

Lock smiled briefly. "Aye, the State Street merchants will be cursing their shortsightedness for months to come."

With another wry glance for the lad devouring his dinner with all the thoroughness of a plague of locusts, Lock decided with grim humor that his own favorite dish was the one best served cold—revenge. It was even tastier when you beat your enemy at his own game. Lock pictured old Alexander Latham, merchant prince and a scion of Boston society, gnashing his teeth when he learned a portion of this whaling season's profits had been snatched from under his long, greedy nose. It was an especially gratifying image considering the ancient rivalry and bitter history between the McKins and the Lathams. Neither family had come away unscathed. The McKins had buried a father, and old Latham's only son had disappeared in the Pacific under circumstances so mysterious that the twenty-five-thousand-dollar reward Latham had posted a decade ago for news of his son had never been collected.

"There's more, sir," Jenkins continued eagerly. "News straight from your own brother's lips back in Lahaina. Your *West Wind* made a Pacific run of three hundred fifty miles in a single day! I've even a copy of the log to prove it. I'm blowed if that's not a record, sir!"

Lock's tension unwound another notch, but he held tightly to his jubilation, only nodding. "Well done, Captain. Good news *and* a full cargo. An owner couldn't ask more."

Captain Jenkins dipped his head in suitable modesty at the praise. "Your *West Wind* earned her fame the moment we passed Boston Light. It's not every naval architect can boast so fleet a craft."

"In truth, the world is speed-mad, but Dylan must bring the *West Wind* home from her China tea run in good time before the skeptics will accept my innovations. I'm still considered something of an upstart in South Boston," Lock admitted as he un-buttoned his now-steaming coat.

It had taken a lot of heartache, backbreaking work, and not a small amount of risk to make the McKin Brothers Shipyard a reality. Even though they'd come far, clawing their way up from the near-bottomless hole their father's death and the Latham vultures had left them in, all their capital was tied up in the current venture, and disaster still lurked around every corner. Yet Dylan's record run aboard the *West Wind* validated every chance Lock had taken, every vision he'd believed in. And good news could make a tremendous difference in the willingness of bankers and ship-hungry merchants to take a chance on a young shipbuilder.

"Publish Dylan's log," Jenkins advised, "and I daresay investors will clamor for you to build them sharp-bowed ships, too."

The lad at the table loosed a resounding belch and Lock grimaced in growing irritation. Notwith-standing the little glutton's abominable manners, Lock hoped Jenkins's prophecy was a true one.

"My *Odyssey* should come off the stocks soon, and I'll need an experienced captain for the Califor-nia run," Lock said, gesturing at the lad, who was now noisily gnawing at a huge hunk of crusty bread. "I regret I've interrupted your first meal on dry land in five months, but perhaps a new com-mand may redeem my discourtesy."

Captain Jenkins's brows scaled his forehead in surprise. "You won't make the maiden voyage yourself?"

Lock shook his head. "I paid my dues in the years I spent at sea in the Canton trade. Though the experience serves me well, it's the building of ships that commands my attention now. Besides, Dylan has the mettle to squeeze the most speed out of a crack vessel. I'll wager he shattered a spar or two during that run."

"Aye, he must have been sailing some," Jenkins agreed with a Down Easter's talent for understatement. "Might we discuss particulars later? I still have duties ..."

Lock nodded. "Of course. Another day for business, then."

"Agreed. There's only one more thing," Jenkins said as he reached for his jacket. "The bairn here."

Lock glanced at the lad still bent over a large crockery bowl. His face was shadowed by the brim of his woolen cap, and he spooned the last of his chowder into his mouth at an amazing rate. With a half-smile, Lock gestured at the debris.

"From the evidence, one might accuse you of keeping your ship's boy on short rations, Captain Jenkins."

"My—?" Jenkins frowned, then shot a glance at his companion. "You'll pardon me, sir, but you're mistaken. I took on this passenger at Lahaina at your brother's behest, with express orders to deliver him to you personally."

"Dylan sent him?" Alarm rang in Lock's head. His younger brother had a notorious sense of humor, and Lock had learned long ago to be wary of his mischief.

"Yes, sir." Jenkins poked the boy's sweater-clad arm. "Take a breather, Con. This is Mr. McKin."

The spoon paused in midair, and the cap tilted upward an inch or so, revealing a fringe of dark hair, a grubby cheek, and a milky mustache. The lad's brief inspection rode from the thick waves of ebony hair spilling onto Lock's brow, across his woolen shirt, all the way down to the arch of his heavy workman's brogues.

"Ain't much like your brother, are you?" The spoon resumed its journey, the soup apparently of more interest than the man.

"Here, now, mind your manners," Jenkins admonished. He flashed Lock a chagrined look. "Had a bad crossing, I'm afraid. Spent most of his time with his head in a bucket. Oddest thing I ever saw. Never did find his sea legs."

"And you're supposed to deliver him to me?" Lock asked suspiciously.

"Aye, your brother said you'd know what to do with him. That's all I know, sir. Now, if you'll excuse me, I'd better get back to my duties."

"But—" Consternated at being given the responsibility for a youngster in such a sudden fashion, Lock bit back a protest. Lauchlan McKin ran a shipyard employing upward of a hundred men, and if among them his reputation was hard, they also knew the Iron Man was fair. The day he couldn't handle one extra green young'un, even if the lad was one of Dylan's practical jokes, he'd hang it up. "Very well, Captain. I'll see to him."

"Good day to ye, then, sir." Jenkins poked the youth again. "You do whatever Mr. McKin says, you hear?"

Con's grunt of assent satisfied the captain, and he nodded once more to Lock and took his leave.

Lock slid out of his pea coat and seated himself on the trestle bench across from the boy. Neck tucked turtlelike within the folds of his greasy sweater, Con ignored him, noisily scraping the bottom of the bowl with the spoon. Finding not a single chunk of potato or a drop of chowder left, he shoved the bowl aside and looked hopefully over the rest of the table, then reached for a saucer of fruit and pastry. Lock caught the youth's too-slender wrist.

"Hold it, lad. I'll have some answers first."

"Bugger off, mate." Con's voice held a husky timbre as he tried to shake Lock off. "I'm empty as a drunkard's whiskey cask."

"Still? What ails you, boy? The salt horse aboard the *Eliza* wasn't to your liking?"

Con's head jerked up at the gibe, revealing a resentful flash of topaz eyes and the flushed features of an underfed waif. But there was something else, a hint of something familiar, yet out of place, even alien, about that face.

"*You* try eatin' that swill while puking up your guts, and you'll see—"

Frowning, Lock ignored Con's indignant splutter. His brain clicked and whirled, conjuring up visions of a lost time and place. The palaces of Canton, another pair of luminous, almond-shaped eyes and delicate cheekbones, a girl named Soo Ling ... *a girl!*

With an angry swipe of his hand, Lock snatched off Con's hat, freeing a raggedly cut mass of shoulder-length hair the weight and color of a sea otter's coat. Accusation burned like blue fire in his eyes.

"What game is this? You're no lad!"

A pink tongue-tip flicked out, sampling the remnants of the soup lingering on the short upper lip, but Con's wide, faunlike eyes never blinked. "You're sure, are ye, Cap?"

With a growl, Lock surged to his feet, twisting his other hand in the worn sweater and dragging Con up and almost over the table between them. "Sure enough, by God, to know the charge wouldn't be sodomy if we both stripped down and inspected the plumbing!"

Con's dark head barely reached Lock's shoulder, but the shrug of utter nonchalance could have come from a person twice the size. "A bastard aboard the *Eliza* already tried that."

"What?" Lock wheezed.

Con pursed milky lips in an attitude of recollection. "Scoggins walked funny for a time afterward. And he could reach the high notes on all the chanteys, too." Con looked at Lock's shackling hand. "You wouldn't be contemplating a similar change of singing careers, would you, Lock McKin?"

The very audacity of Con's bland words caught Lock so off guard that he began to laugh, a creaky, rusty sound for being so little used, but a laugh, and a hearty one, nonetheless. "By Neptune, you've got more grit than sense, you impudent baggage!"

Lock shoved Con back onto the bench and re-seated himself, shaking his head with amusement. Under her dirt, he realized she lacked the Oriental cast of features evoked by his momentary déjà vu, but he'd sailed the Pacific and seen the honey-skinned peoples enough to know Con carried a touch of Polynesian blood. Since she came from the Sandwich Islands, where visiting sailors had been enjoying the favors of the native girls since Captain Cook's first visit in 1778, Con's heritage was un-doubtedly a patchwork of every sailing nationality. An interesting piece of waterfront flotsam, and as out of place in dour Boston as a nightingale in a bear pit. He threw a napkin at her.

"Wipe your mouth, urchin. And if you dare tell me that you're not a female, I'll turn you over my knee."

"That's what Scoggins tried." Though she was straight-faced, an impish mischief danced behind her gold-brown eyes. She gave her mouth a cursory swipe and reached again for the pie. "Luckily for me, most men haven't the sense to see what's what."

Lock shook his head in disbelief. "You're telling me you made a five-month voyage aboard the *Eliza* and no one had an inkling?"

"The captain knew, I suppose." She shrugged. "It was easier to pretend he didn't."

"My God, he's a family man. If this gets out . . ."

She cut a bite of pastry with the spoon but stared at it instead of lifting it to her mouth. "I was . . . ill. No one bothered with me much, least of all that old sourpuss. Dylan said it would be simpler that way, and he was right."

The mention of his brother's name as the author of this affair made Lock's raven-hued brows lower ominously. "Dylan, eh?"

"Oh, yes, this was all his idea, you know. He said you'd know how to take very good care of me." She took a matter-of-fact bite of pie.

Lock choked. Lord, had Dylan really sent him this undergrown island child to take as mistress? Dylan was constantly after Lock about his solitary lifestyle, but, by God, this was extreme even for Dylan! He didn't understand Lock had already learned the painful dangers of giving one's heart unwarily, especially across opposing cultures. Lock's impossible passion for the daughter of a Chinese nobleman had left scars he had no intention of probing ever again.

Besides, he had no time nor inclination for romantic entanglements, much less a liaison with a golden-skinned *wahine* who'd raise shocked eyebrows among the segment of conservative Boston society with whom he had to do business. No, an occasional visit to an obliging and undemanding widow on Ann Street was all he required. He wanted nothing, especially nothing female, to complicate his quest for success . . . and for vengeance.

Con closed her eyes in near ecstasy over the bite of sweet pastry, tilting her head back to expose a delicate curve of slender throat, and she practically purred with pleasure. Her unselfconscious enjoyment had an innocent sensuality that could fire a man's imagination and make his blood run hot. Was this what Dylan had seen?

Lock shook off the image with a groan of dismay. Lord, she was only a child! And only his wild and reckless younger brother would take such a harebrained notion and then act on it. Well, there would be an accounting with Dylan over this bit of madness, but what the devil was he to do with the chit now?

"How old are you, anyway?" Lock demanded abruptly.

"Twenty." She mumbled the word around another mouthful of pie, her dirty face glorious with delight under the straight, shaggy mop of dark brown hair.

Lock gave her a skeptical look. Beneath the bulky sweater and borrowed seaman's trousers, she was too thin, but he doubted he'd find much evidence of womanly curves to back up such a statement. "If you're twenty, I'll eat a hat for every one of my own thirty-one summers."

Her cap caught him full in the mouth. "Then you'd best start chewing."

With a growl, Lock slapped the cap onto the tabletop, but she laughed at his irritation, merriment that seemed too mirthful for such a small joke. But then, her whole air was euphoric, even frenetic, as if she were a convict celebrating her release from prison. His jaw tightened. Lock refused to be anyone's laughingstock.

"Control yourself, urchin. This is a serious matter."

"You're absolutely right." Sobering, she pointed imperiously with her spoon. "What is this, please?"

"Huh?" Lock glanced at the plate. "Apple pie."

"Apples. Real apples." She nearly crooned the words, the dulcet accent of her island tongue giving them a special melodiousness. "'Tis almost worth being sick, starved, and frozen near to death."

Lock was taken aback by her almost worshipful manner over a plate of pie. "You've never seen apples before?"

"Only in books at the sugar colony's missionary school." She licked the back of her spoon, then gave him a blinding smile that transformed her face.

Good Lord, I take it back, Lock thought, stunned. Beneath the bad haircut and grubby face, she was a beauty. Intelligence and liveliness sparkled in those golden eyes. Despite himself, curiosity flickered, and down deep, a stirring of masculine interest. It was a complication he would rather have done without.

Oblivious of the jolt she'd given Lock, Con continued conversationally. "I've never seen anything like this place, you know. A real city. 'Tis fascinating. Only how you stand this perishing cold . . . no wonder you have to wear so many idiotic clothes." She shivered visibly and bent back over her plate.

Lock made an effort to pull himself together. "Now, look here—er, Con, is it?"

"Constance." She sighed at another mouthful of the cinnamon-laced pie.

"Constance, then. I don't know what Dylan told you, but—" Lock felt his ears start to burn. Damnation! How was a man supposed to be delicate about such a thing? "I don't know what kind of arrangement you and Dylan had, or what he promised, but I'm not in the market for a . . . a . . . oh, hell!"

She looked at him, her head tilted slightly to one side, a tiny, puzzled frown puckering the space between her eyebrows. "A what, Lock McKin?"

A flush surged up Lock's neck. He was blushing! Iron Man McKin, who could stare down a dozen cutthroat sailors with one icy look. Lock McKin, who'd sailed into Shanghai harbor right under the Manchu emperor's cannons with nary a backward glance, was now rendered thick-tongued and awkward by a mere slip of a girl!

"Blast it! I don't need a woman in my bed, especially not some skin-and-bones foundling child Dylan picked up in the middle of nowhere, so—"

Constance's incredulous laughter sliced through his bumbling explanation, but this time her hilarity had a derisive, mocking ring that touched a raw nerve.

Lock scowled. "Damn you, girl, are you daft?"

Chameleonlike, Constance drew herself up with

icy hauteur, sloughing off her wharf-rat manner to reply with the precise, dignified diction of a princess royal. "I beg your pardon. Are you accusing your own brother of being a panderer? A dealer in human flesh?"

"Well, no. That is—" Lock tugged the ebony curls at his nape in frustration. "Well, how else did you get here?"

Constance's spoon whizzed past Lock's ear. He ducked, only to be half buried under the avalanche of dirty dishes she shoved into his lap. She was halfway across the room before he even realized she'd moved. Scrambling madly from under the sticky pile, heedless of the crockery smashing to the floor, he flung himself after her and caught her at the door.

"Unhand me, you great, perishing lout!" She spit at him like an enraged kitten, raining a hail of ineffectual blows against his massive chest. "You imbecile! Dunderhead! I'll have you know I paid my own way!"

"I'll just bet you did." Lock grunted with the effort it took to control her puny onslaught without hurting her. Caught in the snare of his brawny arms, she weighed no more than a sandpiper, and beneath his thumbs her wrist bones felt so slender he was afraid he would snap them in two if he weren't careful.

"Idiot!" Her husky voice was scathing. "I paid him with a painting of the *West Wind*! I'm an artist—or at least I will be when I get to Paris."

Thunderstruck, Lock repeated the ludicrous word. "Paris?"

"Of course. All real artists take their final training at the École des Beaux Arts, and I intend to be there by spring." She shook off his constraining hands and looked down her grubby nose at him. "This backwater is only a stopping-off point for me."

Lock snorted. "You mean it's as far as you could

get with your chicanery. I'll wager you haven't got two dimes to rub together, much less the means to buy a packet ticket to Europe."

"I've come this far," she said grimly, suppressing a shudder of—fear? Revulsion? Lock couldn't tell. Gathering herself together, she glared up at him, her strange golden eyes glittering with fury and determination. "I'll make it somehow. And certainly not by selling my virtue to an overgrown baboon with an inflated opinion of himself!"

"Now wait just a damn minute, Miss High-and-Mighty! You may think you can get away with that haughty princess act, but—"

"No, *you* wait, Lock McKin!" Shaking her sable-colored hair out of her eyes, she punched him in the chest with her forefinger. "You may look like St. Michael the Archangel himself, but you've got the devil in you to even suggest such a thing about your own sweet brother."

"Dylan, sweet? That's a laugh!"

"He's the only true gentleman I've ever known. *He* never assumed I earned my living on my back." She poked Lock again. "Share your bed? Ha! You could be dipped in gold dust and you wouldn't interest me!"

Ruddy color spread up Lock's thick neck. "Well, I certainly have no desire to be saddled with a scrawny cat like you."

"That's a relief! So don't you make the same mistake—" She raised her hand for the third time.

He clamped his fist over hers. "Do that again and I'll break it off," he promised. "And my only mistake was thinking you might be a sane, reasonable person in need of a helping hand."

She blinked, hesitating, her dark lashes fanning her cheeks uncertainly. "I can be reasonable."

"Then don't go off half-cocked about Dylan's motives, because nobody can guess them—most of the time not even my lamebrained brother himself.

Since it's clear you don't want my—er, protection, and I'm not interested in taking on a paramour, then we ought to be able to come to some kind of agreement about this situation."

"Of course." She sniffed with haughty dignity. "That's the idea."

"All right, then." Lock released her hand and blew out an exasperated breath. "The first thing to consider is what I'm going to do with you now."

She squared her chin stubbornly. "I can take care of myself."

Lock gave her a disgusted look that took in her boyish garb and dirty face. "Like hell, princess. God knows I'm accustomed to cleaning up Dylan's messes. Whatever he had in mind this time, I won't be responsible for you ending up in some waterfront bawdy house. There's a mission church in Brookline that takes in wayward girls. I'm sure the pastor and his wife would—"

"No!" Constance's cheeks went as pale as the snow drifting outside the window.

Alarmed, Lock caught her arm and eased her down on the trestle bench. "What is it? Your gluttony caught up with you, is that it? Any dimwit knows you can't fill your stomach to that extent without expecting a revolt, but I swear, if you upchuck apple pie on me, I'll—"

"I'm fine." The deep breath she sucked in seemed to fortify her, and she stilled a final convulsive shudder by sheer will. "The only thing I've had a bellyful of is godly folk. No preachy types for me, Lock McKin."

"But we've got to find somewhere for you to stay. I only have rooms over my offices, and I haven't got time to humor your childishness. For God's sake, Constance—"

"Stop yammering at me!" Sinking both of her hands into her hair, she took another deep draught of air to steady herself. "I don't need a handout from a bunch of Bible-thumpers! Dylan said you'd help me find my grandfather."

"You have family here? Hell's bells! Why didn't you say so?" A profound relief flooded Lock, and he smiled broadly. Freeing himself of this unexpected, sassy-mouthed encumbrance was going to be easier than he'd hoped. "What's his name?"

Constance looked at him with guileless innocence. "Latham. Alexander Latham."

"Good God." Lock stared at her as if he'd been poleaxed.

"You know him?"

Lock gritted his teeth to stem a flood of curses. "I know that no typhoon ever stirred up as much trouble as my *sweet* brother." At her perplexed look, his expression grew even grimmer. "Dylan's played a gigantic joke on both of us, princess. I only hope you're ready to run before the storm."

"Great Pele's matchbox! Is this a palace?"

Mouth hanging open, Constance rotated in place on the black-and-white marble tiles checkerboarding the foyer of Latham House. Gas chandeliers illuminated gilt moldings, and antique tapestries decorated the paneled walls. A graceful sweep of staircase rose from the left to a wide second-floor landing flanked by a pair of tall arched windows. Turkey red velvet draperies trimmed with fat gold tassels hid the frigid January darkness that had fallen during the short coach ride from the rough-and-tumble Mermaid Tavern to this luxurious Beacon Street address.

Constance's amazed perusal of her surroundings finally returned to the man beside her, only to find Lock McKin's glowering expression fully as intimidating as the magnificent hall. She suppressed a shiver at a peculiar, smoky feeling in the pit of her stomach, at once unsettled and exhilarated. Though his jaw was taut with annoyance, strength radiated from him in warm, seductive waves, and her fingers tingled with the memory of how his muscular chest had felt beneath her touch . . .

With an effort, Constance drew her tumbling thoughts up short. While there was no doubt Lock was a handsome man, strong-jawed and whipcord-lean, with thick, coal-black curls any woman would covet, it would be madness to think the churning in her middle was anything more than nerves responding to her present precarious situation. And though Lock's mouth was firm and well shaped, so inviting it made her breath quicken with the urge to run her finger over the chiseled outline, Constance could never imagine a man of such tautly held control allowing such a liberty, much less inviting it. He had the determined chin of a man of action, with no softness to humor a woman's affections. Still, there was something oddly dissatisfied in the turbulent blue of his eyes that touched her on a level she had yet to understand, as if somehow the soul of a Scottish poet had been mistakenly placed within his solid American frame. She supposed even a man of such iron strength could have his own private torments and might occasionally welcome a comforting hand or the release of shared laughter.

Staring into Lock's scowling countenance now, Constance instantly dismissed that fancy, for his forbidding manner dared anyone to approach him, much less take him anything less than seriously. But the devil for trouble inside Constance could never resist a challenge. She straightened the borrowed slicker she'd thrown over her sweater and baggy trousers, and shot her companion another considering look from under her lashes. Despite her own nervousness, a streak of perversity insisted she poke a metaphorical stick at the sleeping tiger.

"What a bleedin' fairy land!" Her cocky grin covered the thundering of her heart. "'Tis a good thing you made me wash my face, isn't it?"

"Hold your sassy tongue, urchin!" Lock jerked Constance into place at his side and silenced her with a hard look. He turned to the plump, freckled maid in apron and ruffled mob cap who stood gaping at them. "Tell Mr. Latham it's imperative we see him now."

"But, sir!" the girl protested, the lilt of Ireland in her speech. "The old master is with his guests. I couldn't possibly disturb him."

"Just say Lauchlan McKin is waiting."

The maid's gray-green eyes grew round as dollars, and her strawberry ringlets bobbed madly. "Y-yes, sir. Right away, sir. If you'll be so kind as to wait in the library . . ."

"We'll wait here," Lock said flatly.

The maid took one look at his grim visage and didn't argue any further. She disappeared down the corridor in a flurry of white petticoats, and Constance looked at Lock with new respect. "You must be a powerful man indeed to make so fine a lady jump like that."

Lock frowned, then saw that she was serious. "She's a servant. She's paid to jump."

"Oh." Constance chewed her thumbnail as a tide of rosy embarrassment rolled across her cheekbones, and she hugged her small canvas bag of castoff belongings closer.

How had she ever thought she might carry this off? she wondered. Another glance at the opulence of her surroundings was enough to undermine her confidence completely. Groaning inwardly, she wondered how she'd ever been convinced by Dylan's easy assurances. But then, she'd been desperate and hurting, and *any* haven was worth a chance, even one half a world away across miles of endless, terrifying ocean. She'd paid a heavy price to leave behind a different kind of horror, and until today, when at long last she'd set her feet on dry land again, she'd thought only of escape, never of whom or what she'd find at the end of this journey.

"Do you think he'll come?" she asked in a small voice.

"Latham?" Lock's lips curved into a humorless smile. "He won't be able to restrain himself. Although it'll do your cause no good to be seen in my company, I assure you."

"You won't leave?" she asked in alarm, catching his coat sleeve. However baffled her feelings, however confused her emotions, she was drawn to this stern man with the fierce dark countenance of an archangel, and the thought of losing the only familiar thing in her life at the moment terrified her. "Please?"

Lock stared at her slender fingers, and a muscle in his jaw twitched. "You've a lot to learn, Constance. The first thing is that Lathams don't come to McKins for help."

"Then I've already broken the rule by asking, haven't I?" she rejoined with a trace of defiance. She'd been running against the wind all her life, flaunting rules, bucking authority. It appeared nothing had changed except her location, but she'd come too far to turn back now. She met Lock's blue eyes steadily. "And you and Dylan have broken it by helping me."

"Whether or not you'll thank us for that help remains to be seen."

Bewildered, she shook her head. "I—I don't understand."

"You will."

Constance shivered at his ominous tone and snatched her hand away. "But you must vouch for me."

"I don't know you from Adam's goat, princess." He grimaced and rubbed his nape in distraction, speaking to himself. "Hell, I don't even know why I'm here!"

"But you know I came from Lahaina on one of your own ships. And you know Dylan arranged it. You can say that much."

"Why should I?"

"Because it's only fair."

He was silent for a long moment, his gaze intent on her hopeful, and now well-scrubbed, face. Removing a layer of dirt had revealed a straight nose, a surprisingly lush mouth, and honey-kissed skin blushed with the delicate pink of a seashell. Abruptly, Lock looked away.

"I won't let a Latham say I wasn't fair."

Instinctively, Constance knew better than to thank him. She was jittery enough without Lock's allusions to the ill feelings that somehow lay between him and her unknown family. Though that was puzzling, she was too anxious and guilty on her own account, and too grateful for Lock McKin's solid presence at her side, to worry about that now. The strident click of heels on marble tiles interrupted her thoughts, and she turned to face a pair of formidable figures in black evening dress striding across the foyer.

"You've a hell of a nerve coming here, Lauchlan McKin," barked the older of the two men. His thick silver whiskers began as extended sideburns and sprouted from under his neck like an Elizabethan ruff, leaving his square chin and thin upper lip bare. "Hell of a nerve!"

His elegant companion was a handsome, clean-shaven man in his early thirties whose blond curls were brushed forward to hide a prematurely thinning pate. He added his own sentiments heatedly. "If you've come here to gloat over that so-called sailing record of yours being bruited about the city—"

"This isn't a social call, gentlemen," Lock interrupted sharply.

"And I don't conduct business in my home." The older man's spiky brows drew together in a foreboding line.

"Wait, Uncle Alex." His nephew's hazel eyes were keen with sudden speculation. "Have you come to talk terms over the *Odyssey*, McKin? Don't think you'll drive up the price with these unsubstantiated rumors of superior speed."

"You're a fool to underestimate me, Rodger," Lock snapped. "I'd hardly give my competition the edge by selling my *Odyssey* to you."

"We hear you're strapped," Rodger said slyly. "Latham and Company's offer is a fair one, especially for a ship still in the stocks. Incentive enough to sell to us."

Lock's smile was thin. "When hell freezes over."

"Then my dinner's growing cold for no reason," Alex said, his wide mouth flat with displeasure. Erect and solid despite an age of better than threescore years, he checked a gold watch strung on a chain across the front of his waistcoat with the air of a man wasting precious time. "You've no more manners than your father had, Lauchlan."

Constance, all but unnoticed, watched with growing horror and fascination as twin spots of color ignited high on Lock's cheekbones. But the explosion she thought inevitable didn't come.

"I'll not bandy insults with you, Mr. Latham," Lock said tightly. "Only one thing would prevail upon me to step foot in this house, and that's to deliver a passenger as contracted. We McKins honor our obligations."

His unspoken insinuation made Rodger bristle. "Just a damn minute!"

Lock caught Constance's arm and hustled her forward. "This lady arrived today on the *Eliza*, and if

I were you, I'd take seriously the task of keeping her in victuals."

"Lady? You must be joking!" Rodger wrinkled his fastidious nose at Constance's grimy sweater and oiled slicker. "Who is this . . . this person?"

Constance flashed him a look of dislike from under the dark fringe of her ragged bangs. "You a Latham, too, are you?"

Rodger regarded her with the same mystified fascination he would have if a chair or a toad or a bootjack had suddenly spoken. "You presumptuous snip! I'm Rodger Latham, though whatever difference it should make to you I'm sure I don't know."

"It makes a body think twice about climbing onto a branch of this family tree, I must say," Constance muttered, and heard what could only have been a stifled snort from the man beside her. When she shot Lock a suspicious glance, however, his face was expressionless.

"Young woman," Alex said, his words clipped and impatient, "if you have something to say, please get on with it. My digestion will not tolerate further delay."

Constance studied him, searching the old man's creased features and sharp brown eyes for something she recognized. "You're Alexander Latham, then?"

"I am."

She took a deep breath. "I'm Constance Lilio Latham. James Latham was my father."

Alex's eyes grew cold and hard as the black marble beneath his heels. "Impossible!"

Constance's chin tilted at an angle to meet the challenge, but her voice was soft and musical with the accent of faraway isles. "Improbable, no doubt, but impossible? No, Grandfather. Though my mother's people once served the fire goddess, Pele, I assure you, Latham blood burns as strongly in me as it does in you."

"No." Alex shook his silver head. Rodger's puzzled expression demonstrated that the exchange had been too swift for him.

"But—" Constance began.

"Silence!" Alex thundered, suddenly livid. He turned his back and glared at Lock. "Why does your father's venom against an old partner spew forth this spiteful falsehood now, McKin? What do you hope to gain? Have your crazed dreams made you so desperate you'd invent this tale to collect the fee I offered for news of my son?"

"Your fancies run away with you," Lock responded angrily. "There would be no honor and less satisfaction in such a paltry ruse. I'll bring you down in my own time and in my own way. Until then, I only deliver a passenger to her final destination. Whether or not she's who she claims is none of my affair."

Alex's voice dripped with acid contempt. "Your father's hatred has truly poisoned you, boy, that you should attempt to harm me in this deplorable fashion. It's taken me over twenty-five years to accept it, but my son is dead."

"That much is true," Constance offered softly. "There was an epidemic of fever the summer I was ten. My father took ill nursing me and died while I was delirious. The pastor of the sugar colony where my father helped spread God's word said not to question the Lord's ways, that the missionary calling is often a hard one—"

"Lies! My son was lost at sea."

Constance shook her head. "He's buried in the mission compound in Lahaina."

"That's something that could be verified," Lock pointed out. "Or are you afraid?"

"Get out!" The whiskers under Alex's prominent jaw quivered with rage. "And take this imposter with you! Rodger, see to it."

"At once, Uncle." Rodger stepped forward to do his uncle's bidding.

"You squabble like babes." Constance stood her ground, her voice tart with disapproval. From the depths of her sweater, she drew a shiny silver oval hanging on a finely braided chain around her neck. "Perhaps this trinket will pacify you."

Alex froze, then grabbed the locket dangling from her fingers. When he spoke, his voice was no longer strong, but raspy with the weight of years of sorrow. "Where did you get this?"

Constance shrugged. "I've always had it. Open it. You'll see there's two pictures—"

"I know what's inside."

"Uncle Alex!" Rodger protested, glancing aghast at Constance, then at Lock, who wore as deep a frown as Rodger's own. "You can't mean—"

"Be silent!" Alex's fingers trembled as he pried open the clasp of the engraved locket, and his breath became labored as he gazed on the two open halves and the miniatures inside.

Constance looked up at the tall old man, searching his lined face again. "You don't look like my father."

"No," Alex murmured, touching one of the miniature faces. "James was the image of his mother. Softhearted like Rachel, too. This was hers. She gave it to James before she died, intending he should pass it on to his wife when he married."

"That is what he did, and when my mother died, it was given to me. I've worn it always." Constance peered into his hands, trying to see the two faces inside the locket, linked to the old man by the strands of the chain and soft words of discovery. "Is the lady within my grandmother, then? I've always wondered."

Alex's eyes widened almost imperceptibly. He cast a furtive look at the two other men watching him, then deliberately snapped the locket shut and dropped it back into place. "No. She's a stranger to me. It doesn't matter now anyway."

"Oh." Disappointed, Constance caught the locket in her fist. It was still warm from Alex's touch.

"Constance." Alex Latham tried the name out, and there was a suspicious glimmer of moisture in his eyes. "James's girl. Look at her. My God."

Suddenly, Constance found herself enfolded in the old man's arms, her cheek pressed against the fine wool of his coat. Her nostrils filled with the aromas of witch hazel, sweet pipe tobacco, and peppermint, and she felt his shoulders shake. It was too much for her, his emotion engulfing her, the hope of true affection too painful to endure, the fear of past despairs revisited by his closeness. She panicked, pulling away almost desperately, and hugged herself to conceal her trembling.

"Uncle Alex!" Rodger blustered. "You can't mean to take this outrageous story seriously?"

"Contain yourself, nephew." Alex waved the protest aside, smiling at Constance, oblivious of her inner distress. "She has James's locket. I'd know it anywhere."

"There could be any number of reasons for that, including that she's a thief!" Rodger's face darkened to an apoplectic shade of red. "This is ludicrous! She's obviously some sort of charlatan in league with McKin to dupe you out of an inheritance."

Lock's eyes narrowed dangerously. "Take heed, Rodger. I'll not stand for slander from you."

Rodger was too agitated to restrain himself. "But just look at her, Uncle! A wretched, filthy guttersnipe with who knows what kind of unsavory past, and . . . and a pagan at that. We all know the tales of these island girls—sluttish, whoring vixens who swim naked out to our ships to beg a sailor's favors."

His strident words pricked so painfully at Constance that she winced. Alex scowled at his nephew.

"Enough, boy."

"You're too canny to be hoodwinked in such a fashion."

"We'll hear her out," Alex said firmly. "Why have you waited all this time to come to us, Constance?"

"I knew nothing about you," she replied. She bit her lip and the pain helped to steady her. "I was very small when my mother died, and only ten when Papa went. If he spoke of you or this place, I have no memory of it, and no one in the missionary school on the sugar plantation where I lived could tell me anything about his people."

"Then how did you come to learn of us at all?" Rodger demanded.

"Dylan McKin."

"I knew it." Rodger's voice was acid with scorn. "Fraud and fabrication, all of it!"

The virulence of his adamancy was like a red flag to a bull for Constance. She straightened her backbone and addressed him in her sweetest tones.

"Not at all, dear Cousin Rodger. When Dylan came to Lahaina, he saw my name on a painting I'd made and asked the questions it took to make a connection. You cannot deny that it was a fine Christian gesture to restore me to my family. I wish to study art in France, and as there was nothing to hold me to Lahaina anymore, here I am." Constance's words, sugary with politeness, dripped with acid disdain. "But do not trouble yourself that I expect to find a home or even win tender sentiments from you. As I said, my destination is Paris, and frankly, there is too much strife in this household to suit me."

Rodger choked. "This creature dares to criticize us! By God, I'll not stand for it."

Constance cast a pitying glance at her cousin. "Overinflated dignity is so tiresome in a man."

Alex stifled Rodger's indignant squawk with a sharp gesture. "Then why have you come?"

Constance smiled. "Why, for the reward, of course. And I'd be much obliged if you'd pay Mr. McKin at once so that I may have my share."

Chapter 2

"You mercenary little bitch!" Rodger's snarl shattered the stunned silence following Constance's bald announcement. "We'll not fall for such a blatant swindle, McKin!"

"Now wait a damn minute!" Lock snapped. "I want no part of this."

Constance cocked her head, baffled. "But it was all arranged. We're to share equally."

Alex's brown eyes narrowed in bitter assessment. "So, Lauchlan, this scheme *is* yours."

Lock's face went dark as thunder. "I'd see myself in hell before I'd take anything from a Latham."

"But an agent should be paid for his services," Constance said reasonably, mystified by Lock's attitude. "Why shouldn't you and Dylan take what's rightfully yours? I know I intend to."

Lock's furious blue glance scorched Constance with contempt. "Mammon has always been the Latham god, and I should have known you'd be no different. But I'll be damned if I'll pretend to something that's none of my making to suit some obscure purpose of yours, princess."

Bemused and a little hurt, Constance waved a hand at the well-appointed foyer. "But they're obviously able to pay."

"Then you collect your damned reward—if you can. I've done all that my duty requires." He

27

stormed toward the door, his ire firmly etched in the taut lines of his jaw. On the threshold, he shot them one final look, his lips twisting with scorn. "I wish you joy in each other."

What should have been a blessing sounded more like a curse, and Constance suppressed a shiver of dismayed regret as Lock McKin disappeared into the icy night, leaving her alone to face two outraged men. The astounding realization that she'd already come to depend on Lock's presence was a sign of weakness she could not tolerate, not if she hoped to survive. Summoning up her resources and her determination, Constance turned to her grandfather with a bland look of challenge.

"Well?"

Startled, Alex scrutinized her suspiciously. "Well what, girl?"

"You wanted news of your son, and I brought it, didn't I?" Constance perched her fists on her hips in a belligerent attitude. "Do you intend to make good on the reward, or was that just a humbug?"

"Let me pitch this fraud into the gutter where she belongs, Uncle," Rodger pleaded, his thick hands clenching and unclenching.

"I don't care whether or not you believe I'm James's daughter," Constance retorted. "The fact is, I've come a terrible great way to bring you word of his fate and even produced hard proof of having known him, certainly more than you'd have gotten from mere sailors' hearsay. I demand that you honor the terms of your offer."

"Demand, eh?" Alex's scowl twitched, then dissolved altogether as a chuckle rumbled from his chest. "By God, that's the Latham in you, all right."

"Uncle Alex! You don't mean you believe this preposterous pack of lies?" Rodger asked incredulously.

Alex's gaze flicked between the silver oval hanging on its chain and the rather truculent expression on Constance's face. He reached out, and Constance steeled herself not to flinch or jerk away when he brushed her straight brown hair back so that he could look into her eyes.

"I believe her."

"What—?" Rodger choked, then tried to compose himself. "Sir, I must protest!"

"And the reward?" Constance prompted hopefully over Rodger's gabbling.

"Yes, damn you, it's yours," Alex said with another bark of laughter. "A persistent little businesswoman, aren't you? I like that."

"How else will I get to Paris?" She shrugged. "A woman alone must see to her survival as best she can."

"But you aren't alone—not anymore," Alex said gruffly.

"Oh." Constance swallowed hard and looked away. "I—I hadn't stopped to think of it that way."

"Of course she hadn't," Rodger said, his voice heavy with sarcasm. He took a handkerchief from his pocket and mopped his damp brow. "Nor, I'll wager, has she even considered the fact that she's claiming to be a member of one of the wealthiest families in Massachusetts."

"I want nothing except the reward I've rightfully earned," Constance repeated. "I'm no threat to you. Why, I'll be on my way again as soon as I can buy a packet ticket to Europe."

"Rubbish. You can't expect me to let you slip away so soon," Alex said, scrubbing at his whiskers with the palm of one hand. "I'm an old man, ailing and tired. You must let us get acquainted. There are so many things I want to know."

"We'd do better to give her a gold piece and send her packing right now," Rodger advised darkly.

Alex gave his nephew an exasperated look. "You're more worried about your own interests than grateful for this miracle! And while you're my

cousin's son, and I've welcomed your presence in
this house these past few years, this is my James's
child!"

Rodger drew himself up in stiff disapproval,
tucking his chin into the folds of his perfectly
starched neckcloth. "Uncle, please understand I
would be shirking my responsibility to you as both
relative and business associate if I did not point out
the improprieties of accepting this . . . this female at
face value."

"I may have begun handing over the reins of
Latham and Company to you, nephew, but I'm not
so much in my dotage that I'll stand to have my
judgment questioned." Alex's tone was so harsh
that Rodger's ruddy color faded. "And there are
questions to be answered still, including how
McKin came to be involved in this. But for now, say
no more. Constance is staying."

"Oh, no. I can't," she squeaked, panic rising
again. Freedom was too new and precious a com-
modity to relinquish it lightly.

"Have you somewhere else to go?" Alex demanded. "Or means to do so?"

Her head whirled. "N-no, but if I could have an
advance on my money, I could find a place—"

"Don't be ridiculous. Of course you'll stay here.
This is your home. You belong here now."

"That would be most improper, possibly even
dangerous," Rodger objected. His lip curled in dis-
taste as his gaze raked her unorthodox attire. "At
the very least, we'll have to lock up the silver."

"You perishing, high-nosed prig!" Constance
glared at Rodger, deciding that she could take great
delight in thwarting him. She'd be like a sand flea,
small, infinitely irritating, and impossible to remove. "If my grandfather invites me to stay in his
home, who are you to say him nay?"

"Who, indeed?" Alex laughed out loud at
Rodger's confounded expression. He placed Con-

stance's hand in the crook of his arm, oblivious of the way she stiffened, and swept her toward the stairway. "Come, my girl, I've a thousand questions, but we'll let Maggie take you to a room to freshen up while I get rid of my guests."

"Oh, no, please, don't go to that trouble," Constance said in a faint voice, fairly overwhelmed by Alex's enthusiasm.

"As if I care about those potbellied bores!" he snorted. "Besides, they'll understand when I tell them what a prize I found on my doorstep tonight. Now you just do as I say."

Overcome by his insistence, Constance nodded, dazed and trembling with relief. Everything was going to be all right! She was safe, accepted—at least by Alex—and Paris would soon be within her reach. Jerôme, the kindly, consumptive Frenchman who'd first set brush and paint in her eager hands and been the only friend to a girl whose differences made her an outcast from both her cultures, had filled her head with dreams of Paris—the golden afternoons under the chestnut trees in the Tuileries, high mass below Notre Dame's stained-glass windows, the treasures of the Musée du Louvre. Her palms fairly itched for the feel of brushes and paints. And teachers—oh, what she could learn! While she was wary of Alex's expectations, she could at least express her gratitude.

"Thank you, sir. You're very kind."

The old man paused on the first riser, and his voice was strangely thick. "Kind? Few men in this city would agree with that, but then I've never had a granddaughter before. Until you feel comfortable enough to call me Grandpa, my name is Alex."

"Yes ... Alex."

"Constance," he said, musing. "You even have a proper Bostonian name."

"In Lahaina they called me Lili," she confessed.

"Why was that?"

"From my Hawaiian name, Lilio, I suppose. A child's nickname."

"Would you prefer to be known as Lili here?" he asked.

She stiffened. "No! It—that is, it brings back unhappy times for me."

"In what way, my dear?"

She forced a small laugh. "Childhood cruelties only. After the fever made me so ill, I was confused for a time and could not play or work as the other children did. It made some of them resentful, and so they called me names. 'Crazy Lili' was one of the more hurtful ones."

Alex considered, then shook his head. "Well, then, I'm afraid 'Lili' won't do here in proper society, nor will this mannish attire. So you must be 'Constance,' and dress as a Boston lady should." He glanced back over his shoulder at his nephew. "Rodger, send to the warehouse for some clothing for Constance. Can't have my granddaughter dressing like an orphan."

Rodger's resentment squeezed his well-carved mouth into a mulish pucker, but he nodded. "Yes, Uncle."

"He's really a good and biddable boy, Rodger is," Alex remarked under his breath as he and Constance mounted the staircase. "He'll come around."

"I suppose I am something of a shock," she said in a rueful tone. "I—I don't want to hurt anyone."

"That sounds like your father." Alex's age-spotted hand closed over Constance's with a reassuring squeeze. He didn't seem to notice how she edged free almost immediately. "Don't worry, girl. You're home now."

Constance longed to take comfort in his words, but they echoed like meaningless platitudes in her ears. Perhaps she could pretend for a little while, but she knew she would never again have a real home. It was far too dangerous.

After all, a murderess could never stop running.

At dawn, Constance swam up from the depths of another nightmare and lay panting in the downy softness of her feather bed. Ignoring the chill of the room, she tossed back the quilted coverlets, stumbled to the window, and threw it open. Dressed in just her borrowed flannel nightgown, she took panicky draughts of the frigid air until her heart stopped pounding so fiercely and the sweat on her temples cooled. Only then was she able to focus on the scene before her—a pristine, glistening vista of Boston Common itself, the sunlight streaming through the bare trees and making lacy black silhouettes against the snow.

It was a picture so alien to everything she'd ever known and yet so mesmerizingly beautiful that she couldn't tear her eyes away. Then somehow the vast ocean of white changed, became part of her dream again, demons with death-white skin pulling her under, under. Constance gasped, then took a handful of snow from the ledge and scoured her face, ending the waking vision. Slamming down the window, she sought the haven of the warm bedclothes as the miasma of the dream receded to a manageable level. It was a malady she hadn't been able to so easily control aboard the *Eliza*.

But then, nothing had been easy in the middle of an ocean of vast, paralyzing terror that had kept her sick with fear every minute of every day for five agonizing months. She had lived all her life surrounded by the ocean, but was terrified of the open water. The funny part was that she didn't even know why.

Maybe the reason was hidden in that hazy, murky place in her head where questions weren't answered, but just swallowed up whole or shouted down by demons' voices. She'd known since she was ten and the fever had nearly killed her that she was different.

It was as if a fiendish hand had erased all the details of her life from the slate in her mind. She knew things about herself without knowing how she knew them. Her father's name, but not his face. How to read, but not the schoolroom in which she'd learned. Playmates who should have been familiar were strangers, wary of her differences and often cruel.

Crazy Lili, they'd called her, taunting her for her confusions, her laughable mistakes, her frustrated rages. Devil-touched, her foster uncle had warned, a religious man who, out of Christian charity, had taken in the orphaned, half-caste child of his dead assistant to raise as his own, and punished her for her lies as any good parent would. But that hadn't stopped her from lying, only made her more clever at it, because having no past at all was more frightening than even the most brutal castigation.

But she'd finally escaped all that—at least in part.

Constance shuddered at the thought of the packet boat to Europe that would take her the rest of her journey to freedom. She didn't know how she'd be able to endure it, even if it was only a mere two-and-a-half-week trip. Somehow she had to. Her guilt left her no alternative.

Feet tucked beneath her and back pressed against the carved rosewood headboard, Constance pulled the covers around her shoulders and rubbed her hands up and down her chilled arms. She couldn't feel the marks anymore. That much had healed. But her conscience bore as many guilty stripes as her body had when Dylan McKin's crew had fished her—naked, bleeding, and desperate—out of the harbor that awful night.

She'd gone instinctively to the friendly sea captain who'd talked to her about her paintings and spun tales of her crossing the ocean to a place where she'd be welcome and ... safe. But even Dylan's compassionate help might have been tempered with justice if she'd had the courage to confess what she'd done. Constance shuddered and buried her face in her trembling hands, trying to block out images that wouldn't rest. Like scenes caught in an instant's lightning flash, they played themselves over and over, haunting her.

A bamboo cross and the upraised strap. The old, endless cycle of pain, humiliation, confusion, and the cloying scent of ginger blossoms. Her precious artist's brushes—splintered and destroyed as yet another punishment. Then the anger that forced her to strike back, and the heavy pink conch shell splattered with blood ...

Thou shalt not kill.

She'd broken that commandment, but even though she knew she was going to Hell, she couldn't be sorry, not even if her victim was a man of God.

That was why she'd let Dylan McKin convince her to run halfway around the world to a grandfather she'd never known she had. Constance's fingers sought reassurance and found the silver chain around her neck. She *was* Constance Latham, and she had the proof. If Dylan McKin had been the one to make the connection between her father's name and a reward, then no one in Boston need know. She could happily oblige Alex with any number of lies about James. After all, she was very good at lying, and if it meant half of a twenty-five-thousand-dollar reward to carve a new life for herself in France, shape a new identity, and bury both Crazy Lili and Constance Latham forever, then what were a few more strains on a soul already bound for perdition?

It was just that she was so damnably tired. Constant's gaze ricocheted around the elegantly appointed bedroom with its carved mantel, marble-topped dressing tables, and yellow tea rose wallpaper. It was a far cry from a stinking ship's hold or a grass hut in the sugar fields of a mission colony Uncle Cyrus ruled as his own personal kingdom. And it was tempting—much too tempting.

Huddled beneath the bedclothes, Constance shook her head. Down that path lay a trap and endless trouble, for her guilt was so heavy, so damning, she dared trust no one but herself, dared not respond to the affection she sensed lurked beneath Alex's crusty exterior. It would be unfair to let him form an attachment, and so she stifled her curiosity about her father's home and the enmity that lay between Lock McKin and the Lathams. She had to focus on collecting the reward and making yet another escape.

There was a quiet tap on her door, and Maggie's curly, red-gold head peeked around the casing. "Good morning, miss."

Constance sank further down in the covers and mumbled a greeting as the young maid bumped open the door with her ample hip and carried a tray to the bedside table. The sweet fragrance of chocolate wafted from a squat pot to tickle Constance's nose, and her stomach rumbled. For five months she'd barely been able to choke down enough food to keep body and soul together, and now she was constantly ravenous.

"Thank you, er—"

"It's Maggie, miss." The maid handed Constance a cup of the milky beverage. "Mary Margaret Callahan, actually, but in the old country me da always called me Maggie for short."

"You're not from Boston?" Constance sat up cross-legged and took a sip. The rich sweetness of chocolate exploded against her tongue.

"Lord love you, miss! I'm as Irish as they come." Maggie rattled the coal scuttle and set to work at the hearth, needing no help to keep up her end of the conversation. "Immigrated just three years ago, and found this fine position with Mr. Latham right away. Such a gentleman! I'll soon have enough saved to send after my youngest brother. The Lord does answer prayers, and that's a fact."

Constance pursed her lips at that sour thought. Perhaps He did for good people like Maggie, but not for sinners like her. Still, there was hot chocolate on a cold morning to be thankful for.

"I want to thank you for your help last night and the use of the gown," Constance said, setting the empty cup aside.

"You're welcome, miss. And that reminds me!" Maggie disappeared and returned moments later clutching several paper-wrapped bundles and a freshly pressed gown of cocoa-brown serge with a high, demure collar and tapered sleeves edged with ecru lace. "Mr. Alex had these sent and requests you join him downstairs for breakfast before he goes to the countinghouse."

"Countinghouse?" Constance slid from the bed and began to open the packages, unwrapping a mystifying assortment of fine lawn and flannel garments.

"Yes, miss. Latham and Company, the very finest mercantile and trading company in New England. Didn't you know your grandfather—?" Maggie clapped a hand over her mouth, blushing and chagrined to have revealed the topic everyone in the servants' hall was gossiping about.

Constance sat down on the edge of the bed with a sigh, her hands full of flimsy white underthings. "I'm afraid not. I've just, er—immigrated, too, from the Pacific. I don't know anything about life here. Starting with what you do with *these*."

She held up a ruffled square of fabric with an attached tangle of tapes and ribbons.

"Oh, miss!" Maggie's giggle was nearly a shriek. "Them's your drawers!"

Constance eyed the garment skeptically. The usual female dress in Lahaina was the *holoku*, a voluminous Mother Hubbard introduced a scant twenty years earlier by the first Congregationalist missionaries to cure the Hawaiian natives' lack of proper modesty.

"It's worse than I thought, then," Constance muttered and picked up a strange contraption that seemed to be made of whalebone and boot laces. She cocked an inquiring eyebrow at the other girl.

The redhead's mobile mouth worked with the effort not to crack a smile. "Your corset, miss."

Constance sighed again. She hadn't the least idea how to go about being a dutiful granddaughter! The sooner she was off, the better. "You'd best call me Constance."

That startled Maggie. "Oh, no, miss, I couldn't—"

"It'll be easier, Maggie." Constance scooped up a pile of underthings, threw the young maid a rueful smile, and headed for the dressing screen. "You see, you've got to make me into a proper Boston lady—at least for today—and it doesn't look as though it's going to be easy!"

"You want *what* for breakfast?"

Constance gazed across the shiny mahogany table at her grandfather and repeated her request. "Apple pie."

"Oatmeal is what we eat in Boston," Rodger stated from the seat opposite, folding his morning paper with an emphatic snap. "Every morning."

"Oh. I see." Constance shifted uncomfortably beneath the unaccustomed strictures of corset, petticoats, and heavily boned gown and gave Rodger a limpid look. "Why?"

"Why?" Rodger blinked.

He looked rather like an owl, Constance thought, and his carefully pomaded yellow curls formed twin peaks like ears on either side of his crown to reinforce the image. Knowing her cousin was a man who stood on his dignity, and having no wish to antagonize him further, she steeled herself not to smile too broadly and instead strove to look interested. "Yes, why?"

"Because it's ideal for the constitution, and ... and we just do, that's all."

"Rodger is a creature of rather predictable habits," Alex interjected dryly. "But he is an excellent businessman, so much so I've even been contemplating my retirement."

"Thank you, Uncle." Rodger preened.

"But the conservative inclinations which make him such a valuable asset to the firm sometimes prevent him from readily accepting change." Alex prompted his nephew with a nod in Constance's direction.

Rodger's gaze touched the silver locket Constance wore, and he swallowed as if he had a bone stuck in his throat. "Yes, ah—that is, I wish to apologize for last night, Cousin Constance. My objections were too forceful. I meant no offense and welcome you into our family."

"Why, thank you, Cousin Rodger!" Wary pleasure glowed in Constance's topaz eyes. Though she was sure his statement was made mostly under pressure from Alex, it was a peace offering she would willingly accept. Impulsively, she reached out to touch his hand. "I hope we can be friends as well as cousins."

"Ah, our girl is a charmer," Alex murmured with approval. "Prettily said, my dear. And a night's rest has done you much good. Doesn't she look splendid today, Rodger?"

"Quite ... presentable," he replied somewhat grudgingly.

"Maggie helped." Constance self-consciously smoothed her tight bodice and touched the simple ribbon band that held back her thick hair. Maggie's expertise as a ladies' maid had even extended to trimming the ragged ends of her hair, so that now it cupped gently at the top of her shoulders. "I don't want to disgrace you, but I'm not quite sure . . . everything's so different here."

"Quite nice, my dear."

She beamed at her grandfather's praise. "May I go with you to the countinghouse?"

Alex carefully set down his coffee cup. "To collect your reward, I suppose?"

Constance's grin was ingenuous. "Only if that's where you keep your money."

Alex gave a bark of reluctant laughter. "No, we generally leave it in the bank for the most part. I suggest you do likewise."

"I'll be happy to, Alex, as soon as we can attend to this awkward reward-money business. I'd like to purchase a packet ticket today if possible."

The old man's craggy features tightened, but his tone held a note of genuine hurt. "Are you so anxious to leave us, my dear?"

"No, of course not."

Alex coughed against his closed fist and looked at her meaningfully. "I haven't been well this past year, you see. Lung fever."

"Sudden shock seems to bring on his attacks," Rodger offered.

"Oh, dear." Constance looked around the high-ceilinged dining room for a means to escape this none-too-subtle trap while guilt gnawed at her conscience. "Then all the more reason for me to leave as soon as possible and let your life return to normal."

"Quite the contrary, dear girl," Alex said hastily. "I really think I shall feel much better for your presence here in this drafty old house. Two crusty bachelors make tiresome companions, whereas your being here has already made me feel twenty years younger."

"You're very kind to say so, but—"

"My friends are very anxious to meet you, and you must be so tired of traveling. Surely you see the wisdom of taking your time and regaining your strength before undertaking your grand adventure?"

"Of course, that makes sense," Constance said weakly. "But, Alex, I must insist—"

"We have art galleries." He saw her hesitation, the spark of interest that said he'd touched a nerve, and plunged eagerly forward. "Yes, art galleries aplenty, and instructors, too. Theaters, balls, soirees, sledding parties—we have them all. It would be my pleasure to introduce you to the entertainments of our city." Alex warmed to the idea with enthusiasm, slapping the tabletop until the silver rattled and the lids of the crystal jam pots chimed. "By the saints, girl! What fun we'll have!"

"Really, Alex, I'm sure it wouldn't be appropriate under the circumstances," she said, frissons of alarm racing down her spine. Calling attention to herself had not been her plan.

"Rubbish!" Alex exploded. "You're a Latham. We've been part of Boston society for generations. You must take your rightful place."

Rodger had gone positively pasty at the idea. "Sir, Cousin Constance lacks the—er, polish that would make her comfortable in polite circumstances."

"Then that's what ladies' maids and elocution lessons are for," Alex replied, waving aside all objections. "And that foreign dancing master in Tremont Street—Count what's-his-name."

"Papanti," Rodger offered unsteadily, dragging out his handkerchief to mop his damp forehead and tugging at his high starched collar as if it had suddenly shrunk a size or two.

"Alex, please! I couldn't impose in such a fashion." Constance smiled to hide the desperation that fluttered in her chest. "If only I could convey how important my studies are to me, you'd understand my impatience to have my plans settled. So if we could perhaps visit your bank this morning—"

"Cousin Constance," Rodger chided, "surely even one so inexperienced in these matters as you can understand the difficulties of putting one's hands on such a large sum of cash."

She chewed her thumbnail uncertainly. "Oh. I hadn't thought . . . you will see that Mr. McKin is paid first, won't you?"

Rodger scowled. "The so-called 'Iron Man?' Preposterous! We don't owe the McKins anything."

"Perhaps not, but I certainly do," she said quietly. Indeed, Dylan McKin had probably saved her life. She might be hanged or worse if not for his timely rescue, but she could hardly explain all that. She owed him, as well as his handsome, hardheaded brother, for getting her this far. "If funds are scarce, I insist their portion of the reward be paid first. It's only fair."

As she repeated the same argument she'd used on Lock, Rodger muttered a curse under his breath and tossed down his newspaper in disgust. Constance tilted her head to one side, perplexed.

"I don't understand. What happened to make the McKins and the Lathams such enemies?"

"Business, my dear." Alex's features suddenly appeared chiseled from New Hampshire granite. "Enoch McKin and I were once partners, but we parted friendly company over a number of differences. I prospered, but Enoch was always a fool and a dreamer. Now his sons blame me for their father's failures. I make an easy scapegoat, that's all. Nothing to concern yourself about."

"But it does," she disagreed.

"Never mind. I rather like the thought of a grandiose gesture anyway. I'll see that Lock McKin gets his reward this very day, even if I have to pawn my gold pocket watch—if you'll agree to postpone your plans and stay a time with your old grandfather."

The obligation Constance felt for the McKins warred with the need for self-preservation and the almost overwhelming urge to keep moving. She ought to leave Boston immediately, money or no money, before her guilt and sin brought down God's wrath on this old man. But Alex was family, and she was his only link to his dead son. Was it so very wrong of her to give him a bit of what he wanted?

"You'll pay Lock McKin today?"

"By special messenger," Alex promised. "And you could still be in Paris by the spring."

She drew a shaky breath, wincing slightly at the constriction of her new corset and the fearful thundering of her heart. Wondering if she was making a mistake, she nodded. "All right, Alex."

"Excellent." His mood became expansive now that he had settled things to his satisfaction. "Where the devil is Maggie with my breakfast anyway?"

As if on cue, the maid bustled through the connecting doorway with a laden tray and began setting bowls on the lace mats in front of them. Rodger snapped open his napkin viciously, his handsome face ruddy with irritation.

At least Constance had the satisfaction of knowing her debt to the McKin brothers would be paid. With something like relief, she also recognized breakfast. Dipping two fingers into the gray mush in her bowl, she bent and scooped it into her mouth, then froze as three sets of eyes widened in horror.

Swallowing the gummy mouthful, she licked her fingers, and hid her embarrassment behind a saucy smile. "Some kind of poi, isn't it?"

"Poi?" Rodger echoed. "This is none of your heathenish concoctions. It's honest Yankee oatmeal!"

Constance winced. At her current rate of faux

pas, she would never learn all the ins and outs of being a Boston lady. Well, she'd never been one to be daunted by a few raised eyebrows.

"Not taro root? How curious." She wiped her fingers on a napkin. "It might taste better if you let it ferment a week or so."

Rodger looked as though he might gag, but Alex's amusement burst forth in a loud guffaw, punctuated by Maggie's stifled giggles.

"My dear, you're quite right." Grinning, Alex pushed his own bowl aside. "By gum, girl, I've a feeling you could set this old town on its ear."

Constance hid her trepidation behind an impudent grin. "It might be amusing to try."

"It might at that." Alex's smile grew even wider. "And to make a good start, Maggie, bring us all a piece of apple pie!"

Chapter 3

"Stubborn, blubber-brained, prideful young'un
... why don't you keep the double-damned
money this time? You could use it, cain't ye?"

"Save your breath, Jedediah. My mind is made
up."

Oblivious of the wood dust instantly attracted to
his severe black suit coat, Lock McKin leaned
against a rough-hewn Indian chief, one of several
figureheads and binnacle stands in various stages of
completion in the small ship carver's workshop adjacent to his warehouse offices. His lean fingers
clenched around the heavy paper tube protecting a
rolled sheaf of drawings.

"I'm going ahead with construction of my *Argonaut*, and I won't be beholden to Latham money.
Thrice in two weeks now I've sent it back. I'd have
pitched that last bundle of greenbacks into St.
Agnes's poor box," he complained, "except I won't
have Alex Latham thinking I can be bought."

Jedediah Shoe, a small, wiry man with a face like
a dried apple and a fine cross-hatching of scars on
his knotted fingers from over sixty years' wood
carving, set down the drawknife in disgust. Resting
his arthritic hands on his leather apron, he accused
Lock with eyes glazed by the milky film of cata-
racts.

"But you'll get yourself all gussied up to go

courtin' some fancy-pants bankers and attend all them galas and soir-ees."

"Dammit, Jedediah! Do you think I enjoy the condescension of a stuffy bunch of blue bloods? I can see the questions in their eyes." Lock mimicked the accent of a proper Boston matron. " 'Isn't that Enoch McKin's son? Wasn't he the one . . . ?' "

Jedediah's lined face softened. "Now, lad, surely it's what kind of man you are that interests folk now."

"Gossip dies hard," Lock said in a stony voice. "I need investors if I'm going to get the *Argonaut* onto the keelblocks, so I'll dust off my party graces and waltz every horse-faced merchant's daughter around Count Papanti's ballroom if I must."

"But you won't take Latham's money even though you and Dylan restored his grandchild?"

"Hell, no." Lock's half-smile took the sting from his answer, but his tone said the subject was closed.

Jedediah threw up his hands and went back to work at a block of white oak, muttering under his breath while Lock tried to ignore a twinge of conscience. Since he'd all but abandoned that scrawny cat, Constance, to the Latham wolves that night, he hadn't been able to quiet an uneasy curiosity about the outcome. Still, from what he'd seen, Constance was more than able to take care of herself.

"Come on, Jedediah," Lock cajoled. "I want to know if you'll carve the figurehead for the *Argonaut*."

"It's a wonder you aren't letting one of those newfangled machines of yours chop it out," Jedediah said with a peevish snort.

"The only way I'll be able to compete with the big New York yards is with steam-powered saws and derricks."

"One man with an adz is worth three of your saws, and as for those lathe-turned treenails—"

Jedediah pronounced the name of the wooden pegs used to nail a ship together "trunnels."

"There's still plenty to do around here, even for a lazy whittler like you."

"Insolent guppy! Give me that." Jedediah snatched the tube of plans from Lock, removed the papers, and uncurled the elegant draftings on his cluttered workbench. "*Argonaut*, eh? By the four winds! This design has something to do with all those fancy experiments of yours on the millpond, that hydro-whatsis stuff."

"Hydrostatics." Lock rubbed his index finger over his upper lip in an unconscious, considering gesture. "Science, yes. But I've incorporated my own practical observations as well."

"A clipper that's flat-floored *and* sharp-bowed. Can you do it?"

"I aim to try."

"You're liable to be laughed right out of the stocks."

Lock's features hardened. He rolled the plans together and stuffed them back into the protective tube. "They laughed at Galileo, too."

Jedediah opened his mouth to argue some more, then looked around Lock's shoulder, squinting at the murky outline of a visitor in his open doorway. "Who's there?"

"Excuse me. I was told to come to Mr. Shoe's workshop . . . oh, there you are, Lock McKin."

Lock spun on his heel at the sound of that husky feminine voice, then stared, openmouthed, as Constance Latham swept into the littered workshop with a swish of fashionable skirts. Her transformation from urchin to lady was impeccable, from the crown of her blue silk bonnet to the cut of her velvet-trimmed cashmere mantle to the richness of her large fur muff. Only those slanted topaz eyes struck an exotic and incongruous note, peering out from under her fringe of sable bangs with the wary solemnity of some wild, fey creature, a transplanted Titania surprised by the light of an unexpected dawn. For all her exterior polish, there was a flash of vulnerability and sweet uncertainty in that golden gaze that aroused his protective instincts with primitive impact.

Then she grinned at him, an impudent gamine again despite her finery, and the image vanished. Lock shut his mouth with an annoyed snap. So he'd known some soap and water and a few square meals would make a difference. And some feminine flounces to round out her angles didn't hurt either. No need to make a jackass out of himself just because the little mercenary hadn't wasted any time ingratiating herself into her grandfather's pocketbook and taking her place as a "merchant princess" among the royalty of Boston's moneyed clans. It made him angry at himself that somehow he'd expected better of her.

"What the devil are you doing here?" he demanded rudely.

"You know quite well, I believe." Constance dug in the secret folds of the huge muff, retrieving a rectangular bundle. "You're a very inconsiderate man, Lock McKin. Here, take what belongs to you."

Lock glowered at her suspiciously. "Did Alex send you?"

"Of course not. In fact, I should be at deportment class this very moment, being tutored on Mrs. Farrar's horrid etiquette book, *The Young Lady's Friend.* Fortunately, I escaped. I considered this mission much too important to entrust to the imbeciles Rodger sent earlier."

Lock frowned. "What do you mean, you escaped?"

"Left. Vamoosed. Walked out." She shrugged. "Thanks to you, I've had my fill of elocution, sewing, and etiquette lessons."

"What have I to do with that?"

"I had to promise to postpone my departure to Paris to convince my grandfather your share of the reward must be paid first. And so that I may understand society while I'm here, I've been clipped, plucked, dressed, and instructed to within an inch of my life!"

Lock's mouth twitched. "Is that so?"

"And that's not all. I even had to attend Trinity Church this Sunday past, and you know how I feel about that! Between the visiting, the shopping, the tours of the countinghouse, and Alex's desire to see that I experience every Boston attraction from snow sledding to opera, I'm fair worn out!"

"How very . . . er, tiring." He tried to look sympathetic, but her obvious frustration with a situation that any other young woman would have considered ideal made him grin instead.

Constance cast him a severe look. "I haven't had a moment to myself, or the first opportunity to set a brush to canvas, since I arrived. At least your stubbornness afforded me the opportunity for an outing on my own."

"Your own?" He looked at her closely, noting the wind-flushed pink of her cheeks. "You don't mean you walked all the way down here?"

"Of course not," she said with a sniff. "I rode the horsecar. It was quite refreshing."

"Good Lord." He groaned. "And no one knows where you've gotten off to? That was an idiotic thing to do!"

She tilted her head to one side. "Why? It's come to my attention that most Boston ladies go wherever they wish. Why, just yesterday at the bookseller's, I met a student of the literary arts, a Miss Elspeth Philpot, who said she took a walking tour all the way to Connecticut."

"Even a bluestocking would have better sense than to venture to the waterfront alone!" Exasperated, Lock tugged at the hair on his nape and wondered if Alex Latham would blame this insanity on him. "This isn't the kind of neighborhood a lady goes strolling in! Anything could happen. Besides that, it's freezing."

"Oh, that." Her attitude was offhand. "I understand now why the circumference of ladies' skirts is so generous. I must have on six or seven petticoats at least." She stuck out a dainty booted foot and grabbed up a handful of skirt to show off a shapely, silk-stockinged calf and a rainbow array of ruffled fabric. "Red flannel, batted wool, pleated linen—if anything, I'm overheated."

"Miss, if you please!" Jedediah protested on a high squeak, his lined face as red as her top petticoat.

Lock made a hasty move, sweeping her skirts back in place with a well-aimed swipe of his hand. "Constance!"

"I forget what a preoccupation Bostonians have with underwear," she murmured under her breath, her cheeks flushed with more than cold. "Pardon me, Mr. Shoe. Your work is quite splendid, by the way. Will that not be a porpoise when you're done?"

Jedediah looked at the barely begun slab of white oak, then in pleased surprise at Constance. "You've a clever eye, miss."

"Perhaps we simply see things in the same way," she replied. "May I come again to view it when you're done?"

"Anytime, lass."

"Miss Latham won't have occasion to visit again, Jedediah," Lock interjected firmly. "In fact, she must be on her way right now, so excuse us."

Tucking the tube of plans under his arm, Lock took Constance's elbow and escorted her from the workshop, down the long dusty corridor that smelled of sandalwood, accountant's ink, and nautical tar, past the shipyard's bustling business offices.

Ignoring her squirming and indignant spluttering, he sent a teenage apprentice out to the busy Second Street thoroughfare to hail a hansom cab. As the boy sprinted off, Lock force-marched Constance toward the glass-fronted entrance of the long, remodeled warehouse.

"Come along, Miss Latham. Your cab will be waiting."

"Not before you listen to reason." Constance dug in her heels, forcing him to come to a halt at the base of the wide wooden staircase to the second floor. With lips pressed together in an effort to keep her temper, she thrust the bundle of bills at him. "I've inconvenienced myself quite enough on your account, Lock McKin, so take this and don't argue."

Lock's blue eyes grew hard, and he ignored the package. "Keep it. I've no use for Latham money."

"Oh! You are too ridiculous!" she huffed angrily. "I haven't gone to all this trouble for nothing. It's yours, you foolish man."

"I told you, I don't want it."

"Well, perhaps Dylan does!" Her tone was smug, as if she had trumped his final ace.

"You're wrong," he said flatly. "Now, if you'll excuse me . . ."

He turned away, but she caught his arm, her gloved fingers sinking into the black wool of his sleeve and testing the hard muscle beneath. "I don't understand. Is it this silly feud that makes you so obstinate?"

His expression went glacial, and his voice was so cold she shivered. "Alex Latham destroyed my father. They were partners, but your grandfather betrayed that trust, stripped him of pride and resources, then ruined him. In despair, my father took his own life."

"Oh, no." Shocked to her core, Constance felt her breath freeze in her chest.

Lock's mouth tightened into a grim, unforgiving

line. "I found my father's body. I was fourteen. Do you think I can forget or forgive this *silly* feud, Miss Latham?"

"I—I—"

"I'd rot in hell before I'd touch a dime of that blood money." He shook off her hand, and his eyes burned, scorching Constance with his contempt, his hate, his pain. "*Now* do you understand?"

She couldn't answer. He looked so fierce, so wounded, a proud, raven-browed Lucifer, defiant and unrepentant. Constance knew suffering, and recognized it in this man, but a history of helplessness paralyzed her. Lock dismissed her with a final withering glance, turned, and climbed the stairs two at a time, disappearing into the shadowy nether regions as if recalled by a higher force.

Constance drew a sharp, painful breath and found that she was shaking. Yes, now she understood, at least in part, though there were undoubtedly two sides to this story. No wonder Lock had reacted to her so oddly the day they met. What had Dylan McKin been thinking, sending her to her grandfather via his own brother? The situation was a powder keg of old tragedy ready to explode into new disaster. No wonder Lock wanted nothing to do with any of them.

The bundle of bills she held fluttered like an accusing finger. Repulsed, she shoved the money back into the pocket in her muff. Well, Lock McKin would have his way. But not just yet. Squaring her shoulders, she mounted the worn staircase after him.

On the upper landing she paused, blinking, dazzled by the light pouring into the huge open room through banks of wide windows. As her eyes adjusted, Constance gaped at the macabre scene.

The floor of the room was painted black, and half a dozen men in shirtsleeves crept on hands and knees through a rainbow network of spidery chalk lines—red, yellow, blue, green, white. Some worked with calipers and transit compasses, others hammered nails, and still others drew shapes around flexible wooden battens. Tilted drafting tables lined the walls under the windows where other men conferred over mysterious documents. A five-foot-long wooden half-model of a ship's hull lay on yet another table with a chisel stuck in its bulging middle like a sacrifice to the gods. So fantastic a scene was it, Constance almost searched the black floor for pentagrams and other symbols of magic and witchcraft, for nothing short of an attempt to invoke the spirits of darkness would explain the deadly earnestness and concentration of the men.

No one noticed her hesitating at the top of the stairs. Lifting a hand to her bonnet brim to shield her eyes against the brilliance, she saw Lock at last. He stood silhouetted against a window on the far side, frozen in an attitude of intense concentration, shaggy head bent, staring at the maze on the floor with his index finger pressed against his upper lip. Skirts whispering, Constance glided around the perimeter of the giant room, coming up behind him.

Curiously, she examined the crisscrossing of colored marks, but could make no sense of it whatsoever.

"What do you see?" she asked softly.

His voice came from far away. "The perfect ship."

The sound of his own words seemed to wake Lock from a spell, and he turned with a sharp movement and an exasperated curse. "Hellfire! Don't you ever give up? Get the devil out of my molding loft, woman!"

"Molding loft?" she repeated, letting her gaze roam over the puzzling map being laid out on the floor. "And you mold . . . ?"

"Ships, what else?" he snapped. "Every joint and rib, laid out in sections, like a giant dressmaker's pattern. Is your curiosity satisfied, or are you spying out my design for your grandfather?"

Constance sighed and held up an empty hand. "You win."

"What?" The single word was a suspicious growl.

"About the money. I understand now. I'm sorry ... about everything."

His jaw worked, but Lock merely continued to glower at her without answering. Really, Constance thought, he was the most unforthcoming man she'd ever known! She might be guilty of unmentionable crimes, but she had her standards. She was no thief, and she'd see that the McKin brothers got their part of the reward. It wouldn't be a complicated matter to deposit the money in some local banking institution against Dylan's return. She simply wouldn't tell Lock. That way, they all would get what they wanted. Well, almost. She shrugged, her half-smile wavering with disappointment and a touch of sadness.

"I just wanted you to know," she said, swallowing hard. "And I hope you dream the perfect ship to life someday."

Blinking furiously, cursing herself for her silliness at being hurt by his lack of response, she turned away.

"Constance." His hand closed over her arm, but it wasn't just the contact that made her gasp. Through the bank of windows, she stared down into the panorama of the busy shipyard below.

A tumble of massive timbers spread out in the yard in all directions, beams and stanchions, sholes and rails, tons of lumber aligned as if by a giant's hand. And rising up from this jumble at the edge of Boston Harbor was a clipper's elegant hull. Beyond it lay a glittering expanse of water, and Constance's vision pitched with vertigo before she hastily focused on the nearly completed ship. Scaffolding and ramps rose on each side, supporting borers, dubbers, and mallet men attaching the planking to the ribs of the ship. Derricks hauled curved knees into place to support the decking, and puffs of steam rose from the ovens that were softening the boards that would be bent into place.

"There it is," Constance breathed. Her breath fogged the cold window, and she impatiently scrubbed it clean with her muff to get a better view, then gazed at Lock with something approaching awe. "She's perfect. You've done it already."

"Not quite." Lock shook his head, gesturing toward the cross-hatching of patterns on the black floor. "Perhaps the next one."

Constance's gaze returned to the craft below. "This one's beautiful anyway. What do you call her?"

Lock's fingers tightened on her arm. "The *Odyssey.*"

"You built the *West Wind*, didn't you?" She watched the activity below avidly, longing in her eyes. "I'd give anything to paint your *Odyssey*, too."

"Your grandfather wouldn't like that, princess."

Constance laughed, a low, throaty sound that tickled a man's spine. "So who would tell him? I'd be very quiet, not bother a soul."

Lock released her and jammed his hand through his black hair. "I don't need the complications."

"Oh." She was quiet for a long moment; then she slanted him a look that was both mischievous and challenging. "I wouldn't have thought you'd pass up any opportunity to annoy a Latham."

He surprised himself by laughing at her audacity. "You're a perverse puss."

"I have my own dreams."

Something fragile flickered behind her golden eyes, invalidating her tough facade, and again Lock felt that instinctive tug of protectiveness, and a stirring of masculine desire—both of which were unwelcome and intrusive emotions, considering who she was. What the hell. His quarrel wasn't really with her anyway, and if she was ready to flaunt her grandfather's wishes, who was he to deny himself the pleasure of that?

"Suit yourself," he said with a shrug.

She brightened. "Then I may?"

"Just don't come down here alone again."

"No."

"And stay out of my way."

"Yes."

He eyed her narrowly, mistrusting her unusual acquiescence. "All right, then."

"Thank you." Her smile was more radiant than if he'd presented her with the crown jewels, and for an instant she bobbed in place, as if she had almost given in to the impulse to hug him but thought better of it. "You're an angel, Lock McKin. Aloha!"

With second thoughts already plaguing him, Lock watched her go, scowling like the very devil.

"I'm certain this isn't a good idea," Constance murmured ten days later. "I'm not ready."

Her grandfather tucked her hand into the crook of his arm and tugged her forward through the crush entering Count Papanti's Tremont Street ballroom. Five gilt-framed mirrors reflected the brilliance of an enormous crystal chandelier, and dancers were already whirling about on the first ballroom floor in America built on springs.

"Nonsense, girl!" Alex shouted bracingly over the orchestra music. "You'll do perfectly well. No one of any consequence misses the Winter Assembly, and it's the perfect opportunity for you to meet your social peers. She'll have a wonderful time, won't she, Rodger?"

Looking extremely debonair in evening dress, her cousin concurred amiably, but Constance wasn't fooled. She felt how his regard took in her garnet satin gown with its simple passementerie trim, how his gaze flicked disdainfully over the silk ribbons that caught her locket at her throat and embellished the rolled-back Anne Boleyn hairstyle and ringlets Maggie had coaxed her into tonight. The phrases "silk purse" and "sow's ear" came to mind at the somewhat resentful, slightly contemptuous curl of Rodger's well-shaped mouth, and Constance's courage and her steps faltered.

If only she could be indifferent to Alex's feelings, then she could have refused to attend the function altogether. But it wasn't working out that way. Despite the fact that with his roughshod ways her grandfather tended to plow right over anyone's plans or objections but his own, she was sure that he was motivated out of affection. Dismayingly, she'd found herself responding to the fondness growing between them, even enjoying butting heads with the gruff old curmudgeon over a chessboard, or her self-improvement itinerary, or even the breakfast menu, and no longer flinching when he took her arm or patted her shoulder, a sign that other brutal memories were fading.

He'd looked so hopeful when the idea of the Winter Assembly had been broached, so eager to show her off, so sure that all the tutelage she'd received had transformed her into the ideal granddaughter. And she'd hated to disappoint him, even though she knew Rodger considered her acceptance of the idea just more evidence that she was a toadying sycophant out to get as much as possible from Alex.

"Come along, Constance," Alex said, brooking no resistance. "I want you to meet the Cabots."

Constance put away a fleeting image of herself bolting for freedom, pasted a smile on her lips, and prepared for disaster.

It was worse than that.

By the time they had made the rounds of introductions, her cheeks hurt with the effort it took to keep her artificial smile in place, her head ached from the buildup of temper, and even her teeth throbbed from all the grinding she'd done in an effort not to tell each and every condescending, supercilious snob exactly what she thought of him or her. Oh, it wasn't that they were overtly discourteous. It was just that she sensed the instantaneous withdrawal, as if she were a freak, and one who was none too fastidious in her personal habits at that.

Oblivious of the undercurrents, Alex dragged her from group to group, cheerfully telling a condensed version of her history over and over, apparently unaware that the stiffening features and shocked inspections were anything other than friendly interest. She could appreciate their quandary. While her Latham name gave her a class standing of the highest level, her mixed blood and exotic upbringing would never fit into any predefined niche. For Alex's sake, Constance tried to ignore the matrons' disdainful sniffs, and dodged their husbands' blunt questions with an obtuseness that she knew would probably label her simpleminded as well.

Things became even more intolerable when Alex urged Rodger to take her "among the young people." She received several outright snubs from young women who were total strangers. Worse, she had to pretend she didn't hear the whispered comments about that "brown-skinned heathen" and allegations that she wasn't a legitimate Latham at all, but perhaps one of that rapscallion James's byblows! Even the young men who asked her to dance had speculation in their eyes, clearly wondering what the native girl would be like if they could only get her alone.

Constance was so furious she forgot all her carefully memorized dancing lessons, trodding on toes right and left to further complete her humiliation. It was a replay of all those years in Lahaina when they'd called her Crazy Lili and her differences had set her apart, encasing her in loneliness. And though she fought it, the hurt, angry defiance she'd tried so hard to bury threatened her tenuous control now.

She had a moment's respite when she convinced one smooth-faced Lothario to leave off his attempts to peer down her square-cut neckline long enough to fetch her a cup of lemonade from the heavily laden refreshment table. She hovered near a potted palm, scanning the room for a glimpse of either Rodger or Alex, plotting a sudden indisposition, when a rotund lady in midnight taffeta yanked her partner out of the flow of circling couples and pirouetted to a stop right in front of Constance.

"What a crush!" Elspeth Philpot gasped, pressing her hand to her ample bosom, then offering it for a handshake. "Wonderful to see you again, Miss Latham. Assemblies are such fun, don't you agree?"

"Hello, Miss Philpot," Constance answered, overcome by the middle-aged lady's warm smile after an evening of chilly receptions.

"Let me introduce you to Dr. Tinkerman, my dear," Elspeth said, sliding her blond-going-to-silver topknot from over her left ear and back into place on the crown of her head. As the equally stout gentleman bowed over Constance's hand, she continued to chat away. "Wonderful news, my dear! Mr. Hawthorne has agreed to speak to my literary club this Tuesday next. Say you'll come."

"I'd be delighted, Miss Philpot."

"Do call me Elspeth, my dear. If we're lucky, Mr. William Lloyd Garrison himself may attend. He is the prominent editor of *The Liberator*, an antislavery newspaper here in the city. It will be quite a lively discussion, don't you agree, Todd?"

"Indubitably, Elspeth," the portly physician said, still breathless and red-faced from his exertions.

"Have you had an opportunity to resume your painting since we last met?" Elspeth asked.

Constance's countenance brightened. "Thankfully, yes."

The hours she had stolen over the past days to work on her painting of Lock McKin's *Odyssey* had been among the most pleasant and peaceful she'd had. Fortunately, since Maggie's beau worked at the shipyard, it had been easy to induce her to accompany Constance on the secret horsecar rides to South Boston. True to her word, Constance had stayed out of Lock's path, finding a secluded corner of the yard to set up her new easel. Bundled to the teeth against the brisk February weather, she would lose herself temporarily in the attempt to capture another of his dreams on canvas. When she wasn't able to paint, she added to the sketchbook of island scenes she'd begun. She mentioned this to Elspeth.

"Oh, do bring it when you come," the older woman begged. "We'd all love to see your work."

"Of course," Constance promised, beginning to relax for the first time since her arrival. It was short-lived, however, because Dr. Tinkerman dragged Elspeth off to join him in a new polka just as Constance's latest leering partner reappeared with a cup of punch.

"You aren't friends with that abolitionist biddy?" he asked, handing over the cup. "Eccentric women bore me to tears."

"We wouldn't want that," Constance said tightly, resuming her desperate search for her grandfather over the rim of the punch cup.

It wasn't Alex who caught her attention, however, but Lock McKin. Coolly elegant in evening dress, his dark head bowed in earnest conversation, the shipbuilder expertly guided around the dance floor a rather pinch-mouthed young lady who was one of the people who'd remarked about the hue of Constance's complexion.

"You know who that is?" asked her Lothario, leaning close to Constance in a manner strictly against the rules in Mrs. Farrar's etiquette manual.

"Should I?"

"South Boston parvenu, name of McKin," he snorted. "No friend of your grandfather's, I assure you. My father won't do business with him, either."

Constance stiffened. "Why not?"

"Poor risk. Father died a bankrupt." The rum with which he'd laced his own lemonade wafted to her nostrils as he bent even closer. "Suicide, you know. They say madness runs in families."

His unctuous words pricked a raw nerve, and the fury that had been smoldering inside Constance all evening ignited—for Lock McKin, for herself. Prejudice took many forms—all insulating, hurtful, soul-destroying. She downed her lemonade in a single gulp, but it did no more to quench her anger than if she'd spit on a flame to put out a forest fire.

"This perishing borough is enough to run anyone mad," she ground out, defiantly tossing her cup into the potted palm.

"I beg your pardon?" Her partner's face lit up with avid expectation.

"Mad with boredom," she said recklessly. *To hell with them all*, she thought. Since they weren't impressed with a decorous young lady, she'd give them no more than they expected—or deserved.

With a sultry smile, she ran her fingers up the buttons of her partner's waistcoat, quite flaunting Mrs. Farrar's instructions never to indulge in vulgar familiarity with a person of the opposite sex. "Dance with me and I'll tell you about the hula."

"The what?"

"A native dance I know. Forbidden under pain of death." She lowered her lashes. "Very . . . passionate."

Her Lothario gulped, pulled her into his arms, and within minutes the chaperons were frowning fiercely at the deplorable scene that young Latham woman was making with a succession of dancing partners. Allowing herself to be held much too closely, laughing too loud, her outlandishly colored eyes too bright—it was a disgrace! When Rodger finally plucked her out of a crowd of admirers, he was livid, his face as puffed up as a pouter pigeon's.

"Are you out of your mind?" he hissed, swinging her into the rounds of a sedate polonaise, holding her very properly at arm's length, the pristine square of his white linen handkerchief between his palm and the small of her back as required by the sticklers.

"How very kind of you to come to my rescue, Cousin Rodger." Constance spoke through teeth gritted in a smile. "No doubt you noticed how uncomfortable I was with all the attention."

"I knew you couldn't be trusted. You've made a spectacle of yourself and humiliated Uncle Alex. Now perhaps he'll listen to reason."

"You don't approve of me, do you?"

"You're no more than an adventuress, and nothing about you rings true, Constance," he snapped, rounding the turn toward the refreshment tables. "If that's who you really are."

She lifted her chin at the challenge, and the light caught the silver oval at her throat. "Alex is satisfied."

"Well, I'm not. Why didn't you know James's birthdate? Or what ship he sailed on?"

"I was a child when he died," Constance replied coldly. "Even if they're told, children don't remember such things."

"Don't think I don't know what you're trying to do," he warned, squeezing her hand hard. A sudden predatory gleam lit Rodger's eye, startling Constance and making her reassess her dismissal of her

cousin as Alex's court jester. It occurred to her that
he could be a dangerous adversary.

"And what is that?" she asked uneasily.

"Ingratiating yourself into Alex's affections, trying to influence him against me."

That unwarranted accusation startled her, and she
stumbled over the unfamiliar dance steps, bringing
them to an unscheduled halt beside the punch
bowl. "Rodger, that's not true."

"I've practically run Latham and Company for
the past five years. Slaved and sweated and kow-
towed to that old man from morning until night."
As the music and the dancers eddied past them,
Rodger's mouth flattened with chilling determination. "The company's rightfully mine. I won't stand
for any interference from you, is that clear?"

"Are you threatening me, cousin?" She took a
step toward him. The very softness of her question
should have been a warning that her back was up,
but Rodger paid no heed.

"Let's just say the sooner you leave for Paris, the
better, and I'm sure after tonight, Uncle Alex will
agree."

Constance's lids drooped, giving her the sleepy
look of a stalking lioness. Smiling softly, she
stepped closer, her nearness forcing Rodger backward. "Actually, *Grandpa* has been pressing me to
extend my stay. After the warmth of my reception
here tonight, I simply don't see how I can bear to
leave."

Blood suffused Rodger's face. "You little—"

She trod hard on his instep. Taken off guard,
Rodger yelped, overbalanced, and windmilled
backward into the punch bowl. A pale tidal wave of
lemonade splashed a trio of matrons, cups bounced
and crashed in tiny crystal explosions, and Rodger
flopped like a mackerel in the middle of the debris.

A moment of stunned silence turned into cries
of dismay, offers of help, and—unfortunately—

laughter. Appalled, Constance pressed her fingers to her lips, backing away from the disaster and the disapproving eyes that rightfully accused her of her latest crime. And while Rodger squawked and flapped in mortified dignity like a hen caught under a fence, Constance caught sight of Lock McKin standing at the other end of the table—grinning.

Gulping, she did the only thing a reasonable person could do under the circumstances. She ran like hell.

Chapter 4

The cold wind whistling up Tremont Street did little to cool Constance's flaming cheeks, but at least the darkness hid her humiliation from the odd passerby. She'd fled the ballroom in such a state that she hadn't even retrieved her mantle, and the damp chill of a February thaw raised goose flesh on her bare arms and shoulders, making her regret her vague plan to cut across the Common to reach the sanctuary of Alex's Beacon Street home. Hugging herself, she half ran up the slushy sidewalk, but her physical discomfort was nothing compared with her mental upheaval.

"You diddling fool! What made you think it could work?" she muttered.

Constance hastened across the street between passing carriages, the horses' hooves pounding in her head, drowning out everything but her own erratic thoughts. Scurrying past the canted tombstones of the Central Burying Ground, she plunged into the blackness of the snow-patched Common. The shades resting beneath the markers held their peace in mute denunciation. Pulling a ringlet of false hair from the back of her head, she tossed it at an obelisk.

"This isn't me! Nor this. Or this!" Constance left a trail of curls and garnet ribbons on the path, clawing at her hair until it fell free about her shoulders. "You humbug! Did you really think it could be?"

Shuddering, shivering, the tip of her nose almost frozen, she slogged across the freezing meadow, unmindful of her muddy satin skirts and soaked slippers, scarcely aware of how the illumination of the distant street lamps and lighted windows on the perimeter of the Common barely penetrated the center of the gardens. The frigid air burned her lungs, and her breath rasped in her ears, but on the fringes of her perceptions she heard a shout.

Pursuit! Constance reacted with primitive instinct as past and present blended. Old fears and habits replaced coherent thought, and she ducked under the barren branches of the elms lining the pathway and took to her heels like a doe in flight.

Dragging her skirts through the remnants of snowbanks, she dodged the eerie arms of naked trees that snatched and tore at her hair and clothes. In some places the ground was bare, and dead grass slithered beneath her feet, crunching with the thin layer of night-forming ice. Blood thundered in her ears, magnifying her terror and the sound of footsteps drawing ever closer. In a fever pitch of panic, she threw herself over a low embankment and started down the snowy slope toward the dark open space below. Hands caught her from behind, and she screamed.

"Stop that, you silly twit!" A strong arm caught her across the waist. "You can't go down there."

"Let go!" In the grip of terror, she clawed at him.

"Constance! It's only me." Lock pulled her back against him forcefully, his chest heaving with exertion. "Didn't you realize—look!"

Scooping up a broken stick, he hurled it forward. It sailed into the open space and landed with a crackle and a splash, then sank beneath the thin layer of ice.

"It's the pond," Lock said next to her ear. "You could have drowned."

Constance saw the water then, and in a flash of horror pictured herself trapped beneath the black surface, silver bubbles rising like futile prayers. The sensation was so real, she went unforgivably weak and queasy. Her knees gave way, and before Lock could react, she slid from his arms into a heap at his feet.

"Constance!" Lock squatted beside her, running his hands over her for signs of injury, scowling ferociously through the darkness when he touched her frigid flesh. With a muttered curse, he removed his jacket and pulled it roughly around her shoulders, leaning her against his shoulder for support. The musky scent of warm male skin and shaving soap enveloped her, and she shuddered at the blessed warmth that lingered in the garment.

"Blast it all, what's wrong? Are you hurt?"

"I—I don't like the water," she gasped against his shoulder, shivering uncontrollably.

His arms came around her, hugging her to him, rocking her slightly as if comforting a child. "It's all right. You're safe now, princess."

Safe. She felt it. She sensed it in the solid strength of the muscle beneath her cheek. She understood it in the dependable pressure of his arms surrounding her, supporting her. She knew it in the honesty of his low words. It drew her as a moth to a flame, as inevitable as destiny, as irreversible as the cosmos. She lifted her head, gazing up at him in relief, in wonder, in recognition.

Lock stared down at Constance, stunned by the tremulous vulnerability and naked need shimmering in her smoky eyes. In the chill darkness, a spark of something bright and potent arced between them. With a hungry sound, he covered her mouth with his, and the spark became a flame. With a

muted whimper, she answered his hunger, and the
flame became a fire storm.

Powerfully, he tasted her, lingering at the corners
of her mouth, nipping at her lower lip, the soft teasing caresses adding unexpected nuances to the bold
flavor of his mouth. When the tip of his tongue
laved the seam of her lips, Constance quivered, not
from the cold but from the heat that burned in
her breasts, her belly. Wanting more, she parted her
lips, and touched his tongue with the tip of her
own. Lightning zigzagged all the way to her toes
and lodged low in her core to ignite feelings she'd
never expected.

Oh, she'd been kissed before. She'd been eager to
flaunt the sexual rules along with all the others. But
the island boys were clumsy and as inexperienced
as she was, and she'd known better than to risk her
virtue and health with a foreign sailor. Not that she
wouldn't have if it had been necessary, but Uncle
Cyrus's assumptions had saved her that. So she'd
won a whore's reputation without the inconvenience of losing her virginity, but she'd never even
guessed until this moment what all those fire-and-
brimstone sermons on the weakness of the flesh had
meant. And it was clear that she was very weak indeed.

Somehow, Constance's hands were about Lock's
neck, and she pressed closer, greedy for sensations
and impressions. He obliged with a sense-stealing
swipe of his tongue, tasting her deepest recesses,
sealing his mouth to hers while he pulled her
against his length, showing her the glory of how
they fit, her softness to his hardness.

She couldn't breathe, couldn't think, everything
forgotten but this incandescent splendor, as if he were
truly an archangel who had transported her from
earth to paradise with one touch. But he was real,
and she stroked his cheek, then pressed her fingers to
the corner of his mouth, feeling his lips as they

moved over her own. He kissed her fingertips, the peak of her cheekbone, the corner of her eye.

"Lauchlan," she whispered, her voice an ache.

He went still, the rasp of their ragged breathing the only sound above the tumultuous beating of their hearts. He looked at the passion-stung beauty of her mouth and shuddered.

"Sweet Jesus," he said on a low, raw note. "I must be out of my mind."

She reacted as if he'd slapped her, his withdrawal and repudiation of her safe haven more painful than a physical blow. Reality returned with a vengeance—the darkness, the water, the cold, the man. She lurched away from him with a desperation born of humiliation and hurt, but he caught her hand, helping her to her feet despite her efforts to shake him off.

"Constance—"

"Don't!" she ordered, not looking at him.

He passed a hand over his dazed face. "I don't know what to say."

"Say nothing. Just go away." She took a step and nearly fell again.

"The hell I will!" he exploded, catching her. "It's freezing. You're risking frostbite or worse with this foolishness."

"I hate this blighted place," she muttered, stumbling over her numb feet.

Supporting her weight, he took his bearings, then half led, half carried her back toward a pathway. "You're not going to die of exposure if I can help it."

"The devil take you! I don't need your help."

"Right." He lifted her over a snowy mound, and the sarcasm modulated as his voice became apologetic. "I didn't intend to frighten you—or anything."

That was scarce comfort, so to hide the fact that she was still shaking from the aftermath of his embrace, she resorted to belligerence. "Then why did you follow me?"

"You were upset when you left the Assembly."

"Oh, and you wanted to comfort me? How truly chivalrous," she sneered and pushed at him. "Go away, I said!"

"Don't be difficult. As a gentleman, I can't let you walk home unescorted." His voice was tight with growing temper.

"Since I've just spent the evening breaking every rule in Mrs. Farrar's list, I assure you my reputation can stand it," she said caustically, her nerves raw and overstretched.

"Ungrateful brat. You'd be neck-deep in the frog pond by now if not for me."

Constance bristled. "I'd never have gone off the path at all if not for your sneaking after me. Spare me any more of your *help!*"

"I'm not giving you a choice," he returned, his jaw jutting stubbornly. "Latham House isn't far, and you need to remove those wet things."

They were almost to the Beacon Street entrance of the Common now. Across the thoroughfare well-proportioned mansions stood in solid, dignified lines, every red brick, black shutter, and piece of pristine white trim a daunting reflection of their owners' impeccable breeding and financial success.

"Consider well, Mr. McKin," Constance warned in a nasty tone. "If you insist on following convention and we're seen together without a chaperon, you'll have to marry me. A dismaying thought even for you."

He snorted. "I suppose it's a chance I'll have to take."

"Well, I don't! I'd be obliged if you'd remove your hands and your detestable presence at once."

"So you can sulk in peace?" he drawled. "After that display tonight, I don't blame you. You're hell on crockery, aren't you?"

"Oh!" She took an impotent swing at him through the enveloping coat, fury warming her veins. "Leave it to you to applaud my humiliation. Don't bother denying it—you welcome any trouble that comes to the Lathams. I saw you enjoying it all!"

"Part of it, anyway." The glow from a street lamp illuminated the wry upward tilt of his mouth. They paused on the pathway, his arm around her waist, his other hand pulling the lapels of his coat together at her throat. He used the leverage to tilt her face up to his. "I'll let you in on a little secret. Rodger Latham is a pompous ass. This lowering experience will no doubt have a salubrious effect."

"He's afraid of me," she said, almost to herself, and shivered from a combination of fear and cold and the nearness of the man holding her. "I can't stay here."

"Do you solve all your problems by running away?"

The blunt question took her breath and flooded her with guilt. "You don't understand."

"Don't be absurd." His tone was brusque. "Believe it or not, I well appreciate the galling aspects of society's speculations."

She wilted, defiance draining out of her. "I expect you do."

Hadn't that realization been exactly what had pushed her into making a fool of herself this evening? Hadn't that sense of shared misfortune misled her into thinking for an instant she'd found something precious in his arms? No matter that it had been an illusion, the loss of it still hurt.

"Running is the coward's way." Lock turned their steps down Beacon, guiding her toward the massive granite bulk of Latham House as he spoke. "It only prolongs the problem."

"I'm not as strong as you." Her voice was suddenly husky with tears.

He laughed his disbelief. "You made a mockery of all the dragon-faced gorgons and hypocrites of Boston society tonight. I'd say that's wonderfully courageous."

"No, it wasn't like that at all." Directly across from Latham House, Constance drew to a halt under the lacy arch of trees that she saw each morning from her bedroom window. It was suddenly imperative that she explain herself.

"That wasn't me," she said earnestly. "Not really. I don't know why I do such outrageous things. It's as if I have no control over myself sometimes, as if somebody else is making me do them." Her voice broke. "Maybe I'm possessed. Or crazy."

"Playing for sympathy, Constance? I've never met anyone who needed it less."

"It's hopeless. If you only knew . . ." She shook her head and drew a great shuddering breath that was almost a sob.

"Hey, easy." He looked at her uncertainly. "You've had a shock, that's all, and you're half frozen."

A tear rolled off her lashes, then another, sliding down her cheeks in glistening paths.

"Don't do that, dammit," he muttered. "Come on, Connie, please."

It was beyond her to stop the tears, so she turned to flee yet again, but he wouldn't let her, pulling her into his arms gently yet unequivocally, until the unspoken offer destroyed her resistance and she collapsed against his shirtfront.

Lock held her, not quite knowing what to do, yet doing it anyway, whispering soothing sounds, warming her back under the coat with his large hands, shielding her from the wind with his body. It was a simple kindness, with no overtones of the brief flame of passion they'd shared, but no one except poor Jerôme, her art teacher, had ever offered her such comfort. Though she knew she didn't deserve it, Lock's acceptance was such an overwhelming gift that the tears flowed again, and she clenched her fingers in his shirt as if she'd hold onto him forever.

But that was impossible, another mad fancy born of her loneliness. They were who they were, and her guilt cut her off from even the most basic human ties. To hope for more was to risk her freedom, her life, and the precious little sanity she still possessed.

Pushing out of Lock's arms, Constance crossed the empty street at a run, not even realizing she still wore his jacket. She knew he wouldn't call her back, and he didn't. Taking the coward's way yet again, she fled, not toward the dubious refuge of Latham House, but away from the most dangerous threat she'd encountered since leaving Lahaina.

"Constance? Are you awake, my dear?"

Propped up in her high feather bed, Constance roused from a disgraceful bout of self-pity at her grandfather's knock and soft question. Wiping away the evidence of recent tears, she guiltily rolled Lock McKin's coat into a ball and shoved it back into its hiding place under her sodden pillow. The bands of gray light filtering in through the drapes gave no indication whether it was nine or noon, but after the fiasco of the night before, hibernation was a more attractive alternative than facing up to angry questions.

Another kind of running away, she thought in self-disgust and forced herself to respond. "Come in."

Alex entered, imposing as always in his businessman's stolid black worsted suit, his iron-gray mane and ruff of silver beard giving him a rather natty leonine appearance. He carried a napkin-covered plate and wore a surprisingly uncertain expression.

"Good morning, Constance. Are you quite recovered?"

Huddled against the headboard with her knees raised defensively, Constance watched him with wary eyes as he approached the bedside. "I'm fine, Alex. I want to explain—"

"Not feverish?"

She shook her head, her dark hair lapping about the high ruffled collar of her modest nightgown. "No, I—"

"Good, good. Maggie says you haven't eaten. Would you join me?" He sat down on the edge of the bed, balancing the plate between them on the bedclothes, then pulled the napkin free to reveal an entire apple pie and two forks.

Constance gulped. "I—I'm not very hungry."

"This *is* serious," he jested.

To Constance, the humor seemed misplaced and painful, the spicy scent of cinnamon and apples cloying. She swallowed and forced the words she needed through her constricted throat. "About last night. I want to apologize. I behaved badly. I know you're angry with me."

Alex's dour mouth twisted. "No, with myself. Folk accept my blunt ways and ill humors, but they aren't so generous to a stranger, no matter what her name, and I was too wrapped up in myself to remember it. I threw you to the sharks, didn't I, girl?"

"It wasn't as bad as that," she muttered, twisting the edge of the coverlet.

"It's just that I want so much for you," Alex said. He tapped his fist on his thigh, and his expression turned inward. "The same way I wanted it for James."

"Why did my father leave Boston?" Constance asked. "There was surely much to keep him here."

Alex glanced at her, and his jaw tensed. "We had a falling-out."

"Over what?"

"The usual things a father and his wild son butt heads about—his place in the business, too much hard liquor, the female company he kept." He shrugged. "It was touch and go for the business when the partnership broke up, and I suppose I wasn't in any mood to listen to a young man's excuses. I was actually glad when he shipped out to the Pacific. Thought it would help him grow up, develop some backbone, and then he'd come home again to settle down where he belonged."

"I'm sure he intended to someday." It was all she could offer by way of comfort, for all but the vaguest of memories she possessed of her father lay behind the hazy wall in her head.

"I pushed him too hard and paid a terrible price." Alex was quiet for a moment, then shook off his morose thoughts and focused on Constance's solemn expression. "And again my expectations run away with me. I pushed you to take your place here before you were ready."

"It's not your fault. You've been so generous to me—the clothes, the lessons, everything—but . . ."

Alex's head snapped up in alarm. "But what?"

"But I think it would be best if I left for Paris as soon as possible." She swallowed hard, hating to hurt the old man, but knowing that further complications would arise if she delayed. "I know you're disappointed in me, but if you could arrange for my reward money now, or at least a portion of it for my passage, I'd be grateful."

Alex hesitated, running his forefinger inside of his high starched collar. "I didn't expect this, Constance."

Rosy color stained her face, and she touched her heated cheeks in embarrassment. "I know it makes me sound just like the mercenary Rodger called me."

"Don't worry about Rodger," Alex ordered gruffly. "I can handle him."

"Rodger doesn't trust me, and after what happened, I'm sure an apology won't suffice."

"He'll get over it!' Alex exploded, jumping to his feet to pace back and forth on the gold-and-green Turkish carpet. "For goodness' sake, girl, you didn't try to shoot him!"

She couldn't hold back a smile at that. "No. There's something to be thankful for after all. But I'm sure Rodger will think better of me when there's an ocean between us."

Alex rubbed his neck and looked chagrined. "To be frank, you've caught me at a financially awkward moment, Constance. I've just entered into some rather ticklish negotiations to obtain a new clipper for the San Francisco trade, and my erstwhile partners are demanding cash guarantees."

"Oh." Constance's voice held a wealth of dismay.

Alex sat down beside her again and caught her hands. "You'll get your reward, just as I promised. But since I paid McKin with everything liquid I could lay hold to, I'll have to ask you to be patient just a bit longer."

Constance chewed her thumbnail. "I—I see."

"Haven't you enjoyed anything about your stay?" he asked.

He sounded so anxious, so hurt, she hastened to reassure him. "Of course I have. You've been so kind to me, and I'm very fond of you."

"Yes, yes." Alex waved away her sentiments. "But I should have known a young woman would wish to choose her own amusements. Surely you've found something or someone here to interest you?"

She hesitated as a vision of Lock McKin rose in her mind. Thrusting the tantalizing image away, she answered the question carefully. "I have my painting, and Miss Philpot was very friendly last evening and invited me to her literary club."

"Well, that's the ticket, then!" Alex said firmly. "Rather than trying to fulfill any of my asinine expectations, you must follow your own heart. From now on, all classes are canceled."

"But, Alex—"

He bussed her cheek clumsily before she could shy away, then placed the pie in her lap and stood. "Now, I won't hear another word on the subject, so eat up."

"It's a lot to swallow," she muttered, caught somewhere between amusement and frustration.

Alex paused at the door. Chuckling to himself, he winked at her. "Literary society, eh? We'll show them there's more than one way to skin a Massachusetts cat."

Constance watched the door close behind her grandfather, looked at the pie she held, and shook her head in defeat. She was certain the shrewd old man had steered her in his chosen direction yet again. But what was she to do? Without funds, she couldn't get across the Charles River, much less the Atlantic.

Maybe it wouldn't be so bad now, she mused, breaking off a section of the fluted crust and nibbling at it thoughtfully. If her grandfather had truly resigned himself to more realistic expectations, she could be meek and mild and self-effacing for the duration and avoid further trouble.

Maybe.

Picking up a fork, Constance stabbed the center of the pie, then laughed as she retrieved a succulent wedge of cooked apple. But the taste of it brought to mind a certain ebony-haired shipbuilder, and she sobered again. Balancing the pie, Constance dragged Lock's coat from under her pillow and laid it over her knees.

It was self-indulgent, she knew, to find an ephemeral kind of comfort in the fact that he'd worn this garment, and that he'd given it to her still warm from his own body. It was dangerous to think that his brusque protectiveness was anything but a form of Yankee chivalry. And it was rash and foolhardy to remember how sweet and hot and powerful his mouth had been.

With a soft moan, she set aside the pie, the sudden quivering of her stomach killing all interest in food. It was the man who fascinated, intrigued, and frightened her. But hadn't she already decided she ought to stay as far away from Lock McKin as she could?

When had she ever done as she "ought"? an inner voice wondered.

No, this time was going to be different, she vowed and threw back the covers. Trouble would simply have to find someone else to plague.

She would give Alex a week, and if he still couldn't come up with her share of the reward, she'd advance herself a loan from the money she'd deposited for Dylan and his troublesome brother. In the meantime, there were loose ends to tie up before leaving for France: apologize to Rodger, attend Miss Philpot's meeting, complete her painting, investigate the packet schedule and gather her courage for the voyage, return Lock's coat.

She snatched the garment from the bed, but her fingers lingered on the fine fabric, and she inhaled the subtle scents of wool and soap and man that still clung to it. Realizing what she'd done, she folded the coat irritably, annoyed at her own susceptibility. The sooner this reminder of an incident best forgotten was out of sight and mind, the better. With luck, she could tease Maggie into a painting excursion this very day, finish the portrait of the *Odyssey*, and return the coat to the shipyard office without even seeing Lock McKin.

Nodding firmly to herself, she prepared to dress, not even considering what kind of luck it might turn out to be.

Lock threw down his pen and leaned back from the drawing board, stretching his tired shoulders and rubbing his grainy eyes. A steam winch had broken down, two of his more nervous investors wanted out for reasons that sounded suspiciously lame, and none of his calculations were making any sense. Between those headaches, the shipyard's normal daily crises, and Lock's edgy, unsettled emotional state, it had been a hell of a day.

A fire glowed behind the isinglass window of the stove located in the corner of his combination sitting room and workroom. The chamber was cluttered with a bachelor's few luxuries—a large comfortable chair, worn on the arms; shelves laden with shipbuilding treatises, mathematical texts, and a batch of experimental models; a spacious drafting table lit by both an oil lamp and a shuttered window overlooking the shipyard. One door led to the outside staircase of his second-floor quarters, the other to the bedroom where luxurious Oriental silk coverlets, a carved ebony tea chest, and a folding screen embellished with a red-eyed dragon made a surprising contrast to the sitting room's bare-bones austerity. The apartment over his offices was private, convenient, and as much home as he either needed or wanted.

Pegged on the board in front of him, the hull elevations and tonnages he'd struggled with this afternoon mocked him, ridiculing his efforts to concentrate on something other than a golden-eyed enchantress. With a growl, Lock untacked the scroll and rolled it up, stuffing it into a small cask to stand along with a dozen other rolls. Maybe some supper shared with Jedediah at Mrs. Pibb's excellent boardinghouse would improve his mood. He reached to close the shutters against the gloaming and froze. All his workmen had finished for the day, and for an instant, it seemed his thoughts had conjured up the lone figure seated in the lee of a massive beam. Then he stifled a curse.

Damn the troublesome woman! After everything

that had happened last night, what was Constance
Latham doing back in his shipyard? He'd seen her
dabbling with her paints and brushes on other occasions, noticing her from the molding loft or when
he'd made his inspections of the *Odyssey*, but they'd
stayed well out of each other's way. Until last night.

Improbable, absurd urchin! Thumbing her nose at
society, dunking her pompous cousin in a punch
bowl, then leaving with such a stark, haunted look
on her beautiful face that Lock had been compelled
to follow. Before last night, he would have laughed
outright at the insane notion that Iron Man McKin
would end up sitting in a snowbank kissing the
granddaughter of his sworn enemy, much less that
she would have kissed him back to the point that
they were both nearly senseless!

What still appalled Lock was his loss of control.
He'd seen his father's gradual disintegration in
those awful years after his mother died, and he'd
sworn never to let the same happen to him. A man
controlled his emotions at all times, used that
strength to coolly assess problems and accomplish
goals. It was insupportable that a sultry-voiced *wahine* had been able to knock him off-balance from
the very first moment of their acquaintance. It was
intolerable that at least a dozen times today he'd
found himself thinking about how sweet her mouth
was. It was unthinkable that when he'd touched
her, he'd realized she was a fraud. Her tough-girl
facade hid a soft, vulnerable center, and all he'd
wanted then was to bury himself in her need and
give himself up to his own.

Lock hissed air between his teeth at these dangerous thoughts and slammed the shutters closed. His
jaw working, he muttered an oath, then rolled his
shirtsleeves into place and reached for his pea coat.
He'd find no peace of mind until Constance Latham
was off his property and out of his thoughts for

good. He'd just have to make it clear once and for all that no Latham was welcome here.

Moments later, Lock strode across the yard, circling the shed that housed the deep saw pits where timbers were shaped, once by two men on a long saw—one above and one below in the pit—now by a steam-driven apparatus that was the latest innovation. His heavy boots were muffled by a year's thick layer of sawdust. Rounding a pile of timbers, he came up short.

Constance sat on a beam with her back to him, her head wrapped in a knitted muffler, wielding a brush and palette over a canvas propped on a pile of scrap lumber. It was the *Odyssey* in her painting, all right, the masts sketched in but still lacking sails, her bow plunging through high seas, running before purple storm clouds roiling over the horizon. It was so real, Lock could almost feel the spray. Frowning, he realized he'd have to retract all his assumptions about Constance being a dilettante. The luminous, living impact of the picture showed enormous talent and infinite control. She was certainly no amateur. Lock took another step to get a closer look.

"Another minute, Maggie," Constance murmured, her brush flying. "The light's going, and I'm almost done . . ."

"It doesn't appear finished to me," Lock said.

Constance jumped, and her uncontrolled motion produced a white smear on the picture. "*Parbleu!*"

She cast a resentful look over her shoulder, then rapidly went to work to fix the mistake. "You're making a tiresome habit of sneaking up on me, Mr. McKin."

"Beg your pardon, Miss Latham," Lock returned with a sarcastic edge to his voice, "but I can scarcely be accused of skulking about on my own property. And while I admire your work, I must repeat, aren't you missing something?"

The error corrected to her satisfaction, she wrapped brushes and palette in rags that smelled of linseed oil, stuffed them in a cloth sack, and rose to her feet.

"I'm quite satisfied with the harmony of my composition. And at least my masts are in place," she said, glancing toward the real *Odyssey*. "You're due to launch her soon, I see."

"A few more weeks, perhaps."

"Then tell me how you plan to rig her so that I may complete my portrait."

Mildly amused at her imperious demand, Lock obliged, giving her a complete list of royals, mainsails, and spankers, then asked, "Wouldn't it have been simpler to paint her docked, with all sails furled?"

From beneath her wisp of bangs, her look was contemptuous. "Is that how you see her? Or flying through the seas ahead of a nor'wester?"

"A romantic notion, but a sailor always prays for clear weather," he said. "The reason she's fast is to command top freight rates, certainly more likely now that the *West Wind*'s set a record for me. Unloading a fortune in tea and goods is how I'd like to picture the *Odyssey*—and hopefully will before another year passes."

"Does that practical streak ever get in the way of your dreams?"

"Never."

"It must be gratifying to be so sure of oneself." She looked at him thoughtfully in the gathering twilight, then lowered her lashes to veil her expression. "I returned your coat to your office. Thank you. I'm glad to see you didn't suffer for its lack."

Lock dug his hands in his jacket pockets, forcibly reminded now of their previous encounter and his mission. "You're welcome. It was nothing."

"Not to me."

The soft quiver in her voice was infinitely revealing, and Lock looked at her in alarm. Then it was back, that fine-tuned awareness, that breathless sense of stepping off a cliff into nothingness. He could have drowned in the golden depths of her eyes or willingly lost himself in the wild magic of her mouth, and he knew with a touch of male ego that she wouldn't resist, might even welcome him as she had before. His hands turned to fists inside his pockets with the effort not to reach for her.

"You shouldn't come here anymore," he said abruptly, surprised at the hoarseness of his own voice.

Startled, she looked at him with widened eyes. "Why?"

"You know why."

"No." She laughed without humor. "I don't."

"It's impossible."

"Because you say my grandfather betrayed your father? How? No one will tell me that!"

Lock's mouth firmed into a harsh line. "Alex Latham withdrew his financial support at a critical time and ruined us. My father lost everything after that. His marriage, his business, eventually his life."

"But why?" she cried. "Why would Alex do that? There must have been a reason."

"A Latham doesn't need one."

An angry, defiant color stained her cheeks at his condemnation. Pulling aside her muffler, she shook out her sable-colored mane and stepped close to him, her look sultry and challenging. "Is that why you're afraid of me, Lock McKin?"

"Don't be absurd."

"Then why is it you who's running this time?" she asked, trailing her hand up the front of his jacket.

He snagged her wrist in a viselike hold, and his voice deepened into a low growl of warning. "You're playing with fire, Constance."

"'Tis better than freezing in this wasteland," she

murmured, swaying against him, her gaze fastened on his mouth.

"You'll only get burned." *We both will*, he thought with an inward groan.

That reckless, fey look was back in her eyes. "Maybe I don't care."

Mysterious shadows chased across her face, and the breeze whipped her hair against his cheek, bringing with it the fragrance of flowers. Lock could feel his control slipping by degrees, and he thrust her away.

"Damn you! What kind of game do you think you're playing?"

"One of little consequence, it seems. Especially to a man so sure of himself." Constance rubbed her wrist and gave him a knowing smile, then reached for her bag and the wet painting. "Ah, there you are, Maggie."

Lock turned to see the red-haired maid and one of his laborers, a broad-shouldered, pug-faced black Irishman by the name of Tip Maddock, picking their way through the timbers. Maggie's eyes were bright, and she looked well kissed. Her smitten beau kept a protective hand on her elbow.

"It's sorry I am, miss," Maggie said, breathless and blushing. "We were talking . . . and forgot the time."

"'Tis well at least one of us didn't miss the opportunity at hand," Constance said.

The look she slanted at Lock tweaked his temper and made his blood boil with frustration. He ground his teeth. So this was his reward for being sensible! God, the woman was maddening.

Maggie bobbed a curtsy in Lock's direction and looked at Constance curiously. "Tip's ready to see us back now, if you're ready, miss."

Constance caught Lock's hard gaze and smiled again. "Yes, Maggie. I'm quite done here."

Chapter 5

Miss Elspeth Philpot's establishment was situated near the intersection where Summer Street became Winter Street, along a block lined with small shops not far from Trinity Church. She lived over a store whose canvas awning proclaimed, in scarlet-and-gilt letters, "The Attic— Stationers, Periodicals, and Books." Since Miss Philpot's apartment was fairly bursting with printed matter of all types, as if somehow the bookstore had once exploded, spewing its inventory like spores that mushroomed in the most unexpected and often inconvenient locations, Constance was scarcely surprised to learn that her hostess was a partner in the enterprise.

"It was the only way I could support my reading habit," Elspeth admitted cheerfully, setting her empty teacup on a wobbly pile of *Scientific Gazette* in lieu of a parlor table.

"Do not be misled, Miss Latham," an angular gentleman with deep-set eyes advised. He rose from the circle of ornately carved armchairs and horsehair settees, where a heated literary discussion had taken place for the better part of two hours. "Our Miss Philpot is a catalyst of the first order. Our most respected authors have generated ideas around her tea tray, then brought them to publication with her enthusiastic support."

"My interests aren't all altruistic, you know," Elspeth denied modestly. Her jet earrings bounced against the crocheted snood bundling her gold-and-silver chignon. "I must encourage the book trade for the sake of my business, and this is more enjoyable for me than other methods. But you aren't leaving so soon, Mr. Garrison?"

"Another issue of *The Liberator* demands my attention." He bent over Constance's hand. "It's been a pleasure, Miss Latham. I hope we meet again soon."

Constance made suitable murmurs of appreciation. The warmth and welcome she'd received among this elite group was a striking contrast to her experience at the Assembly Ball. With Elspeth Philpot as her mentor, she had been readily accepted, plied with intelligent questions about her Pacific home, and her answers listened to respectfully by the eclectic group, some of which were famous writers and artists, others relatively unknown supporters of Boston's cultural endeavors, but all devotees of the literary and artistic life.

As the meeting broke up, Elspeth elicited a promise from Constance to stay a while, then saw her guests out through the maze of crammed bookshelves, potted ferns, and stacks of odd newspapers, files, and boxes of old and rare books. On her return, Elspeth flopped down beside Constance, fanned herself with a lace handkerchief, and gave a satisfied sigh.

"What a truly enlightening afternoon! Mr. William Garrison is a great orator, is he not?"

"He speaks quite eloquently," Constance agreed, smoothing the vandyked flounces of her green silk visiting gown and adjusting the tilt of her silver locket, pinned today with a rosette on the lapel of her bodice.

"His work for the antislavery society is untiring.

And," Elspeth added, "he is remarkable in that he also favors equality for women!"

"I found all of your guests fascinating," Constance replied, "especially Mr. Hawthorne."

Elspeth bobbed to her feet. "I promised to lend you a copy of his *Twice-Told Tales*, didn't I? Now, where could I have put it?"

Constance glanced around the cluttered chamber dubiously and raised a hand to stop her new friend. "Please, I couldn't put you to such trouble."

"No, no trouble at all. I've a knack for remembering things. Just because I have thirty years' worth of reading materials stacked about . . ." Elspeth looked distracted for a moment, then her expression cleared, and she hastened to a tall dresser dripping with antimacassars and poetry journals and pulled a volume from under the deepest pile. "Eureka!"

Constance smiled her thanks as Elspeth placed the book in her hands. "I know I'll enjoy it."

"Some of his stories are quite droll. There's one about—but I shan't spoil it for you," Elspeth said with a laugh. She settled herself once again on the slick horsehair sofa and looked at Constance expectantly. "May I see your sketches now, my dear?"

"I shouldn't expect too much," Constance hedged as she retrieved her portfolio from under her feet. "They're just working sketches for the ship's portrait I've completed recently, and some studies I made for my own amusement."

"You must have confidence in yourself and your work, especially if you wish to excel in Paris," Elspeth instructed stoutly, pulling the ribbons free and opening the sketchbook. She drew a pince-nez from a pocket on her ample bosom and set about examining each page. "After all, if you don't believe in yourself, who will?"

"You're right, of course," Constance said. To cover her nervousness, she rose and went to the fireplace to examine an ornately carved fire screen in the "naturalistic" style, dripping with sheaves of wheat and clutches of pheasants. "It's something I've dreamed of for a long time, and now that it's almost within my grasp, I can't help being afraid that I won't be good enough."

"I shouldn't worry about that point, if I were you," Elspeth said dryly. "These are marvelous!"

Constance turned back to the older woman with a look of relief. "Do you really think so?"

"Absolutely. The ship studies are well done and of interest to you considering your family's success in the seagoing trade, but these other drawings! My dear, they're fascinating."

Constance frowned, puzzled by Elspeth's enthusiasm. "You mean the drawings of Lahaina?"

"Not Lahaina—the *people* of Lahaina." Elspeth flipped pages again. "These cherubic children, and the young men with this wonderful canoe. And this old woman—you can see the compassion and love in her beautiful, wrinkled face. Who is she?"

Gazing down at the portrait, Constance frowned and rubbed her temple. She felt on the verge of remembering something significant, but then the feeling slipped away. "I—I'm not sure. A priestess, perhaps."

"All your pictures tell a story about life on your island. Constance, you must let me find you a publisher!"

"A publisher?" She was astounded. "Why?"

"Because these drawings are wonderful, but also because interest in the Sandwich Islands hasn't waned since the first Congregationalist missionaries left here over thirty years ago. The audience for such a publication would be ready-made, and while I don't purport that you'll become wealthy overnight from such a venture, here's a chance to use your art to become self-supporting."

Elspeth's runaway enthusiasm made Constance's head spin. "I don't know what to say."

"Just say yes, and I'll do the rest." Elspeth's pale blue eyes sparkled behind her spectacles. "Mr. Evans on Washington Street is a fine printer and would do a handsome job. We can approach him first."

"How can I say no to such a proposition?" Constance asked.

To actually earn something from doing what she loved best! The thought was exhilarating. Nor would she have to borrow on the McKins' account or wait on Alex's promises to pay for her ticket abroad if things went forward quickly.

"You're so kind," she said, smiling her gratitude. "I can't thank you enough."

"I abhor waste in any form," Elspeth replied primly, tying up the portfolio again. "And your talent is too exceptional to squander on ship's portraits alone."

"Painting the *Odyssey* was something I wanted to do for myself," Constance explained, wandering back to the fireplace. "Lauchlan McKin's ships are truly works of art."

Elspeth's ears perked up. "McKin, you said?"

With a grimace, Constance turned back to her friend. "Yes, I know it seems unreasonable for a Latham to be dealing with a McKin. It's all rather muddled." Without thinking, she touched the locket on her lapel. "I only wish I knew what really happened . . ."

"Surely you have no wish to dredge up that old gossip?"

Constance looked startled. "Is there something I should know, Elspeth?"

"No, no." Elspeth waved her pince-nez. "It was all so long ago . . ."

"Please, Elspeth!" Constance sat down beside her, overcome by a sense of urgency. "I only know bits and pieces of what brought on this feud. It would help me so much if I could just understand."

"It started out as a business disagreement, I suppose," Elspeth said thoughtfully. "Latham, McKin and Company could do no wrong in those early days. Enoch—that's the present Mr. McKin's father—was the shipwright and your grandfather the merchant, and I must say everything they touched turned to pure gold."

"So what went wrong?"

"Well, that's the point, isn't it? No one really knew, but when they fell out with one another, they fell out with a vengeance. Old Enoch lost everything without your grandfather's financial support, and after that . . ."

"I know. He killed himself."

"A bitter thing. So sad for those sons of his, especially Dylan, having lost his mama so young, too." Elspeth shook her head sorrowfully. "A real pity, because the company had put some fine ships into the water under its banner, a real boon to the city. But here, I think I can even show you . . ."

Elspeth went over to a tall bookcase, pushed a pile of books into place, and used them to scale the shelves. After a moment and some little muttering, she retrieved an old volume of the *Shipbuilder's Almanac* from the top. Returning to Constance's side, she fanned the pages until she came to an engraving of a ship-launching ceremony.

"There, you see?" she asked, pointing at a group pictured on the deck of a sleek-bodied packet. "Those were happier days for everyone."

Frowning, Constance took the almanac to examine the cluster of figures more closely, then gasped softly. "That's my father! And Alex, too. 'Owners of the *Silver Crest*, Alexander and James Latham,' " she read softly, tracing the accompanying text with her forefinger, " 'and Mr. and Mrs. Enoch McKin with son Lauchlan.' "

She smiled at the portrait of a grinning youngster in knee britches and straw boater standing proudly at his parents' side. He'd been a handsome lad, but it was hard to translate that carefree youth into the man she knew now.

Constance stifled a sigh. She wasn't sure what devil had prompted her to bait Lock McKin on their last meeting. It was just that he was so infuriatingly cocksure of himself, warning her off as if he were so irresistible she was sure to lose her heart over a few kisses! Just because things had gotten out of hand in a moment of weakness didn't give him the right to make assumptions about her intentions. Although it had done her impetuous heart good to see him squirm, she had no desire to become intimately involved with a man whose soul and emotions were under such rigid control that they seemed encased in glacial ice.

Her gaze wandered over the smiling, boyish features in the picture again, and a feeling of sad regret stole over her. The trials Lock had undergone since that day must have been arduous indeed to have cast and molded him into the Iron Man. She knew herself how hard it was to have lost both parents. Her fingers touched the picture of Lock's young mother, a pretty blond woman with a solemn expression, and she sucked in a startled breath.

"Dear God!" It was the woman whose picture was in her locket!

"What is it, dear?" Elspeth asked, then frowned. "I see you've already heard the vicious slander about Enoch's wife and . . . and your father."

"Tell me," Constance demanded in a strangled voice.

"The gossips reported a . . . a liaison. Now, it was true Eliza was a great deal younger than Enoch, and she and James were much thrown together by the business association, but that was certainly no proof! It was truly tragic how malicious lies destroyed two innocent people's lives. James went off to the Pacific, and poor Eliza was so devastated by the scandal and the troubles after the partnership dissolved that she died of a wasting sickness only a few years later. Of course, the gossips put it down to a broken heart, but it was pure rumor all the way 'round, I say."

"You're wrong,' Constance said unsteadily. Hands shaking, she removed her locket and opened it for Elspeth's startled perusal.

Elspeth took the silver oval, amazement written on her plump features. "Why, that's—"

"Yes." Constance nodded and swallowed hard. "My grandfather told me she was a stranger, but it's Eliza McKin, isn't it?"

Elspeth looked uncomfortable. "The resemblance cannot be denied, but there's still no cause to make rash assumptions . . ."

"This was my father's locket, a sentimental heirloom from his mother intended someday for his bride, and yet it holds the portrait of another man's wife." Constance's expression turned stark. "If the rumors were false, Elspeth, why did my father carry Eliza McKin's image with him halfway around the world?"

Latham House was quiet, crouched on the rosy-hued hearth of sunset like a slumberous gray cat awaiting the master's return. Upstairs, Constance sat in the gathering twilight at her grandfather's desk in his richly appointed private study, pensively sucking on Alex's favored peppermints and staring at her father's portrait.

Her critical eye thought the picture hanging over the desk was poorly executed, and she searched in vain for a sense of the bearded young man who looked across time with soulful brown eyes, a poet's forelock falling over his white brow. A Bible lay open on the table beside him and a hound worshipped at his heels. Had James Latham been the kind of man to steal another's wife? A scoundrel

and a womanizer? Or merely weak, as Alex had often hinted? Perhaps he had truly loved Eliza
McKin. Whatever the circumstances, only tragedy,
hate, and vengeance had come of his passion, the
repercussions widening across the years like the ripples in a pond to touch lives even now.

Constance could guess how James might have
thought to make reparation for his sin by a life of
penance and service and missionary ardor—or at
least to find deliverance from temptation and disgrace and his father's heavy hand in the far Sandwich Isles. But instead he'd found Constance's
mother.

"Namaka," Constance whispered.

The only things she knew about her mother were
a name she'd found on the mission's marriage reg-
istry and the date of her death when Constance was
scarcely two years old. Now she wondered if
Namaka and her baby daughter had ever meant
anything to James Latham, of if they had both been
poor substitutes for a life he couldn't have. Constance closed her eyes at the painful thought. Perhaps that was why she remembered so little about
her father. Perhaps he had never really cared, never
loved her, never thought that his neglect would
condemn his child to a life of torment and fear. And
maybe it hadn't been the fever that made her memory a hazy cloud, but her own desire to forget a
father who found her unlovable.

Constance bit down on the peppermint, shattering the sugary confection between her teeth, and
pulled her Shetland shawl around her shoulders.
Well, damn James. She hadn't needed him in the final account. She'd killed her dragon and escaped
without anyone's help. Never again would she let
herself be placed in a dependent, defensive position, at the mercy of someone who hated her. There
was no trust, no affection, no loyalty worth losing

her freedom over, and that was the way it was going to stay.

Through her musings she became aware of the sounds of arrivals below, the slamming of the front door, masculine voices raised in demand, the deferential replies of servants as Rodger and Alex returned from the countinghouse. Constance's mood was so bitter she didn't bother to bestir herself, though the study was so nearly dark she could make out only the outlines of the Empire-style chairs and tables. She would have to join the men soon enough at the dinner table, and she needed the time to compose her thoughts.

"Where is she?" Rodger's strident demand echoed up the stairwell, followed by Maggie's anxious but unintelligible reply.

Constance turned her head toward the study door, frowning. Beyond the wedge of illumination from a gas light on the landing, she heard the sound of footsteps pounding up the stair treads, then striding down the hall, doors opening, sibilant cursing.

"God's breath! I swear the vixen's fled, Uncle! Check your valuables."

"Calm yourself, boy." Alex's gruff words vibrated with tension. His silhouette appeared in the study doorway. "I'll just—who? Constance?"

"Yes, Alex." She rose from the desk, standing with her fingers pressed to the marbleized blotter. "Is something amiss?"

"Rodger! I've found her," Alex announced, fumbling his way into the room. "What are you doing sitting here in the dark, child? Maggie, come light the lamps at once!"

Maggie appeared immediately, moving around the study to ignite the gas jets that only the wealthiest could afford to pipe higher than the ground floor.

"Just as I would have expected," Rodger declared

from the doorway. "She's been going through your papers, Uncle Alex."

Constance blinked in the slowly brightening room, bemused by Rodger's hostility. She thought she'd made peace with her most recent apology. Sighing, she wondered what she'd done now to set her cousin to squawking like a crow yet again.

"That's not true, Rodger," she protested tiredly. The perfume of the pomade on his yellow curls made her nose itch. "See for yourself. I haven't touched anything."

"Only for lack of time, I suspect. Where the devil have you been all afternoon?"

Confused, Constance glanced at Alex, then back at Rodger. "Miss Philpot's literary meeting. Should I have been anywhere else?"

"Perhaps conspiring with Lock McKin?" her cousin sneered.

Constance stiffened. "I don't know what you mean."

"Then perhaps you would care to explain *this*." His lip curling in disgust, Rodger heaved Constance's portrait of the *Odyssey* into the middle of the rug. "Or did you think we'd never find out?"

Icy rage frosted Constance's expression and chilled her voice. "You had no right to go through my things."

"Your things?" Rodger scoffed. "Since we've supplied every morsel you've eaten and every stitch you've worn since you arrived, how can you say they're *your* things?"

"I beg your pardon. I was under the mistaken impression that they were gifts," Constance returned, infuriated, scalding color staining her cheeks. She ripped off the shawl and threw it at Rodger's feet, then began to unbutton her cuffs. "I'll return everything immediately. I wouldn't want to be called a thief, and I'd much rather go naked under a tapa cloth than wear this *haole* garb I'm begrudged."

"Constance!" Alex interjected hastily. "That's not necessary, and certainly not what Rodger meant."

"Oh, he didn't mean to be offensive?" she questioned sweetly. "But, Alex, it comes to him so naturally."

"I told you she couldn't be reasonable," Rodger muttered angrily. "She knows full well what enmity lies between us and McKin, and yet she chose to flaunt your feelings openly, Uncle! And you!" He jabbed a finger at Maggie, who'd been edging toward the door, trying to make a strategic retreat from the scene of this family brawl.

"Me, sir?" Maggie squeaked.

"You're discharged, miss!" Rodger barked. "You helped in this escapade, didn't you? That's the reward for those who forget where their loyalties lie."

Maggie's freckled face crumpled pitifully. "But, sir—"

"Out! Pack your things and clear out!"

Maggie burst into tears, threw her apron over her face, and fled. Constance made a tentative motion to go after her, then turned to her grandfather furiously. "That's not fair! She was only doing as I bade her. There's no reason to punish Maggie because I displeased you."

"Displeased him?" Rodger lifted his eyes to heaven for strength. "You traitorous hussy! You have no idea, do you? Will all our work go for naught because of your willful ways? You're not to see Lock McKin or go anywhere near his shipyard again, is that clear?"

As always, a direct order transformed Constance from an otherwise reasonable female into a human mule, with all of the breed's characteristic stubbornness. She tilted her chin. "I do as I please, cousin."

"By God, you'll—"

"Rodger! That's enough." Alex's bellow froze the younger man in mid-stride. He took Constance's hand, urging her into a chair, his voice soothing.

"Constance, please. This is too much for my old heart. It upsets me to see you children arguing."

"I'm sorry, Alex," she replied stiffly.

"It's just that when we heard reports of your visiting South Boston, naturally we were concerned."

"Do you have spies watching me, then?" Her words were tight with disdain, yet beneath her composed facade she shivered.

In Lahaina, they'd kept a close eye on Crazy Lili, a girl whose fancies were condemned as lies and who was always severely disciplined by Uncle Cyrus. A wild child, full of insolence and rebellion. So strange and unpredictable that the adults on the plantation and in the mission school watched her with wary suspicion and fearful superstition. Her mildest transgressions never went unreported or unpunished, and she was often blamed for someone else's mischief, which increased her resentment until it exploded again in another offense so that she never gained a moment's respite from the condemning scrutiny. Had she been a fool to think she could escape that, even here?

Now a lifetime's built-up resentment made her glare her defiance at her cousin. "I've done nothing save paint a beautiful ship."

Rodger gave an exasperated snort and pulled his fingers through his artfully arranged blond curls, revealing the thinning patch of hair above his forehead. "We can't afford to arouse McKin's suspicions, not after all the effort I've made to convince the senator, not to mention—"

"Rodger." Alex's voice held a warning note.

"But, Uncle, we'll have to move immediately now, don't you see?"

"What is it?" Constance demanded. "You're planning something, aren't you? More warfare for this damned feud! Hasn't everyone suffered enough?"

"It's business, child." Alex patted her hand. "You

wouldn't understand. It's just that it would be better if you avoided the McKin shipyard right now."

She rose to her feet again, shaking him off. "The fact that you won't answer me says a lot."

"Only that we've come to care deeply for you, my dear," Alex said gently, his hands lifted in appeal. "I want you to be safe and free from worry, and that's why . . . well, that's why I've altered my will to name you my legal heir along with Rodger."

Constance gasped and her hands flew to her mouth. Rodger gawked in stunned silence, the color draining from his face to leave him pale with resentment.

"Oh, no," Constance moaned. "No, Alex, don't do this."

"Doesn't it please you?" her grandfather asked, his manner hurt. "I only wanted to spare you the complications of an involved probate and provide for your future."

"But you don't understand," she said desperately. "I came to Boston neither expecting nor deserving anything but my half of the reward you offered. Rodger has been your support, your right hand all this time. I have no desire to deprive him of the rewards he's earned with his service and loyalty. Don't pit us against each other this way by making us rivals!"

Alex's brown eyes glistened with emotion. "Do you hear that, Rodger? Is she not the most admirable, unselfish, and generous of women? Small wonder I love her!"

Rodger's glittering hazel gaze flicked her with contempt. "She certainly knows how to cement your devotion, Uncle."

Dazed, Constance touched her temple. "Cousin, I'm sorry. I had no idea—"

"I've only just issued my instructions to the lawyers today," Alex explained. He smiled, as smug as a well-fed lion. "You'll be pleased at some of the other arrangements I've made, too."

"No." She backed away, stricken by the virulence in Rodger's expression and the terrifying and imprisoning affection in Alex's. She grabbed up the forgotten canvas and held the portrait of the *Odyssey* against herself like a shield. "I can't accept this."

"It's for your own good, my dear," her grandfather said kindly. "You'll simply have to trust me."

She shook her head. "No, no. Just the reward money so that I may go to art school. Paris—"

"You must see that's out of the question for now, don't you, Constance?" Alex smiled and tried to smooth her hair, but she jerked away, and his smile became a scowl. "What do you need with that pittance when my entire fortune is at your disposal? Don't worry about anything from now on. I'll take care of you."

Bile rose in her throat and terror constricted her heart as she felt her freedom slipping away. "You don't understand. I can't. If you truly care about me, you won't force me to do this."

"Constance, my dear, calm yourself. You'll make yourself ill."

The word shocked her into stillness. She'd been ill from fear before, so sick in her mind she'd done the unspeakable. No, she wouldn't, couldn't, let that happen again. With a shuddering breath, she took hold of her jangled emotions, forcing the most terrified part of her soul into a tiny box in the back of her head, somewhere near the hazy borders of her sanity.

"Of course, Alex," she said quietly. "I'm being a silly, emotional woman, aren't I? It's just that this is so sudden."

"I knew you'd see it my way," Alex said with satisfaction.

"Somehow, so did I," Rodger muttered.

"Here, let me take that from you," Alex said, tugging the painting from her nerveless fingers. "It's really quite good, isn't it, Rodger? A trophy of our latest prize. Perhaps we'll hang it in the counting-house someday."

She nodded helplessly as he leaned the portrait against the wall. "Whatever you say, Alex."

Beaming, he clapped his hands together in self-congratulation. "Well, now that that's all settled, let's go to dinner, shall we? Eloise has prepared sweetbreads and croquettes tonight."

On Alex's arm, Constance somehow managed to negotiate the stairs without a bobble. But as her grandfather continued to regale her with his plans, she felt trapped in another suffocating nightmare, and her desperate thoughts focused on one thing—escape.

At dawn, Constance was much calmer. By the time she'd dressed, breakfasted with Alex, and spoken vaguely of an afternoon's browsing in Elspeth Philpot's bookstore as a diversion, she was coolly in possession of a plan. She was so amenable and cheerful, so full of easy lies, she was certain she raised no suspicions when she donned her mantle and bonnet against the threatening rain and left Latham House later, although she carried a parcel wrapped in brown paper rather than an umbrella under her arm.

Constance was composed, even philosophical, when she withdrew a sum of cash from the account she'd set up for Dylan McKin. Luck was with her, too, so that when she inquired at the commercial shipping offices, it took her only three tries to find a vessel scheduled for a London departure the very next day. Since she considered her circumstances dire enough to warrant desperate measures, she had no qualms about using McKin money to purchase her ticket, which she tucked carefully into her reticule with mixed feelings of vast relief and infinite trepidation.

Calling at the McKin Brothers Shipyard, she convinced Tip Maddock to deliver her apologies and a wad of greenbacks to Maggie. Tip's sullen expression softened at Constance's generosity, and her conscience eased a bit when he solemnly assured her that Maggie had already found a new position. But when she gathered her courage to attend to the last item on her agenda, she was told Lock had gone to State Street on urgent business, and none of his clerks knew when he would return. Frustrated, Constance went to see Jedediah Shoe.

"Would you see that he gets this, Mr. Shoe?" she asked the old wood-carver.

Straightening from his work, Jedediah squinted at the package. " 'Tis your painting of the *Odyssey* you be givin' him, then?"

"Yes. It seems little enough thanks for the trouble I've caused him." Constance ran her gloved hand admiringly over the smoothly polished snout of the old man's wooden porpoise. "Even though my efforts cannot compare with your wonderful work, I wish Mr. McKin to have it. I'd thought to have a word with him as well, but I must get back before I'm missed."

Although something urged her to warn Lock of the vague threats she'd gleaned from Rodger and her grandfather the night before, she couldn't afford to arouse any further suspicion.

"There's no knowing when the lad will be back, so navigate a surer course, lassie." Jedediah tugged a narrow leather thong strung with a key from around his scrawny neck and handed it to her. "Leave your present in the boy's rooms. Around the corner and up the stairs. I'd do it myself, but my old legs aren't what they used to be."

"You don't think he would mind?"

" 'Twould be a nice surprise to find, I think."

"Well, if you're certain . . ."

"Go, go." Jedediah waved her away with his chisel. "Just leave the key on the hook beside the door."

"Yes. Thank you, Mr. Shoe." She took a final look around the cluttered workshop, marveling again at the beautiful sculpture and bidding the old man a silent farewell.

Slow drops of cold rain pelted her as she stood on the wooden landing and knocked loudly at Lock's door. She received no answer, and feeling more than a little nervous and guilty, but determined to see this through, she inserted the key and went in.

Constance was surprised at the small size of the apartment, and interested, despite her resolve to hurry, in the various accoutrements with which a man of Lock's talent surrounded himself. Pale afternoon light filtered in through open shutters, and books lay everywhere. Through an open doorway she saw exotic fabrics covering a bed and hastily averted her eyes, somehow feeling she was intruding on something intimate that Lock McKin never shared with the world.

Hastily, she unwrapped the portrait of the *Odyssey* and set it in the seat of an overstuffed armchair where Lock could not help but see it when he came in. She was at a loss how to warn him to be on his guard against Alex's and Rodger's machinations without his suspecting her motives. She wasn't clear about them herself, really, only that she wanted nothing to do with carrying on the feud her father had been responsible for starting. At Lock's drawing board she found a pencil and a scrap of paper, removed her gloves, and began a brief note of explanation. Chewing at the end of the pencil, she deliberated, lost for a moment in the memory of his arms about her, the flavor of his mouth. No matter what lay between them, the "might have beens" of their brief acquaintance made her heart ache with a bittersweet poignancy. But she had made the only choices she could. Determinedly, she shook off the feeling of loss and bent to her task.

The door burst open and Lock McKin strode into the room, his face an impenetrable icy mask, his blue eyes glazed with preoccupation. Without even noticing Constance, he slammed the door, then, surprisingly, rested his forehead on the panels for an interminable moment. His black hair was plastered against his brow from the rain, and beneath his heavy double-breasted coat, his shoulders heaved in vast shudders. Mouthing a vicious curse, he swung around in a sudden burst of violence and kicked an ottoman across the room. He came up short at the sight of the bonneted woman frozen over his drawing board.

"What the hell are you doing here?" he thundered. "Come to gloat?"

"What? No, I—"

He was across the room in two steps, his hands digging into her arms, shaking her. "Blasted thieves, all of you!"

Bewildered, she shook her head. "I don't understand."

"It's simple enough," he snarled. "You goddamned Lathams have stolen my ship!"

Chapter 6

"S tolen?" Constance's eyes darted to the window in disbelief. Glistening through a gray curtain of rain, the sleek hull of the *Odyssey* rose from her keelblocks as usual. "But—"

"Not physically, you hen-wit!" Rivulets of moisture dripped down Lock's lean cheeks, but his expression was too blazingly contemptuous for the droplets to be mistaken for tears. "Though sleight of hand and black magic might explain how Latham and Company forced out the other stockholders to gain majority ownership of my vessel!"

"Forced? How?"

"The usual methods—corruption, bribery, coercion, pressure applied to the weakest link in the chain. I wouldn't sell out, so they went at it behind my back to take control of everything for a mere pittance. As if you didn't know," he sneered.

"I didn't!" The wild light in his ice-blue eyes made her voice go shrill. "I mean, they spoke of plans, but I had no idea, I swear! I came here to warn you—"

"God! Spare me any more of your lies, woman! You and that nest of serpents made me look a clown!" His lips twisted bitterly. "So now I end up working for Latham, and the hopes I had for turning my fortunes around are dashed. By God, I

ought to break her keel and turn her into kin-
dling—"

Constance's eyes grew wide with horror. "You
wouldn't! She's too beautiful!"

"And it wouldn't fit in with the scheme, would it,
princess?" His fingers tightened on her arms. "I
give you marks for guile. Using your little witchy
games to divert me so that I couldn't see the real intention until it was too late."

"That's not true!" She struggled, trying to shake
him off, but he jerked her against his chest.

"Isn't it?" His eyes narrowed, and he caught her
chin, crushing the back of her bonnet against the
crook of his arm and forcing her to look at him.
"What a liar you are."

"Not about that," she said, gasping a little.

"So the reason you kept coming around unin-
vited wasn't to keep me intrigued and off-balance?"

"No!" Outraged, she pushed against his chest. It
was like pushing against a mountain. "You flatter
yourself overmuch. I told you the day we met you
were wrong about that, but I suppose that colossal
ego of yours has misled you again!"

"Perhaps the memory of your tight little bottom
in those boy's trousers is more than I can resist."

Her eyes flashed, molten gold with ire. "Suspicious swine! Your imagination runs away with you,
and you see malicious intent where there is none."

Cynicism made him lift his eyebrows in mock astonishment. "All the blather about the cursed
money, and 'what Alex won't know won't hurt
him,' and setting up camp in my shipyard to paint
your damned picture—that wasn't to blind me to
what was coming?"

"Of course not!" she said furiously, jerking her
chin free. He merely readjusted his grasp, holding
her so close she felt his thighs flex and the liquid heat of his body through the billow of her
burgundy-colored skirts. Unnerved, she ceased

struggling, resorting to an icy hauteur. "How could I possibly do anything like that?"

"By showing off your pretty ankles and crying on my shoulder." Looking down into her upraised faced, Lock tightened his jaw, and his words came out in a husky rasp. "And by teasing me with those mysterious golden eyes and that smart mouth and the scent of your skin until I'm nigh crazy wondering what it would feel like to have you naked beneath me."

"Let me go." Her voice was a hoarse whisper.

He smiled slowly, his gaze lazy with speculation. "You've wondered, too, haven't you, Connie? Hell, we've been circling each other like cats at howling time. Alex either has a rare confidence in you or cares not a whit for your virtue, since it's a wonder we haven't both gone up in flames before now."

"You're wrong." She shook her head. "Daft as a coot. Imagining things. I feel nothing but loathing for you, Lock McKin."

He brushed his thumb over her lower lip and felt the invisible tremor his touch evoked. "And I despise liars."

Constance's pulse leaped, and she found it suddenly impossible to take a breath. "Lock, please . . ."

Behind his dark lashes the angry blue flames smoldered and became something else. "Sweet revenge indeed on your thieving grandfather and twofold pleasure for me if I give you what you've been asking for."

"You bastard." Choking, she tore free of his arms, half blinded by the prickle of sudden tears at words that echoed accusations from her past. That Lock's assessment of her character should parallel Uncle Cyrus's cut surprisingly deep, and she lashed out in retaliation.

"What would a perishing great clod with an icy lump instead of a heart understand about anything important? Believe what you want! I came to bring you a farewell gift, and I heartily regret the impulse that led me to such a futile gesture!"

Frowning, he looked where she pointed and saw for the first time the finished portrait of the *Odyssey*. He went rigid, and bitterness settled into the creases on either side of his mouth. He laughed harshly.

"So this is all you Lathams leave of my pride—a painted image."

Constance hadn't considered until that moment that her gift would only be more salt on his wounds, and she gasped as if she felt the sting herself. "I'm sorry. I only thought . . ." She looked at him helplessly.

Peeling off his damp coat, he turned to her, tugging at his rain-sodden neckcloth and unbuttoning his waistcoat with angry, impatient movements. His voice was silky with menace. "Pity, now? How admirable. Just what I needed from a Latham."

His cool contempt for her sympathy and her gift made her furious. "I do pity you, Lock McKin. You have no notion of human warmth. What's happened is deplorable and disappointing, but you'll never admit you need consolation, because you're too afraid it would make you seem less a man."

He slung his waistcoat across a chair and unfastened his shirt, his expression growing darker and darker as he all but ripped the buttons from the placket. "Save your pretty platitudes for the fools who can believe in them. Life has taught me better."

"Oh, yes, I know what they call you. Iron Man McKin." Her scathing tone made the appellation an insult. "Hard. Tough. And so caught up in vengeance and hate you've forgotten how to feel."

His shirt hanging open to reveal a swath of tanned chest sprinkled with black curling hairs, Lock glared at her, his blue eyes hot and dangerous. "I feel plenty."

"But you can't show it."

"Why would I want to reveal myself to you? To a Latham?"

"It never occurred to you that you weren't the only victim of this senseless feud, did it?" As she thought of the two tiny portraits preserved inside her locket, her expression was both furious and pitying. "I'm the only one who really understands, but it would take more courage than you have to see it, much less use it to end the enmity. But perhaps that's not what any of you really want, since you find war so much more satisfying than peace."

That stunned him, and he stared at her with a confused mixture of frustration and stubborn disbelief that Constance knew mere words would never change. What was left of her patience vanished in a white-hot flash of temper. "Blind, arrogant, vengeful fools, the lot of you! I'm leaving, and you can all go to the devil!"

Head held high with disdain, Constance started for the door, but Lock caught her arm. The angry pulse in his jaw throbbed, and his voice was tight. "Should I call you Solomon now, since you apparently have all the answers?"

"At least I'm not too proud to welcome some human comfort occasionally," she retorted. "Or to give it, either. Everyone needs it now and again."

"Then comfort me, my dear," he said on a low, furious growl. "For right now I'm the neediest man on the face of the earth."

Dragging her into his arms, Lock caught Constance's small panicky cry with his mouth and consumed it voraciously, devouring her resistance in a sense-stealing kiss that went on until the edge of forever. He was rapacious, punishing, his tongue tasting her deeply, his fingers working loose the ribbons of her bonnet, then dragging it aside so that he could stroke her throat, the delicate underside of her jaw, the sensitive patch behind her ear.

Crushed against his chest, Constance felt her

heart hammering against her ribs as his tongue took uninhibited liberties, sampling the deepest recesses of her mouth to leave her weak-kneed and breathless. He was insatiable, hungry for everything she could give and more. It was beyond her in that first stunned instant to deny him, and she gave willingly, melting against him until his hold gentled. His mouth became more persuasive as desire replaced anger, and they forgot everything but each other.

Somehow, he'd unfastened the frogs on her mantle and tossed the garment aside, and now his large hands roamed freely over her shoulders, traced the narrow line of her collarbone beneath the fine burgundy gabardine of her gown, smoothed her breasts spilling over the edge of her corset, and thumbed their sensitive centers. Even through the fabric of her bodice the action produced an almost unbearable thrill of pleasure, and a burning heaviness settled between her legs.

Deluged with sensation, Constance groaned a protest against the wicked expertise of his skillful hands, the insistent heat of his mouth, and her own undeniable response. He took her hand and guided it inside his open shirt, and she felt the tremor that traveled through him as her fingers tangled in the crisp bramble of chest curls and scored the coin of his male nipples. That she could produce such a reaction in him made her more light-headed than ever.

Dragging his mouth away, he gave a low rumble of satisfaction and arousal at the sight of her dazed features, then lifted her and carried her to the silk-draped bed in the next room. Hastily ripping off his shirt, he half lay across her, one knee insinuated aggressively between her thighs, and she gasped at the shocking contrast between the heat of his bare skin and the coolness of the colorful coverlets at her back. His fingers plundered the tiny buttons at her collar, and he nipped at the delicate cords of her neck until his relentless foraging across her skin led him to the indentation at the base of her throat. He licked at the sheen of moisture gathering in that shallow well, and the rasp of his tongue made her cry out in surprise and bury her hands in his thick hair.

"You taste like honey," he muttered against her throat. "All golden and smooth and sweet."

"Lock." She gasped his name and stirred restlessly against the unbearable pleasure coursing through her veins. His hair was like midnight silk sifting through her fingers. Daringly, she traced the powerful muscles of his neck down to the wide flare of his shoulders, lost in wonder. He was hard as the iron of his name, but warm, the taut skin a velvety miracle over sinew and bone, and he shivered violently at her touch.

Capturing her mouth again, he rolled over, pulling her on top of him, and even through her petticoats she could feel the hard outline of his arousal pressed against the soft concave platform of her belly. The sheer carnality of his lovemaking overwhelmed her senses, his tongue deep in her throat, his hand seeking beneath her skirts to stroke her thigh encased in thin muslin drawers. When his palm moved over her buttock and his fingers found the sensitive cleft of her womanhood, she arched, pulling her mouth free to gasp a startled cry of shocked pleasure and growing uncertainty.

Deprived of her lips, he took wild and unrestrained license, suckling at her breasts through the fabric of her gown, stroking her intimately, seemingly lost to all control, all discipline. He was the essence of primal male, intent only on mating with the female, all trappings of civilization sloughed off in the primitive savagery and fierce excitement of mankind's most basic act.

It was nothing like she'd ever expected, not careful, not safe, certainly not caring, and she shuddered with a trepidation and rising dread she could no more control than the tide. Pushing at his shoulders with her hands, she strained away from his questing, tormenting mouth, wriggling toward escape. "Lock, please! I don't . . . we can't!"

In the blink of an eye, she found herself on her back again, staring up into a face she no longer recognized. Eyes narrowed, teeth bared as his breath rasped between his parted lips, he was a hard-eyed stranger intent on plunder, the power of his need brooking no denial, no second thoughts. Constance made an involuntary movement to rise, but his hard hands thrust her shoulders into the silken coverlet. Trembling, she knew that she'd pushed him to this with her impulsive words, taunted him with her judgments, dared him to show his true feelings, and, rash fool that she was, unleashed the tiger—on herself.

"Don't hurt me," she whispered.

Lock blinked, his eyelids quivering. The predator faded, and he shook his shaggy head as if rousing from a dream—or a nightmare. With an oath, he levered himself painfully to his feet. He stood with his bare back to her and his fists clenched, swaying like a drunken man, sucking in great gusts of air.

Quaking in every molecule, Constance rolled to the side of the bed, relieved, unnerved, and shamefully disappointed by her sudden reprieve. She closed her eyes in mortification, guilt pounding in every cell. Lust was her sin, and not only had she wallowed in it, but in the end she'd wanted Lock to take her, making her a double-damned sinner! "Lock, I—"

"Shut up." He didn't look at her, and his voice was harsh and strange. "Say another syllable and I won't be responsible for what I do."

She went crimson, then paled and came unsteadily to her feet, smoothing her skirts and fumbling with the buttons at her neckline. Feeling awful and hollow, she hesitated, obligated somehow to apologize, to offer reparation for his anger. Overcome with remorse, she touched his shoulder.

"Don't!" He swung around with a snarl, throwing off her hand, his blue eyes iridescent with hate. "Just another step in the plot, eh, princess? Reduce me to a mindless rutting idiot and I'll be no threat to any Latham."

She flinched, and what was left of her color leeched out of her cheeks, leaving her as pale as an ivory statue. "You mustn't think that."

"You don't want me to think at all!" A flush rose on his chest and neck as anger replaced passion. He took a threatening step toward her, then another. "Get out."

Gulping, she stumbled to the sitting room, snatching up her bonnet, mantle, and the reticule that held her precious packet ticket. It had been a disaster to come here, for now she had more to forget, more to regret.

Lock stood in the bedroom doorway, his cold facade firmly back in place, a transformation Constance found both staggering and infinitely sad. Her nerves shattered, her pride smashed, her body still throbbing from Lock's touch, she struggled for a semblance of his control, with much less success. Her nose stung and her throat constricted, but she vowed she wouldn't let him see her cry—she wouldn't!

"I'm sorry," she murmured, her tone totally wretched. "I wish—"

"Go, damn you!" His lip curled in contempt. "And tell Alex it didn't work."

She quivered. "You're wrong about me, you know. If I could prove it to you, I would."

"Out, goddammit! Before I do murder."

She fled then, running out the door into the drizzle, nearly slipping on the wet stairs, not even paus-

ing to don her bonnet or mantle as at last her tears
fell and mingled with the rain. Lock's final caustic
words drifted down from above like the wrath of
God.

"If you come back, I'll kill you."

"Am I interrupting a celebration?"

Constance's strident words startled Alex Latham,
and the lip of the brandy decanter he was holding
clattered against his tumbler. He hastily returned
them to the silver coffee tray as Constance pushed
past a young, very flustered clerk and entered her
grandfather's private office at Latham and Company.

Green velvet draperies and Belgium tapestry
chairs balanced burnished leather sofas. Bookcases
filled with gilt-lettered volumes towered between
even taller windows overlooking State Street and
the Merchant's Exchange, the Old State House, and,
in the distance, Long Wharf itself. Files and ledgers
and a thick folder of legal-looking documents were
stacked neatly on the green felt blotter in the center
of Alex's desk beside his usual afternoon tray, a
large silver affair laden with Chinese porcelain
cups, sugar-dusted cakes, liquor decanters, and a
carafe still emitting the rich aroma of the best Java-
nese coffee.

"Sir, I tried to tell Miss Latham you weren't to be
disturbed," the clerk said, his fuzzy cheeks bright
pink with chagrin.

"It's all right, Perkins. Judge Freidel left some
time ago," Alex replied, waving a dismissal. His
brown eyes grew wide at the sodden and bedraggled state of Constance's apparel. "My dear, you're
soaked!"

Constance snatched off her ruined silk bonnet
and sopping mantle and threw them into a chair
without regard for the expensive upholstery. Pushing the wet rat's tails of hair out of her face, she

reached across the wide expanse of Alex's mahogany desk and poured herself a drink. Tipping the glass, she downed the contents, grimacing and shuddering as fire raced down her gullet. She slammed the tumbler down on the desk and gave her grandfather a belligerent glare.

"It's raining."

"I can see that," he said, somewhat alarmed. "Constance, are you quite all right?"

"No." She reached for the cut-glass decanter again.

"I think you've had quite enough, my girl," Alex remonstrated, corking the decanter firmly. "You're not accustomed to spirits. You'll become inebriated."

"Yes, that might be the best way," she muttered, shuddering again. Perhaps if she were drunk, she'd be able to face crossing another ocean tomorrow. And maybe if she pickled her brain in alcohol, she'd stand a chance of forgetting today's humiliation.

Constance licked the mingled flavor of rain and brandy and Lock McKin's kisses off her lips and nearly groaned aloud. She'd ridden the horsecar from South Boston all the way to State Street before she'd realized she'd made such a decision. It was as if that other person inside her was controlling her again, but this time her mood was wild and aggressive, boiling with frustration and angry demands.

Slapping her palms on the desktop, Constance bent forward to stare into her grandfather's startled eyes. "I want to know *why*."

Alex blinked and gave her a guarded look. "Why what?"

"Why did you steal the *Odyssey*?"

"Steal, my dear?" Alex leaned back in his tall leather chair, tucking his silver ruff of whiskers into his black silk neckcloth. His expression took on a foxy shrewdness. "That's a rather harsh word for a perfectly legal business acquisition. Several of

McKin's backers weren't as committed to his outrageous design ideas as they had believed. It took only a little persuasion to convince them a slight profit now was worth more than losing everything later. But how did you come to know about this so soon? We've only just executed the papers today."

"I heard."

Alex's well-shod feet hit the floor, and he scowled. "You saw McKin, didn't you? Even after I forbade it!"

"Obedience has never been a virtue of mine," she retorted. Shrugging insolently, she took a linen napkin and began to blot her damp face.

"It's clear you need a firm hand to keep you from such shenanigans," Alex said, growing ruddy with annoyance. "You might have run wild before, young lady, but this unconventional behavior of yours will stop immediately. I'll see to that!"

"Better men than you have tried, Alex," she said with a short laugh, crumpling the napkin and tossing it over her shoulder to flutter to the floor. "What you've done isn't right or fair. If you needed a ship, why, out of all the vessels in the world, did it have to be Lock McKin's?"

"I shouldn't have to explain something as simple as that to you, girl," Alex snapped. "It made good financial sense, and since McKin beat us out with the whalers at Lahaina last season, it's only right that he should pay a forfeiture for that piece of audacity."

"Don't tell me it's just business!" Constance marched up and down in front of the desk, gesturing angrily. "This is the most dishonest, vindictive piece of treachery I've ever seen, and Lock McKin even thinks I had a part in it! It's absurd to carry a rivalry to such lengths, no matter what my father did!"

"James? My boy was guiltless," Alex said, his mouth compressing into a thin slit. "It was Enoch

McKin's senseless accusations that ruined everything!"

"But Enoch's dead, and so is my father. What's
the point anymore?" she demanded.

"Someone has to pay," Alex muttered, his brown
eyes hard as New England agate.

Constance stopped pacing, chilled by what she
saw and by the realization that Alex and Lock
weren't so very different from each other. Her pitiful attempt to change the course of a generation's
worth of hate and vengeance was as effective as a
butterfly battling a hurricane. A graceful withdrawal from the field of these old battles was the
best she could hope for. And that would happen on
the morrow.

"It's useless trying to make either of you see reason," she said, and reached for her mantle. "I'm
leaving."

"Just a moment, miss! I'm not through with
you—"

A brief rap at the door interrupted Alex, and
Rodger burst in. "Uncle, a word, please."

Rodger stopped short when he saw Constance,
then frowned at her bedraggled appearance, touching
his own pristine cravat as if to ward off contagion.
"What the devil happened to you?"

"Fits," Constance said succinctly. "Falling sickness. St. Vitus's dance. The passersby on the street
found it all exceedingly interesting, but as no one
offered an umbrella, I got rather wet—"

"My God!" Rodger's hazel eyes widened in horror. "You don't mean . . ."

"You believe her humbug for a moment and
you're a bigger fool than I thought!" Alex snapped,
his irritation showing in the twin flags of color on
his cheeks. "Did you investigate that report from
the shipping office as I told you?"

Rodger's own annoyance at appearing a gullible
dunce manifested itself in the sour downward turn

of his handsome mouth. With a fulminating glance at Constance, he drew a folded paper from his coat pocket and slapped it down in front of his uncle.

"There it is, Uncle Alex. It appears dear Constance plans to leave us. She purchased a packet ticket for England this morning."

Struggling with her damp mantle, Constance caught her breath. Alex ignored her, his eagle gaze focused on his nephew. "And?"

"I canceled it, of course," Rodger replied.

"What!" Constance's mouth fell open, then snapped shut angrily. "You had no right! Now I'll have to go and *un*cancel it!"

"I've made it clear to the booking agents that your grandfather hasn't approved your travel plans." Rodger's smile was smugly vindictive. "You'd find it difficult to secure passage to Cambridge under that condition."

"But—" Constance's throat constricted with dismay, and confusion muddied the clear topaz of her eyes. "I'd have thought you of all people would welcome my departure, Rodger."

Her cousin flashed a quick glance at Alex, then looked down at his stubby fingers folded piously at his waist. "I . . . thought better of it, Cousin Constance."

Fury made her mouth pucker, but her voice held a shadow of growing desperation. "Neither one of you has the right to interfere with my plans. I'm going to Paris!"

"Now, that's just what I was talking about!" Alex retorted firmly. "Running wild, behaving rashly, even dangerously. It's clear to me, Constance, that you're simply much too young and empty-headed to be considered responsible for your own fate. That's why Judge Freidel has agreed that I should be named your legal guardian."

"Legal—what does that mean?" she demanded suspiciously.

"It means that I'll have the lawful means to guide you as you make decisions that could affect your entire life, my dear. A safeguard for your future security."

She didn't like the sound of that. "I'm quite capable of deciding what's best for me, Alex. I don't want this guardian business, and I don't want to be included in your will. All I want is my reward money so I can further my education in my chosen profession."

"Posh and piffle!" Alex snorted. "A lady of your standing and—er, spirited nature doesn't need a profession, she needs a husband!"

Constance was so astounded she began to laugh. "You've had too much brandy, Alex. What would I want with a husband?"

"Well, aside from the obvious feminine accomplishments of children and a home, you'll want someone to help you run your half interest in Latham and Company." He riffled through the thickest folder on his blotter and shoved a document across the desk to her. "See for yourself."

As if the paper were a cannonball ready to explode, Constance lifted it with two fingers. "'. . . and on her marriage be immediately invested with fifty percent interest in Latham and Company . . .'" she read incredulously.

"It's all perfectly legal, I assure you, my dear," Alex said. "Signed and notarized by Judge Freidel himself and filed this day for record in the state of Massachusetts."

Constance stared at her grandfather, aghast at the enormity of the bequest. "But why would you do such a thing?"

Alex glanced at Rodger, then shrugged. "I've been thinking about retiring anyway, and nothing would give me greater pleasure than to see you happily settled here in Boston and producing a passel of great-grandchildren for me to dawdle on my knee."

The image made Constance choke and shake her head. "You must be joking!"

Alex lifted one hoary eyebrow in sly inquiry. "Half of my estate is reason enough to stay in Boston, isn't it?"

"My God, Alex," she gasped, "you're trying to *bribe* me! Rodger, have you ever heard anything so incredible? Don't you have anything to say? Alex is trying to give me your inheritance!"

Rodger shifted uncomfortably and thrust a hand through his thinning yellow hair. "Well, that is—"

"Your cousin won't have any objections, because I've made similar arrangements for him to receive his half of the company upon *his* marriage," Alex explained.

Constance plopped down in a tapestry chair and shook her damp head in admiration of Alex's deviousness. "How neatly you've tied up this package."

Alex beamed. "Well, it certainly makes sense to preserve the company intact by keeping everything in the family."

"Now if only you can provide suitable fiancés for both of us, we'll be all set," Constance said, her tone dry with sarcasm. "Rodger will have no trouble, I'm sure, for he's handsome, somewhat charming, and very eligible, but as for myself, after the Assembly, I'm sure there's not a proper Boston gentleman who'd touch me with a ten-foot pole. So unless word of this arrangement gets out and the fortune hunters begin to line up—"

"Constance, I'm afraid you don't understand." Perturbed, Alex scratched his chin whiskers, then gestured sharply at Rodger.

Looking strained, Rodger bent to pick up Constance's discarded napkin, smoothed it out carefully, then spread it on the floor at her feet and went down on one knee.

"Cousin Constance, would you do me the very great honor of becoming my ... my wife?" Rodger strangled on the word "wife," so that it came out like a blue jay's squawk.

Constance looked at him as if he'd gone mad—as she was indeed sure he had. "You aren't any good at jokes, Rodger. Get up—you look like a jackass down there!"

Rodger flushed crimson, but he plodded on doggedly. "I assure you, I'm most serious in my proposal, Constance."

"But you don't even like me!" She cringed back in her chair in sheer disbelief.

"While it's true we don't know each other very well," Rodger intoned stiffly, "I'm sure that our common interests will lead us to a Christian union of mutual respect and benefit."

"Alex, make him stop!" she cried, springing to her feet.

"Think, my dear," Alex advised. "It's a most sensible arrangement. You'll have a secure position and future after I'm gone, and that's my most important consideration. I think you and Rodger would suit admirably."

"I agree, Cousin Constance," Rodger began from his kneeling position.

"Oh, do shut up, you imbecile!" she shouted, giving Rodger a push that rolled him onto his backside. "You may be willing to sell your soul to this cunning old devil for a sack of gold, but I'm not!"

"See here, granddaughter," Alex said, rising from his desk, "you've got to be reasonable."

"Reasonable!" She pointed at Rodger, who was scrabbling to his feet and dusting himself off with the soiled napkin. "You want to tie me to that cawing jackdaw, and you think that's reasonable! I'll *swim* to Paris before I marry him!"

"Now, Constance, since I'm your guardian, you'll have to let me be your guide," Alex soothed. "Perhaps Rodger didn't phrase it to you in the most romantic light, but after you've had time to consider—"

"No!" She leaned over the desk, glaring at her grandfather nose to nose, the stubborn jut of her chin a match to his. "Not ever!"

"By God, girl, you'll listen to me!" Alex roared, losing his temper. His brows pulled together ominously, and his face suffused with blood. "This is for your own good, you stubborn hellion!"

"Ha! None of this is for me!" Constance screeched. "It's all what *you* want. Grandchildren, bah! Sniveling little gnatcatchers like Rodger nesting all over Latham House—the idea is positively nauseating!"

"I'm trying to protect you, girl—give you something to build on. You have a heritage here, a responsibility!" He was practically purple with frustrated rage. "You can't go galloping across Europe all alone. You need stability, and, by God, I'm going to see that you get it one way or the other!"

"Whether I want it or not?" she demanded haughtily. "What about the free will God gave me?"

"Arguing won't accomplish anything," Rodger interjected, his hands raised placatingly.

"*Shut up!*" Constance and Alex shouted it simultaneously, then went back to glaring at each other as if they hadn't been interrupted.

"You're a mean, selfish old man, Alexander Latham," Constance yelled. "And I heartily regret the day Dylan McKin sent me here!"

"If you'd half the wit of a dormouse, you'd see that I'm just trying to help," her grandfather blustered. "I'll be damned if I'll let my own flesh and blood make unnecessary mistakes."

"They're my mistakes to make, you old fraud! If you tried to run my father's life the way you're trying to run mine, it's no wonder he left!"

"You leave James out of this!"

"He's the one who started it, didn't he, falling in love with Eliza McKin? What did you do when that happened, threaten to disown him?"

"James had to learn a lesson, just like you do," Alex bellowed, so furious that small specks of spittle dribbled from the corners of his mouth.

"Well, you're teaching me the same lesson you taught my father!" Constance said, angry tears glistening. "How to hate you!"

Enraged, Alex swept the coffee tray off the desk. Cups and decanters shattered, and the pungent fumes of brandy mingled with the aroma of coffee.

"You wretched little liar! James didn't hate me!"

Constance's voice dropped to a triumphant whisper. "Then why didn't he ever come home?"

Alex's expression changed painfully, and his eyes widened in surprise. Grabbing his chest, he gave a sharp cry and toppled to the floor amid the mess of glass and liquor and crushed cakes.

"Alex!" Constance dropped to her knees beside him, afraid to touch him, afraid not to. "Grandpa!"

"Get back!" Rodger pushed her aside to examine the stricken man, fumbling with Alex's cravat and feeling in frantic haste for signs of life.

Her heart thundering in her ears, Constance felt her own limbs go numb with fear and shock. Blackness danced at the edges of her vision, and from a great distance she watched in icy horror as Rodger placed his ear against the old man's chest. When he raised his gaze again, his eyes were filled with such virulence and condemnation that her blood congealed.

"You bitch. You've killed him."

Chapter 7

"But why can't I see him?"

"I told you, Constance. The doctor's with him now." In the gloomy corridor adjacent to Alex Latham's bedroom, Rodger's features were shadowy and implacable. Death hovered in the still air, along with the faint scents of damp wool and hair pomade. "And the Reverend Mr. Whitaker's here. In case—"

Constance gave a small strangled cry and pressed her knuckles to her mouth in distress. In the frantic hours since Alex's collapse, in the confusion of doctors, panicky clerks and accountants, and the harrowing job of transporting her stricken grandfather home, she'd never felt more helpless, more terrified, more guilty. She regretted every impetuous word with the fervency of a damned soul, but in her heart she knew it was too late. Though Alex still held onto life by a thread, she knew she had killed again.

"You don't understand," she said in a voice thick with grief and tears. "I must tell him . . . he's got to know I didn't mean . . ."

"Stop thinking of yourself," Rodger ordered coldly. "You're the last person he wants to see now."

Her cousin's callous words pierced Constance like daggers, but she couldn't deny their truth. Her chest full to the point of bursting, she sank down in one of the straight chairs that lined the damask-covered walls and went back to chewing the ragged remnants of her thumbnail.

If only she could tell her grandfather ... what? That she was sorry? That in spite of everything he'd become important to her? That the ties of blood *did* mean something, and she loved him? With a little moan Constance buried her face in her hands.

She was the one who didn't deserve to live. She'd broken practically every commandment in the space of a few hours—lied, cheated, lusted, misjudged, and now, because of her thoughtless, angry words, perhaps murdered again. All the sermons she'd ever heard promising damnation for the wicked echoed in her head. But her punishment was not to be postponed to the next world. It had already begun in the here and now. Rocking back and forth in the chair, she moaned again in an agony of remorse and tried to pray.

Oh, God, let him live. I'll do anything ...

The bedroom door opened and Dr. Callum appeared, his lined face solemn. Constance raised her head, her expression bleak with resignation. No God, not even her mother's people's ancient savage ones, would hear her prayers. Her grandfather was dead. Rodger took a step forward.

"Doctor? Is he ... ?"

"Resting. He wants to see Constance."

A fit of trembling rendered Constance incapable of movement for several terrifying moments. Then, gathering strength from some unknown reserve, she shook out her burgundy-colored skirts and rose, forcing her shaking legs to bear her weight. Reluctance and eagerness tugged her fragile equilibrium in painfully opposite directions, but her prayer for a chance to make amends had been answered, and she dared not ignore it lest there be no more opportunities. Steeling herself, she moved toward the door.

Rodger blocked her path. "If you do or say *anything* that upsets Uncle Alex again—"

"I won't." Constance shuddered. "I swear."

"See that you don't. Or by all that's holy, you'll answer to me."

Constance looked at Rodger's grim visage and nodded. Silently, he stepped aside.

The soft, warm glow of a single lamp illuminated her grandfather's chamber, spreading a golden circle on the parqueted floor and heavy carpet and into the dim recesses of the enormous half tester walnut bed that dominated the room. At the head of the bed, his Bible in hand, the Reverend Mr. Whitaker intoned a verse from the Book of Job to a figure only partly visible behind the swaged veil of filmy bedcurtains. Constance's guilty regard glanced nervously off the minister's clerical collar, and she swallowed hard against the knot in her throat that threatened to choke her. Resolutely, she approached the side of the bed, then gulped for air.

A much-diminished Alex lay propped against a mound of pillows, his ashen color relieved only by dark mauve circles beneath his closed eyes, a frail figure in the enormous expanse of the feather bed. When he inhaled, his chest barely moved under his flannel nightshirt, and his hands, resting on top of the covers, seemed pale and bloodless.

"Grandpa," she whispered, and tears spilled over her lashes and slid down her cheeks.

Alex stirred fretfully, then opened his eyes and focused on Constance. He lifted a hand to her. It was more than she could have hoped for, and with a sob, she took his hand desperately and fell to her knees beside the bed.

"That's enough, Whitaker," Alex said in a gravelly voice.

The minister immediately stopped his reading but hovered protectively at the head of the bed, slightly apart from Constance's sobbing form. Alex lifted his other hand to stroke her sable hair, the straight, silky locks long since loosened from her pins to spill recklessly across her shoulders. "Constance ..."

"I'm so sorry, Grandpa," she said brokenly, clinging to his hand. "I'm wicked and horrible, but I never meant to hurt you. Say you forgive me."

"Hush, child. My temper is a cross I have to bear."

His gentle remonstrance was like a hot brand across her guilty conscience. "You must get well. I'll never forgive myself ... you will get better, won't you?"

He sighed deeply, and his eyes drifted shut again. "If the Lord wills it. Life is so uncertain. That's why ..."

Constance pressed his cool palm against her wet cheek and hiccuped on a ragged sob. "Why what, Grandpa?"

"Why I wanted to see you safely settled ... before I go."

"You're going to be fine!" she cried, squeezing his hand urgently. When she felt no answering squeeze, her heart lurched with fear, and her voice became panicky. "Grandpa? Alex!"

He roused slowly, the fatigue and strain dragging his features into tired folds, as if his face were collapsing in on itself. "I worry about you ..."

"You mustn't! Please, you've got to concentrate on getting well."

"So hard ... no one to take care of you. If I could only be sure. If you'd only promise ..."

"Promise what, Grandpa?" She leaned closer to hear his muttering. "I'll do anything you want!"

"No, no. Couldn't ask it again." He rubbed his chest and grimaced as if in pain. "But it's such a terrible burden. James's girl. I'm responsible for you. If only ..."

"What? Just say it," she begged in alarm, chafing

his limp hand between her own. "What do you need? What do you want me to do?"

"Marry ... and stay in Boston. Then I could rest easy."

The room seemed to dip and sway. The light from the lamp grew brighter, then dim again. Give up Paris to take up a life in Boston? Marry, pretending she wasn't a murderess who might be discovered at any moment? Surrender herself body and soul to a man who would only tolerate her, who would surely come to hate her? Life had already taught her a bitter lesson about that kind of bondage. But she'd known the dangers of this trap almost from the beginning, known her own neediness for affection and family would make her vulnerable to the calls and ties of blood. God would exact a high price for his mercy to Alex.

"I—I don't know whether I can," she whispered in a tortured voice.

"Then go, damn you," Alex said, turning his face away. "I'd rather die alone than with ungrateful children."

The Reverend Mr. Whitaker touched her heaving shoulders, urging her to her feet. "Perhaps it would be better if you left."

Constance shook him off. "No! Grandpa, please."

"I love you, girl, but it hurts too much to know I've failed you as well as James." Alex's breath rasped painfully. "I'm done. Leave me to my Maker."

She wanted to be heartless, selfish in her own defense, but it was beyond her, even though her dreams were dissolving beneath her feet like the sands of Lahaina at storm tide. She sat down beside the old man and laced her fingers through his.

"Don't give up, Grandpa." Dread pressed heavily on her chest, but she forced herself to say the words. "I'll do what you want, I promise."

He swiveled his head on the pillows, his brown

eyes catching the lamplight with a gleam of gold. "Swear it on the Good Book."

The Reverend Mr. Whitaker proffered his black leather Bible. "You are a believer, aren't you, child?"

Constance stared at the book, trying to keep the trepidation from her voice, but for years she'd found neither comfort nor salvation between those holy pages, and her voice trembled with fear and resignation as she placed her hand against the worn cover. "I was raised on it."

"Swear it, Constance," Alex whispered hoarsely, struggling to raise his head. "So you'll have an inheritance. Swear you'll stay and marry—"

"I swear," she said hastily, then snatched her hand away and gently eased the old man back into the nest of pillows. "Now rest. I'm not going anywhere."

"Yes." His eyes closed again, and he sounded drowsy and self-satisfied, a little half-smile playing across his pale lips. "I think I can sleep now."

Numb with the implications of her promise, Constance sat beside her grandfather long after he'd fallen into an easy slumber and the Reverend Mr. Whitaker had gone home. She held Alex's age-spotted hand while a single question tickled her whirling thoughts with little hysterical bubbles of silent laughter.

Now that Alex had gotten his way, how was she going to break the good news to Rodger?

When her cousin came later to take over the vigil, however, neither he nor Constance was in the mood for conversation, so she was spared that ordeal, at least for a time. Weary in body and soul, she stumbled to her bed, but spent a restless night wrestling with her dreams, nightmares of great white monsters with flapping wings and snapping teeth that berated her for her wickedness and pushed her under in pools of molten tears.

Constance rose early to another overcast dawn,

unrefreshed and burdened with the weight of her promise to her grandfather. But she'd taken an oath on the Bible, and even for a sinner like her, to break it was unthinkable. She dressed in a sedate dark skirt and shirtwaist, her locket her only ornament, and hastily scraped her hair back in a single shoulder-length braid. The only way to survive was to take one step at a time. The first step was to vow to hold her tongue, no matter what the provocation. The second was to see that Alex recovered his health through expert attention and nursing care—hers.

A short time later, Constance looked dubiously at the selection of dishes Eloise, the cook, had prepared for the sickroom. Eloise was the freewoman of color responsible for Constance's favorite apple pies, a woman of formidable size in a white apron and calico tignon who ruled her kingdom in the basement kitchen of Latham House with all the imperiousness of Queen Victoria herself.

"Are you certain this is what Dr. Callum ordered?" Constance asked, eyeing the tray uncertainly.

"Calf's foot jelly, stewed prunes, and oatmeal porridge," Eloise recited, pointing at the various bowls. "I tol' that doctor this won't do no good unless he adds a good dandelion tonic to purge the system, but he ain't got a lick of sense, that man!"

"I'm sure the doctor knows what's best for his patient," Constance murmured.

Her brows puckered as a vague memory peeked its fuzzy head over the wall in her head. At some other time, in some other place, she'd carried a tray like this one. It had been heavy and hard to balance, difficult for a little girl to manage. Had the tray been for her father? The more she strained, the faster the memory receded, vanishing entirely as Eloise continued her litany.

"Mr. Rodger said he'd come to get Mr. Alex's

breakfast soon as the doctor finished with the old master."

"Dr. Callum's here already?" Automatically, Constance glanced overhead in the direction of the bedrooms. If she was going to be involved in her grandfather's convalescence, then she'd better obtain the particulars of his condition and prognosis from the physician now that she was calm enough to absorb them intelligently. She reached for the tray. "I'll take this up."

"Well, they ain't sent for it," Eloise said, "but they ain't hired a girl to take Maggie's place, either."

"I—I hear from her beau that she's working for a greengrocer and living with his family."

"I'll look for her at Quincy Market, then, come shopping day. She was a good girl, and a hard worker," Eloise said, "and I'm not going to turn down an offer of help in her stead, even if it ain't fittin' for a lady like you to be fetching and carrying."

"Believe me, Eloise," Constance replied, hefting the tray, "it's the least I can do."

She took the service stairs, mounting the steep, twisting staircase to the second floor, arriving unobtrusively as a good servant should, just in time to see Rodger's well-dressed back disappear into her grandfather's chamber. Puffing slightly, she paused outside the room to catch her breath, then froze at the sound of robust male laughter drifting from the partially open door. It was Alex's!

Amazed, Constance nudged open the door with her hip, then came up short. Alex and Dr. Callum sat opposite each other in a pair of wing chairs before the glowing fireplace. A chessboard lay on the small table between them, and Rodger bent over it, examining the game. Alex, freshly shaven and wearing a burgundy satin dressing gown, his ruddy color completely restored, grinned around a lit cigar clamped between his teeth and deftly maneuvered his black queen into place on the board.

"Checkmate, Doctor. By gum, Matthew, when are you going to learn I'm too smart for you?"

"Only because you cheat, Alexander," the doctor grumbled, and dug in his waistcoat pocket for his watch. Glancing at it, he stood. "I've wasted enough time with you, you old charlatan. I've patients to see who are really sick."

"Grandpa?" Constance blinked, hardly believing her eyes. "Should you be up? Doctor, his heart . . . is this wise?"

"His heart?" Dr. Callum's brows lifted in surprise, and he gave Alex an accusing look. "What's this, man? You didn't let the poor girl think it was your heart, did you? These fits of yours are always provoked by an excess of choler . . . and one day they will kill you. Until then, my prescription is a few days' quiet and meditation on the benefits of retirement."

"The only thing liable to kill me is this swill you keep trying to feed me," Alex complained, stubbing out his cigar. A flicker of apprehension crossed his face, quickly concealed behind a good-humored smile. "But here's my darling granddaughter, come to help me forget about my little scare and the unappetizing menu. Rodger, help her with that tray."

Dr. Callum bade his adieus, and Rodger relieved Constance of the breakfast tray and placed it beside the chessboard. He wouldn't quite meet her eyes, but she was too befuddled to notice, overjoyed on the one hand by Alex's overnight recuperation and appalled on the other by the depths of his treachery.

"I—I thought you were dying," she faltered.

"A false alarm." Alex shrugged and reached for the calf's foot jelly. He took one bite, grimaced, and set it aside. "Appalling stuff. Eloise knows better than this! Where's my codfish balls and brown bread?"

"You tricked me." Her tremulous voice held a wealth of hurt.

With great temerity, Rodger placed a hand on her arm. "Now, Constance . . ."

"You both did!" she accused, shaking him off. "You let me believe . . . you let me think . . ." Burying her face in her hands, she shuddered violently. "How could you? How *could* you!"

"My dear, it was all confusion," Alex said soothingly. He nodded sharply to his nephew, and this time Rodger took her arm with a bit more force, urging her down into Dr. Callum's vacated chair.

Constance rubbed her temples, her expression dazed and vulnerable. Cigar smoke mingled with the sharp odor of Alex's witch hazel. "I underestimated you, Alex."

"A misunderstanding. I wasn't myself, muddled and in pain. It's the price I pay for an overly sanguineous nature. But the episode did have a purpose, if you will but see it."

She gave a low, bitter laugh. "To make me suffer?"

"Of course not! I'd say this crisis brought us all closer, made us all realize what's really important. Wouldn't you say that's true, Rodger?"

"Indeed, Uncle Alex." Rodger leaned against the mantelpiece, watching Constance closely, but the light in his hazel eyes was more acquisitive than affectionate. "Adversity often reveals our true feelings."

"And cuts through needless posturing," Alex added. "Considering everything, I see no reason why you and Rodger should wish a long engagement period—"

She gasped. "You don't intend to hold me to a promise made under duress and false pretenses?"

"You made a solemn vow before God, Constance," Alex said severely. "Would you risk eternal damnation by ignoring it?"

Constance gaped at him. "You aren't serious! Rodger, tell him this is impossible!"

"It really would be better if you accepted the situation," Rodger advised calmly. "We wouldn't want Uncle Alex to have another episode. As soon as we're married, we'll both receive our legal settlement, and I'll be taking the full load of Latham and Company from his shoulders. I believe we could arrange with the Reverend Mr. Whitaker to have a simple ceremony at Trinity Church by the weekend, if that's agreeable."

"No, it's not!" she said, a knot of panic growing in her middle.

"You promised!" Alex snapped. "Why delay?"

She turned to her cousin in appeal. "What kind of marriage would this be, starting out on such a poor footing? We both deserve better, Rodger!"

"Affection will grow, I'm sure." Rodger cleared his throat and arranged his yellow curls with a nervous hand. "I'm really quite fond of you already, Constance."

"And you don't lie worth a damn, cousin!" Her hands clenched in angry fists. "This is obscene, and you both know it! I'm going to Paris even if stealing Lock McKin's ship left you too broke to ever pay me the reward you promised!"

Alex and Rodger exchanged a look, and Constance knew with a certainty she'd been lied to about that, too.

"You've had my money all along, haven't you?" she asked bitterly. "God, I'm so stupid, I actually swallowed your tales about financial embarrassment. I should have realized you've always had pots of money, and that telling me you didn't was only another way to force me down the path you wanted. Well, it won't work!"

"Your eternal soul is at stake here, girl!" the old man insisted with a growl.

"God has much more reason to strike me down

than over this puny vow. I won't be a victim of your manipulations, Alex Latham."

"You'll do as you're told, girl!" Alex roared.

"Or you'll have another 'attack'?" she sneered. "Go to it! And this time I hope you turn your toes up for good, you old bastard!"

"Don't speak to your grandfather in that manner!" Rodger ordered angrily.

"Or what?" she demanded, cold and haughty as a born princess. "You'll lock me in my room?"

"Since that's the usual practice when dealing with recalcitrant children, it's not a bad idea, at least until you can come to your senses!" Alex replied. "Rodger, see to it at once!"

Nonplussed, Rodger hesitated. "Uncle, are you sure?"

"Don't argue with me!" Alex thundered.

Rodger took a step toward Constance. She narrowed her eyes. "Be careful, Rodger. I bite."

When some minutes later Rodger turned the lock on the screaming, spitting wildcat he'd just barely managed to incarcerate behind her bedroom door, a daintily etched half circle of tooth marks on the edge of his palm proved that for once Constance had spoken the truth.

The saloon on the ground floor of the red brick Ferry Street tenement boomed with roisterous laughter, and a pipe and a fiddle filled the air with a lively Irish jig. Lock McKin hesitated at the well-lit entrance. Through the etched glass he could see the clientele of mostly Irish immigrants, working-class folk with tales to tell and drinking to do on this cold, sloppy evening. Friendly, joking men and their pretty "biddies," sharing a moment of respite before the morrow's poverty and drudgery began again. The atmosphere was warm and inviting, but Lock knew his black mood and loner's temperament would make him a misfit. He tried not to mind.

"In here, sir." At Lock's side, burly Tip Maddock gestured toward the alley that separated the tavern from a greengrocer's stand. "I can't be thanking you enough for coming like this, sir. My Maggie is right worried, but she's only boarding here herself, and the Fitzgeralds can't really afford to take anyone else in. We didn't know aught else to do."

His features stiff with suppressed vexation, Lock followed Tip down the muddy, littered alley toward a side door. It had been a hellish, frustrating day, spent futilely trying to convince his investors to reconsider, racking his brain, and calling in every favor in an effort to find a way to recover his *Odyssey*, all to no avail. Latham had seen to it that all the doors were closed. Now this summons was the absolute topper. "This one's a natural troublemaker, Tip."

"If you say so, sir," Tip replied, his tone doubtful as he rapped on the door. "Though my old gram would blame it on the wee folk or call it drunk on Queen Og's hell-soup."

The door opened a cautious crack, then swung wide to reveal a glimpse of the grocer's storeroom, cluttered with boxes of cabbages and turnips, sacks of onions and parsnips, baskets of orange pumpkins and butternut squashes. Nets of potatoes and strings of dried peppers hung from nails on the low overhead beams, and pickle casks and apple barrels of assorted sizes lined the plaster walls.

"Bless you, sir, come in," Maggie said, her freckled face anxious in the wan light of the smoking whale oil lamp she held. "Maybe you can help."

"Where—?" Lock began, but broke off when he saw the form crumpled in a corner behind Maggie. "Constance?"

Dressed in the same boy's garb in which Lock had first seen her, Constance sat on the sand-scrubbed wooden floor, next to an apple barrel, hugging her knees and staring sightlessly at the wall. She twisted the old woolen cap in her hands, and her expressionless face twitched occasionally, her lips moving in soundless conversation. Her hair fell in wisps out of a clumsy braid.

Maggie drew Lock inside as Tip closed the door, and began whispering as if she were in the presence of a mortal illness. "She won't hardly say a thing. She was wandering Quincy Market, dressed like that, near out of her head."

"What happened?" Lock demanded.

Maggie stepped closer to Tip, as if for protection from Lock's ferocious expression, and shook her head. "I don't know, sir, but she won't go back to Latham House, and since the young master sacked me, I won't either. I couldn't think of anything but to bring her here. I knew you were as close to being a friend to the lady as I was likely to find. I hope I did right, sir?"

"We'll see," Lock said. He was suspicious, having walked into too many devious Latham traps of late to take even such a pitiable picture as Constance made in her greasy sweater at face value. Somehow this sly female always managed to slip under his guard, and although he had full control over his emotions again, his disgraceful, dangerous lapse of the day before was enough to make him as wary as a thrice-burned child. "Let me talk to her alone."

"Of course. I've some straightening to finish up front, anyway." Maggie set the lamp atop a tall cask, then dragged Tip toward the front of the store. "Come along, boyo, I've need of your strong back."

Unbuttoning his pea coat, Lock dropped down on one knee beside Constance and wiped an uneasy finger over his mouth. She stared at the wall, rocking herself slightly, totally oblivious of his presence.

"Constance?" Lock touched her hand. "Princess?"

Her head snapped around, and she stared at him

without recognition for a blank moment, her golden eyes wide and dazzled as if she had drunk of some enchantment. Then, though she didn't move, the tension seemed to drain out of her body, and her sight cleared, perceptions once again in focus.

"Lauchlan." Her tremulous smile hovered for a fleeting moment, but then an almost instantaneous cognizance replaced the warmth in her remarkable eyes, and she cringed away from him in fear.

It nearly killed him.

"Dammit, I'm not going to hurt you!" he muttered.

He felt as though he'd kicked a kitten. But it was his own fault. He shouldn't have been so hard on her the day before. God, when he thought of the lustful, angry beast he'd loosed on her, he wanted to cringe himself. No wonder she was afraid of him.

"Why are you here?" Her face was a mirror of confusion. "I didn't come to you. I knew better . . ."

He winced inwardly, haunted by the viciousness of his final, threatening words of yesterday. He would never really hurt a woman, it was just that this particular one had a knack for rendering him totally out of control with the greatest ease. It was something he couldn't tolerate within himself, that feeling of careening headlong and unchecked, like the wild toboggan rides down Breakneck Hill he and Dylan had taken as children. Exhilarating, dangerous, and, in his position as a responsible adult, something to be avoided at all cost. Only it wasn't working out that way.

He cleared his throat and said in a gruff tone, "Maggie sent for me."

"Maggie?" Constance blinked, taking in her surroundings, visibly shaking off the cloud of vagueness. That brief moment of recognition and welcome he'd seen vanished as if it had never existed, leaving him with a curiously bereft sensation in the pit of his stomach. The tilt of her chin and the compression of her mouth registered her wariness and hostility. "She shouldn't have done that."

"Well, it's done, so you may as well—" Lock broke off, shocked by the sight of a coin-sized bruise the color of a pansy mottling the tip of her round chin. "Good Lord."

He reached to turn her face so that he could get a closer look, but she jerked back, batting him off with her cap. Annoyed, Lock pulled the cap out of her grasp, then scowled at her gasping cry of pain. He grabbed her hands and sucked in a ragged breath at the raw scrapes, torn flesh, and thorny abrasions covering her bloody palms.

"What the hell happened?" he demanded roughly, dragging her up and pushing her to a seat on top of the apple barrel. She was on eye level with him now, and he turned her palms up in his hands and swore. "Who did this to you?"

She shrank from the force of his anger. "N-no one. I mean, I did. Climbing down the rose trellis—ow!"

Ignoring her protests, Lock blotted her palms with his handkerchief, cleansing them of the worst of the dirt, plucking out several thorns as he went. "So you're masquerading as a cabin boy again to climb trellises? Dare I inquire why?"

"Rodger locked me in my room." She yelped as Lock pinched a particularly pernicious thorn free with his thumb and forefinger. "He and Alex and I had a . . . difference of opinion."

Lock's blue eyes grew dark as a thundercloud. His jaw working, he touched the tip of her chin and asked in a dangerously quiet voice, "Did Rodger do this, too?"

She followed the path of his fingers with her own, frowning in consternation at the tender spot, then shook her head with a little snort of disdain. "He got the worst of it. I probably did that to myself when I bit him."

"Jesus Christ." Lock neatly tied his handkerchief around the worst scrape, then stepped back and rubbed his nape in amazement. "Is there anything you haven't managed to do since yesterday?"

"I wasn't fortunate enough to catch the packet ship and get the bloody hell out of Boston." She picked at the makeshift bandage too casually, her brittle smile belying her nonchalant tone. "I had my ticket, but Alex . . ." She shrugged.

"Ah. The difference of opinion. So you've come up against Alex's ruthlessness, have you?"

Constance abandoned her inspection of the bandage and slid off the barrel. "I'm practically a prisoner in this wretched city. Alex is a master at boxing you in! But I suppose you know that."

"I think my experiences speak for themselves," Lock said dryly. He watched her pace, poking restlessly at the boxes of vegetables, inspecting the crocks and casks.

"He lied to me, and tricked me into making an impossible promise, then had the gall to say it's because he *loves* me, for God's sake!" The words spilled from her in a cascade of bitterness. "Well, if that's love, heaven spare me, for I've never felt less a person and more a possession, a chess piece to be pushed around the board at his whim. My *beloved* grandfather may have swindled you, Lock McKin, but he's done far worse to his own flesh and blood!"

Behind her angry words, Lock sensed the hurt, and something twisted inside him. For all her bravado, she was as defenseless as a babe. "No wonder you risked the rose trellis," he murmured. "Maggie said you were . . . er, distracted."

"Was I?" Constance dipped a red apple from an open barrel, passing it from hand to hand and frowning. "I don't remember. God bless Maggie for her kind heart. She thinks I'm crazy. I'm not . . . exactly."

He smiled at that. "What are you, then, *exactly?*"

The wild light that dawned in Constance's eyes was sudden, savage, and purposeful. "I'm your revenge, Lock McKin."

His laugh was rather uneasy. "Damn, but you're a woman who loves to talk in riddles!"

"Maggie did us both a favor, bringing you here." Constance tossed her hair back and impaled Lock with a direct, challenging look. "Do you want your *Odyssey* back again?"

"You know damn well I do!"

"I can help you." She smiled and took a bite of the apple. "All you have to do is marry me."

Chapter 8

"Holy Mother, woman! Have you gone stark, raving mad?"

"I'm extremely clearheaded at the moment," Constance said, deadly calm for the first time since she'd clung to a rickety trellis two stories above Beacon Street. "Alex is planning to marry me off to Rodger—"

"What?" Robbed of his normal composure, Lock gave a bark of astonished laughter. "That ass?"

"Exactly so." She waved the apple in airy explanation. "It's all for my own good, you see. Simpleminded female that I am. Or so he thinks."

Her expression changed, and Lock was taken aback by the sudden fury that flashed in her eyes.

"By the bloodthirsty goddess Pele," she vowed in a fierce voice, "Alex will soon learn differently. My life is my own. I won it at great price, and *no one* will take it from me again."

"I surmise you're not in favor of the plan?"

"Hardly!" She pitched the half-eaten apple back into the barrel. "Until now I didn't really understand to what lengths Alex was willing to go to get what he wants, and as for Rodger—that lickspittle would do anything short of murder to stand at the helm of the company!"

"You lunatic!" Lock shook his head in disbelief.

"Foiling their schemes by marrying me is no solution."

Constance leaned against a crate of leafy cabbages and gave him a provocative look through her lashes. "Not even if I stand to inherit half of Latham and Company the minute I'm wed?"

"The devil you say!"

"Oh, aye, my grandfather is clever as Satan, but he's outsmarted himself this time." She plucked a ruffled cabbage leaf from the crate and twisted it between her fingers to fashion a crude flower. "The old schemer had the documents drawn up and filed to tempt me. You can check with Judge Freidel himself if you want, but there's enough legal rope to hang Alex. He pretended to be ill last night, and scared me into a vow to stay in Boston and marry."

"One of those tight little Chinese puzzle boxes your grandfather is so fond of designing for other people," Lock commented dryly. "Quite a dilemma."

Constance tucked the little blossom behind her ear, island-style, and smiled, a feline, feminine grin of pure malicious triumph. "Except I never exactly promised *whom* I'd marry."

Lock crossed his arms and glowered at her. "So you've decided I'm a likely candidate for a husband? Princess, you are deranged!"

Her color heightened, but she held her ground. "Don't misunderstand. I'm talking of a business arrangement that will give us both what we want."

"After what happened yesterday," he muttered, raking her with a look she felt from eyebrows to ankles, "I'd want quite a bit more than what you're apparently prepared to give."

"With my interest in the company, we can recover your *Odyssey*. Alex wants me under his thumb, and you can deprive him of that pleasure, too. Isn't that enough for you?" she asked in a haughty tone.

Lock smoothed his forefinger over his upper lip,

his eyes narrowing in speculation, then answered in a lazy drawl. "It's getting close."

"Very well." She licked her lips, then gave him a direct look. "I'll sleep with you, too, if that's what you want. Then your vengeance on all the Lathams will be perfected."

Lock stared at her. "My God. And you call Alex Latham ruthless."

She shrugged. "It would be a complication, surely, since ... intimacy between us would make an annulment impossible. I leave it to your choice, although even that would make it no true marriage, since I fully intend to leave Boston as soon as the legalities have been arranged to our mutual satisfaction."

"It seems that I would be the one reaping all the benefits from this—er, arrangement," he said in a tight voice.

"Not entirely. I'll have the protection of your name and your presence as long as I'm with you here, and some kind of settlement so that I may live modestly and study in Paris. Should you wish to legally dissolve the marriage at some later date, I will not contest it."

"You've got this all worked out, I see."

"It's a daring concept, is it not?" Constance's smile faltered at Lock's forbidding expression, and she looked away. Taking a deep breath, she squared her shoulders, gathering her determination. "Once again Alex must accept the consequences of his actions. He will learn I am not to be trifled with."

"And you'd trust me to keep my end of this bargain?"

"If anything, you hold your honor too dear, Lock McKin, and in your own way you've been kind to me, though I'm certain you'd never admit it. I believe we can be allies, at least for a time, and ..." She swallowed, then recovered her nerve. "And I would rather trust my fate to you than to Rodger."

"Scarcely flattering, my dear." His lips compressed. "I think I'll pass on your gracious offer—tempting though it is. Somehow the bad taste it would leave in my mouth wouldn't be worth the trouble."

"But what about your *Odyssey?*"

"There are other ways."

"Can you name one?" she demanded in growing frustration. "I hand you your revenge on a silver platter, and you spurn it! Are you a fool?"

"Not so big a one that I can't foresee what a disaster this insane scheme would be!" he said in disgust. He took her elbow. "Come on. Jedediah's landlady will give you a room for the night, then tomorrow—"

"Tomorrow Alex may have found another way to maneuver me to his will!" she cried in exasperation and rising fear. Feeling trapped resurrected old horrors, and she shuddered, whispering, "I might do something desperate again . . ."

"You don't call contemplating marriage with a stranger desperate?"

"I know more about you than you think," she muttered angrily.

"Not nearly enough!" Lock grabbed her other arm, looming over her, his face hard with his own fury. "Especially if you believe you can dismiss me like some kind of damned eunuch."

Her sore palms pressed against his chest. "I—I didn't say that."

"That cold-blooded display wasn't meant to disgust me into staying out of your bed?" He saw the flicker of uneasiness behind her eyes and laughed, nuzzling wickedly at the little cabbage-leaf flower behind her ear. "Don't play games with me, Constance. I've had more practice than you at dealing vengeance."

The warmth of his breath and the feel of his lips against her skin raised goose bumps, and she shivered, aware once again of the strength of his male body and the intangible but potent pull of his magnetism. This wild plan was suddenly as inconceivable and dangerous as he predicted, yet it was all she had. Desperation made her risk a bold question.

"Then why do you hesitate now?" she goaded, swaying against him. "Do you fear the snickers and snubs if you take an island bride? It would only be for a time, and there would be compensations, I assure you."

He stiffened, then threaded his fingers through the hair on either side of her temples. The little flower fell unnoticed to the floor, and he growled down into her upraised face. "Damn you and your heathen tricks! You know that's not true."

"I know you're a man who sets great store in his own reputation, and yet you won't take this chance to avenge your wronged father or the slur on your own mother's name!"

That startled him into releasing her. "What the hell do you mean by that?"

"I know." Reaching beneath the neck of her sweater, she pulled out her locket, opening it so that he could see the two tiny faces within.

"My God." He touched the pictures with fingers that shook. "Mother."

"And my father. Didn't you wonder about what really happened? It wasn't all business that destroyed the Latham and McKin partnership. You must have been old enough to remember the whispers, the scandal."

"None of it was true." Lock's face went livid. "None of it!"

"There's no way I can guess the truth. I only know James Latham must have felt something for Eliza McKin to have carried her portrait." Constance's eyes clouded, and her fist closed over the silver oval. "And that Alex must have punished

him and pushed him and driven him away just as
he's doing to me now."

"That's why you're so hell-bent on this madness!"

"Alex has much to answer for—and you'll deny
me my just reprisal as well as your own! I give you
the means to achieve the most perfect, the most
ironic, revenge, yet you will not grasp it, Lock
McKin." Her lip curled in contempt. "What does
that make you?"

Lock jerked her into his arms, cupping her jaw
with his splayed hand. She made him crazy, turning
him inside out, racing him through a gamut of emotions so that he couldn't think straight, causing
more upheaval in his carefully ordered life than an
earthquake. But just because she lived her life on
the edge didn't mean he'd let her topple him off the
precipice, too. His nostrils flared with the angry
breaths he drew, and his eyes were thin slits of blue
ice.

"You damned shrew. I'm no coward."

Daringly, she lifted her face even higher and
brushed her mouth against his. "Prove it."

Something primitive and forbidden flared within
Lock. His arm tightened around her waist, and the
hand positioned about her jugular flexed experimentally. Constance didn't flinch. The skin across
Lock's cheekbones stretched, and the crinkles in the
corners of his eyes deepened. His mouth twitched,
and something approximating a grudging respect
crossed his face. "Damn you."

"Very probably," she answered with a strange little catch in her voice that twisted Lock's heart. The
door creaked open behind them.

"Excuse me, sir," Maggie said. "We were wonder-
in' if—oh!"

Maggie and Tip hesitated in the doorway to the
storeroom, but Lock made no move to release Constance and she made no move to go.

"Pardon us," Tip gulped, dragging a dumbfounded Maggie back from the sight of two lovers in a close embrace.

"Don't go," Lock ordered, his eyes never leaving Constance's. "Do you have a gown Constance might borrow, Miss Callahan?"

"Well, yes, sir," the girl said uncertainly. "That is, I think—"

"Good." Bending, Lock took Constance's pliant mouth in a brief, hard, possessive kiss, staking a claim. Somehow in that swift exchange, the balance of power shifted. When he lifted his head, he was again in control of the situation, bizarre and queer as it was, and it was Constance who was dazed and shaky.

Satisfied, Lock turned to the other couple with a bland look. "Miss Latham has agreed to become my wife. Where do people get married around here?"

It was surprisingly easy. Father Prelowe had just finished evening prayers at St. Agnes's. Lock's glib tale of orphans and true love and a premature appropriation of his husbandly privileges resulted in a hurried dispensation of the banns and a brief ceremony, complete with a slender gold circlet provided by the obliging padre that Lock placed on Constance's finger. Maggie and Tip stood as witnesses and even toasted them with elderberry wine during the wedding dinner that Lock insisted upon at Mrs. Pibb's Boardinghouse afterward. The reality of what she'd done only hit Constance later, when she and Lock climbed the wooden steps to his little apartment above the shipyard offices, and she realized that the time was upon her to pay the price of revenge.

Lock let them in with his key, then lit a lamp while Constance waited awkwardly in the middle of the chilly sitting room in her borrowed gown and knitted shawl. She watched him strip off his coat, then add coal to the stove and punch up the fire. In her jangled frame of mind, the domestic chore seemed totally incongruous in its simple normalcy.

"We'll need a bigger place, I suppose," Lock said, rattling the poker among the embers, "depending on how long this takes. I want you to be comfortable."

"This is fine." Her words seemed stiff to her own ears. "I shouldn't want you to go to any trouble."

He slammed the stove shut and dusted his hands. "I thought a bridegroom's job was to see to his wife's every care?"

"Ours is scarcely a traditional arrangement."

"True enough." Lock's eyes were a deep, enigmatic blue as he came to her. Placing his hands on her shoulders, he slowly tugged her shawl free. "We could have gone to some place like the Tremont Hotel, but it seemed wiser not to draw attention."

"I understand." Her heart thumped against her rib cage, and she found it increasingly difficult to breathe normally. "What will be the best way to advise Alex that Latham and Company has a new partner?"

Lock touched her hair, now slipping from the soft chignon that Maggie had pinned up for her. "I'll have my lawyers see to it. Best to avoid any face-to-face unpleasantness for a time, don't you think?"

"He'll be livid."

"Isn't that what you wanted?"

She lifted her chin, trying to ignore the way her body responded as he stroked her throat. "Maybe I'd like to see it."

"You are a bloodthirsty creature."

Constance took umbrage with that. "Simply because I desire justice? I have the right."

"I can't argue with that. It's been an eventful day for you. Would you like to prepare for bed?"

Her heart tripping over at double time, she swallowed hard and looked away from the light burning in his eyes. "I'm afraid my trousseau is sadly lacking."

Chuckling, Lock picked up the lamp and led her toward the bedroom. "We can remedy that tomorrow, for your dowry is most handsome. In the meantime, what's mine is yours. Here, this might suffice for a nightgown."

He removed a heavily embroidered robe of scarlet silk from a hook on the back of the door and placed it in her hands. Constance stared at the fantastic creations of mythic Oriental scenes adorning the fine fabric. "How beautiful."

"A memento of my Canton days." His expression was strangely wistful for an instant. "A gift from a lady."

Then he turned and stripped the bed of a couple of its silken quilts and pillows. "There's water for washing in the pitcher and the usual amenities behind the screen. Good night, Constance."

Astounded, she gaped at him. "You—you're sleeping out there?"

"It seems advisable."

She didn't know whether to laugh with relief or cry with disappointment. And the robe she held clutched to her breasts seemed to mock her for her stupidity. Why had it never occurred to her that Lock might love someone else? It accounted in part for why he seemed cool and unreachable except when she goaded him into a display of anger . . . or passion. But Constance had made a bargain, and an inexplicable sense of honor demanded that she see it through, even though trepidation made her voice quiver when she spoke.

"You don't have to do that, Lock," she murmured. "I told you . . . "

He paused at the door, and his features were stiff. "Your offer is duly noted. But on reflection, I believe you're right. It will be better to keep this a business relationship only."

"If that's what you want."

"It's not," he said, suddenly harsh. "I want you, Constance, and I think you've an idea how badly. But I've learned the hard way that it's best to control what one wants in favor of what's sensible. So if you know what's good for you, you'll stop looking at me like some kind of sacrificial lamb and get the hell to bed before I change my mind."

With an irritable oath, he turned on his heel and pulled the door shut behind him with a slam that echoed of finality. An irrational prickle of tears burned behind Constance's eyes, and she cursed herself for a confused fool. She was afraid of what intimacy with a man like Lock McKin would mean—afraid of his size and masculinity, afraid of the injudicious feelings his touch evoked, afraid of the ties that would inevitably be formed, at least for her, if they should come to consummate this farce of a marriage. And yet she couldn't suppress a delicious shudder of anticipatory pleasure at the pictures her imagination drew of them together; so, irrational as it was, his rejection hurt.

With a murmur of distress, Constance went to work on the buttons of Maggie's modest gown. Before she was done, she was half cursing, half laughing at her contortions, for it took quite an effort to reach all the fastenings. Maggie had surely assumed there would be a helpful husband at hand to do the honors. When at last Constance put the scarlet robe on over her chemise and drawers, a film of tears blurred her vision, and she had to remove her hairpins by feel. Pulling the voluminous robe about her, she threw herself down on Lock's bed to lie in a miserable huddle while her thoughts foundered erratically.

Somewhere on the outer edge between wakefulness and true sleep, she dreamed she was back in Lahaina. She was on the beach, running, pursued by nightmare beasts the color of ivory that were chanting hymns. The sand held her back and she sobbed, knowing she could never outrace her enemies. Louder and louder, the luau drums beat in her head—

Gasping, Constance sat up in Lock's bed, disoriented, and stared into a pair of demon-red eyes straight out of her dream. She cried out in terror and scrambled off the bed, flinging herself toward the door, tripping on the overlong hem of the robe, which seemed to hold her back just as the sand had. She fumbled at the door in an agony of fright, finally wrenching it open, and stumbled into the next room with Lock's name on her trembling lips.

But she never uttered it, for her voice froze in shock at the sight of Alex and Rodger, in tall hats and overcoats, standing in the doorway blocked by Lock's rangy form. He'd removed his shirt, and a briar pipe smoldered on a plate by the stove, but there was no evidence that he'd gone to bed. Swaying, she tugged the lapels of the scarlet robe around her, realizing on some level that the drums she'd heard in her dream had been the strident pounding on Lock's door.

"There she is, Uncle!" Rodger peered over Lock's broad shoulder at the barefoot, wild-eyed woman hesitating on the sitting room rug. His lip curled at her disheveled appearance. "Just as I suspected. I was right to have this place watched. I knew she'd run to him."

"Stand aside, McKin," Alex said sharply. "I've come to collect my granddaughter."

Lock half turned, and he frowned at Constance's stricken face. Instinctively, he knew there was something more to her distress than this unexpected visit. He took a step toward her. "Connie? What is it?"

With a gulping sob, she launched herself into his arms, holding him fiercely around the waist, her cheek pressed to the hard muscle of his chest, shuddering uncontrollably. Lock's arm settled around her shoulders, and he gave Alex a hard look.

"Apparently my wife doesn't wish to be collected."

"Your *what?*" Alex staggered as though on the verge of an apoplectic stroke. "Constance, what is this madness?"

Constance closed her eyes and burrowed against Lock's chest. The musky scent of his skin and the sweet pungency of pipe tobacco mingled pleasantly, and he felt warm and solid and safe, his arms a haven from all danger, both imaginary and real.

Lock tenderly cupped the back of her head, every protective instinct aroused. "She's not yours any longer, Latham. We were married this evening at St. Agnes Church."

"My God!" Rodger exploded. "Uncle, do you realize what that means?"

"He's bewitched her, that's what!" Alex took a step closer, his voice gruff with appeal. "Constance, selling yourself to this ruffian isn't necessary. I'll fix everything, no matter what you've done. All will be forgiven. We'll begin again."

"Only this time you'll make certain there are locks on the windows as well as the doors?" Lock sneered. He caught one of Constance's hands and opened it so that they could see the slashed and punctured skin. "She did this to herself to escape from you this time. She'll likely kill herself the next. Is that what you want?"

"This is none of your business, McKin!" Alex bellowed. "I know what's best for my granddaughter! You set out to seduce this innocent child just to get back at me. I'll disown her before I allow you to use her against me."

Lock laughed. "I vow it's too late for that, and you have only yourself to thank. My lawyers will see you in the morning regarding my bride's inheritance. I believe she's entitled to a tidy sum upon her marriage. And so that the launching ceremonies can proceed as I originally planned, you can begin the transition by signing over full title to the *Odyssey* to Constance Latham McKin."

"This—this is outrageous! Impossible!" Alex blustered.

"I knew this little bitch was up to something all along," Rodger wailed in frustration. "Didn't I try to tell you, Uncle Alex? Didn't I warn you that McKin was a part of it, too? Now look what you've done!"

"Shut up, you imbecile!" Alex snarled. "Don't worry, they won't get away with this!"

"We already have," Lock said.

"Constance! You must be reasonable, girl!" Alex reached out, but Lock set her into the big armchair, then caught Alex by the collar.

"Lay a finger on my wife, threaten to harm her in any way, and I'll tear you to pieces!" Lock shook Alex as a dog would a rat. "That goes for both of you. Now get off my property before I have the law on you for trespassing."

"By God, that's enough!" Beet-red with fury, Alex twisted and flailed wild fists at the younger man.

Lock dodged easily, then shoved Alex into Rodger's arms. "Get him out of here before he hurts himself."

"You haven't heard the last of this, McKin," Rodger sputtered, dragging Alex, who was muttering indignantly, toward the door. "I'll find a way to make you both pay!"

Lock slammed the door behind them with great satisfaction, then knelt in front of Constance and took her icy hands. "Are you all right?"

"That was awful." Her teeth chattered, and she didn't resist when he rose and took her in his arms.

"Revenge isn't as sweet as you hoped, is it?" he said.

"No." Shuddering, she clung to his neck as he

slid his big hands up and down her arms and her back to warm her.

"Regrets already?"

How could she answer that? Cold-blooded plotting hadn't prepared her for the heat of direct confrontation, or for the conflict within herself. No matter that Alex undoubtedly deserved a comeuppance for everything he'd tried to do, still her conscience ached. And though the Lathams and the McKins had a long history, now her impetuous actions had made Lock a central target in all this turmoil. Would what he stood to gain outweigh the costs to come?

"It's too late for regrets," she said, swallowing. "We made a bargain, and I'll see it through."

"You're not as tough as you try to appear."

Her laugh was a trifle wobbly. "Neither are you. But I liked the way you came to my rescue."

"All part of the McKin matrimonial services, ma'am." He brushed her temple with his lips, inhaling the sweetness of her fragrance. "You'd better go back to bed."

She stiffened, remembering. "I can't. I'll sleep out here. It's not fair of me to take your bed, anyway, and I—"

"You're babbling, princess. What's the matter?"

"You'll think I'm silly," she murmured, trying to pull away.

"Tell me."

"I saw something." She pointed at the bedroom. "In there."

"Let's take a look."

"Lock, no." She resisted his urging hands. "I was dreaming, but then the knocking woke me, and . . . and there was something!"

"Don't you know by now I won't let anything bad happen to you?" he asked quietly.

Her lips parted but nothing came out, for quite suddenly, she believed him. And trusted him. *God help me*, she thought dizzily, *it would be easy to love this man.*

But it couldn't be. She mustn't allow such disastrous folly to complicate an already convoluted situation. Lock would never forgive her if she let her foolish heart interfere with their business arrangement. He would never have willingly shackled himself to her if he'd known of her terrible crime, and she owed it to him to keep her part of the bargain by leaving Boston and his life as she'd promised. Unless she controlled her wayward emotions, leaving would be another thing that was a lot harder than she'd planned.

Lock held out his hand. Trembling a little, Constance slipped her fingers into his. He smiled encouragingly, then took a lamp and led her into the bedroom.

"Well? Do you see anything?" he asked. He moved a chair and peeked under the bed. "I'll admit you looked a bit unstrung. I wouldn't doubt a wood mouse might have worked his way up from the yard, but they're harmless."

She wandered to the side of the bed, trying to remember. "I sat up, and then I saw—oh!"

Lock whirled at her sudden cry. "Jesus! What is it?"

"The dragon," she whispered, pointing toward the ornate lacquered folding screen in the corner. "It has red eyes."

"He's a fierce fellow, all right." Constance stared at the skillfully painted image with such intensity, Lock frowned and set the lamp aside. "Is that what you saw?"

"Yes." She gasped suddenly and turned her back, old demons and afflictions rising to haunt her. "Put it away. Please."

Mystified, Lock carefully folded the screen so that the dragon's head faced the wall. "It's gone."

"Don't pay any attention to me." She sank down on the edge of the bed, her mouth quivering. "I have bad dreams sometimes."

"Is that what it was?"

Constance shuddered and gave him an oblique look through her sable tresses. "Yes. It was a nightmare."

Lock sat down beside her and placed a comforting arm around her shoulders. "Not surprising, considering all you've been through. But I'm a pretty fair dragon-slayer, if you'll have me."

Constance leaned her cheek on his bare shoulder, letting his strength and the safety it guaranteed seep into her skin like a balm.

"You break my heart when you say things like that, you know," she whispered, suddenly tearful.

"Why?"

"Because I'm so tired of fighting my own battles."

Lock used his thumb to brush the moisture from her lashes; then he shifted so that he lay against the headboard with Constance sheltered in his embrace. "Maybe I could fight them for you. Just for a while."

"It wouldn't be fair to you."

"I believe that little ceremony today made your problems my problems."

"It was a crazy thing to do. I didn't think of all the complications for you." She plucked fretfully at the embroidery on the robe. "That you might be . . . involved with someone else."

Lock frowned, then suddenly took her meaning and covered her restless fingers with his own. "Rest easy, princess. I made the choice with my eyes wide open."

"But you said—" She broke off. "I'm sorry. I don't mean to pry."

"I suppose a wife can be forgiven for being curious. Her name was Soo Ling. She was a Cantonese noblewoman, and as far above the attentions of a wet-behind-the-ears seaman as my topgallants are above the deck of the *Odyssey*. A disaster from start to finish."

"But you loved her?"

Lock shrugged. "I learned the hard way the price of infatuation, the lack of control, the stupidity. One experience like that was quite enough to convince me never to repeat it, so don't worry that my emotional life will suffer from this arrangement of ours. It suits my plans and inclinations quite well for now, and I won't mind another battle or two on your behalf if the cause is worthy."

She trembled, knowing Crazy Lili's crime made her far from worthy, but she could never confess that. "St. Michael come to slay my dragons, are you? I hope you don't become disillusioned before this crusade is over."

Lock's large hands smoothed her back, and he chuckled. "I'll tell you when that happens. Until then, you wear this robe for me. All the symbols are supposed to bring good luck. I've a feeling our enterprise will flourish."

And Constance had a feeling they would need all the luck they could get, but she was too weary to warn him, too tired to deny her heart the sweet solace of Lock's reassurances, and it felt so good just to be held. Her drowsy murmur barely reached his ears.

"I pray you're right, Lauchlan McKin. I pray you're right."

Holding her, Lock found something within himself he hadn't known was missing, a genuine wish to comfort, to share a connection with another person that was based in peace and compassion.

Lying in his arms, Constance dreamed a little, a waking dream this time, of peace and wholeness and someone who'd always fight her battles no matter how unworthy she was.

In silence, they shared a single unspoken regret that the vows they'd taken were only fantasy and this wedding night wasn't real.

Chapter 9

"You should be out there on deck with that new husband of yours, sharing the glory," Elspeth Philpot scolded, "not standing here with the old maids!"

"I'm as close as I care to be, Elspeth," Constance replied nervously. "And I'm very glad you're here."

Constance tore her giddy gaze from the silver expanse of Boston Harbor and focused on the flag-trimmed and banner-festooned hull of the *Odyssey*, perched on her launching cradles like a majestic bird ready for flight. All three of her temporary masts streamed with colorful pennants, and she sparkled with new black paint, fresh copper, and gleaming varnish.

A multitude of artisans, sailors, journeymen, businessmen, reporters, and spectators of all sizes, ages, and descriptions thronged the McKin Brothers Shipyard, their murmurs of excitement building to a crescendo as this much-heralded ship's christening festivities continued apace. Even the weather was cooperating, for in the three and a half weeks since Constance's impulsive marriage, winter's back had been broken, leaving behind a few late March gusts, perfect sunshine, and crisp air that smelled, at least for a time, more of spring, black earth, and growing things than Boston's ubiquitous fishiness and salt.

From her vantage atop a pile of timbers well back
from the water's edge, Constance strained her
eyes for a glimpse of Lock's dark head among the
black-coated dignitaries standing high above on the
Odyssey's deck. As the ship's designer, he rated a
position among those who would ride her down
the bulge ways and be among the first to see how
she took to her true element. As the newly court-
appointed owner, Constance should have been with
him, but as a first-rate coward, she had been forced
to make her excuses.

Even though she knew she'd disappointed Lock
by her adamant refusal even to consider joining
him, she still could not fathom why any sane person would wish to ride tons of out-of-control ship
down a flimsy, tallow-greased railing into the briny
deep. Why, anything could happen! Chewing her
thumbnail, she offered up a silent prayer for her
husband's safety just as the convocation of notables
on deck parted and Lock escorted a bent figure forward.

Holding her broad-brimmed white chip hat
against a playful breeze, Constance brushed back
the trailing pink ribbons that matched her new
glacé silk promenade gown and pointed. "Look, the
invocation is over, and here comes Mr. Shoe to perform the christening."

"Silliest thing I ever heard," Elspeth muttered,
wrestling with her striped parasol, "letting the old-
est sailor perform the honors. Why, he looks too
feeble even to lift a bottle, much less smash it!"

"Jedediah will do splendidly, I'm certain," Constance replied.

Sure enough, though the wind whipped the
speeches shouted from the deck into incoherent
sounds, when the time came, Jedediah gamely shattered the christening bottle over the *Odyssey*'s bowsprit with all the enthusiasm of a much younger
man. At a signal from Lock, two men waiting on

the scaffolding along the hull swung their axes, cutting ropes that released the weights on the dog shoes, short timbers that angled against the cradles to hold the ship back.

For an endless moment all was still, and Constance held her breath with the rest of the crowd. A knot of panic jumped into her throat. What was wrong? Lock had planned everything so carefully for this day. His pride would be crushed if anything went amiss!

Constance's flitting thoughts hung suspended just like the great ship; then a distant creaking of timbers rent the still air. The *Odyssey* seemed to tremble, the whole hull coming alive.

"She's moving!" Elspeth cried, grabbing Constance's arm and bouncing up and down on her toes like an energetic India-rubber ball. "Oh, watch her go!"

Slowly, then faster, the ship slid in her cradles, accompanied by a high-pitched screeching of wood against wood. The rails smoked from the friction, then flamed. A swell of sound came from the onlookers, and Constance found that she was shouting, too. With a final rush, the *Odyssey* slid down the ways, plunged into the water with a gigantic splash that soaked the nearest spectators, then floated free. The crowd roared.

"Oh, well done!" Elspeth chortled, clapping madly. "Well done, indeed!"

Constance blotted a film of nervous moisture from her upper lip with the back of her gloved hand and managed a shaky smile. Her knees felt like jelly and her heart pounded, but then, after almost a month of living under the same roof as Lock McKin, that was nothing new.

Close proximity to a man of Lock's blatant masculinity was enough to make any maiden entertain foolish fancies, and Constance had the added complication of vivid memories of the way his mouth felt against hers, hot and hungry. The daily intimacies of living in the same household were seductive, giving her notions that had nothing to do with their agreement. Yet the scent of his shaving soap across the breakfast table or the way his shirt stretched across his broad shoulders had a way of undermining her good sense. Under these trying circumstances, it was a miracle that she was able to retain any degree of equanimity whatsoever!

"Whatever are they doing now?" Elspeth asked, shading her eyes and squinting at the plethora of skiffs and tugs that had quickly surrounded the bobbing *Odyssey*.

"They'll tow her to the rigging yard to ship the masts and lay on the shrouds," Constance said. "Won't she be a thing of beauty then!"

"Just as you painted her, my dear." Elspeth twinkled at Constance. "That's a mighty proud husband who's displayed your ship's portrait on his office door for the public's enjoyment today. I'd say you've been busy."

Constance wondered at the understatement of that simple declaration. Considering the unusual circumstances of her life, it was a wonder she was accomplishing a thing, but since the day Lock had moved them into a modest furnished house on Devonshire Street, she'd been a veritable workhorse, and the rear parlor she'd commandeered as a studio was already littered with over a dozen canvases of Boston street scenes, tropical flowers, Hawaiian mythical depictions, and more.

Perhaps her restless energy could be ascribed to the tension over Alex's vehement legal protests regarding her marriage settlement. These objections had been partially resolved when, to prevent dissolution of Latham and Company assets by the courts, Alex had reluctantly deeded the *Odyssey* to her. That was all Lock really wanted, but her grandfather had appealed the ruling, and until the issue was settled, Lock's attorneys insisted they keep up the appearance of a newly married couple, since the terms of Alex's initial bequest had stated that as an express requirement.

Perhaps, Constance thought, her productivity was the result of her anxiousness to move on to Paris. After all, she'd been delayed too long already, and the frustration of another postponement of her dream made her edgy and nervous, not to mention the intermittent bombardment of abuse and pleading she received in letters from her grandfather. It was especially difficult to harden her heart when his missives described in great and pitiable detail the sudden failing of his health due to his disappointment in her.

But if Constance were critically honest with herself, she'd admit the reason she'd plunged into her work was that only when she was engrossed with her paints and brushes was her mind free of Lock McKin. He'd been equally busy, preparing for this launching ceremony and laying down the keel for the *Argonaut*. He'd used his work just as she had, as a buffer that, if they were lucky and worked hard enough at it, might actually help them both ignore the physical awareness that kept the air perpetually charged between them.

It wasn't that either one of them had forgotten their agreement. They both behaved with the utmost circumspection, with none of the flare-ups of temper that had marked their relationship to this point. Indeed, never had Constance acted with or been the recipient of more civility. Neither had there been any occasions when a touch or a look had led to anything other than a hasty apology, and there had been no repetitions of the strange and intimate interlude they'd shared on their wedding night. They were as polite as strangers living temporarily in the same house. The trouble was, Constance groaned to herself, she didn't know how much longer she could stand it!

That was why she could honestly tell Elspeth, "I've been working very hard."

"Every artist should be so devoted. And you a newlywed, too!" Elspeth noted Constance's heightened color and smiled. "Don't mind my teasing, dear. Every comment I've heard today about your portrait has been most favorable. But then, I'm not surprised."

"I'll grow swellheaded if you keep this up, Elspeth," Constance protested with a laugh.

"Your modesty is most becoming, but positive publicity will help to sell more copies of *Sandwich Islands Sketchbook*. Did I mention that Mr. Evans thinks he can have it printed by midsummer?"

Constance's mouth fell open. "You mean he agreed to publish it?"

Elspeth nodded, quite proud of herself. "Wonderful news, isn't it? And cause for another celebration for you. Come, treat me to a cup of something adventurous. While your husband is ferried off his vessel, we can't let all of his lovely refreshments go to waste!"

Still reeling from the good news, Constance readily agreed. They threaded their way through the milling crowds to the sawhorse-and-board tables laid out with acres of food and drink. The launching of a ship was a celebration for everyone from owner to lowliest caulker, and already a fiddler had begun to play as part of the dancing and merrymaking that would last well into the evening.

Constance helped herself to a cup of tea from a steaming samovar, then watched, wide-eyed, as Elspeth did the same and daringly added a dollop of a potent concoction of rum and cider known as stonewall to her own cup.

"For medicinal purposes and body heating only, my dear," Elspeth quipped with a wink.

"Mrs. McKin!" Eyes shining and cheeks flushed apple red with excitement, Maggie appeared at Constance's side, dragging Tip along behind. "Ain't it a grand day? You must be right proud of Mr. McKin."

"It's a happy time for all of us. You had no trouble getting Mr. Fitzgerald to give you a free day?" Constance asked.

Maggie laughed, making the daisies on her straw bonnet bob in tandem with her strawberry ringlets. "He's come, too, with his whole family—all thirteen of 'em!"

Constance chatted with Elspeth and Maggie while Tip loaded a plate with generous helpings of the salads, cold meats, cakes, and savories laid out in abundance. Maggie was happy with her job with the greengrocer's family, but glad to get the extra money she earned on her off days helping with the McKins' small household chores which were still such a mystery to Constance. The two women had shared more than a few giggles over Constance's attempts at housekeeping, in the end deciding an artist's time was better spent in the studio than on her knees scrubbing. Thanks to Mrs. Pibb's boarding-house kitchen and a convenient laundry, Lock and Constance weren't likely to starve or go dirty, and Lock's bachelor routines went more or less uninterrupted except for his having to make polite, if stilted, conversation over meals with his new wife.

It was a reasonable system, but one that Constance found rather maddening. Sometimes it took all her self-control not to stir something up just to see if she could find a crack in Lock's impassive facade again, to somehow release the tension building up between them like electricity crackling before a thunderstorm. So far, she'd been able to resist the impulse, but she knew herself better than to think such forbearance could last forever, and though she lectured herself sternly, she couldn't suppress a tiny thrill of excitement at the prospect.

When in due time Lock arrived, Constance experienced the same small tremor of annoyance she felt during those polite breakfasts, for his manner was far too dignified and restrained for a man who should be in the heights of delight over a successful ship launching. His dark head caught the sunshine, glistening like a raven's wing, as he strode through a clutch of reporters, answering questions gravely. Constance thought she'd never seen him look more handsome, his black business suit setting off his tanned good looks in a manner that turned more than a few feminine heads. But the animation that should have been in his expression was severely controlled, and it made her sad and angry at the same time to see it.

"Here he comes, lads!" Tip shouted to the yard hands gathered around the tables and led a round of spontaneous, congratulatory applause. "The McKin himself! Speech, sir!"

Workmen tugged Lock forward, pressing a glass of something potent into his hand, refusing to hear any demurral. Lock caught Constance's eye and shrugged slightly, then stepped onto a chair so that he could be better seen and heard.

"It's you men who should be congratulated," Lock said, his words clipped and forthright. "I dreamed the *Odyssey*, but you built her. I salute you."

Tip led a rousing "Hurrah!" Lock held up his hand so he could continue.

"The New York firm of Tugwell and Kent has contracted with McKin Brothers for a vessel, and we'll be laying down the keelblocks starting tomorrow morn. With the *Argonaut* begun and now a New York commission, there's work here for all who'll have it." Lock lifted his glass. "Gentlemen, today I give you the *Odyssey*, and a toast: May she fly!"

Cries of "Here, here!" and "Aye, McKin!" accompanied a general tilting of glasses and another cheer.

Constance saw the trust and the pride reflected in the men's faces, and her own heart swelled. Lock might be a hard taskmaster, but he had his employees' respect. With a sudden jolt, she considered what that must mean to a man whose life had been shadowed by family scandal and disgrace. She smiled, fiercely glad she had been a small part of his triumph, and, catching Lock's glance again, raised her teacup in mute salute.

Something in Lock's expression intensified, and Constance's cheeks warmed and her heart thumped. The heat in his blue gaze made a curl of something smoky tickle the back of her throat and lodge low in her feminine center, licking at her resolve like a flame set to tinder. Thirsty for the taste of him, her lips parted in unconscious invitation, and Lock's eyes became the shade of a thundercloud, dark and just as dangerous.

Recalled to herself by a thrill of alarm, Constance hastily averted her gaze, disconcerted by her involuntary response. How could she hope to keep things businesslike if her recalcitrant body betrayed her in such an obvious fashion every time she met Lock's eyes? She had to get hold of herself! With difficulty, she schooled her features into a semblance of composure as he climbed down from the chair and made his way through the throng, accepting backslaps and congratulations from all and sundry.

"Mr. McKin, this is a fine day for Boston," Elspeth said as Lock joined them. She pumped his hand furiously. "You'll make this city the premiere shipbuilding center of the East Coast, if I'm any judge of fleet vessels—and I've been watching your family build them since you were a mere wee thing yourself!"

"Thank you, Miss Philpot."

Lock had replied in his usual urbane manner, but Constance knew instinctively that beneath his cool and serious demeanor, he was bubbling with exhilaration. Again it vexed her sorely that he would not allow himself to enjoy this moment to the fullest extent. Didn't he realize that to cheat himself this way was to deny the joy of life itself? Really, she thought, someone should teach him a lesson. With an inner grin, Constance realized it was a mission she could embrace with gusto. It would be a small enough way to repay him for all he'd done for her.

"Just don't neglect your bride in favor of work, mind you," Elspeth cautioned mischievously. She relieved Constance of her teacup and urged her hand into the crook of Lock's arm. "Now, off you go, you two! This is a day to enjoy."

"It's useless to argue with Elspeth," Constance murmured, mentally thanking the older woman for giving Lock a metaphorical shove in the right direction.

"Then I won't even try," Lock said with a brief smile. "Shall we?"

Bidding Elspeth good-bye, they strolled through the crowd, greeting Lock's friends and business associates, even stopping to visit briefly with Captain Jenkins and his pudgy, mule-faced wife. The captain was cordial, and made absolutely no mention of having recognized the new Mrs. McKin as Con, his former passenger, much to Constance's amusement.

"It appears Captain Jenkins has had a lapse of memory," she remarked. "I pray it doesn't interfere with his command of your *Odyssey*."

"As a matter of fact, he's decided not to wait on her. He'll take the *Eliza* on the California run come Wednesday. With luck, we'll turn four times the profit of his last trip."

"After meeting the captain's wife, I understand why he prefers to spend his life at sea," Constance commented, her lips twitching.

"Married woman or not, you're still an incorrigible brat," Lock returned under his breath, but for the first time that day, his tone held an element of humor that Constance found vastly encouraging. He nodded politely and passed a few words with a trio of financiers, then moved on.

"You don't really enjoy this, do you?" Constance asked out of curiosity, tilting her head up at him as they completed a round of the shipyard. While most of the important personages, dignitaries, and politicians had taken their leave, the fun was only beginning for the shipyard employees gathering around an impromptu dance floor cleared near the now-empty ship's cradles.

"Enjoy what?" Lock asked. He scanned the sunny yard, taking in every detail. The festivities had gone without a hitch, his only disappointment that Constance hadn't been at his side during the *Odyssey's* wild slide to freedom. Why that should bother him was a mystification he chose to ignore.

"Having to be convivial to all these people," Constance answered. "You're quite good at it, very dignified and courteous, but you don't really like it."

They stopped on the edge of the dance area to watch the couples whirling in a high-spirited polka, and Lock shrugged. "I'll admit it doesn't come easily for me, but such duty is part of the job. Good public opinion can do wonders, but it can just as easily turn and eat you alive."

"How very cynical you are," she protested. "Today is a wonderful achievement, with news of a new contract to boot!"

"That's why I can't afford to let up." There was determination in the granite line of his jaw. "The world craves fast ships now, and I can build them, but it won't last forever. Something new will replace the clippers eventually. Why, steam technology is improving every day."

"So you'll construct steamships when the time comes." Her voice held complete confidence. "You can do anything."

"It's sailing ships I know and love. Has been ever since Dylan and I build our first dory as boys." Lock's blue gaze swept out across the bay and settled on the ship being towed slowly around the curve of the waterfront. "The *Odyssey* could pay for herself the first time around the Horn, but this contract with Tugwell means I can push ahead the *Argonaut*'s completion as well."

"That's the one I saw chalked in the molding loft?" she asked.

Lock nodded, and for an instant his eyes grew shadowed with a poet's dreams of glory. "She's the one who'll make my name, Constance."

Constance understood then that it was more than ambition, more than money, that was important to Lock. Somehow his drive came from a desire to clear the McKin name, to erase the shame of his father's failure and suicide from the collective consciousness of Boston society with one great work that would stand for all time.

"I know you'll do it, Lock," she said softly. "But dream your great ship into life tomorrow. You've worked hard for today, and the Iron Man needs a rest."

Lock brought his wandering attention back to her then, somewhat startled by her curious words. She was a fetching sight in her stylish chapeau with its floating pink ribbons, and as she held out her hand, she dazzled him with her gamine's smile.

"Come dance with me?"

A bolt of pure desire shot through Lock, and sweat broke out on the back of his neck. He'd managed to keep the fire in his belly dampered for over a month, but there wasn't a day that went by that

he didn't curse himself for a damned fool. Having
Constance close at hand, smelling her perfume in
the hall, seeing her in all her moods—drowsy at
breakfast, engrossed in her studio, hurt and furious
over one of Alex's guilt-making letters—were trials
to any normal, healthy man's sanity. Forget all the
sensible reasons why making love to her was a complication neither wanted! Why hadn't he claimed
her for his own when she'd offered? Damn his stiff-
necked pride! His only hope was that she didn't realize what an effort it took to keep from making a
complete jackass of himself now. Holding her close
would only drive him completely around the bend.

He shook his head, answering hoarsely. "Not
now. I've got some things—"

"Lock, please." She caught his hand. "I saw a picture of you at the *Silver Crest*'s launching. Surely
you haven't totally forgotten what it's like to have
fun?"

He blinked, taken off guard. That boyhood day,
before his mother's death and before his father had
grown hard and distant, rose in his memory, carefree and innocent. Those same things tempted him
now from the depths of Constance's warm golden
eyes, urging him to cast off cares and seriousness
and simply *live*.

"This isn't particularly wise," he warned, moving
to take her in his arms anyway.

"It wasn't a wise man who first climbed to the
volcano's summit, but look what wonders he
found." She smiled up at him, and her expression
was bright with challenge and invitation. "Come, be
foolish with me for a while. It will do you good."

He wanted to say, *"You* do me good," but he
wasn't sure she'd understand. Hell, he barely understood himself! He only knew that, despite everything, with Constance he felt more alive inside than
he had in years. But he couldn't find the words to
say it, so he whirled her into the stream of dancers,

showing everyone a side of Iron Man McKin few even knew existed.

It was heaven and hell all rolled into one.

The feel of Constance in his arms, the warm fullness of her breasts brushing his chest, the ribbons of her bonnet tickling his cheek as they circled the makeshift dance floor, were all exquisite pleasures. And he knew that he wasn't the only one aware of these sweet tortures. Constance's hand trembled ever so slightly within his, and when their eyes met, a peachy blush invariably mounted her cheekbones, and her lashes fanned down in coquettish allurement.

Every sense was heightened. Her scent was the sweetest nectar of paradise. The music was the liveliest melody this side of heaven. The sunset had never been as lovely and the stars had never shone with greater incandescence. After a while, it was easier simply to give in to the sensual enchantment, so Lock relaxed as the warmth of Constance's presence flowed through him like honey, and just let himself enjoy the moment.

It was well past midnight when they stumbled through the doorway of their Devonshire Street house. Constance carried her hat and gloves, and her hair had long since come down from its sedate coil, but she glowed with good spirits and healthy exertion.

"What a glorious day it's been!"

In his shirtsleeves, his muscles aching pleasantly from hours of dancing, Lock watched her with an indulgent smile as she made pirouettes through the shabby sitting room. Though he hadn't had much to bring from his old quarters, it was Constance who'd found a home for all of his books and scientific instruments, and arranged the bright silk cushions and his comfortable old armchair so that the rented house felt familiar and cozy.

"You've worn me out," he mock-complained. "I'm too old for such shenanigans."

"And who insisted on an encore polka with Maggie that nearly brought the house down?" Constance teased back, setting aside her things and twirling in place. "It was so much nicer than that stuffy Assembly, don't you think? I love to dance!"

Lock tossed his coat on a horsehair settee and turned up a gaslight, illuminating a dreadful flocked rose wallpaper. But even that couldn't dampen his mood. "You're good at it."

She wrinkled her nose. "All Alex's lessons." For an instant her expression wavered, but then she smiled, lifting her hands in a series of graceful gestures. "And, of course, my clandestine training in the hula. Did you know my mother's people tell stories this way? The missionaries forbid it, but still the stories are passed on. Every motion means something—palm tree, ocean, moon."

She fit her gestures to the words, swaying her hips gently in a series of flat-footed steps, her expression far away. Although there was nothing salacious about the dance, Lock's mouth went dry.

"It's lovely," he murmured. "Who taught you?"

Constance looked blank for a moment. "It's not important." She grinned, her euphoria returning with a rush. "I'm starving, aren't you?"

"What, again?" He feigned a groan. "I know Mrs. Farrar's book must have something crushing to say on the subject of a lady's appetite."

"I refuse to eat like a bird for anyone. Besides," Constance said, smoothing her trim form with both hands, "the island folk admire an Amazonian figure. Most of the royalty weigh upwards of three hundred pounds."

"When you attain that weight, I can use you as a counterbalance on the shipyard windlass."

"A useful occupation at last," she quipped. "Let's see if there's anything in the cupboard."

Constance caught Lock's hand and pulled him into the stone-flagged kitchen at the rear of the house. It was a homey room with a large cast-iron stove, a stone sink, and a well-scrubbed pine table. She pushed Lock down into one of the heavy high-backed chairs, then rummaged in the pie safe, emerging with an armload of bread, apples, cheese, and a decidedly deformed pie.

"It's my first attempt," she said proudly, cutting Lock a huge wedge. Her laughter gurgled delightedly at the expression on his face as she poured milk into crockery mugs. "You may laugh at it all you wish without fear of hurting my feelings. I may be an atrocious cook, but I do other things well."

Lock paused over a bite of the surprisingly tasty pie, dumbstruck. It was true. She did many things well—amuse him, fascinate him, irritate him, make him crazy with desire, replace the loneliness in his life with the slightly off-centered brilliance of her wry wit and intriguing personality. Sitting here with Constance, sharing apples and cheese and conversation, he felt the ice-encased center of his heart thaw in a way that hadn't happened since he was a boy and his mother had made them a family. He'd been too busy fighting his own dragons to realize until now what he'd been missing by depriving himself of this sweet and simple pleasure.

Lock considered his situation logically, scientifically. Today, with the launching of the *Odyssey*, he'd reached a certain level of success. A man in his position needed a wife to support him as hostess and helpmeet, to make a home and bear sons to inherit what he'd built. But he had a wife now, he reminded himself, albeit a temporary one, wed under the most unusual of circumstances. Lock tried to imagine his life once Constance was gone, and the stark image chilled him.

But what if he could persuade her to change her mind? Constance said she was set on Paris, but she'd seemed content enough these past weeks with her work and her new friendships, and he could not deny the pleasure her company had given him today. She'd badgered and teased him into forgetting his dignity for a while, and he'd seen how his employees warmed to her. She would be an asset in many ways, even without the added attraction of her usefulness as an instrument of revenge. And what could be more convenient than keeping a wife one already had?

For all her flirtatious shows, she was skittish when it came to passion, but he knew she wasn't indifferent to him. He stifled a wry laugh at that gross understatement. Hell, it was a wonder they didn't spontaneously combust, the way things heated up between them sometimes. There was nothing wrong with pure, clean lust, and his instincts said they'd have quite a time before the flames burned out. It wouldn't be love, he told himself staunchly. He'd had a stomachful of that overrated emotion with his unrequited adoration of Soo Ling. No, this was something more substantial, a mature and sensible arrangement that could provide security and companionship for both of them. Other marriages succeeded on less.

If only she would see it.

Watching Constance from across the table, her upper lip coated with a childish-looking milky film—just as it had been the first time he'd seen her—Lock felt the familiar tightening of his loins. But instead of forcing the sensation back, which he'd done these past endless weeks, he allowed it to uncurl slowly, heating his blood as he watched her pink tongue lick her lips clean.

There was one certain way to show her.

Constance reared back in her chair, arching into a stretch, fluffing her dark hair as she stifled a yawn. "What a day. I swear my feet are ready to disown me, they ache so!"

"Let me help," Lock murmured. He knelt, fishing one of her feet out from the frothy confines of her pink hems, then slipped off the offending shoe and pressed his thumbs against her arch.

She jerked convulsively, then relaxed, shuddering with the pleasure/pain of his ministrations. "Ohhh, that's lovely . . ."

He repeated the operation on her other foot. "Better?"

"Mmm." She looked at him through her lashes. "You're different."

Lock slid his fingers around her trim ankle, then up to her stocking-covered calf, kneading the muscle gently. "I'm the same as always."

"No. Something's changed."

"Because I rub your feet?"

A smile quivered on her mouth. Pointing her toes, she pressed the ball of her foot against his bent knee. "You must admit it's rather a unique position for the McKin."

"It must be your influence. Being with you is a unique experience." He took her hand and kissed her palm. "I enjoyed today. Thank you."

Her eyes were sherry-colored and startled. "I—I enjoyed it, too."

"I'm glad." Carefully, he unbuttoned her cuff, pressing his lips against her leaping pulse. Involuntarily, her foot flexed against his knee, and Lock smiled to himself. He turned his attentions to her other wrist. "Very glad indeed."

"Lock?" His name was a breathy question, and her fingertips caressed the side of his jaw, lingering over the tactile pleasure of taut male skin beneath a shadow of dark stubble. "What are you doing?"

Rising, he bent over her, burying his nose in the fragrant curve of her neck, whisking his lips over the translucent skin in the hollow beside her ear. "I'm kissing my wife."

Constance shivered. "W-why?"

"Because I'm a man." His fingers found and began to release, one by one, the buttons that ran in a row from her nape to her waist. "And if I don't taste you again very soon, I'm sure to go out of my mind."

"But—"

He captured her soft gasp with his lips, melding their mouths sweetly, sensuously, sipping at her like a connoisseur. She was nectar and honey and a thousand delightful, exotic things he couldn't identify. She gave an inaudible groan, and her lips clung to his when he finally lifted his head.

"When I encouraged you to have some fun, I didn't realize you'd take my advice quite so much to heart," she whispered shakily.

He rubbed his thumb back and forth over the luscious curve of her lower lip. "It's unnatural to deprive ourselves of something we both find so pleasurable."

Constance's eyes widened. "But what about our agreement? I thought you decided—"

"A man isn't allowed to change his mind when he's found he's made a grave mistake?" His ebony brows drew together in a doubtful frown. "Or was your offer to share my bed an empty one?"

"N-no." She gulped. "But you were right. It seems terribly cold-blooded just to . . . and then to leave."

"But I want you to stay."

She went pale, then crimson. "What?"

"I've been thinking about it hard for nearly a month." His fingers made persuasive circles on her shoulders, slipping underneath the loosened neckline of her gown to trace the delicate line of her collarbone. "Hadn't you ever considered the possibility?"

"B-but Paris, my studies . . ." she began weakly.

"Why is it so important? You have a budding career right here, what with your *Sketchbook* and the inquiries I had today from some shipowners who'd like portraits of their own vessels. You'd be a stranger struggling on your own in Paris. You're already making a name for yourself here."

"Lock, stop!" Agitated, she shot to her feet, but he merely put his arms around her, one hand sliding beneath the open back of her dress to rest between her shoulder blades. They stood pressed breast to breast, thigh to thigh, and Constance's breath caught and tarried in an unsteady rhythm that revealed her confusion. "It's not fair to you! You can't know—"

"You wouldn't suffer for it, I promise," he said, his voice gruff. "I'd see to it you didn't want for anything. I'll even be in a position soon to take you abroad myself, if that's what you truly want. We'll see Paris together, London, Rome, Florence. Isn't that what all artists rave about, the light of the Italian countryside?"

She shook her head, looking somehow lost and miserable, her mouth trembling. "It's not that."

He kissed her eyelids, the curve of her cheekbone, the line of her jaw, and she quivered in his arms like a palm shoot in the wind, her hands unconsciously clenching and unclenching in the fabric of the shirt tucked into his waistband. Giving in to his body's desperate urging, Lock pressed her into the cradle of his thighs, letting her feel the strength of his arousal.

"You see what you do to me, Connie. Maybe we started off differently from other couples, but it could be a good life."

"But this isn't what we'd decided," she said, her words growing more frantic, her body stiffening against his in panic. "This isn't in my plans."

"Would you find it so very hard?"

She looked at him with her soul in her anguished eyes, and her whisper was rawly honest. "No. No, it wouldn't be hard at all. That's what frightens me."

"I'd never hurt you. Believe that. And this."

Lock kissed her with all of his expertise, wooing her gently, holding his strength in reserve though he longed to crush her against him, to end the distance that physically separated them forever. Constance jerked and shivered as her resistance faded. With a little moan of defeat, she parted her lips to his insistent urging, and as their tongues met and melded in sinuous union, Lock felt passion rising within him like a sweet tide.

God, he wanted her so much he hurt, and the strands of his control shredded into gossamer filaments that could no longer hold back his raging heart. Deepening the kiss, he swept the open gown off her shoulders, and, freed from the sleeves, her arms slid around his neck. With a trembling hand he explored the angle of her elbow, moving up her arm to cup her round shoulder, then straying over the soft swell of her breasts heaving beneath the flimsy chemise and bone stays. Muttering an exclamation, he undid the corset laces, releasing her from the garment, pushing it and the gown down and away so that she stood in only her petticoats and chemise. Afraid he'd be tempted to take her on the cold flagstone floor, he tore his mouth from the magic of hers and buried his lips in the tender hollow of her throat.

"Jesus, you're sweet," he murmured, shuddering with need. "Come, love, let's go to bed."

Lock felt Constance freeze for an awful instant of suspended time; then she strained free of him, choking on a dry sob. He was too surprised to resist. "Connie?"

"I can't." Her voice cracked on a hoarse note, and she pressed her knuckles to her mouth as she struggled for control. "I can't be what you want. I'm sorry. Oh, God, I'm so sorry!"

She turned her back, holding herself as if to restrain a tidal wave of tears. Frustrated, mystified, Lock reached for her again, then froze in horror. Laced across the delicate skin of her exposed upper back was a cross-hatching of fine white marks, some old, some not so old, revealing a brutal history.

"My God." A rage like none he'd ever experienced scalded him like red-hot lava. He grabbed her so swiftly she squealed in alarm. "Who did this? Goddammit! Who beat you?"

Her eyes opened wide. "N-no one."

"Damnation to Satan and all his fork-tailed demons!" he roared, giving her an infuriated shake. "Don't lie to me! Who hurt you? I'll kill the son of a bitch!"

"He's already dead." Her voice was as flat and lifeless as the tarnished pools of her dilated irises. "Crazy Lili killed him."

"Who the hell's Crazy Lili?"

Her mouth twisted. "Me."

"Christ!" Lock released her as if stung.

Constance snatched up her gown, holding it against her nakedness, her features etched with stark despair. "Christ can't help me, even if He did send an archangel to try."

Lock took a step toward her. "Connie. Princess—"

She caught her breath on a strangled sob and backed away. "It can't work, Lock McKin, so it's better not to start. I'll go tomorrow."

Then she fled. For the second time that day, the sensation of sliding out of control sent Lock reeling. Was Constance running from her past—or from him?

Chapter 10

She'd been wrong to believe nothing else could surprise her, Constance thought wretchedly. Roused at dawn by a grim-faced and taciturn Lock, she'd been both surprised and hurt by the rapidity with which he seemed intent on sending her packing. Ordered to dress simply, she'd barely been given a chance to wash her sleepy face while he'd haphazardly scooped her things into a canvas seabag. Then, without addressing a handful of words to her, he'd hired a buggy and told the driver to take them to Long Wharf.

Now, shivering under her mantle and thin sprigged gown in the damp pea-soup weather, Constance stood on the rough cobbled wharf, wondering which of the tall ships anchored amidst the forest of masts was meant for her. The smells of fish and tar were strong, and the sound of water lapping all around behind the enveloping curtain of mist unnerved her. She tried to contain the thudding fear that made her heart race at the thought of setting sail again.

Lock slung the seabags over his shoulder and took her elbow. "Come on."

"W-where?"

"You'll see."

Her feet dragging with reluctance, she prayed she wouldn't further disgrace and humiliate herself with a show of cowardice, or worse, an emotional display over this farewell that would only embarrass them both. She tried to focus on Paris, but couldn't conjure up the golden image that had sustained her before. All she saw was the man whose stern visage and tightly clamped mouth indicated how much he despised her.

With the collar of his pea coat turned up against the chill, Lock led her past dozens of oceangoing vessels, turning at last onto a small outshoot of dock. He leaped into a small single-masted yawl with the painted legend *Valiant* emblazoned on her stern and began to roll up the protective canvas that covered the roof of a tiny cabin and the highly varnished deck. Constance stared, openmouthed with shock.

"Cast off that line, will you?" he ordered, busy with shrouds and cleats. "Then climb aboard."

"I may be crazy, but I'm not mad enough to get into that thing!" Fine droplets of moisture gathered on her dark lashes and the tendrils escaping her hasty braid. "I know I'm not going to Paris in that."

"We've got some things to sort out first," he said, his tone hard with annoyance, "so save your arguments, Constance, and get the hell in!"

She backed away from the edge of the slip. "No."

With an oath, Lock threw down the rope he'd been coiling and vaulted in one sleek predatory movement to cut off her retreat. "You're a great one for running, but we're going where you can't run away."

"Lock, please," she begged. "You don't understand."

"Not yet." He caught her under the knees, scooping her up so quickly that she gasped and grabbed for his neck. "But I will. We're going to talk, Constance, and we can't do it here."

"But—but you're supposed to start on the New York commission today!" she protested wildly.

"My foreman knows what to do, and we can stand a few days to get things straight." Lifting her high, he stepped into the boat.

"Days?" A whimper escaped her, and she clutched his neck even tighter. "But I'm leaving anyway, so it serves no purpose—"

"You're going to tell me," he insisted grimly, gazing into her frightened topaz eyes with a determined blue fire burning in his own. "*All* of it. Now, stay put."

Lock plopped her down gently on top of the seabags and cast off. Before Constance could gather her scattered wits, they were gliding away from the slip through the lifting fog toward the outer reaches of Boston Harbor. Cringing, shuddering, Constance sank down on top of the lumpy bags and clenched her eyes shut. But it didn't help, for she felt the lift and sway of the yawl and knew that liquid death lay underneath the boat and on all sides.

"Oh, God," she moaned in terror, her fingers digging into the canvas spasmodically, "I'm going to be sick . . ."

"Then get it over with," Lock ordered brusquely. He adjusted the sheets and took up his position at the tiller. "You'll feel better afterward. Just don't foul the deck."

She wasn't entirely successful, then or later. And as the day brightened with sunshine that burned off the fog and made them shed their coats, a snapping breeze kept them scudding up the coastline like a miniature *West Wind*. But Constance's white-faced misery didn't relent. Only an occasional spasm of sickness gave physical release from her vertigo and the throat-clogging sense of imminent doom, but such relief never lasted long.

Lock found there wasn't an opportunity for any of the quiet questions he had planned for this easy sailing trip, and his concern for Constance grew intense. She was withdrawn and silent, her color pasty and her brow beaded with sweat despite the breeze. Nauseous and dizzy, she lay on the narrow bunk in the tiny cabin or leaned over the railing to heave up her juices, and Lock finally realized it wasn't simply a matter of waiting out a case of mal de mer. This was her body's defensive reaction to something that quite literally frightened her to death.

"Jesus, is this how you were aboard the *Eliza?*" he asked after a particularly violent bout. He placed his hands on her waist to steady her as she knelt at the railing in a spineless collapse.

"Mostly." She rinsed her mouth with water from the boat's cask, then blotted her face with a wet towel. "I told you I didn't like the water."

His respect for her courage trebled. "But why?"

"I don't know. I have nightmares about drowning sometimes. It's been like that since I was small."

Constance breathed in shallow gulps, holding herself as still as the plunging motion of the yawl would allow, praying that this moment of respite would last longer than the ones that had gone before. To her disappointment, her stomach began to lurch again almost immediately, and she moaned softly.

Cursing himself for not taking her earlier protests seriously enough, Lock inspected the rocky shoreline, picking out familiar landmarks, a spectacular jut of black rock, a half-moon of sandy beach, a stretch of virgin hardwood forest still untouched by greedy shipbuilders like him. He and Dylan had sailed this rugged, island-dotted coastline as boys, and though it had been too many years since he'd come this way, he knew it still and realized they were well past the point of no return.

"Hang on a bit longer, princess," he urged. On impulse, he pulled her back to the tiller, seating her between his legs with her back resting against his chest. She was too limp to protest. "We'll be there soon. I had no notion this would be such an ordeal for you, or I'd never have insisted."

"I've been nothing but trouble to you since the day we met," she murmured with a tiny smile. "Had enough?"

"Lord, does nothing quail your impudence?" He laughed ruefully, then tilted her head back and kissed her gently. Much to his amazement, a smidgen of the sick tension in her limbs eased. Frowning, he intensified his gaze on hers.

"Look at me," he ordered in a low, commanding voice. "Watch my eyes, my hands. I know the sea. Let me share my love of it with you. I won't let anything harm you."

Weak, with no reserves left, she wanted to believe him, and somehow the strength in his strong body and the power of his will over hers made it possible. Whispering in her ear, Lock spoke of the ocean, the winds, the tides. Placing her hand over his on the tiller, he let her feel how he controlled the water, guiding the yawl across its shining surface. The sail swelled and the shrouds vibrated as he skillfully caught every breath of wind. Constance's senses began to fill with the force of Lock's vital masculinity, crowding out everything else so that she was half hypnotized by him and forgot to fear.

The husky timbre of his voice cocooned her as Lock spoke of sailing around the Horn, of the scents that blew off the Chinese mainland, of the thrill of sighting Java Head for the first time. Mesmerized, she forgot everything but the sweet sensuality of being held so close. His scent enveloped her, mingled with the salt spray to become uniquely and indelibly linked. The warmth of his sun-kissed skin against hers burned through the chill terror, melting it, and her blood ran like molten honey. His strength enfolded her, protected her, cherished her, and as time swept by like the waves rushing beneath the hull, her trust built, her stomach settled, and her limbs relaxed.

It was really a miracle, Constance decided hazily several hours after the sun had passed its zenith. Cradled in Lock's arms, touching his hand, she wasn't afraid any longer. She really ought to be angry with him, charging in like a bull and inadvertently forcing her to face her terror in this fashion, but her fear was gone—or at least held at bay. Either way, it was a success she had not expected, a precious gift from the man she loved.

Constance snapped out of her delicious, half-dozing reverie with a gasp. Stripped of all her defenses, she faced a truth she could no longer deny. God help her, she was in love with Lock McKin, with her own husband! The irony of it made her want to weep.

"Easy," Lock soothed, feeling her renewed tension. "We're here. You made it."

Constance blinked, coming fully aware of her surroundings even as her heart brimmed over with love and anguish. No longer was her fear of the open water her greatest concern. How could this disaster have happened? Loving Lock only meant leaving him would be a hundred—a thousand!—times harder, for it would be the ultimate selfishness to act on this wayward emotion, even if he had convinced himself it was what he wanted.

"I have to trim the sails so we can dock," Lock said, easing from his seat at the tiller, watching her carefully. "Will you be all right?"

"Of course." The terrors of the voyage were forgotten as she looked up into his concerned face. Lock smiled, squeezed her shoulder in encouragement, then hastened to his work, and Constance could almost believe he cared for her, just a little. It might truly be possible to conquer her dragons with the love of a man like Lock McKin.

No, she cautioned herself firmly, Lock had married her for only one reason, and this fervor of the blood that confused and beguiled was merely an illusion, best set aside at once in favor of their original, sensible business agreement. He was an honorable man, too good to be permanently tied to the likes of a murderess like Crazy Lili, and she couldn't ever let impossible, unrealistic dreams of wedded bliss make her forget that.

Swallowing hard, Constance let her gaze skip over the water of the little bay to take in the vistas of this lonely and beautiful place. The heart-shaped inlet with its double arc of sandy beaches was surrounded by glistening black rocks tumbling down from a breathtaking stretch of cliff dotted with sheep sorrel and bayberry. Nestled in the protective curve of the hill was a fisherman's tiny clapboard cottage, its shingles gray and weathered with age and salt air. A small dory lay upside down under a lean-to shed cluttered with lobster traps, cork floats, and old fishnets.

With exquisite care and infinite skill, Lock reefed the sails at the precise instant that brought the boat up beside an ancient, canted pier protruding from the point of the heart. When he held out his hand to help her from the yawl, Constance needed no second invitation.

"W-where are we?" she asked, squinting against the westering sun, clutching Lock's arm to ward off a final, lingering flash of vertigo as they walked up the uneven dock. The surf surged and roiled against the shore with a ragged murmur, and wheeling sea gulls cawed and cried above them.

"A place I used to love." There was a remembering look in his eyes, and he readjusted the seabags he'd thrown over his shoulder. "Skye, my father called it, after his father's birthplace in Scotland. It's quiet here. Peaceful. My mother and I spent the whole summer here before Dylan was born. Later, he and I came as often as our father would let us. We built our first dory together right over there."

"Dylan couldn't have been much help."

Lock supported her as they stepped from the end of the pier onto the sandy path leading over the low, grassy dune toward the cottage. "He was young, but he was company. Father didn't have much time for a rowdy kid like Dylan. Then there were only the two of us . . ."

Dry land under her feet again had given Constance back enough strength to ask an impulsive question. "Is that why you've brought me here? For company?"

"Not exactly." Lock paused on the porch steps, examining her returning color closely. "How are you feeling now?"

"Better." She considered for a moment. "Hungry!"

Lock gave a relieved chuckle. "I'm not surprised. Well, I can set out the lobster pots and dig us up a few clams for supper. Would that suit?"

"Yes. I'll help." At his raised eyebrows, she explained. "Though I'm a coward when it comes to sailing it, we lived off the ocean's bounty in Lahaina, and I know how to do my part."

"Very well. Want to see inside first?"

At her nod, he ushered her into the sparsely furnished cottage. It was pleasantly warm inside, and as they shed their outer garments, Constance inspected her surroundings nervously.

A small fireplace dominated the main room and faded pink cotton curtains hung at the dusty windows. Someone had lined up an assortment of seashells on one windowsill. A rustic table with two trestle benches stood on one side, and a scarred settle on the other. Against the back wall, a dry sink held an assortment of thick, brown-glazed crockery. Through an opening Constance could see the only other room, furnished with an old sea chest and a tarnished brass bedstead covered with an assortment of tattered patchwork quilts. Constance gulped audibly.

"Don't look so worried." Lock tossed the seabags down beside the bed. The roughness of his voice was tempered by the gentle hand he raised to smooth the windblown sable tendrils back from her anxious face. "Nothing's going to happen here that you don't want. *Nothing.* I guarantee it. But the offer I made last night still stands."

Constance paled. "Even ... even knowing what I've done?"

He crossed his arms, observing her impassively. "You say you killed a man."

"I did!" Guilt and horror shimmered behind her eyes, and she shuddered uncontrollably at a vision of dead-white skin and scarlet blood. Her voice came from far away. "I didn't mean to ..."

"Tell me."

She gulped. "No, please ..."

He took her hand. "Trust me, princess."

"I—" She stared at his strong fingers locked around her own, and her soft words trembled as she forced herself to remember. "I'd been to the waterfront and talked with Dylan. Uncle Cyrus was waiting. Somehow he always knew when I disobeyed ..."

"Daughter of Satan! I'll teach you to mend your whoring ways!"

She dodged another blow from the shadowy figure looming before her. "No! It's not like that—"

"Lying Jezebel! I know where you've been."

The night breeze blowing off the ocean was balmy and fragrant with the perfume of exotic flowers, but the air inside the dark hut felt icy against the beads of terror-induced sweat pearling her temples. "Uncle Cyrus, please. I haven't done anything wrong, I swear."

Only dreamed of escape, her heart whispered guiltily. Only listened to the young sea captain with laughing eyes who'd admired her painting of his proud, sleek ship and talked of her crossing the oceans to places she'd merely read about in the mission school's textbooks, to a city where her pictures wouldn't be called the devil's work, to a family and a home where she'd be safe ...

"You dare to profane the Lord in my own house?"

The Reverend Cyrus Tate rumbled the demand in the awful voice he used from his pulpit to convince unrepentant heathens of the reality of eternal hellfire and the sinful consequences of sloth in the sugar fields of Holy Sanctuary colony. "Ten years since your papa died and I took you in to raise as my own, but you've learned nothing! I praise God my Eleanor didn't live to see your shame, but I'll not let you slide into Gehenna unchecked!"

"None of the other girls—"

"Are products of sin and lust! Do they see visions? Do they hear voices? Satan wants you, girl. And once he's got his teeth in you, he'll drag you under like a shark to drown in the molten waters of Hell."

She hesitated, assaulted by images she could not control. "I only meant—"

"Down on your knees!" His hand, slim and white as a girl's yet surprisingly strong, caught the sleeve of her *holoku* and thrust her down before the simple altar adorning one wall of the hut. His fingers cruelly twisted her tender flesh, but she stifled her moan. She'd learned long ago that no one dared interfere when the spiritual leader of Lahaina disciplined his devil-touched, recalcitrant foster child, no matter that she was a woman full grown. On the bamboo altar table an offering of sweet ginger blossoms spilled from a large pearlescent conch shell, and the cloying fragrance made her retch.

"Unclean woman! Your very flesh reeks with the stench of fornication. Pray that the Lord Jehovah will strike the wickedness from your tongue!"

Leather hissed as he pulled his heavy belt free. It cracked across her back, and she arched in white-hot agony. Again and again the blows fell. Reduced to sobbing, whimpering mindlessness by the searing pain, she struggled to her feet, trying to protect herself, trapped before the altar.

When he paused for breath, the look on his face was like none she'd ever seen before, a mixture of transfigured power and bizarre ecstasy. She knew with a certainty that this time he wouldn't stop until she was dead.

"Thank the Lord I'm here to help you wrestle with your sinful nature," he ranted. "Mortify the flesh if ye want life everlasting! Purify your thoughts and deeds. Destroy the tools of the devil!"

He pulled a small bundle from his pocket, revealing her most precious possession, the priceless and irreplaceable bouquet of artist's brushes that was her single anchor to sanity. Then he calmly snapped it in two between his strong fingers.

"No!" The scream that had been so long withheld ripped from her throat in an outburst of rage and despair. After years of submission, she struck back in sheer desperation and perhaps a spark of madness.

The heavy conch shell caught him squarely across the bridge of his nose, bone and cartilage crunching sickeningly with the force of her blow. Water and ginger blossoms and blood sprayed everywhere, and he dropped without a sound, sprawling at her feet, his hand still clutching the bloody leather strap.

The shell slipped from her nerveless fingers, and she caught her breath on a sob of joy, of relief, of renewed terror. One look at his still, crimson-streaked visage told her the worst. Scalding panic bubbled like the lava in Pele's fiery mountain, and she stumbled from the hut.

A cry of alarm rose from the dark compound behind her. She lurched down the beach toward the water, frantic images of tribal justice and white man's law churning in her shocked brain while the salt of the ocean breeze bit at the bloody stripes on her back.

She was as wicked and evil as they'd always said, and now she'd defied Jehovah's just punishment, cut herself off from all human and divine compassion. No one would understand she'd only meant to make Uncle Cyrus stop hurting her. No one would believe or forgive Crazy Lili, who had always been like the smoking mountain, ready to blow to pieces at any second. And that was what she felt now, as though she were shattering right before her own eyes, crumbling to nothing, like the sand cliff beneath her feet at the water's edge.

Around the curve of the bay, the masts of tall ships rose like black fingers into the navy blue sky. Shouts drifted from the compound, and she gazed in stark terror at the foaming sea.

Nowhere to run. Perhaps it would have been more merciful to die at her uncle's hand than to face what island justice would surely mete out to her. But it seemed God wasn't finished with her yet. He wasn't through making her suffer. The shouts increased in volume, came closer. No, the Lord had one more trial for her before she would be allowed to join the legions of the truly damned. Dropping her gown, she forced herself into the crest of a giant, curling wave . . .

Bars of golden sunlight speckled with floating dust motes illuminated Constance's stricken profile as she fell silent at last. She pulled away abruptly, showing Lock the defensive curve of her shoulder.

He scowled, remembering the lacy etching of scars he'd seen there.

Her uneven breathing sounded loud and harsh in the little cottage, and she mumbled wretchedly, "Now you know. Now you can despise me even more."

Lock went to her, turning her around so that he could peer into her averted face. "I think you know I don't despise you."

"You should!" Her head jerked up, and she glared at him, all false bravado and defiance. "Then you'd give up this crazy notion! I'm not the wife for a good man like you, Lock McKin. Anyone with half a brain can see that! I'm a child of sin, willful and disobedient and bound for hell, but I don't want to drag you there, too . . ."

Lock mouthed an obscenity. "Is that what the bastard told you? Christ! I've seen bloodthirsty mutineers flogged with less violence! Did you really believe all that?"

"I *killed* him!" she cried. Her hands curled into fists and she pounded Lock's chest. "A man of God!"

"Hellfire! From the looks of it, he was trying to kill you!"

She hesitated. "I—I thought he was, that last time. I suppose Uncle Cyrus was trying to guard my virtue. Not that he thought there was much left to protect."

"Don't defend the bastard!" Lock roared. "No matter what you did, you didn't deserve ten years of that kind of abuse! What else did he do? Force you to sleep with him?"

Shock widened her eyes. "No! I've never been with a man that way!"

"But this Tate accused you of it, right?" Lock guessed. "When he beat you, I'll wager he enjoyed it, loved touching you." Constance's face flamed, and Lock knew his guess was right. "No wonder you killed the bastard! I'd have done it for you if I could. And no wonder you're afraid of me now."

"I'm not afraid of you!" she flared. "And I certainly don't want your pity!"

"Then how about some of that human comfort you once lectured me about, Constance? Or don't you think you deserve it?"

Her expression went bleak. "No."

"Hell, can't you see? *You* were the victim, not this Tate!"

"It doesn't change what I did," she cried in anguish.

"Self-defense! No jury in the world would convict you."

"I don't believe you."

Lock stalked her across the bare room, his expression hardening. "And that's why you're always running. What happens when you get to Paris, Constance? Will you go on to St. Petersburg? Then to Canton? What happens when you run all the way back to Lahaina?"

"Stop it!" she screamed, covering her ears. "I won't listen to this!"

"You've got to stop running sometime," he said, jerking her into his arms. He cupped the back of her head, forcing her to look at him, and his voice was husky with emotion. "Make it here with me."

His offer, now that he knew the worst, completely undid her. Tears trickled over her lashes and streamed down her cheeks. "Oh, God, I want to. I don't know if I can."

Tenderness transformed his harsh expression into one of dazzling promise. "You can. I'll show you how."

Constance licked salt from her lips and shivered. Could she believe him? Dared she hope this fierce, dark archangel of a man was the key to her salvation? She needed his strength and solace, and even though he didn't love her, he offered her something she'd never had—a resting place, safety, and peace. And even though her heart leaped to her throat at the thought of what would happen between them, because she loved him, and because she was too weak to do the right thing, there was really only one answer she could give.

"Yes," she whispered. "Show me."

"God, you're brave." He praised her, marveling, sweeping the moisture from her cheeks with the pad of his thumb. "And beautiful. And smart. And I want you so badly I ache."

Lowering his head, Lock kissed her fiercely, molding his mouth to hers in a feverish staking of possession. Her lips trembled and he thrust his tongue between them, tasting her deeply. Fire surged through his loins and gathered in his sex. Constance moaned inaudibly, and the vibration ignited a raging hunger in him that had been too long denied.

With a murmur, he lifted her and carried her to the bedstead, laying her on the old quilts and following her down. The metal frame creaked, and Lock groaned with the heat that surged through his bloodstream at the feel of her beneath him. It was a fantasy he'd dreamed too many times, the soft thrust of her breasts against his chest, the way his hips fit so perfectly against her pelvis. Releasing her mouth, he drew back, in a frenzy to rid them of their impeding clothing, but something about the tension in her impinged on his last rational moment.

Lock looked at her face and saw the same sick dread as when he'd placed her in the yawl that morning. But this was more than virginal shyness. Suddenly, all the times she'd frozen in the heat of his embrace made sense. That goddamn monster Tate had punished her so viciously for imagined sexual behavior, he'd no doubt given her a fear of the real thing. Lock pulled away, swearing softly.

Constance opened her clenched eyes, bewilderment shadowing her stark white features. "Did I do something wrong?"

"Not you, princess. Me." With a deep, frustrated breath, he sat up on the side of the bed, hanging his head and rubbing his face until his ragged breathing modulated and he could look at her again. "Forgive me. I didn't mean to frighten you."

"It's all right. You didn't ..." Hesitancy and a raw vulnerability made her voice shake. "You want this, don't you?"

"You don't know the half of it," Lock muttered with painful irony. He touched her face gently, and his eyes darkened to the angry indigo of a thunderhead. "But we'd better not, not just yet. That bastard marked you in invisible ways more serious than the physical hurts. I'm not going to compound them by forcing you into this."

She was dazed, aching herself in a dozen secret places, and thoroughly confused. Her lower lip quivered. "But I want to."

"We will make love together, Constance, make no mistake about that. But when you're ready. And that's for you to decide."

"I don't understand you." Petulance and hurt feelings made her lower lip sulky. "Don't you want me?"

He caught her hand and pressed it to his swollen manhood, letting her feel his hardness through the fabric of his trousers. "Does that answer your question?" he said with a groan.

She gasped and pulled her hand away as if scalded, her face crimson.

"We've got time here, Connie," he said in a hoarse tone. "Time to explore each other. Time for you to learn what it's like to be with a man. You can touch me in any way and at any time you like, and I'll touch you and kiss you because I just can't help myself. But until you show me you're ready for more, until you're no longer afraid of me, I can be patient for the rest."

Wonder filled her eyes, and her brave facade slipped to reveal the relief she felt. When she spoke, her voice shook. "I never knew there were men in the world like you, Lock McKin."

"Don't attribute high motives to this gesture, my dear. Until I have your complete trust, it's just not worth the risk of a wrong move making you run again, this time from me."

Constance marveled at his generosity and forbearance. He was willing to wait for her to make the decision? He was giving her the right to control her destiny and her body, and he wasn't turning away? Rather, his simple words hinted at a greater commitment than she had yet dared to dream of. It was a heady, exhilarating freedom such as she'd never known.

She touched his cheek, then rubbed her forefinger over the outline of his upper lip. "I never thought I'd have reason to be grateful for the Iron Man's self-control."

"No, you like to see me lose it, don't you?" Lock laughed wryly, pressing a kiss into her palm. "Well, I'll wager you'll try it sorely before we're done, but I'll do my best."

"Thank you."

Lock cleared his throat, shifting uncomfortably as if already regretting his decision. "That's my noble gesture for the millennium, so make the most of it. In the meantime, a cold dunking and a siege with the lobster pots will help me keep my good intentions."

Constance blushed furiously, and Lock chuckled again, although it sounded a trifle strained. Rising from the bed, he headed for the door. "Can you build us a fire? The nights here can be frigid this time of year."

"Yes, of course." Constance nodded miserably,

uncertain if he referred only to the weather or if his words were a dire prediction regarding her ability to respond to him.

Catching sight of her ambivalent expression, Lock hesitated, then came back and kissed her with such gentleness, she wanted to cry all over again.

"Don't worry, love," he consoled her. "We have time now, and together we'll outride this storm."

At sunset, after several hours of solitude in which she had tried to sort through the mass of conflicting emotions that held her in thrall, Constance finally gave up and joined Lock on the beach. Careful to keep her gaze directed away from the surf, she helped him build a driftwood bonfire, then watched as he dumped the fat lobsters he'd trapped into a bucket of boiling seawater for their dinner. They dined outdoors beside the fire, feasting on the lobster and steamed clams Lock had provided, accompanied by boiled heart of cattail and orache salad, which was the result of Constance's foraging.

Afterward, Lock shoved another dried branch into the glowing coals and threw himself down on the sand beside Constance. She sat with her back toward the water, watching the sun disappear over the western cliffs in a blaze of tangerine-and-violet sky. The chill evening wind caught at her hair and whipped it around her face, but she wore her mantle and didn't seem to notice.

"You aren't cold?" Lock asked quietly, watching her from where he reclined against a driftwood log.

"No." She glanced at him from under her lashes. "It's nice here."

"Like Lahaina?"

"Oh, no. Lahaina's much warmer, and the palms and cane fields are so green they hurt your eyes, but there are places that are as rugged as here. Once I even made the journey to Haleakala."

"Hale-what?"

She smiled. "House of the Sun. A very ancient and sacred volcano. Before the Christian God came, my mother's people believed the demigod Maui captured the sun there to make it slow its transit of the sky so the people would have more time to harvest their crops and dry tapa cloth."

"It must be something to see."

"Like walking on the moon, I think," she said, gazing upward at the sprinkling of stars that were just appearing. "In the crater Pele's fire once flowed, leaving only ash and desolation, but even in such a place, life will not be denied. The sacred silversword plant grows only there, springing from the rocks like a miracle."

"Adversity often produces the hardiest souls," Lock murmured, thoughtful. "Like tempered steel, the trial by fire results in greater strength and resiliency."

"Aye, the silversword is famed for its beauty, but the fire flower bears its purple bloom only once before it dies. I find that rather sad."

"Better than never blooming at all, I guess." Lock scratched designs in the sand with a stalk of sea grass.

"Yes." She drew a deep, shuddering breath. "You're right."

Frowning, Lock shifted his position, sitting facing her, one knee drawn up, his wrist resting on it. Beyond her, the silver curl of the surf glistened against the dark water, foaming up the beach, then withdrawing in a rhythm as ancient as the moon itself.

"Connie, what is it?"

Her hands twisted in her lap. "What if I can't please you? What if I never bloom?"

With a tender smile, he toyed with her earlobe. "You worry too much. Things will happen all in good time, as they're meant to be."

"But I don't know how or if I can do what you

expect," she nearly wailed. "Oh, I wish you'd taken me this afternoon! Then at least it would be over!"

"A coward's way, and I know you're no coward. Some things, even good things, just have to be faced, princess." Gently, he drew her around onto his lap and pointed at the water. "You've already conquered one demon today."

"Because of you," she whispered.

"Look at the sea," he urged. "Your artist's eye can't help but appreciate the beauty of it. The movement, the mystery, the spindrift rising to the stars like a prayer."

"You are a poet," she said softly. "I knew it."

He laughed. "Just a man who likes to build ships—the bigger the better, except for my little *Valiant*. There's a spur of the Massachusetts and Western Railway about ten miles inland from here. We could go back to Boston by train, but I'd prefer to go home the same way we came. Do you think you can do it?"

Constance shivered. She might have some artificial control over her fear, but she knew that it wouldn't last without Lock. "If you'll hold me again."

His arms tightened around her, and his voice held an element of lazy humor. "My pleasure."

"You're a rogue to tease me about this," she accused in a shaky voice. "I've already confessed I have no experience."

"What a man and a woman do together can be a beautiful thing." He nuzzled her neck, lightly nipping at the fine cords straining there. "And what leads to the act is nearly as important as the act itself. If it's experience you want, all you have to do is touch me."

"I want to touch you," she murmured, swallowing hard. "But I'm afraid . . ."

Tipping her chin up, he searched her face. "Can you trust me again as you did on the boat?"

"I—I can try," she breathed.

"That's all I ask, love. Come, it's getting late, and it's been a long day for both of us."

Her heart stirring with trepidation, Constance walked with Lock back to the cottage. Inside, she stood awkwardly while he lit a lamp and stoked the fireplace. Passing by her, he touched her shoulder.

"Why don't you get ready for bed? There's water for washing in the pitcher, and you can have first turn at the necessary out back." Unbuttoning his shirt, he pulled it up from his waistband. "I'll clean up outside."

"All right." She gulped, her eyes locked on the ridges of muscle revealed by his open shirt.

"Constance." Taking her hand, he put it inside the shirt to rest against his heart. Her fingers flexed involuntarily, threading through the crisp black hair that covered his chest from his shoulders to his navel. The movement made him suck in a silent breath. If ever he needed all of his self-control, this was the most crucial time. "We'll share the bed and get used to each other. That's all."

"Oh."

"Princess." He kissed her, then gave her a serious look. "I never break my word. Never."

After Lock stepped outside, Constance nervously undressed, washed, and tugged on a voluminous flannel nightgown. She found her brush in the bottom of the seabag and went to work on her wind-whipped braid, unthreading it and brushing her dark hair in a ritual that was meant to be soothing but somehow wasn't. Despite Lock's assurances, she wasn't certain she could maintain her composure. What if she giggled? He'd think her inane and silly, a child. What if she cried? He'd think she was the most craven of cowards.

She was so lost in her thoughts, she whirled and dropped her brush when he came through the door again, wishing she'd at least had sense enough to be under the covers already.

Shirtless and shoeless, his hair damp from his ablutions, and his skin prickled with goose flesh from the rapidly cooling night air, Lock tossed his things onto the sea chest and reached for the brush. "Here, let me do that."

Throwing back the covers, he sat down on the edge of the bed and drew Constance down in front of him. Silently, he brushed her hair, smoothing the sable mass until it jumped and crackled with life.

"You have beautiful hair," he murmured.

"It—it's grown a lot since I came," she managed to say.

Though Constance sat docilely, her pulse leaped, and she was supremely aware of his hard thigh pressed against her hip. She wanted—what? She didn't know exactly, only a yearning to be close to him warred with her fear—of the unknown, of the sinfulness that lust created, of her own insecurities and failures.

"You're so tense I could use you as a poker," Lock said, dropping the brush to massage her tight shoulders. "Relax, sweetheart."

Her voice was breathless. "I—I'm trying."

"You need something to take your mind off yourself," he said. "I believe you need to think about me instead."

"What?" She stood up at his urging, glancing over her shoulder at him with a puzzled expression that quickly turned to wide-eyed bewilderment as he shucked off his trousers. He reached for the waistband of his long johns, but one look at her face made him think better of it. He lay down on the bed, patted the empty space beside him in invitation, then crossed his arms under his head.

"A little experiment, Constance. Something I learned in the Orient. I give you leave to touch me, stroke me from head to toe, anywhere, except for one or two—er—extremely sensitive spots. You lead the way. There's nothing right or wrong, just touching for the simple pleasure of it, for both of us, with no pressure to go any further."

She swallowed, overwhelmed by his dark masculinity, spread out on the bed like a pagan sacrifice. "You really want me to do that?"

"Very much. Come on. Don't be shy." His lips twisted wickedly. "Unlike you, I don't bite."

"Oh!" She became instantly huffy, excited by the prospect of unlimited freedom to explore his beautiful body, challenged by the light in his eyes that said he thought she couldn't do it. Well, she'd show Lock McKin!

Gingerly, she scrambled onto the bed, kneeling beside him, looking anything to Lock but childish in the enveloping gown. Though she was swathed to the throat in flannel, he could still see the outline of her breasts pressing against the fabric. His grin didn't waver, but his mouth went dry, and he had to resist the urge to swallow convulsively as she reached out a tentative hand. When her fingers lightly touched the center of his breastbone, Lock could have sworn an electric current arced through him, and he braced for the sweetest torture ever endured by man.

Frowning slightly in concentration, Constance trailed her fingertips over the muscular contours of Lock's chest, raking paths through the soft black curls, circling but not touching the bronze coins of his flat nipples. Warming to the task, she bent closer, stroking his collarbone with both hands, then exploring the width of his strong neck. His Adam's apple bobbed revealingly, and she smiled as his lashes fanned down to cover his eyes and the expression they held. She fingered the velvety underside of his earlobes, then plunged her hands into the ebony silk of his hair, enjoying the texture before rubbing his temples and then his beard-shadowed jawbone.

She skimmed his upraised arms, following the paths of blue veins to the sensitive crooks of his elbows, then down the sides of his rib cage, counting each muscular ridge. Engrossed, she pressed his hipbones, but at her movement toward the point where the arrow of body hair tapered and disappeared beneath the waistband of his underwear, his hands flashed downward, capturing her wrists.

"Uh-uh, sweetheart," he said, a flush on his cheeks and his voice husky with strain. "I'm only human, after all."

"Hmm?" Dazed, she took a moment to catch his meaning. "Oh!"

"Not that I'm complaining. You're doing a wonderful job," he told her with a raspy chuckle. Releasing her, he rolled over onto his stomach and crossed his arms under his chin. "Try this side for a while."

His amusement rankled a bit, canceling out any embarrassment she'd felt, and the urge to rattle his iron composure made her redouble her efforts. She explored him from nape to heels, smoothing and stroking the sleek, powerful muscles of his legs, the indentations of his vertebrae, the dimples above his buttocks just peeking over the edge of his waistband. The texture and scent of his skin were intoxicating, addictive, and she saw that the pleasure she achieved by giving to him in this way was in proportion to the pleasure he experienced as the recipient of her attentions. It was a powerful notion, this giving and taking, something to be contemplated thoroughly at a later date. Now she could only follow her instincts, and giving in to an impulse, she pressed her lips to the hollow of Lock's back in the softest of feather kisses. He jumped, showing her that his relaxed attitude was more feigned than not, and she smiled and did it again.

"That's enough," he croaked, rolling onto his side. "You're an apt pupil, as dangerous to my peace of mind, not to mention my good intentions, as the sirens who lured mariners to their destruction in ages past."

"My wish is to please you," she answered demurely, sitting back on her heels in the middle of the mattress.

"Good." He caught one of her hands. "For it's your turn now."

Her eyes flew open wide, and she gulped. "My turn?"

"Just touching, Connie. Promise." He came up on his knees facing her, gently rubbing his thumbs over the pulse that beat in her wrists. "May I look at you?"

Drowning in the blue fire of his gaze, Constance reminded herself it was all a question of trust. She'd been drawn to Lock's strength from the first, but now his utter gentleness and surprising sensitivity revealed facets about him that called out to her deepest needs. If she loved this man, how could she not trust him? Licking dry lips, she nodded.

Slowly, he drew the gown off over her head and tossed it aside. His breath caught, for she wore nothing underneath to mar his view. Shimmering in the feeble whale oil lamplight, her skin was the color of honey, her breasts high and full, crowned with delicate rosy-brown peaks. She knelt with her head bent, the raw sable silk of her hair spread over her shoulders like a royal cape. Lock felt a surge of primitive possessiveness. She was as beautiful and perfect and untamed as a pagan princess, and she was his. Exultation filled him, humbled him. Jesus, but he wanted her! Exerting every ounce of his control, he banked the fire that surged through his loins. He must take care even yet, lest this wild, fey creature take wing.

"Lovely," he murmured, cupping her shoulders and gently pressing her back into the bed linens. "You are so damned beautiful."

She made a small negative sound, shaking all over with fright—or anticipation?

"Yes, you are," he insisted. "I'll show you."

Just as she had, he smoothed and stroked her arms and legs, the tops of her straight shoulders, her neck and face. Knowing she wasn't really ready to accept more intimate attentions, he stayed clear of her breasts and the dark triangle between her thighs, though he thought he'd go insane with the intensity of his desire. After a while, her shivering abated as she warmed to the unhurried sensuality of his wanderings.

She was limp and languid when he rolled her over onto her stomach, dazed by the completeness of his ministrations, for it seemed that he'd missed no square inch of skin with his skillful fingers. She tensed for a second when his surveying hands paused on the marks on her back; then she sighed when his lips anointed each place with a satiny benediction, dispelling her fears that he'd find her scars repulsive. Quiet pleasure drifted through her veins, and she was floating, sailing on an ocean of sensuality, relaxing beneath the warmth of Lock's hands, for the first time in her life, warm, safe, and pleasured . . .

Incredulously, Lock listened to the soft regularity of Constance's breathing, then gave a pained, ironic grimace. She was fast asleep, trusting as a babe under her mother's safeguarding hand! With a ragged groan, he kicked off his underwear, doused the lamp, then drew the covers over them both. He lay stiffly beside her, not daring to touch her again, trying to ignore the throbbing ache between his legs.

His plan to win Constance's trust had been per-

haps a mite too successful. With a sigh, Lock prepared to wait out his body's screaming demands,
hoping the rewards of this campaign would outweigh a restless night.

Chapter 11

Constance awoke at the first rosy streaks of dawn, faintly surprised by her dreamless night and the fact that she was nude beneath the bedcovers. She was too cozy and refreshed to give the subject more than fleeting attention, snuggling closer to the pleasing warmth next to her. With a jolt of returning awareness, she realized it was Lock, and he was as naked as she was!

She held her breath for a long instant, but the chest on which her cheek rested rose and fell with the regularity of sleep. He sprawled on his back, and she lay tucked protectively under his brawny arm. Raising her head a little, she looked at him.

Relaxed in sleep, he was boyishly handsome, yet his features retained the essence of his iron-hard strength and determination. On further examination, however, Constance discovered faint plum shadows under his eyes, evidence that Lock had not enjoyed as restful a slumber as she had. With a wry half-smile, Constance realized that she was probably to blame.

Good Lord, she'd fallen asleep on the man! Was that an insult to his masculinity? It was merely that what he'd done to her with his hands had felt so good, so right, just as lying pressed against his heart did now. Her legs tangled with the hair-dusted length of his, and she could feel the pulse of his blood through her skin. Remembering how they'd explored each other made her own blood heat, and a place low in her belly tightened. She wanted more. Tentatively, she slipped her palm across Lock's broad chest down to the narrows of his waist, then stopped, suddenly uncertain. How did she convey that need without seeming immodest, or worse, wanton?

"Go ahead, princess."

Constance snatched her hand away at Lock's sleepy rumble of encouragement, but he caught her with his arm when she would have rolled away and turned himself to face her.

"I'm sorry," she gulped, crimson-faced. "I didn't mean to ... to wake you."

"Sweetheart, it's one of the best ways I know." Pulling her close, he kissed her deeply. "Good morning."

"I—ah—" Constance panted for air, shocked and thrilled by the pressure of his hardening manhood against her bare thigh.

"Curious, love?" His voice was amused. "Feel what you do to me."

Kissing her again, he pressed her palm against himself, letting her feel his growing tumescence, the shaft rising from the soft nest of hair, the sensitive globes beneath. He jerked convulsively when her fingers closed around his arousal. Embarrassed, wondering, Constance gasped against his lips, too shocked to stay, too curious to pull away.

Lock smiled against her mouth, then made her jump when he teased his fingers through the fluff at the juncture of her thighs, lightly caressing the delicate folds of her womanhood. Flushed and uncertain, Constance strained away.

Lock raised his head, judging her expression, and swallowed back a groan of frustration. *Not yet*, he ordered himself. *Not yet!* But even a man of iron could stand only so much, so he cupped the lush

mounds of her breasts in his hands, flicked the pebbled nipples with his thumbs, then tasted one rosy
crest—just to keep himself sane.

Constance's gasp was almost a squeal, but before
she could react in fear, Lock gave her a friendly slap
on the hip and rolled out of bed. "Cast off, princess.
Time to get going."

Still in a daze, Constance averted her gaze from
her husband's nakedness, but not before she got a
very clear view of his rampant maleness. It made
her weak and dizzy, and her palms burned, knowing she'd touched him so intimately. The place
where his mouth had been on her breast felt wet
and cool, and she hastily dragged the covers up to
her neck.

Lock reached for his clothes and tugged them on.
"Have a taste for mackerel? I'll net us some for
breakfast."

Eat? her brain screamed. He wanted to *eat* at a
time like this? Well, she was hungry, too, but it
made her blush all the more to think of what she
wanted. Insecurities and doubts surfaced anew. Was
Lock merely being considerate, or had she disgusted him with her aggressiveness? It was clear
she was out of her league when it came to the nuances of this relationship. Maybe breakfast was a
safer topic at that.

"I—" She cleared her throat and began again. "I
think I saw some coffee in the supplies you
brought. I can boil some oatmeal, too."

"Can't abide the stuff," he said cheerfully, dragging on his boots. "But suit yourself. Find a skillet
for the fish, will you? I'll be back in a bit."

Constance stared after him as he left the cottage,
then threw back the covers with a gusty breath, indignant that he should be so unaffected when she
was a mass of quivering nerves! She dressed in a
plain white shirtwaist and a dark blue skirt, then
piled her hair into a loose knot on top of her head.

Pausing by the window as she inserted pins, she was gratified to see Lock standing knee-deep in the surf, hauling in a small hand net full of silvery, glistening mackerel fingerlings. Maybe he was in the same itchy state as she was and had chosen a dunk in the cold Atlantic as a means of cooling his ache. Feeling somewhat mollified, she went to work on the coffee, not even noticing that her perusal of the water had failed to evoke her usual frightened response.

On the surface, breakfast was an easy meal, and as they gobbled the tasty pan-fried fish, Lock discussed his plans to make some minor repairs on the cottage and dock while they were there. Undercurrents of awareness that Constance knew with a feminine surety were not all one-sided flowed between them, but Lock was so matter-of-fact she had no notion how to proceed. It seemed simpler for the time being to stay out of his way, so while he hammered and nailed and painted, she spent several hours under a perfect blue sky exploring the cliffs, seeking out the flowers that were beginning to bloom in the warmest crevices, and gathering wild rose hips and early raspberries.

The sun was high when she returned, pleasantly flushed from the hike. She'd undone the top buttons on her shirtwaist to let the air cool her throat, and rolled up her cuffs as no true lady of Mrs. Farrar's school of etiquette would have dreamed of doing. For the first time she missed Lahaina, for she'd wandered its fertile sugar fields and lush upland valleys to find peace, especially after the worst episodes with Uncle Cyrus, and now the solitude and rugged beauty of this New England landscape soothed her in much the same way.

Following the sounds of construction, she found Lock hard at work under the lean-to, sanding a layer of cracked and blistered red paint from the bottom of the old dory. Strips of sunlight filtered through the cracks in the board roof, making patterns on the raw wood and his shirtless back, and the pungent scent of fresh sawdust reminded Constance of Jedediah's workshop.

"Enjoy your walk?" Lock smiled when he saw her hovering at the edge of the lean-to, cautious as a wild wood sprite entering a bear's den. And she looked rather otherworldly, a golden-eyed fairy queen with daisy chains of yellow flowers and braided grasses around her neck. He set the planer on the prow of the boat and straightened with a groan, stretching and twisting to loosen the muscles in his back.

"Yes," she replied. "Your Skye is a beautiful place."

"I'm glad you like it. I used to bring Jedediah fishing here. Maybe I ought to offer again." Lock picked up a dipper from an oak water bucket and drank thirstily. A fine layer of wood dust clung to his sweat-dampened chest curls, and rivulets of moisture trickled down his corded arms and ribs. He dipped again and offered the ladle to Constance.

"Thank you." She accepted it gratefully, her mouth suddenly dry and her heart pounding as arousal sped through her veins at the sight of him. She sipped the cool liquid with a sigh of enjoyment and a shiver for the knowledge that her lips now rested where Lock's had. She fancied the water even carried a hint of his taste to her parched tongue. Raising her eyes, she found him watching her, and blushed. He turned back to his work.

Replacing the dipper, Constance drifted around the dory, inspecting the progress and surreptitiously watching the flex and play of Lock's strong back as he shoved the planer back and forth. A large hogshead stood on end against the wall of the cottage, and after a moment or two, she hoisted herself to a seat on top of it. Her feet hung well off the ground and she swung them like a little girl, absently drumming her heels against the curved staves while withdrawing a handkerchief from her pocket.

"Look what I found." She unfolded the square of cloth, revealing a handful of purplish raspberries. Mischievously, she popped one into her mouth, smiling as the tangy flavor exploded against her tongue. "I'm thinking pie."

"I've had your pie," Lock teased, coming around the dory. Swiftly he stole a couple of berries, chewing appreciatively. "How about dumplings? With cream like my mother made."

"I don't know how to make dumplings." She swatted playfully at his next attempt at thievery. "But if you keep stealing my bounty, there won't be enough for either one!"

"You dare threaten me, woman?" he asked mock-seriously, the corners of his mouth twitching. Dropping the planer, he leaned toward her and rested both hands on the barrel top.

"I've merely heard that the way to a man's heart is through his stomach," she replied with a sniff. "But if you're not interested in pie . . ."

"I like simple fare," Lock murmured, leaning closer. The tang of honest male sweat and wood shavings clung to him, and the breadth of his bare shoulders blocked out her view of everything but him.

Constance's eyes widened momentarily; then she chose a particularly succulent specimen and bit it in half. Sucking on the sweet fruit, she arched one eyebrow in mute inquiry, offering Lock the other half. His blue eyes narrowed, and, never taking his gaze from hers, he nibbled the juicy berry from her fingertips. Constance's smile was lazy, flirtatious.

"I always wanted to have a man eating out of my hand," she said with a gurgle of breathless laughter.

He hooked a finger in the open neck of her blouse, slipping under the top hem of her chemise to rest between her breasts, and tugged her closer.

"Be careful who you try to tame, my girl. The virgin's unicorn may turn out to be a tiger."

"I don't want to tame you." The scent of wildflowers enveloped Constance, and she shivered at the pressure of his fingers against her flesh.

"Just as well," he murmured, and deliberately worked a button free.

Daringly, she offered him another berry, letting her fingers linger against his lips as he crushed it between his teeth. Catching her wrist, he licked the purple juice staining her fingertips, laving each digit with a gourmand's diligence while he continued to open her blouse with the other hand.

Lock was pleased to see she had forgone the constrictions of a corset. He spread open her shirt and, ignoring her swiftly indrawn breath, released the shoulder tabs of her chemise so that it slipped and puddled in folds at her waist. Her hands twisted in her handkerchief, and a pink flush stained her cheeks, but she made no move to forestall him. Fondling the ropes of blossoms, he let the backs of his knuckles graze the contours of her breasts, smiling as the rosy crests puckered in response. "Pretty."

"The lei is a traditional symbol of welcome in my homeland," Constance said, swallowing to clear the sudden husky tremor of her voice.

"Most appropriate. But I wasn't talking about the flowers."

Selecting a final raspberry, he gently pulled the kerchief out of her stiff fingers and set it aside. Automatically, her hands balanced on his forearms, and her eyes were large and wary as he bit the berry in two as she had done. Lock touched it to her lower lip, painting it with the ripe juice, then bent to kiss and suck the flavor of the fruit from her mouth.

"Delicious," he murmured, then took the berry and anointed her nipples. His lips followed, and Constance gasped and arched, clenching her fingers on his arms and throwing back her head in a spasm of shocked delight.

The rasp of his tongue against her sensitive flesh sent bolts of sensation deep within her, tightening her core and producing a heaviness in her womb. Moisture collected between her thighs.

"You wicked, wicked man," she whispered, pleasure coursing through her veins like sweet, thick syrup. "You're full of surprises."

"Because I like these berries best?" Lock leaned into her, pressing her knees open with his hips as he stroked and lifted the fullness of her breasts, kneading them with his palms and lightly pinching the pebbled tips between his fingers. "They're just the way I like them, sweet and salt."

Constance squirmed restlessly. "I'm sure we shouldn't . . ."

"What? Enjoy each other?" He flipped her skirts back, spreading her legs open, running his large hands over the garters holding her stockings at her knees and up the soft naked skin of her inner thighs. Constance quaked and shuddered when he gently thrust his hips against the apex of her thighs, the thin stuff of her drawers barely veiling the dark, mysterious triangle there.

"It's the way God fashioned us," he said on a low groan, and caught her mouth in a drugging kiss. When he broke away again, both of them struggled for breath. "You're not as smart as I think you are if you pay any heed to the sanctimonious hypocrites who say differently. We were both made for this."

Lock massaged her thighs, then cupped her mound intimately. When his thumbs flicked a spot that shot sparks through every nerve, Constance cried out and clutched his neck.

His breath was a hot rasp against her ear. "Touch me, Connie, like you did this morning. I swear I'll go mad if you don't."

Her whole body throbbed, demanding release.

She slicked her damp palms down his muscular arms, pressed the pads of her fingers against his bronze nipples, then followed the whorls of body hair lower, lower. He muttered encouragement in a strained voice, and she found the buttons of his trousers, releasing them one by one until the heavy, hot velvet of his manhood lay in her open hands.

Lock cupped her buttocks, shifting her to the edge of the barrel top, urging her closer as he stood between her thighs, the tip of his shaft probing against her feminine entrance gently, provocatively. He found her mouth again and his tongue mimicked the movement, thrusting and withdrawing.

Awash with sensation, Constance responded unequivocally, twining her tongue against his, using her hands to offer resistance to his thrusting tumescence in a way that made him gasp and shake.

Fighting for control, he cupped her face, kissing her fiercely, then plucked the pins from her hair. As it fell in lush waves about her shoulders, he stripped the flower leis from her throat, crushing them against her swollen breasts. He could feel the tension building within her as she panted against his lips, and he hurried to bring her to the edge before his own control completely deserted him.

Lock pressed over Constance, fighting the urge to penetrate, to bury himself within her sweet body. Instead, he teased her through the slit in her thin drawers, dragging the tip of his arousal along her dewy folds, then found again with his thumbs that sensitive locus of feminine hunger hidden beneath the hood of flesh, rhythmically rubbing, increasing in tempo until she arched with a cry of surprise.

Thunder exploded in Constance's center. Lightning sizzled from Lock's skilled fingers down every nerve, through every extremity, and stars sparkled behind her eyes as overwhelming ecstasy shattered her. Gasping, shuddering, every muscle contracted in exquisite release. All she could do was hang on and ride out the storm.

It was barely in time. Pushing aside her limp hands, Lock pulled her even closer, thrusting against her thigh; then his own completion overtook him. Groaning against her neck, he crushed her in his arms until his spasms ceased.

Breathing hard, they clung together, limp and spent.

"Oh . . . my." Constance panted.

"Sweet Jesus, is that all you can say?" he asked hoarsely.

"Oh, my!"

Grinning, Lock cupped her chin, tilting her face to his. He kissed her nose, the fans of her lashes, the corners of her mouth. "I suppose that does just about say it all."

Constance glanced down at herself, her disarrayed clothing, her wanton position. Half dazed, she touched the moisture on her thigh, then looked up at Lock.

"The pleasure's enough for now," he said gruffly. "We'll plant the seed properly in good time."

Her mouth dropped open. "You . . . you want me to have your child?"

"God willing, yes." He frowned. "You are my wife."

Until that moment, she hadn't really believed that he meant it to last between them, that it had been anything more than physical hunger that had driven them to this point. Now she understood. Lock meant them to be together, to make a life, a family. This was forever. And he never broke his word.

With a little cry, she flung herself into his arms. Half laughing, one hand dragging at his waistband to hold up his loose trousers, Lock staggered under her onslaught. She pressed her cheek against his salty skin and blinked back tears.

"Connie? What is it, princess?"

She drew a deep, shaky breath. "I love you, Lock McKin."

His expression was uncertain as he smoothed her hair back from her damp brow. "My God."

She caught his hand, her face a mirror of joy and desire. "I'm your wife . . . and I want you to show me how to do it properly."

"Jesus!" He swallowed, and something wild ignited in his blue eyes. His voice was hoarse. "Now?"

In her disheveled state, she still managed a demure look through her lashes. It made his blood burn all over again. "If you don't mind."

"I'll show you how much I mind!" he growled. Scooping her up into his arms, he carried her inside.

They left a Hansel and Gretel trail of clothing from the lean-to to the bedroom and fell naked and hungry into the old brass bed. Murmurs and sighs of pleasure and appreciation accompanied a new exploration, and this time there was no rush, no impediments, nothing to push them forward too fast or hold them back too long. They had the leisure to explore, to stoke the flames slowly until again they came to a fever pitch.

"That tickles," Constance managed to say sometime later. From his position above her on his knees, Lock conscientiously traced every rib with his lips, then brushed his mouth lower over the indentation of her navel. Her fingers tangled in the black silk of his hair, and her body curled, involuntarily tilting her pelvis upward.

"I'll stop if you don't like it."

"Yes. No. I—"

His throaty chuckle interrupted her, and he moved back up her slender form, dropping kisses on her breastbone, her chin, and finally her mouth. The diminishing daylight cast him in planes of light and shadow that made him mysteriously male and powerful.

"Maybe we'll save that particular lesson for another time."

Her eyes widened with the thought of where his exploration might have ultimately taken him—and her. "Do people do that?"

"Sometimes." He nibbled at her lower lip. "If they both want to."

Constance considered that, and his unspoken implication that she was as much a part of this experience as he and had as great a voice in the decisions of their being together as he did. It was liberating, and the last stultifying tendril of fearfulness withered and died, leaving only trust and love. Stroking Lock's back, Constance gloried in the feel of her man, his weight pushing her down into the bedclothes, his skillful hands busy on her breasts. That restlessness, that tension, were back, and she stirred against him, speaking wordlessly of her need.

"Sweet heaven, woman," he muttered hoarsely, "you drive me out of my mind."

Oh, that pleased her! To be the one who could push the Iron Man out of control. To be the one he lost himself in. She tugged at his hips, pushing against him, wanting him past anything she'd ever desired before.

"Show me," she whispered. "Please, Lock."

He hesitated. She was so sweet and responsive, how could he spoil what she was feeling by telling her the first time wouldn't be good? But she deserved to know.

"You aren't afraid?" he asked, holding her face between his hands and gazing deeply into her eyes. "It likely won't be . . . comfortable for you this time."

Her pulse pounded in her throat, and she gulped,

but shook her head. "I'm more afraid of how I'll feel if you don't hurry!"

Lock laughed, a mixture of tenderness and triumph. "All right, have it your way."

He kissed her, arching her over his arm and delving into the deepest recesses of her mouth with a soul-stealing sweep of his tongue. Stroking the folds between her legs, he found her wet and aroused. She quivered at his touch, but opened for him, humbling him with her trust, and he vowed to make it as good for her as was humanly possible. He tormented her—and himself—by touching her intimately with little feather touches interspersed with longer, harder, lingering strokes, finally inserting a fingertip into her body.

Constance shuddered, clutching his shoulders, her lips clinging to his as he pressed in and out, readying her, stretching her feminine opening. She was small and tight, and stiffened when he used two fingers to examine the fragile barrier of her virginity, but his drugging kisses and the building need within her made her almost frantic.

"Lauchlan, I can't . . . oh, *now*," she whimpered. Desperate, she reached for him, finding him steel encased in velvet, glorying in the way he groaned his own need against her lips.

Unexpectedly, he rolled onto his back, dragging her atop him, his hands at her waist to guide her.

"You do it, love," he said, gasping, his features strained and flushed. "You lead the way."

Too bound up in the throes of passion to protest, she bent her knees and settled instinctively into place. Her body cried out for him, demanded that he fill the emptiness within, and she pressed herself against the heated tip of him, letting the liquid slide of gravity bring her inch by inch closer to fulfillment. The momentary pinch and burn of tissue tearing caught her by surprise, but Lock's large hands on her hips steadied her, holding her poised until she could no longer withstand her body's urgings and sank down fully against him, filled at last.

"Oh ..." Her sigh was full of wonder. *This* was what he'd meant when he said they were made for each other. How they fit together was a miracle of creation. How she felt was a revelation. Even as her body stretched and adjusted to the wondrous fullness of him, she knew there was more. Placing a kiss on the center of Lock's chest, she lifted her hips experimentally, and was rewarded with a groan.

"Oh, Jesus, woman, Jesus, Jesus ..." he chanted, his fingers flexing on her hips.

Exultant, she began to move, and in a moment the tenderness between her thighs disappeared, forgotten in the heat and rush of sensation that flung her high as the sun and deep as the valleys of the ocean. Constance gasped for air, for it was like drowning, no nightmare but a dream in which she could breathe under water. When she broke the surface to the light, her sun exploded again, rocketing her through the heart of the starry universe.

Constance collapsed against Lock's damp chest with a cry of stunned delight, and his fingers dug into the soft flesh of her buttocks, pulling her even closer as he drove upward, once, twice, thrice. With a hoarse shout of triumph, he climaxed powerfully, surging against his woman as his body emptied and his mind flew skyward.

After a long, long time, when breath and consciousness returned, Lock felt Constance begin to shake. Coming up from the lethargy of total surcease, he withdrew regretfully, running his hands over her back, concerned about her trembling.

"Sweetheart, it's all right," he soothed, kissing her ear, smoothing her damp hair back from her face. "Did I hurt you? I didn't mean—"

"Foolish man," she chided, giggling and drowsy and sated. "How could something so wonderful hurt? I was only thinking ..."

"Hmm?"

"No wonder Mrs. Farrar's guide never said a word about this!"

They stayed a week at Skye. It was a week of such discovery and joy, Lock never managed to finish sanding the dory and Constance never once made a raspberry pie. On the other hand, they shared picnics and loving in the grassy places on the cliffs, walked barefoot on the beach under the stars, and after easing the hunger of their bodies, talked late into the nights with their heads on the same pillow, making plans for the *Argonaut*, for a studio for Constance, for the name and the family they would build together, a new dynasty of ship-builders. Constance even dared to voice a hope that some sort of peace could be made with Alex, and if Lock was skeptical, he merely kissed her and kept his doubts to himself.

After such a week, anything seemed possible, even a truce between the Lathams and the McKins, even a sail back to Boston. Constance sat with Lock at her back as before, but this time it was his caresses and kisses that kept her mind from the terrors of the water, so when they finally sailed into Boston Harbor, she actually left the *Valiant* with a feeling of regret.

The shabby little house on Devonshire Street had never looked more welcoming, but Constance sensed an eagerness in Lock to return to his work. It was a need she sympathized with, for the faint lingering odor of oil paints evoked an urge in her to rush to her canvases, to somehow capture something of her happiness and the time they'd spent at Skye, to defy the ephemeral and fleeting nature of life by rendering the perfection they'd shared into works of lasting substance. So, understanding as well as loving Lock, she encouraged him to look in at the shipyard, shooing him away with the excuse that she needed to visit the market if they were to have any supper.

"I'll have to do some shifting about of my belongings, too," she informed him with an arch look. "Unless you don't want me sharing your bedroom?"

Lock took her shoulders and gave her a hearty kiss that left no doubt as to his answer. "Just see that you're finished before I return, for I've plans for you, Mrs. McKin."

"Oh, be off, you rogue!" Her smile held a sweet promise as she added softly, "But hurry home."

But it was well after the supper hour, well past dark, and still Lock didn't come. Constance sat cross-legged among the colorful silken coverlets he'd brought from his previous rooms, clad only in his crimson silk dressing gown. She found both coverlets and dressing gown surprisingly luxurious and sensual in a man so outwardly controlled, but she'd come to know the inner sensitive man, the dreamer who could leave pragmatism behind for a time to simply enjoy beautiful things and take unabashed pleasure in their lovemaking.

She distracted herself from worry over his delay by making sketches of some preliminary ideas on a large drawing pad. But the landscapes of the cliffs and inlet at Skye kept turning into studies of her husband's face, some severe or angrily determined—the face he showed most often to the world—but more smiling, softened with amusement and affection—the face she'd seen this past week.

Constance didn't try to pretend that Lock loved her—yet. She was intelligent enough to know how hard a man of his background would find it to admit that to himself, much less say it to her. But he would someday, if her prayers and determination and devotion had anything to do with it. Lock cared for her. He was too generous, too loving when he held her, for their relationship simply to be a pragmatic business arrangement. Even when she managed to drive him to the edge of insanity, as he did so often to her, she sensed his gentleness.

Her dreams of Paris seemed childish and pale beside the brilliant reality of living with and loving Lock McKin, of being his in all ways. His understanding and defense of her almost had her believing she might even be forgiven for her worst crime. If a good and honest man like Lock believed in her, how could she not believe in herself? And that knowledge gave her freedom to be patient. The depth of emotion her inner heart cried out for would surely come when he grew to trust what they had together. The future that she had feared and dreaded for so long now stretched out before her full of hope.

A key grated in the front door downstairs, and she threw down the sketch pad, hurrying to the top of the dim stairway. "Lock?"

"Yes." He dropped his key on a marble-topped hall table and slung his coat on the many-armed coat tree.

"You're so late. Is something wrong?" She came halfway down the stairs, looking pagan and exotic in the flame-colored robe, her hair hanging loose about her shoulders. Lock paused at the first step, his features impassive.

"No, everything's all right. I simply got . . . tied up at the yard. Sorry."

"Do you want something to eat?" she asked. "I bought some cheese . . ."

"No. I'm not hungry. Go back to bed. I think I'll have a drink."

Something didn't ring true in the innocuous words, and she came another step down toward him. "You're not telling me everything. What is it?"

His deep breath held a barely controlled exasperation. "Constance—"

"I mean it, Lock. A wife shares her husband's life."

He looked at her closely, taking in the determined golden light in her topaz eyes, swallowing harshly at the way her nipples poked against the thin silk of the embroidered robe. If that was the way she wanted it, so be it. He removed a packet of letters from his pocket and held them out to her.

"Your grandfather evidently hasn't conceded the game, princess."

"Alex?" She took the papers, frowning. "Why? What's he done now?"

"I'm summoned to court day after tomorrow."

Opening the pages with a crackle, she examined the gibberish of legal terms on the official-looking documents, then gave up in confusion. "What does it mean?"

"They intend to fight the marriage settlement."

"Oh, no. The *Odyssey?*"

He reached up and touched her concerned face. "Don't worry. The law's on our side. This is no more than a tantrum Alex is throwing because he didn't get his way. I'll take care of it. You won't even have to appear."

"I most certainly will!" Her chin firmed stubbornly. " 'Twas my choices that brought us here, too, you know. I can do my part, testify, whatever."

"I only seek to spare you the tug of conflicting loyalties."

Her expression softened. "You've given me so much. I stand with you now, Lock. Together. Don't you know that?"

"I guess I'm not accustomed to thinking about it that way," he returned gruffly, stepping closer to her. His hand cupped her waist.

"Then you'd best get used to it, Mr. McKin." She put her arms around his neck and smiled. "I'm here to stay."

There was no answer to that but to kiss her, and

somehow his hands found their way beneath the silken garment that had been driving him to distraction since the moment he'd realized she was naked underneath. She whimpered against his mouth when he thumbed her nipple, and tore at his clothing with an eagerness that inflamed him all the more. Having won her trust, he let go of his control, relishing the matching power of her response, sucking in his breath when she caressed him boldly, intimately, without shame or reservation.

They made it only as far as the upper landing before their passions overcame them, and somehow Lock was inside her, pressing her against the wall, her heels locked in the small of his back, the silk of the robe whispering around his thighs. Mouths hot and insatiable, they strove together, welding their hearts into a marriage with the white-hot fire of lust. Constance cried out, arching her back at her completion, and Lock convulsed within her sweet recesses, his lips open against her neck as her ripples of pleasure became his own, and for a long time neither Lock nor Constance was sure where one ended and the other began.

Two days later, dressed in her best spring bonnet and lavender promenade gown, Constance sat at her husband's side in the somber legal chambers of the Boston Court House. Much to her dismay, news of the conflict and the renewal of the Latham and McKin feud had gone round the community like wildfire, filling the paneled courtroom with spectators and reporters. At a table on the other side of the railing, Mr. Carlisle, the earnest, chipmunk-cheeked young barrister who attended to Lock's legal affairs, rustled through a portfolio of documents. Meanwhile, the Latham lawyers presented Alex's petition to Judge Simpson Haynes, a formidable figure reigning from behind an elevated mahogany bench.

"At least it isn't Judge Freidel," Constance murmured to Lock. "Though I wouldn't be surprised to learn Alex tried to have his friend hear this case."

"Even Alex doesn't have that kind of influence in this town," Lock answered, and gave her hand an encouraging squeeze.

Constance smiled her gratitude, but then could not prevent her gaze from straying across the aisle. Arms crossed over his chest and chin tucked pugnaciously into his silver ruff of whiskers, Alexander Latham watched the proceedings while pointedly ignoring his granddaughter. At the sight of Alex's stern profile, Constance felt a pang of regret, instantly quashed by a firm self-admonition not to forget how ruthless Alex had been in his handling of her. That he'd painted himself into this proverbial corner with his machinations was only poetic justice, and while she could never condone what he'd tried to do, she pitied him. His high-handed actions had alienated both James and her, depriving him of the family that might have succored his old age, leaving only bitterness and loneliness.

If he'd been just a little less tyrannical, they might have come to some understanding, Constance thought sadly. But then, she might never have jumped into an impulsive marriage that had given her happiness beyond her wildest dreams. No, she couldn't regret a single step along the way that had brought her to Lock, her slayer of dragons and her heart's refuge. Constance returned Lock's squeeze with a warmth that made him send her a quizzical look.

Before he could frame a question, however, the doors to the rear of the courtroom burst open, and Rodger Latham hurried in. Impeccably dressed as usual, yellow curls shining with pomade, he strode down the aisle with an air of urgency. Ignoring Alex, he leaned over the railing and whispered something to one of the trio of Latham lawyers.

"What do you suppose he's up to now?" Lock muttered.

Constance shivered and shook her head. Whatever it was, she was convinced that they shouldn't underestimate the virulence of Rodger's resentment or his determination to stand at the helm of Latham and Company, no matter what the cost. The attorney speaking to Rodger nodded, then turned, interrupting his colleague's monologue about clauses and subparagraphs.

"Your Honor, we beg the court's indulgence. New information forces us to amend my clients' petition to disallow ownership of the property in question. We will submit documents requesting that all bequests and transfers by Alexander Latham be declared null and void."

Mr. Carlisle came to his feet, objecting. "Sir, this is most irregular! We have proved Mrs. McKin has concurred with all of the stipulations of the bequest and deserves to be placed in full possession without further harassment or delay!"

"Gentlemen, order!" Judge Haynes banged his gavel irritably, then addressed Rodger. "On what grounds do you interrupt these proceedings in such a fashion, sir?"

"In the interest of justice, Your Honor," Rodger replied. "My uncle wished to donate a legacy to his granddaughter, but he has been made the dupe of a criminal conspiracy to defraud him of his property."

"What absurdity is this?" Lock thundered, surging to his feet. "Now the Lathams invent scandalous fictions to wiggle out of a legal and binding provision of their own making!"

The force of Lock's fury at being publicly maligned made Constance catch her breath. Across the aisle, Alex spluttered incoherent questions.

"Counselor, restrain your client!" Judge Haynes directed, slamming the gavel down.

"Mr. McKin, if you please—" Carlisle began.

"The charge is valid," Rodger interjected heatedly, "and we have a witness to prove it!"

Rising to stand beside her husband, Constance touched Lock's hand in support. He gripped it hard, glaring at Rodger with eyes as cold as Arctic ice. "This is a puny charade, Latham. Produce your witness—if you can."

At Rodger's signal, a bailiff opened the courtroom door, and Constance craned her neck along with the rest of the spectators. For a long moment, her incredulous brain refused to accept what she saw; then a silent scream rose in her throat. She was trapped in a living nightmare, and a phantom drew closer, step by fateful step. The shock of death-white hair, the stand-up clerical collar looking no whiter than the pallid skin it circled, the ever-present smoked-glass spectacles, the flawless hands, slim and pale as a girl's, yet strong—so brutally strong.

The chill of the crypt brushed her skin, and the overpowering funereal sweetness of ginger blossoms nauseated her. But this was no walking corpse, risen from the grave to haunt her days as he'd so often possessed her nights, no cadaver pointing a bloody finger to demand retribution for murder. No, this preternatural vision was a thousand times worse, for it was real.

"My child." The pious voice reverberated in the stunned and silent courtroom.

Unhooking the curved wire earpieces, he dragged off the dark, concealing glasses. He sighed loudly, and Constance recoiled as if from a serpent's hiss. His unnatural pink eyes flashed red as blood.

"Lili, Lili. What have your lies brought you to this time?"

Chapter 12

"You see, Your Honor?" Rodger crowed triumphantly. "This woman is an imposter! She's not, and has never been, Constance Latham!"

The courtroom erupted in a tumultuous wave of noisy speculation. Reporters scribbled in their notebooks, lawyers conferred in hushed tones, and Alex Latham loudly demanded of his nephew what the devil was going on. Judge Haynes's shouts for order and repeated hammering with his gavel punctuated the furor.

"He isn't dead," Constance whispered, her eyes dilated so wide that only a thin ring of topaz showed around the enlarged irises. Her skin was clammy, her lips almost blue from the lack of blood.

Lock looked at the tall clergyman, so freakishly cheated of all coloring by Nature's capricious hand, and thought, *He's the one.*

This white-skinned stranger with the darting, red dragon eyes had to be none other than the Reverend Cyrus Tate, sprung from a grave half a world away.

Lock had seen albino birds, and once an idiot in a circus who shared the minister's milk-white skin and hair, but the deformity seemed all the more bizarre for Tate's affectation of an all-white garb. He was beardless and even-featured, with skin as smooth and cool as alabaster marble, and he could have been twenty or sixty.

Despite the turmoil flowing around him, the cleric's demeanor was serene and unruffled, almost pontifical, and evoked from the curious onlookers a certain involuntary respect and no little awe, as if he spoke as the Lord's own special messenger. A small wooden cross hung on a chain at his breast, and his expression was one of enforced piety underlaid with a cunning intelligence. Lock scowled, thinking of the marks the bastard had left on Constance and of this new attack against her very identity.

"It's him, isn't it?" Lock asked Constance under his breath. "You didn't kill anyone. You've felt guilty all this time for something you didn't even do."

"He isn't dead," she repeated in a stunned voice. It wasn't relief that colored her words, but horror. "Oh, God!"

She made a panicky movement, looking for escape. Lock restrained her with a hand on her shoulder. "I'm here, Constance. You don't have to run anymore."

She didn't appear to hear him.

"Order!" Judge Haynes roared. "I will have order! What is the meaning of this, Mr. Latham?"

"A way to get at the truth, sir," Rodger answered. "The Reverend Tate has come from Holy Sanctuary Mission in the Sandwich Islands with intimate knowledge of this woman who calls herself Constance Latham."

"Then perhaps you would care to shed some light on this matter, Reverend, before this hearing becomes a total shambles?" the judge suggested testily.

"Indeed, Your Honor, my duty compels me to free an innocent family from a web of lies." Squinting against the light, the minister again turned his unnerving regard toward Constance. "I know this woman. Her name is not Constance Latham, but Lilio Young, an orphan child I fostered at the mission school in Lahaina."

"But she must be Constance!" Alex Latham's lined face went slack with incredulity. "She had my son's locket!"

Constance covered the silver oval hanging around her neck with both hands, utter bafflement in her stark expression. It was an unthinking movement that could have been a gesture of either self-reassurance or guilt. "Lilio Young? No, it's a lie . . ."

"It was my mistake to have given the token to Lili," Tate explained in sorrowful tones. "I thought it would bring some small comfort to a distraught child."

"Explain yourself," Alex demanded. "What is this riddle?"

The Reverend Tate's smooth features fell into sympathetic lines. "Your son, James, answered the Lord's call in Lahaina, assisting me worthily in spreading God's word to the heathen. He took a wife there, but she died, leaving him to raise his daughter alone. Then ten years ago, during a fever epidemic, the Lord called James to his reward."

"Yes, yes," Alex snapped impatiently. "I know all that."

"What you can't know is that the day we buried James, little Constance drowned in the Auau Channel."

Constance moaned, and her knees gave way. Sinking down into her chair, she buried her face in her hands, undone by the nauseating resurrection of some intolerable, half-known memory. But was it guilt or fear that made her tremble?

Across the aisle, Alex sputtered in astonished indignation. Lock frowned at Constance's reaction, and the first infinitesimal crack formed in his shell of certainty. The Reverend Tate continued.

"Lili was so inconsolable over her dearest friend's death, I feared for her mind. Oh, aye, it broke your heart to hear her prattle afterward, pretending Constance was still alive, carrying on conversations with a dead girl, even eventually answering to her name. It seemed a harmless game, a way to calm such a high-strung child." The minister shook his head sadly and held out his hand to Constance in appeal. "But, Lili, you cannot claim Constance's place now. Can't you see how wrong it is to lead these good people astray with your lies?"

Constance moaned again, unable to answer, rocking back and forth like a child trying to comfort herself, her head full of images of watery death—black ocean, silver bubbles, incandescent waves curling against an endless sky.

"Well, girl, is this true or not?" Alex demanded hotly, his expression a ferocious mixture of betrayal and despair and chagrin.

"Don't badger her," Lock ordered. "Can't you see she's had a shock?"

"She obviously felt herself safe from discovery of her fabrications," Rodger snapped. "Well, the truth will out! Look at her! She can't deny what her own guardian says."

Lock's blue eyes narrowed dangerously. "You tell a glib tale, Reverend. Raising a little girl with such terrible memories must have been hard."

"Lili was always a difficult child."

"You beat her into submission." It was not a question.

"I admit I was forced to administer a switching occasionally." Tate's eyebrows, so white as to be almost invisible against his skin, pressed together, and he gave a long-suffering sigh. "What good parent has not? 'For whom the Lord loves, He disciplines,' says Proverbs. But the wages of sin have always been strong in the girl. The Lord knows my late wife and I did our Christian best for her, but her lies grew continually worse and she consorted with low companions."

"So you flogged her so unmercifully that she'll bear the marks for life?" Lock demanded. "Small wonder she ran away from Lahaina."

" 'Twas her own drunken-sailor father who laid those marks on his bastard child's back," Tate explained. "When I took Lili into the mission school, it was to save her life, but the ungrateful child repaid kindness with disobedience! One scandalous episode after another, illogical, impulsive, devil-touched hellion that she is—the girl's run mad most of her life."

Constance's head jerked up. Her expression reminded Lock of a small furry creature caught in the teeth of a trap, and she couldn't seem to catch her breath.

"I'm . . . not crazy. I'm not!"

The Reverend Tate ignored her outburst, and his explanations flowed easily, persuasively. "Like the father of the prodigal son, I am always ready to welcome Lili back into the fold. That's why I did not hesitate to come here when I heard she might have taken passage on a Boston-bound ship. I welcomed the opportunity to make my report to the church offices in person, of course, but now I rejoice to have found my foster daughter again. Lili belongs at home with those who can care for her and understand how to deal with her excesses of emotion."

"No." Constance pressed her knuckles against her mouth, a look of utter abhorrence on her face. "Oh, God, no."

"It's your word against his, Connie," Lock said. "Tell us it's not true, and we'll go home."

"Yes, Mrs. McKin," Judge Haynes intoned. "What have you to say to these assertions? Can you offer anything in your defense to refute the reverend's statement? Are you or are you not Constance Latham?"

"I—I—" Her chest heaved as if she had run a race, and her eyes darted from side to side, searching out any avenue of deliverance, but all around her she saw only accusation and doubt.

A chill knot formed in Lock's gut. "Constance?"

"Lili?" The Reverend Tate's tone had changed, now sweetly cajoling and full of understanding. "You know what to say."

Her temples throbbed painfully, and she pressed her fingers to them, shutting her eyes. But the visions inside her head were even worse, disjointed images flashing against the hazy wall in her mind, spinning kaleidoscopic forms of the past and present, reality and illusion. Lili. Constance. Who were they? Memories ran together, undermining her confidence, shattering the carefully constructed framework of her existence. Doubts toppled the precariously balanced self-images that had allowed her to function in a world too harsh to face completely. What was the truth? Battered, she couldn't recognize it anymore, even about herself.

"I don't know," she whispered, agonized. "I can't remember."

"Constance!" Lock gripped her shoulders between his two hands and jerked her to her feet. "What are you saying?"

She whimpered. "It's too hard . . . I can't remember!"

"Lili is a very confused young woman," Tate said kindly. "And I have no reason to wish her ill, only the Lord's injunction to speak the truth."

"Shut up, blast you!" Lock snarled. A heavy sinking weight pressed down in his chest.

"I forgive your curses, my son," Tate replied. He folded his hands in an attitude of benediction and compassion. "I see you have been a victim of Lili's lies, too."

"The damn fool *married* her, Reverend!" Rodger hooted, gloating, and a titter swept through the crowded courtroom.

Lock released Constance so abruptly that she staggered and clutched the arm of her chair. A deep red stain flowed up his neck and burned his ears. Had he been a fool? Everything Tate said sounded so plausible. Had Lock been so caught up in his own need for revenge that he'd stepped blindly into a trap? He'd swallowed Constance's stories and tidy explanations with the gullibility of a besotted lad and outwitted himself! The worst part was the chagrining realization that he had *wanted* to believe her, because he'd wanted her in his bed even then.

The confusion on Constance's face confirmed her guilt, and scalding humiliation poured through Lock's veins. She'd used him, betrayed him with falsehoods, seduced him with the illusion of passion and affection, ensnared him in a web of deceit so complicated he might never be able to unravel it. Constance—Lili—using him and the Lathams in an attempt to swindle them both. The ins and outs of this maze went far beyond his power to comprehend it.

And even though she was found out, she still couldn't be truthful. Rage burned in Lock's soul, but he'd give Rodger no more fodder for the bonfire of his contempt, so he poured ice onto the heat of his anger, preserving it within himself as he took up the Iron Man's impassive mask again.

Judge Haynes cleared his throat. "Do you have anything further to say, Mrs.—er—McKin?"

Stricken, Constance sat silently, too stunned and dismayed by Lock's withdrawal to frame a defense, too sickened and scared to fight back.

"I see." The judge stroked his jaw for a moment, then made a decision. "In light of these revelations, I have no choice but to rule in favor of the Latham petition, revoking all previous donations by Mr. Alexander Latham. Case dismissed."

"Thank you, Your Honor," Rodger said, smiling broadly. The lawyers gathered up their papers. Carlisle leaned over the railing and muttered something to Lock about an appeal while Rodger clapped Alex on his back in congratulation. "We're most grateful, aren't we, Uncle?"

Alex's jaw flexed, and he stared at Constance, his brown eyes gleaming with a dark mixture of hate and hurt. "I nearly loved you, girl," he said roughly. "May you rot in hell for that."

Constance swayed as if from a physical blow, and her cheeks blanched even further, making her almost as pale as Tate himself.

"Take me home, nephew," Alex said gruffly. He set his shoulders carefully, looking suddenly ancient and fragile. "You've preserved the company, and for that you'll step into my place as I've always meant you to. After today, I have no more heart for business."

A look of supreme satisfaction colored Rodger's owlish smile. "Yes, sir."

The judge glanced sharply at Constance. "Fraud of this nature could be further pursued on a criminal level."

"As long as Mr. McKin surrenders the *Odyssey*, I don't think that will be necessary, Your Honor," Rodger replied. His expression was smugly magnanimous. "I'm sure nothing would be served by incarcerating this pitiable, demented woman, and Mr. McKin has problems enough with a wife wed under false pretenses."

Constance flinched, each word like the flick of a whip, and another ripple of laughter flowed over the courtroom. Pain twisted in her stomach. She'd made Lock a laughingstock, the butt of jokes and scorn. Sweet Jesus, he'd never forgive her for this dishonor!

"You'll get what's coming to you, Latham," Lock said in a stony voice.

Futile thoughts darted through his brain. The *Odyssey*, lost again, and two half-finished ships in the stocks, including his beloved *Argonaut*. Counting on the *Odyssey*'s profits, he'd stretched his finances to the limit, but the foundations he'd laid were built on quicksand. His business, his reputation, his pride, his honor—all brought to the brink of ruin again because his illogical, overemotional desire for this woman and the revenge she'd falsely represented had clouded his judgment. He focused his anger on those things, refusing even to acknowledge the loss of secret dreams. The sweet companionship, the happiness and security of a loving family, were all a seductive, destructive illusion. Never again would the Iron Man be betrayed by softer emotions. Ruthlessly, he locked all those burgeoning feelings away, then ground his teeth to keep from howling his pain like a mad dog.

"Your position is not an enviable one, Mr. McKin," Judge Haynes said. "Misrepresentation is grounds for immediate annulment of a marriage. I suggest you consult your attorneys."

Something burst inside Constance, and she turned to Lock with a faint cry. "Lock, you must believe . . . I never meant to do you harm, to hurt you—"

"Shut up, damn you! Must you complete my humiliation with these puny excuses?"

"But it's the truth—"

"Coming from such a liar as you, that's hardly reassuring."

"I care for you!" she said desperately, feeling him slipping away. "That's real, I swear!"

"You cared only for your dupe!" he snarled. "You used me like a whore, beguiling me with the tawdry trappings of your body, illusion wrapped around a putrid truth. Well, it's over—all of it. May God forgive your harlot's heart, for I surely never will."

His repudiation of what they'd shared together stripped Constance of her last defense. She felt as though she were falling into a deep pit, clutching vainly at a life rope that Lock jerked from her desperate, grasping fingers with his callous words. The Reverend Tate smiled benignly, and she knew a dragon waited in the bottom of the pit for her. She cried in vain for help, clutching her husband's arm. "Lauchlan, please . . ."

Lock impaled her with one long, contemptuous look, then shook her off as if she were something vile and leprous, and turned his back.

Rodger laughed again, a nasty, insinuating, vindictive sound. "Well, McKin, since you'll not see a penny of any Latham prize now, at least I hope you got *something* for your trouble from this little tart!"

Lock's fist caught Rodger square on the nose, spinning him backward onto the floor, blood splattering. Lock stood over him, fists raised threateningly as the bailiffs converged, but Rodger lay stunned, crimson gushing from his smashed nostrils.

Over the angry roar in his own ears Lock heard a woman's shrill cry, but for a moment he was too stunned by his own explosive reaction to register the sound. Then he whirled, taking in the Reverend Tate's unctuous smile, the pristine handkerchief he used to blot speckles of blood from Constance's lavender bodice, and the look of abject, mindless horror on her face as she screamed and screamed and screamed . . .

Constance floated in a blue-green sea, rocked by the gentle undulations of the waves, dazzled by the sunlight dappling the sand beneath the clear water.

A shadow moved under her dangling feet, something dark and sinister with long white wings. Frightened, she swam toward the shore, where palm trees beckoned her like welcoming hula hands, but the sky darkened and the waves dashed her back. The harder she tried, the faster the shore receded, until the cloud-crowned mountain sank from sight beneath the water and she was alone, the salt of her tears mingling with the ocean as she wept . . .

Take your medicine for Elspeth, there's a dear. It will help you sleep . . .

Sleep, my little one, my Lili, urged the soft voice from the past. All will be well. No *kupua* will harm the daughter of Namaka, for Chieftess Kanai spoke it so.

Constance murmured with pleasure as gentle fingers smoothed her hair and rocked her against a warm and ample bosom, but then hard hands tore her out of that comforting embrace, and she stood shivering and naked as the rain fell and Kamapuaa, the Pig-man, laughed and snorted and gnashed his tusks to make her run . . .

She won't drink the broth, sir. I've tried.

It's all right, Maggie . . .

Don't drink it, Papa, she pleaded, but he wouldn't listen, and the sickness came and the sour odor like death made her gag and retch until her sides ached. Then the other appeared, patting her head with hands that smelled of ginger blossoms. When she tried to run he bade her sing, or else the angry dragon would carry her beyond the fiery mountain to die. So she sang "Make Me a Captive, Lord" until her throat was as dry as old bones . . .

That's right, drink some more, and just a spoonful of this so you'll feel better . . .

And Lock was there, a fierce dark archangel with buckler and sword, and she cried out at his beauty, full of love for him. White wings covered the sky and she cowered in fear, begging for protection, but his eyes were full of poetry as he boarded a magnificent ship of gold with sails black as hell itself. The dragon caught her in his ivory claws and burned her with his red eyes, whispering, Too late, too late . . .

No more laudanum.

But the dreams, sir!

Let her have them. Nothing else is working . . .

She was both observer and victim, inside and outside her body, jerking as the blows landed, watching from afar yet intimately involved as pain scorched her flesh. She painted the scene with brushes that flowed with that other self's blood while old Jerôme gave her lessons in technique and criticized her efforts. The face she struggled to paint was too dark, too light, too full, too flat, too old, too young—she'd never be an artist if she didn't try harder! But she couldn't see it clearly, she protested. So *look*, he said and pointed.

The face wasn't the one she expected, and in her terror she dropped her brushes and fled for her life, into the night, into the beckoning surf. But something dark and powerful caught her, pushed her under, held her as the salt filled her mouth and her lungs burst. In the last helpless moment she looked up through the green-and-blue layers . . . and saw that the dragon was really an angel.

Constance sat up with a gasp. Blinking back the images in her head, she struggled for breath, sweat-drenched and shaking. She pushed her lank hair out of her eyes with trembling hands, vaguely aware that she was in her own bed in the Devonshire Street house, wearing her own nightgown. Her head ached abominably, and her mouth tasted as foul as a South Street sewer. Every muscle in her body was sore and stiff, and she knew the dreams had been bad this time even as the details slipped away.

A soft spring breeze parted the filmy curtains to reveal an early evening twilight. It was much too early to be abed. Disoriented, she wondered if she'd been ill. Lock would know.

"Lock—" Her voice was a mere croak.

Constance struggled to her feet, amazed at her weakness. Lock's embroidered silk robe lay over the back of a nearby chair, and she reached for it gratefully, pulling it over her chilled limbs, finding familiar reassurance in the feel of the delicate fabric against her skin. She hesitated in the dim upper-story hallway, her bare feet making no sound on the thin carpet.

"Lauchlan?" she called uncertainly.

A plump figure carrying a covered tray appeared on the stairs. "My dear, you shouldn't be up!"

"Elspeth?" Mystified, Constance clutched the door casing for support.

"Well, praise God, you're awake at last, and lucid, too, but you're weak as a kitten, aren't you?" Elspeth Philpot bustled forward, the silver-and-gold sausage curls on the sides of her head swinging like pendulums. "And I shouldn't wonder after six days in bed, but that doesn't mean you should get up all at once."

"Six days?" Constance rubbed her temple, confused.

"Yes, since your . . . episode. Maggie and I have been helping out. Come back to bed, dear. I've got some broth for you. Dr. Tinkerman said you must remain calm."

But the hazy wall in her head was too close, and Constance was afraid something grave had occurred. She wanted the one person who always made her feel safe. "Where's Lock? I want my husband."

Elspeth set the tray on a nearby table, her expression troubled. "Yes, dear. I'll fetch him."

Moments later, Constance breathed a sigh of relief as Lock followed Elspeth up the stairs. He was in his shirtsleeves, his cravat dangling untied under his open collar, and his black hair bore evidence of his having plowed his fingers through it. He looked tired, Constance thought at once, but simply seeing him reassured her, and she smiled. "Lock."

There was no answering smile. Instead, his features were grim and implacable, his blue eyes cool, impassive, unreadable. For a flicker of a heartbeat she didn't understand; then it all came back to her in a rush, and her smile died.

"Oh." Constance shrank against the door casing, the pain and confusion her mind had denied for six days of delirium back in full force.

Elspeth came instantly to her side. "Constance?"

"I—I'm all right. I'll not go hysterical again." She lifted her eyes to Lock's. "It—it was the blood."

"Convenient." Lock's expression was patently skeptical, and so cold with condemnation Constance shivered.

"Now, see here, Mr. McKin," Elspeth protested. "She was upset enough that Dr. Tinkerman had to sedate the poor thing!"

"Yes, sympathy has its uses."

Constance gulped at his suspicions. He didn't believe that her overstretched nerves had snapped or that her retreat from the world had been involuntary. In despair, she knew he'd drawn the worst conclusions from the Reverend Tate's damning testimony and her own inadequate defense. Lock would never accept that she hadn't meant to mislead or betray him, even though she herself was as much a victim of this situation as he was. But she loved him, needed him too much not to try, especially now.

"I *am* Constance," she said on a desperate note.

He snorted. "Sure."

"But I'm Lili, too," she whispered miserably, her voice no stronger than the rustle of crimson silk that covered her trembling limbs. "I was sick when I was a child. The fever—it made this confusion in my mind like a wall of smoke. I know things. I just can't remember how. What does it matter what I call myself? Can't you see I'm still *me?*"

"It matters, especially considering the tangle you've spun us into with your tales. Latham is even demanding I return a reward I never accepted!" Lock's look was hard and accusing.

"I have it," she admitted, feeling herself sinking further into the quagmire of his contempt. "Most of it, anyway." She named the bank. "The account's in Dylan's name."

"I'll see it's returned. Have you perpetrated any other deceits I should know about?"

She winced. "Please, Lock. I do love you."

"Your delusions are exceptional, especially this one that lets you believe I'll swallow any more lies."

Hurt, she let anger lift her chin. "Then why am I here?"

He looked away, only a slight tic in his jaw indicating any tension. "You'd have rather I pitched you penniless into the street in such a state? Though no doubt it's where you belong, I'll not give the gossips and the newspapers in this town more to snicker about."

So his decision was all for appearances and pride, and nothing of compassion or any residue of tender feelings for her. That he was able to shut away the sweetness of the time they'd shared as if it had never been wounded her deeply. He was the Iron Man again, and the gentle and sensitive lover who had quelled her fears and led her to paradise in his arms might never have existed.

"I won't stay," she said, feeling a little frantic. "I'll

go to Paris. That's all I ever wanted. I won't trouble you further."

"Paris?" Elspeth sputtered. "You're not fit to go next door! Mr. McKin, you mustn't let her even think such a thing. She'll kill herself."

"I know my responsibilities, Miss Philpot," Lock returned coldly. "I've had enough difficulties squelching the misgivings of my New York investors since this story hit the papers. I won't have them thinking I can't handle my personal affairs. Constance stays, at least until she's stronger and the precarious nature of the situation abates."

"There, dear," Elspeth said, patting Constance's shoulder and beaming, "I knew everything would be all right."

But Constance knew that things were far from right. She'd made Lock look a fool. Contempt and resentment radiated from him in chill waves, killing all hopes of forgiveness and reconciliation or even explanation. His high-handed pronouncement that they would stay together to keep up pretenses was not a kindness but a punishment, and her first impulse was to fling his oh-so-gracious offer in his teeth. After all, he'd hurt her, too, abdicating his role as her champion, leaving her to face her demons alone again.

Banshees raised their voices inside her head, taunting her. She pressed her hands to her ears in a futile attempt to shut them out, drawing a startled look from Elspeth. Abandoned, powerless, with no real financial resources and no strength left to fight, she questioned how she could leave here to go to Paris or anywhere else. For a while at least, she had no alternative but to accept the grudging charity of a man who despised her.

"Lock, try to understand," she said desperately. "I *am* sorry."

"Spare me that." His tone was scathing. "Circumstances may warrant your continued presence, but you don't belong here and you have no claim on me. You never did."

The voices sang a triumphant paean to her humiliation, then ceased as abruptly as they'd begun. Constance trembled with the force of her annihilation. "I—I understand. I don't wish to cause you any more trouble."

"No. I'll see to that," he replied grimly, ignoring Elspeth's soft, disapproving murmur. He stared at Constance, and his eyes were hard. "Make no mistake. From now on, the only thing we'll share is a roof."

Constance shuddered, and the last vestige of hope died, for above all, Lock McKin was a man of his word.

Three weeks of teeth-clenching and jaw-setting had a way of making a man raw inside, no matter how cold was the face he showed to the world. It could also make him damned careless.

Cradling his throbbing right arm, Lock let himself into the Devonshire Street house early one mild May afternoon. A makeshift bandage covered the bloody scrape on his forearm and bruised hand, and he muttered an oath at his stupidity. He'd faced down nosy reporters, speculative acquaintances, and nervous investors since the courtroom debacle with Constance had robbed him of his ship, his pride, and nearly his business, but he'd paid a price with a single-minded abstraction that rivaled Constance's increasingly vague moods.

If Tip Maddock hadn't had a quick mind as well as a strong back when the stringer beam that Lock had been helping set on the *Argonaut* had slipped, Lock might have suffered far worse than a mauling. It was a wonder he hadn't lost his whole arm, a hell of a notion for an architect who drew ships for a living. On a certain level it wasn't his own negligence he blamed, but Constance for creating the entire distracting situation, and his resentment boiled like acid, eating away at his middle, so that his gut hurt all the time and his temper, usually so well controlled, was cocked on a perpetual hair trigger.

Lock stalked through the little house, intent on cleaning the wound at the kitchen sink. The odor of paint and linseed oil indicated Constance was again busy in the parlor she'd claimed as a studio. Lock told himself he wasn't the least bit curious, even though Elspeth had been quick to assert that these past days had produced some of Constance's best work yet.

The older woman was staunch in her support, a loyalty Lock questioned but had to admire, and it was thanks to Elspeth and Maggie that Constance had recovered her physical strength so quickly after what Lock cynically thought of as her "unfortunate collapse." To his intense irritation, however, since then Constance had affected a show of despondency worthy of the greatest melodramatic actress.

Lock stripped back the tattered flags of his ripped shirtsleeve, and his lips twisted with scorn. As if anything could really touch Constance's conniving little heart. Still, he hadn't been oblivious of the nightmares that continued to plague her, finding himself listening through the thin walls to her restless tossing and muttering long after he should have been asleep in his own solitary bed. The rewards of a guilty conscience, he thought with a sour grimace.

If anyone deserved to be wan and unhappy, it was Constance—he couldn't bring himself to refer to her as Lili even now—and if her reclusive and at times erratic behavior was a bid for his sympathy, he was determined not to be moved. At first she stayed in the house and its tiny, weed-infested rear yard from sheer weakness, but now her purported fear of seeing the Reverend Tate on the streets kept her incommunicado. Meanwhile, the clergyman had become something of a celebrity, making a creditable report to the Congregationalist Board of Supervisors and impressing the various Boston congregations with the flair and power of his sermons, not to mention his rare and awe-inspiring appearance.

Constance had also responded strangely when Elspeth reported that the most eminent doctors in Boston had been seen visiting Latham House on a regular basis since Alex had resigned from the helm of Latham and Company in favor of his nephew. From Constance's worried frown, one might have thought she had real feelings for the old man, but Lock knew better.

Besides, Lock didn't fully believe that Alex Latham had abdicated completely, poor health or not. Even if that was the case, Rodger was doing a fine job of following in his uncle's vindictive footsteps. Supplies were suddenly hard to come by and expensive. Credit disappeared overnight. Heretofore loyal laborers found other employment. It was a subtle harassment, but it was beginning to tell, and Lock had a feeling he was going to pay dearly for breaking Rodger Latham's nose and besmirching his manhood before a courtroom full of reporters. To all appearances the Lathams had achieved everything they'd wanted, but Lock knew they wouldn't be content now with anything less than the total destruction of the McKin Brothers Shipyard in order to win a feud that had begun more than twenty-five years earlier.

But Lock was equally determined to win—or at least to endure. Survival was everything now, and vengeance would have to wait, but Lock knew the value of patience. He worked feverishly to all hours at the shipyard, overseeing double crews, pushing forward the New York commission as well as the labor on the *Argonaut*'s innovative hull. Since losing the *Odyssey* again, the hope of turning around the yard's finances was grim unless both ships reached the earliest completion. With the threat of bankruptcy staring him in the face, his name and honor at stake, Lock drove his crews as mercilessly as he did himself, returning to the house only to rest briefly, eat, and clean up before leaving again for the yard. He could have moved back to his cramped rooms over the office, but the appearance of normalcy had quieted all but the most persistent rumors about his so-called marriage.

Besides, his continued presence in the Devonshire Street house was a form of masochistic punishment, a payment he extracted of himself for being not only a dupe but fool enough despite everything to still be affected by Constance's nearness. Though he was invariably civil, cool, and aloof when they met in the house, the physical awareness that had been such a part of their relationship refused to die, and he resented that most of all.

Lock cursed as the bandage stuck to the dried blood beneath. The soreness and swelling made him grit his teeth, and though impatience demanded he say the hell with it and rip it loose, prudence advised he soak it off. Reaching for a tin basin beneath the stone sink, Lock caught the flash of something white through the narrow paned window overlooking the tiny back garden. He paused, then his heart leaped to his throat, and he dropped the bucket with a clatter and raced out the rear door.

Vaulting down the worn brick steps, he ran toward the figure sprawled in the middle of the patchy grass. Constance lay on her stomach in the sunshine, clad in her muslin chemise and petticoat, barefoot and unmoving, her hair spread like a dark counterpane across her shoulders. Lock fell to his knees beside her, fearing the worst. His hands trembled when he touched her, and relief burst like a bubble in his chest to find her bare skin warm like honey, sun-kissed and rosy with life.

Then anger blossomed, and he shook her. "Constance? Answer me, dammit! Are you hurt?"

"Hmm?"

She stirred reluctantly, her sable lashes fluttering like a butterfly against the exotic orchid blush of her cheekbones. The city sounds were far away, drowned out by the buzz of hidden insects, and the sweet scent of crushed grass and rich earth rose in a cloud around them. She lay with one cheek pressed against the warm ground, her fingers twisting the strands of tough grass.

Lock took in the state of her undress, the rickety fence that was the only barrier between them and the well-traveled alley, and what was left of his temper ignited. "What the hell do you think you're doing?"

"Trying not to fall off the earth."

"What the—" Dumbfounded, he stared, and an awareness of the slimness of her limbs and the supple curves of her waist and hips beneath the thin, lace-edged fabric stole in under his anger to lodge low in his groin. He swore and dragged her to a sitting position. "Get up!"

Constance tossed her head, flinging the heavy mass of hair back from her flushed face. Her eyes were overbright with too many dreams. "If you don't hang on when you're adrift, you'll fly right over the edge of the world."

"I've had enough of your nonsense," he snapped. "You're not even dressed, for God's sake! Anyone could come along—"

"Leave me alone!" She shook him off, an angry goddess with eyes of molten gold. "You have no privileges here, *haole.*"

He hesitated, struck by the notion that she was possessed by one of her people's ancient deities. She'd said sometimes another person inside her made her act impulsively. Had it been Lili all along?

With a snort, he discounted the fancy. "This is absurd, Constance. Let me get you inside."

A royal prophetess could not have stared at him with more disdain. "The gates of Honaunau, the City of Refuge, are always open to those afflicted and accused. Not like your heart, Lock McKin."

"I'm not interested in your heathen philosophy. Get up!" Out of patience, he stood, jerking Constance to her feet, then swore because he'd used his injured arm without thinking.

Instantly, that other presence left Constance, and she focused on the grimy bandage with concern. "You're hurt! Let me see."

"Forget it," he growled, dragging her through the back door into the shadowy coolness of the stone-flagged kitchen.

"Don't be afraid of Crazy Lili," Constance chided with a soft laugh. "She's perfectly harmless, even if she does bathe in sunbeams."

"I'm not afraid." His tone was sullen.

"Then let me." She plucked at the oozing bandage, and a flicker of infinite sadness crossed her face. "It's little enough for me to ask or for you to give."

Lock hesitated for a moment, then silently extended his arm. Seating him at the old pine table, she retrieved the basin and soaked the bandage free, sucking in only one sharp breath at the sight of the deep gouge and ragged abrasions running from knuckles to elbow. The flesh was already purpling with bruises, and her touch was gentle as she bathed the clots away, anointed the injury with salve, then made a tidy new bandage from several clean kitchen towels. She tied it up with more strips of towel, then stood at his side as he moved his arm experimentally.

"It feels better already," he said grudgingly.

"How did it happen?" Constance chewed her thumbnail as he related an unemotional account of the incident. With great temerity, she touched his swollen fingers as they lay on the tabletop. "You were lucky this time. Please take more care."

He stiffened, pulling his hand away, and leaned back in the wooden kitchen chair to inspect her face. "I'm overwhelmed with this show of wifely concern," he drawled, "but I don't quite know what to make of it."

"Make of it what you will." Her lower lip trembled, and for an instant her face reflected naked longing. "I didn't lie about everything, you know."

A giant hand punched Lock in the belly. Moved by rage and frustration and a tension that had been building for these past excruciating weeks, he reached out and dragged her across his lap, bending her across his good arm, holding her chin with his sore fingers, forcing her face up to his.

"You're such a liar, you'd even lie to yourself. Don't be a fool, Constance," he snarled. "It wasn't love."

Her voice was barely a whisper. "It was to me."

"No. It was only this."

He kissed her savagely, letting his hand cup her breast, kneading the flesh until she moaned into his mouth. His tongue was rapacious, hungry, and he searched out every drop of sweetness, consuming her. Her fresh, sun-warmed scent, the soft texture of her skin, the pressure of her body against his, all made him sick and desperate with desire. Liar and dissembler and half-mad woman she might be, but his body recognized hers and, remembering, responded totally. Blood surged through his sex, through his brain, heating and destroying him, making him want, making him hurt, making him vulnerable again.

He couldn't allow it.

Lock shoved Constance to her feet. She grasped the edge of the table for support, her eyes dazed, her breath coming in ragged gulps.

"You see?" he sneered, rising. His breathing was no steadier than hers, the irregularity only better concealed. "It means nothing except you're a woman and I'm a man and it's been too long since either of us had any satisfaction. Lust, pure and simple, so don't put any fancy names to it."

She took a step toward him, her pride gone, only the need left. "I don't care what you call it."

"I do." His face was hard. "I'd as lief slake this urge on some Ann Street whore as on you. At least I'd know who she was."

Constance gasped and pressed her fist against the pain inside her chest. Her eyes filled. "First you wanted to hate me because I was a Latham. Now you hate me because I'm *not*. It's not the name that's important to you, Lock McKin, it's the hate."

"It's all we have." He saw a tear slide down her cheek and hardened his heart until it was as cold and brittle as the iron in his name. "And it's all you're likely to get from me. You'd best remember that and stay out of my way."

She laughed, a soft, tearing sound. "How could Crazy Lili forget the day the McKin broke his word?"

Chapter 13

⌒~⌒○⌒○⌒~⌒

The next morning, Constance was gone.

Lock's first reaction was surprise. He hadn't expected her to simply walk away, no matter how awkward their situation. After all, as his wife, she had the legal right to his support, at least until the courts ruled otherwise. Considering the hostility between them, he was further surprised to find she had taken only his old Chinese robe, a few clothes, and her paints. There was no note.

Then fury replaced surprise. No doubt she'd run crying to Elspeth or Maggie and he'd hear from her soon enough with the usual demands one would expect from a mercenary witch on the lookout for the main chance. Hadn't she gone first to the Lathams, then to him, looking for such an opportunity? No doubt she was hoping to sponge off Elspeth for a time before moving on to her next victim.

It was really better this way, Lock told himself, considering how Constance was still able to turn him inside out with her impetuous ways and feigned innocence. Whatever sense of outrage had possessed him to touch her the day before, it had recoiled on him, showing him, despite his bitter denunciation, that she could still move him to dangerous depths. Her leaving now saved him the trouble of sending her away.

But after three days without any word, Lock's anger over Constance's abrupt departure and this silent war of nerves had risen to the combustion point, so he went to Elspeth's to demand a showdown.

"What do you mean, she's not here?"

"I'm certainly not trying to hide Constance from you, if that's what you're accusing me of, Mr. McKin," Elspeth replied with some heat. Her ample bosom heaved under an expanse of tartan gabardine, and she gestured at the book-cluttered and magazine-heaped condition of her second-floor rooms. "See for yourself if you don't believe me."

"I beg your pardon, Miss Philpot," Lock said stiffly. "I merely assumed Constance would come here first."

"This is most distressing," Elspeth said, wringing her hands. "Why in heaven's name did you wait to come after her? Dear Lord, anything might have happened, the state the poor girl's in!"

"You needn't worry about Constance," Lock said. He jammed his fists into his trouser pockets, and his voice was caustic. "She's like a cat. She'll land on her feet no matter where she falls."

"Faith, you're a coldhearted man! Just like your father." Elspeth shook her finger in Lock's face. "And you needn't glower at me, either, Lock McKin. You took Constance for better or for worse, yet you've driven her away with your unfeeling attitude when she most needs your help!"

"You can't begin to know or understand the complexities of my relationship with Constance, Miss Philpot," Lock said between gritted teeth. "I'll thank you not to make presumptions that are totally unfounded."

"Oh, yes, that stiff-necked McKin pride again. We mustn't let anything get in the way of that, especially a child so head over heels in love with you she'd rather die than cause you harm!"

"Merely a disguise, part of the charade she concocted to obtain what she wanted. Unfortunately for her, at least that didn't work."

Elspeth snorted her disgust. "Ah, you're a bigger fool than I thought, then! Perhaps Constance is confused about herself, but who wouldn't be, I ask you, after what she's obviously suffered? I saw her scars when I was nursing her, and although something even worse torments her mind, I'll wager my first-folio Shakespeare that Constance never intentionally misled you. Why, to my way of thinking, her feelings for you were always as easy to read as an open book."

"Since she's gone, I don't suppose it's relevant." He turned to go, his face rigid.

"What's relevant is that you've made her situation so intolerable she's run away, and you'd best find her again with all haste if you ever hope to know the whole truth!"

"Constance has obviously made her choice," he replied stonily, trying to quell a growing unease.

But the pattern was there. When confronted with something she could no longer cope with, Constance fled. Only this time, she'd run from *him*. But he was no monster, and his anger was justifiable, Lock assured himself. Why, then, did that uneasy prick of conscience persist? And why did Elspeth's comparison to his father jab him so painfully? In his memory his own boy's voice piped a question: *Why, Papa? Why did you make Mama cry?*

Exasperated at his lack of a proper response, Elspeth grabbed Lock's sleeve and shook him like a terrier with a rat. "Have you not thought of what you stand to lose if you let her go? Have you not considered she might even be carrying your child?"

Elspeth's blunt words shocked him like a bucket of ice water to the face. "Is it true?" he croaked.

Elspeth shrugged, her expression bland. "You

should have a notion of that better than I. All I know is I wouldn't want to take the chance."

Put on those terms, Lock knew then that he couldn't, either.

But Constance's trail proved elusive. Neither the shipping offices with their packet schedules to Paris nor Maggie at her greengrocer's job in Quincy Market nor anyone at the shipyard nor even discreet inquiries at Latham and Company turned up any trace of her. The proprietor of the Mermaid Tavern hadn't even seen a scruffy cabin boy. As far as Lock could discern, Constance had vanished from Boston like a fairy sprite whisked out of sight by a magic spell. With each dead end, with each failure, Lock's anxiety multiplied. She'd had few funds and no other friends that he knew of. How far could she have gotten under those conditions? There was no knowing what dire predicament that unpredictable, impulsive female might land in!

Stymied for the moment, Lock finally went back to Devonshire Street, but he found no comfort there. Every shadow made him jump, half expecting it to be Constance coming home, and everywhere in the shabby little house her presence haunted him— images of her smiling, distressed, thoughtful, distracted, and, most painful of all, lost in passion.

By God, he hadn't meant it to end this way! Could he stand forever having things unfinished between them? And what if Elspeth were right? What if Constance carried his babe? The thought made him weak. Where had she run to this time?

Lock paced the house like a caged tiger. Eventually, his restless steps led him to the back parlor studio. He hesitated on the threshold, almost as if it were the sanctum sanctorum, for he'd never intruded here before except to peek in from time to time. A collection of canvases leaned against the far wall, and an unfinished landscape sat on her easel.

Squaring his shoulders, Lock resolutely began to examine the paintings.

He found they could almost be a calendar that charted Constance's presence in his life, beginning with her portrait of the *Odyssey*, which still hung in the main office of McKin Brothers Shipyard. The gentle yet intriguing assortment of vivid tropical flower portraits, pastel scenes of island sunsets, and bright Boston panoramas dated from the quiet time following their marriage, before passion had led them to another kind of relationship, and before the appearance of Cyrus Tate had destroyed that illusion, too. The next group of canvases bore silent witness to Constance's unhappy frame of mind since then, scenes of dark blue, wind-whipped clouds in the shape of dragons, bent and tragic figures with no faces whirling in macabre purple dances, burnt-orange forests of fire-ravaged trees on desolate ocher slopes.

Lock turned over a final painting, then swallowed hard. He stared into a pair of ice-blue eyes—his own. Shirtless and sun-bronzed, the Lock in the portrait sprawled at ease on a sandy dune, a red-painted dory pulled up in the surf farther down the beach and a small, weathered clapboard cottage in the distance. She'd done a credible job on the portrait, but he doubted he'd ever looked quite that carefree and smiling. Or had he?

With a pounding heart, Lock knew there might have been one time he'd risked showing his softer self, one woman who'd evoked a tenderness he couldn't deny, one place he'd let go the reins of control for a time and simply *lived.* And he knew then of a certainty where Constance had gone.

The Massachusetts and Western railroad agent remembered her, saying he'd arranged for a rented team to take her down to the coast. The helpful agent wanted to jaw for a while, but Lock had no patience after another restless night and a grueling morning breathing smoke and cinders aboard the noisy spur-line train. He rented a mount and left the watering stop at a gallop, but it was still well toward sundown before he reached Skye.

He topped the last rise of sandy, saw-grass-covered hill, reining in the horse at the sight of the familiar clapboard cottage. The surf pounded in his ears, and when he licked his lips he tasted the tang of salt. To his dismay, there was no sign of habitation, no friendly curl of smoke rising from the chimney.

Lock urged his tired horse the rest of the way down the incline, then dismounted in a tumble of impatience, vaulting up the rickety wooden steps and throwing open the cottage door.

"Constance!" His call echoed in the empty house. Scowling, he scanned the room and sucked in a breath. There was no doubt that Constance had been here. And she'd been busy.

Paintings of all sorts and sizes, all techniques and forms, produced on scraps of tarpaulin and badly tacked canvas and even on bits and pieces of board and driftwood, decorated every cranny of the tiny house. They adorned the dresser and shell-filled windowsills, lay propped against the walls, decorated the mantel. They represented a prodigious effort, a feverish compulsion that had clearly taken precedence over everything, including the body's most basic needs to eat and rest.

He'd never seen anything like it. Jarring, bizarre, yet strangely compelling, each painting told its own story and somehow connected with all the others, evoking emotional responses that had no basis in reason yet tapped something deeply primal. Lock found the pictures breathtakingly beautiful—and vastly disturbing, echoing resonances of memories from his own past, from the time when his father's black moodiness cast a pall over his entire existence.

Mesmerized, Lock studied each one. He found his own face in a series that seemed snatched from a medieval tapestry in which royal purple banners and flourishing silver swords adorned swirling scenes of battle filled with white-winged dragons and drowning sailors. But there was no sign of triumph, only rout and ruin and the silent screams of the vanquished.

Even more unsettling was a quartet of small pictures painted on wooden blocks, for the centerpiece of each was a tiny, supine female figure, an exquisitely shaded nude with long sable hair he recognized instantly as Constance's self-portrait. Vulnerable and defenseless in her nakedness, she lay prostrate in submission, making no move to fight the demons that crowded the pictures. In one, her prone figure formed the pupil of a teal-green eye overlooking a smirking ivory otter. In another, she floated in an ebony abyss beneath a magenta moon etched with a grinning gargoyle's face. The angry amethyst eye of a spinning hurricane whirled her above a writhing moray eel the hue of milk. But the fourth was infinitely disquieting, for the figure was only partially visible, buried under an avalanche of silver and blood-tinted boulders. Or were those bubbles?

Gulping, Lock understood that he was looking straight into Constance's worst nightmares. But was this an exorcism or a surrender?

With an exclamation of dismay, he came up short at the sight of her precious art supplies laid out in the dry sink. The bottles and tubes were aligned in precise rows, the brushes cleaned to their original softness. And each brush had then been deliberately broken and laid aside with a finality that made Lock's heart lurch to his throat with a nameless dread.

He left the cottage at a dead run, calling her name. The shed was empty and the beach deserted. The air was warm and thick with salt spray, and sweat popped out on his brow and drenched his armpits beneath his sedate blue jacket.

He yelled again, but the sound was lost in the roar of surf and wind. A rapidly dissolving line of indentations led up the sandy beach. A sign of life at last! Constance's footsteps, and made not long ago.

Telling himself his anxiety was unfounded, that she'd simply gone for a walk along the strand, Lock strove for calm, but a rising dread sent him jogging after her. He followed the tracks until the sandy verge changed to black rocks, but there was still no sight of her.

Splashing through sun-warmed tide pools, he sent crabs scuttling in the shallows and sea urchins shrinking from the disturbance. Spiraled whelk shells and acorn barnacles made walking hazardous, and the rust-colored fronds of sea dulse clung to his ankles. All the familiar creatures and plants of his boyhood seaside rambles were enemies now that thwarted him, and made him growl with frustration as he slogged onward with waterlogged shoes.

He broke off in the middle of a curse at the sight of the still figure perched like a mermaid on an outcropping of rock several hundred yards farther up the beach. Constance! And she was perfectly safe.

The wind whipped his yell away, lost in the raucous cawing of gulls, as relief sluiced through his system like mulled wine. Swathed in his silk robe, Constance sat silhouetted against the plum-colored sunset, her gaze fastened on the limitless expanse of water before her as if it held all the answers to the mysteries of the universe.

But she'd never been able to look at the ocean with such calm equanimity. The uneasiness returned, insidious fingers of apprehension squeezing Lock's throat. Even as he hurried toward her, Constance rose and walked to the water's edge. The wind pressed the flame-colored silk against her, and her sable hair flowed behind her like a dark banner. Her movements were easy, deceptively calm, deliberate. Opening the robe, Constance let it flutter to the sand, and Lock's breath stopped. She was completely naked, a pagan sacrifice of heart-wrenching loveliness.

And then she walked into the sea.

"No!" Lock's roar of denial came from his deepest soul, his most powerful fears. Memories of his father's death—the guilt and shame and fury— burned through his soul like acid. *Not again, dammit! Not again.*

Scrambling over rocks and splashing through the shallows, Lock flung off his coat and shoes on the spot where she'd entered the water, then plunged in after her.

The temperature of the water took his breath away. A dozen strokes into the surf, and he couldn't feel his arms or feet any longer. Beyond the foaming curl of whitecaps, he saw a dark head bob. Lock forced his body to respond to the directions he gave it, driving through the watery peaks and troughs with all his strength. There was no contest between his iron will and mere frail flesh.

He breached a wave in a burst of tortured gasps, then out of the corner of his eye saw a graceful feminine hand emerge from a dark comber and point toward the heavens. Calling on every ounce of his will, he kicked hard and made a desperate grab . . . *Got her!*

Constance's hair streamed around them like a silken web, slithering into Lock's eyes and mouth, so that when he broke the surface again, he was half blind and choking. Another breaker slapped him in the face, and he strangled on a lungful of frigid seawater. Coughing, Lock dragged Constance's limp form into his arms and grimly kicked for shore.

It was an excruciating journey, made even more painful by the numbing cold, Constance's dead weight, and the tug of the receding tide. When at last Lock dragged them both onto the sun-warmed sand, his ears rang and black sunbursts sparkled on the edges of his vision. Fighting the faintness, he rolled her over, then pressed the heels of his hands against her back to expel the water from her lungs, willing her to be alive, to breathe, to *live.*

"Come on, princess," he urged in a voice raspy with salt. "Dammit, Connie, you're not going to do this to me!"

She moaned, convulsed, and coughed up fluid.

"Fight it, Connie! Fight the darkness." Shuddering with fear and cold, Lock blinked away seawater and tears, pleading with her, commanding her to respond as his hands pressed heavily. "Come back to me. I won't let you go!"

Constance coughed, then gasped in a deep breath, drawing a knee up in an automatic response to the pain the effort produced. She clawed at the sand, arching her back, naked and shivering as a newborn, but *alive.*

Grateful emotion clotted in Lock's throat. With trembling hands, he turned Constance over in his arms, cradling her protectively against his sodden garments. He smoothed back the tangled strands of wet hair and dusted the damp, clinging sand from her pale cheeks and blue lips. "Connie. Answer me."

Her eyelids quivered; then wet, spiked lashes fluttered open over unseeing topaz eyes. "Oh, God, let me go."

"Damn you, woman." He groaned and kissed her hard, striking a blow for life, denying the brush with death in the most elemental way he knew. "Damn you! What the devil are you doing?"

Her sandy fingers dug into his forearms. "Voices . . . calling me."

Then she'd heard him? And plunged into the water anyway? Angry suspicion returned, and his jaw worked.

"Was this just another of your damned fool stunts gone wrong? Something to punish me, to gain my sympathy? What did you think to gain from this madness?"

Her face was chalky now, her lips white and bloodless. With great difficulty, as if she could barely see him over a giant chasm, she whispered, "Only peace."

That scared him, and his rage left him as quickly as it had come, leaving him foundering for answers, for understanding. "Sweet Christ, woman, why? *Why?*"

With a ragged sound of pain, she leaned her forehead against his chest and wept in helpless defeat. "The dragons are back."

Remorse built within Lock's tight chest. Dear God, had he driven Constance to this? How profound had been a despair that convinced her the only relief was to surrender her very existence? And if that wasn't bad enough, what demonic force had compelled her to choose the form of death she feared above all others as extra penance? All the surface toughness, all the spit and fire and strength with which Constance met life, concealed a fragile soul so vulnerable and yet so valiant, only the most coldhearted, unfeeling individual could remain unmoved at her struggles. Or a damned, icy bastard like Iron Man McKin.

With a silent oath, Lock buried that self-recrimination in his deepest soul, along with that dangerous moment of illuminating pain when he'd thought Constance was lost to him and he'd known what true despair was.

"There aren't any dragons, dammit!" he shouted, roughly chafing her arms and legs, trying to bring life and warmth back into her icy limbs.

"Go away," she moaned, tears slipping down her wet cheeks. "Haleakala awaits. The fire flowers bloom and angels bleed. I'm coming, my people. Oh, Kanai, oh, Namaka—"

"Shut up!" Unable to fathom her mumbling, he resorted again to anger. "I won't let the McKin name suffer the stigma of another suicide. Do you hear me, you selfish little bitch!"

Her weird laughter made the hairs on the back of his neck prickle. "I thought if I faced it . . . I tried to conquer the fear and destroy the bad feelings, but I couldn't. Can't you see? I've fallen off the earth."

"Then I'll catch you, goddammit!" Lock shook her so hard her head snapped back, and she gasped. For an instant there was a flicker of the old Constance in the golden flash of her eyes, and Lock tried to reach her the only way he knew she couldn't ignore.

"Princess, look at me!" He held her face between his gritty palms, his expression so fierce his blue eyes burned like twin flames. "Who am I? Say it. Say my name."

She blinked, shivering, struggling. Her lips moved soundlessly. She tried again. "Lock."

"Yes. You're here, with me. Not falling off the world. Not in some otherwhere. I'll keep you safe, but you've got to *try*."

Her lips quivered, and her lashes drooped. "I'm so tired."

"Look at me!" he ordered. "Do you love me?"

Her eyes flew open, wide and startled, as if she were again fighting her way up from the bottom of an ocean. "I—"

"Do you?"

Her tears flowed faster. "Yes."

"Then hold onto that. Hold onto *me*."

With a faint cry, she reached for him, clinging desperately to his neck as if he were her only life-line to salvation.

"Hush, princess. I've got you now." The words sounded lame, but they were all he had to offer, except for physical succor. Worrying now about the consequences of exposure, Lock scooped Constance up into his arms. "You're going to be all right, I promise."

He wrapped her shivering form in their discarded garments, but she wept silently against his neck all the way back to the cottage. She remained inconsolable even when he toweled her dry and tucked her into the tarnished brass bed. Then he stripped, built a fire, and crawled under the quilts with her, ignoring her incoherent objections and warming her with his hands and his own body heat until the chills began to subside.

"Don't cry, Connie. Talk to me." His voice was low, his hands firm. The sun was gone, and only the flickering light from the fire illuminated Constance's stricken features.

"How . . . how did I get into the water?"

He smoothed back her damp hair, swallowing hard. He was a scientist, a dealer in concrete facts and logic, a rational man struggling with irrationality, at a loss to know what to say, what to do. But trusting instinct and emotion had landed him in this mess, and he shied away from that avenue, opting for reason. And reason said she couldn't take much more.

"It doesn't matter," he said in a gruff tone.

"Nothing's real anymore. I'm so scared . . ." Her gaze turned inward again, spying something so terrifying she shuddered.

"Don't, Connie. Stay with me." He drew her closer into his arms, fitting her against his length in a protective embrace, letting his fingertips trace the delicate valley of her spine, demanding her attention with physical sensations. He felt her skin warm beneath his touch, the involuntary tensing, the charge of summer lightning as the awareness that never failed sprang up between them again. "This is real. You and me. We've always had this much."

She trembled with need, swaddled in a patchwork of misery and desire. "If I hurt you again, it will kill me."

"I can take care of myself." His jaw squared. "And I can take care of you. You're my responsibility, and you aren't going to hurt anyone, not even yourself. I won't let you."

"I want to remember the truth, but I'm drifting, drowning in thoughts and feelings I can't stop. I only imagined I could control it, but it's worse."

"Anchor yourself in me," he said in a voice that brooked no dispute. "Not in dreams, not in visions. In *me*, here and now. In this."

He kissed her, letting her feel the heat, the power. When he lifted his head again, the first glimmer of hope burned behind her eyes, tentative, unsure, yet wanting desperately to believe.

Constance tried to free herself from the black depths, tried to focus on the only solid and stable thing in a universe gone mad—Lock. Even if he couldn't truly forgive or believe her, and even if his talk of mere responsibility was like a hot blade through her soul when all she really craved was his love, at least he'd put aside his abhorrence long enough to hold her. She was a beggar, and not too proud to accept a morsel of compassion. Maybe it would give her enough strength to withstand the fierce tempests to come.

"I want to," she whispered, touching his skin. "But it's so hard . . ."

"Don't think of anything else but me, but *this*."

He stroked her breast. "We'll find safe harbor together."

A soft sob bubbled from her throat. "I never meant to lie. Not to you."

"Connie." He rested his forehead against hers. "Latham or not, it was the truth as you knew it. I shouldn't have blamed you for that, but I have dragons of my own."

It was as much as he was able to give her, and more than she deserved. Constance couldn't really blame him for holding a part of himself back. She was at the very least untrustworthy, at the most stark raving mad, and a man could only surrender so much control when involved with a lunatic. The reserve she sensed in him hurt, but to be without him hurt more. It might be wrong, but she had no pride left. Besides, when you were drowning and someone threw you a rope, you didn't quibble over philosophy, you just hung on. And she was hanging on for her life.

Constance touched Lock's hair as if it were a talisman against evil. "Hold me, Lauchlan," she whispered. "Chase the dragons away."

Her lips were still cool, but warmed beneath his kiss, opening with sweet desperation so that he could deepen it as he willed. What began as comfort and reassurance changed as passion ignited, burning Lock's loins, scorching his mind. It was always the same, this hunger between them, yet always different, and, right or wrong, he could no more deny her—or himself—the physical surcease than the tides could defy the moon.

Her fingers kneaded the muscles in his arms, drawing him closer. He nosed aside her still-damp hair and found the hollow behind her ear, tasting salt and woman and the essence of what he desired. Shivering, but with growing heat rather than cold, she shifted restlessly against his hair-dusted length, tracing the ridges of his ribs; then, with a small seeking noise, she turned her head until she found his mouth again.

She was needy, but he was needier, the craving for her sweetness taking him over, leading him to places within himself he'd never explored. Tongues entwined, darted, teased, stealing sense and breath. Lock held her breasts in his large palms, stroking the rosy nubs until she writhed in frustration. Then, with infinite gentleness, he rolled her beneath him and slowly sank into her wet, silky depths.

They didn't dare breathe for a long, endless moment. There was a poignancy and a desperation to their joining that mingled with the basic and tumultuous pleasure. Lock throbbed for release, but his heart ached and yearned, trying to reach Constance, trying to ease her fears, trying to show her that together they could weather the wildest storm.

Slowly he began to move, and she clung to him as if to a lifeline, arching against his powerful thrusts in search of a solace she could find only in his arms. With a shuddering cry, she tensed, and wave after wave of exquisite release flooded through her. Humbled, exultant, Lock kissed her passionately and took his own reward.

Afterward, Lock held Constance as she slept, exhausted and wonderfully dreamless, but slumber was a long time coming for him. One question haunted him.

Would what they shared be enough to keep her safe—from herself?

Chapter 14

The full moon dusted the crooked Boston streets with silver, disguising the mean warrens and summer-ripe gutters of Devonshire Street with magic. From her perch on the wide sill of the bedroom's open window, Constance watched the shadows march across the cobbles and limn the chimneys with iridescence. Striving for calm, she inhaled deeply. The balmy midnight breeze that stirred the muslin curtains and cooled her sweat-dampened temples carried a tang of the harbor, and the city's muted voice whispered and murmured an incomprehensible accompaniment to the images that lingered behind her eyelids.

A pair of strong hands gently cupped her shoulders from behind. Constance jumped, then sagged back against the reassuring bulk of her husband's bare chest. "Lock, I didn't mean to wake you."

His voice was a sleepy rumble against her ear. "Another dream?"

Lock ran his palms up and down her arms, sliding over the sleeves of the silky Chinese robe. Constance placed her hands on the backs of his, following his warming movements, shivering slightly.

"It wasn't too bad. I *am* better." She said it firmly, as if to convince herself.

"Yes, you are, but it's only been a couple of weeks . . ."

His unspoken words hung in the air. *Since her senses had betrayed her and she'd nearly abandoned her life at Skye.*

But thank God Lock had come for her when he did. The fortuitous nature of his arrival almost reestablished Constance's belief in a merciful Creator. Of course, for a time she'd thought a truly benevolent God would have let her suffering end, but her love for Lock McKin was an anchor line to this world that she could not cut. Also fortunately for her, Lock's damnable sense of responsibility and honorable behavior made him too stubborn to give up on her. His concern that she might be with child had proved unfounded, but still the Iron Man was ruthless, using her feelings for him with no compunction, filling her mind and body so completely that most of the time there was no room left for demons.

He'd brought her back to Boston and continued his campaign of tender, healing magic, mingling raptures of physical delight with sometimes painful, probing questions, determined as only the Iron Man could be to uncover reasons, dissect problems, and construct solutions. Though Constance doubted that the causes and effects of her disturbances could be charted on a drawing board like one of his great ships, she didn't want to disappoint him. So she tried hard to find her balance, to develop a sense of equilibrium, going about her day-to-day existence as best she could, even painting again. Only that morning she'd completed a landscape of the silversword-covered slopes of majestic Haleakala that pleased her and contained no undertones of darkness, as the paintings she'd done at Skye had. But nothing completely stopped the dreams.

"I'm trying, Lock," she said, fighting to keep the

desperation out of her voice. "Only when I close my eyes—"

Lock's breath stirred the tendrils at her temple. "Don't push so hard, princess. What was it about this time?"

"The same. Water. Going under. Something ... bad frightens me and I'm running. Uncle Cyrus—" Constance broke off, shuddering, and Lock wrapped his arms around her.

"Never mind. It's over."

She shook her head, frustrated. "It's agony to doubt one's own memories. Why does my mind play such tricks?"

"To cope with something even worse, perhaps. Something that happened when the fever scrambled your memory."

She swallowed. "Uncle Cyrus said my father beat me nigh to death."

"A child's mind could not deal with a beloved parent doing such a thing." Pushing the sable-colored mass of her hair aside, Lock massaged her tense shoulders, and his thumbs traced the residue of welts beneath the silk. His face was stony. "And even if the Reverend Tate was well meaning, he never 'spared the rod,' did he, Connie?"

She froze, searching her thoughts, attempting to sift truth from the chaff of her inner confusion. "No. He punished me quite harshly—" She broke off again, this time with a low sound of distress, and rubbed her temples. "At least I think he did!"

"You couldn't be entirely mistaken about something like that."

"You believe me?"

Releasing her shoulders, Lock propped his hip on the windowsill and sat down facing her. Clad only in moonlight as he was, his face and chest were cast in sharp planes and softly shadowed angles. He took her fingers between his. "I *know* the bastard hurt you. Your reaction was too intense to be imaginary. If I wish to be charitable, I'll say he was simply a clumsy disciplinarian, with no notion how to handle a high-strung little rebel like you. Or, on a more sinister note, maybe he likes to inflict pain on a helpless victim."

A queer, knowing weight settled like lead in the pit of her stomach. "Yes."

"Either way, it certainly explains why he frightened you into striking back and then leaving Lahaina. Small wonder you have nightmares."

"At least it was a relief to find I could cross murder off my list of sins," she agreed in a shaky tone. "Of course, I have plenty of others to take its place."

A corner of his mouth twitched. "None of any significance."

A sudden lump of emotion clogged her throat, and her fingers tightened on his in wordless thanks. He had good hands, strong, callused from hard work, yet long-fingered and artistic, as skillful and creative on a woman's body as with a well-rigged ship. On impulse, she brushed a kiss across his knuckles.

It was a silly thing to do, but a woman in love had to be allowed a few freedoms, especially when the man she cared for held such a tight check over his emotions. Not that she had any reason to fear Lock's desire for her was feigned. His enjoyment of their physical relationship was too intense to be a sham, but at the same time, it left her somehow empty. She found safety and surcease in his arms, but what she truly wanted was a place in his heart, to be allowed past his iron shell as she had those first glorious days at Skye. To regain Lock's trust was another imperative reason to strive for sanity.

Her brief kiss evoked no response, and she released him with a stifled sigh. "You work so hard, and I've disturbed your rest long enough. Go back to bed, Lock. I'll be all right."

"In a while." He grimaced and gazed out the window at the deserted street. "I'm a bit restless myself."

"Something wrong at the shipyard?" she asked. *Or is it just your crazy wife?*

"Nothing to worry about, princess. It's simply going to be nip and tuck for a while, and as always when it's crucial that things should go right, we've had a rash of mishaps."

Alarmed, she straightened on the uncomfortable sill. "Anything serious?"

Lock shook his head and tunneled his fingers through his hair. "Nothing other than a few bumps and bruises. Just annoying, stupid mistakes, tools mislaid, machinery on the blink, that sort of thing."

"Will you be able to keep to your schedule on the New York commission? And on the *Argonaut?* You have to finish her, don't you?"

"If we ever hope to climb out of this hole." He rubbed a forefinger over his upper lip, frowning at the darkness below. "The *Eliza*'s profits got us started, but my designs have scared off more than one potential investor. I've taken quite a beating in the press."

She winced. "Because of me. Lock, I'm sorry—"

"No, princess, not because of you." Reaching for her, he pulled her around so that they fit together like a pair of spoons. "Because the critics who think they know took one look at the *Argonaut*'s lines and are now trying to laugh her out of the stocks. But they're wrong, Connie. She'll be fast, faster than anything afloat. I know it."

His conviction made her proud. "Then don't listen to those naysayers, Lock. If you believe in yourself, that's all that's important. Isn't that what you've been telling me?"

He grinned against the top of her head. "So you have been listening."

She would not allow herself to be cajoled. "Tell

me you won't let anything stop you from building your dream."

Lock heaved a sigh. "Unfortunately, it's more complicated than that. Money is the problem at the moment. Cash for wages and materials. Hell, I can't even sell my shipbuilder's interest in the *Odyssey* unless Rodger agrees, which isn't likely. I'm sure he sits up nights at Latham House gloating at the bind he's managed to put me in."

"If only I could remember, if only there was some other way to prove I'm a Latham, then you could go to court again and get the *Odyssey* back. That would solve everything, wouldn't it? There's got to be a way—"

"Don't, Constance." His tone was stern.

She turned to look up at him, pressing her palm against his chest, feeling the strong beat of his heart through her own skin. "Why?"

"Because it's time to move forward, and you can't if you continue to delude yourself that you're Constance Latham instead of Lili Young."

She gasped as though he'd slapped her. "But, Lock, I *am*—"

"Before you claim any name, think!" he interrupted roughly. "You have to accept yourself for who you really are, or those secrets are going to remain locked in your head along with all the pain."

"You think I'm Lili?" she asked on a tremulous note.

He hesitated for only a split second, then nodded decisively. "Yes. From what you've told me and what the Reverend Tate said, it's the most logical conclusion. The reason you're terrified of the ocean must be because you saw the real Constance drown."

"But if even *I* don't know, how can *you* be so certain?"

He caught a fistful of her hair and inspected her

features in the milky light filtering through the curtains. His words were fierce.

"Can't you see that it doesn't matter anymore? Whatever tales you made up to survive in Lahaina, you're safe now. Call yourself Constance if you want, but let the rest go so you can heal and get on with the rest of your life."

"I can't." Her breath came in tortured spurts. "It's not that easy."

His fingers gentled, and he smoothed her hair back from her brow. "It could be."

"I can't wish away things I know and feel simply because it's more convenient!" She made a move to get up, but he held her firm. His assumptions distressed and upset her, and as a defense against the fear, she lashed out, flinging her flowing hair out of her eyes and glaring at him. "I can't pretend nothing moves me, nothing hurts. I'm not encased in ice like you!"

Lock's voice was flat. "Then you'll have to do it the hard way."

"I thought that's what I've been doing," she muttered, resentment making her mouth mulish. "Not that I'd dream of complaining."

His smile gleamed unexpectedly in the dimness. "That's right. Get angry. Show me you can fight."

Constance struggled against his grip. "I can. I am!"

"Good. You'll have to, because as much as I'd like to keep you safely here in my bed, the world doesn't exist just inside this house, and it's time you rejoined it."

She went very still. "I—I can't trust myself not to disgrace you again."

"You have to start somewhere, and staying cooped up isn't normal or healthy. I'm not running an asylum, and you're no timid *wahine*. You need to see other people, get some exercise, go to the market. You can't brood if you're busy."

"But, Lock," she wailed softly, "what if I'm not ready?"

"You can conquer anything you choose, princess, no matter what you call yourself." Holding her still, Lock kissed her, offering his strength and reassurance. She drew a shaky breath when he lifted his head.

"You're very persuasive, Lock McKin."

He rubbed his thumb over her cheekbone in an unthinking gesture of tenderness. "You can start tomorrow by visiting Miss Philpot. She's been asking after you."

"Elspeth." Constance nodded in relief. "Yes, I can do that."

"Mrs. Brack can go with you if you need company." He referred to the middle-aged matron he'd hired to do the heavy work around the house.

Constance made a face and stood up. "I don't care for Mrs. Brack. She moves my things and then denies it."

"Careful, my dear." Magnificent in his unabashed nudity, Lock stood and chucked Constance under the chin. "People *will* think you're mad if you accuse the housemaids of persecuting you."

"Leave it to you to make a joke of it," she replied in a huff, batting his hand away. "If you think I need a watchdog, why couldn't it be someone pleasant like Maggie?"

"Because Maggie already has a position and a beau who takes all her time," he said reasonably. Chuckling at Constance's annoyance, he pulled her close and slowly untied the sash of the robe. "I'll discharge Mrs. Brack if you insist."

Constance shivered with the heat of his hands against her bare flesh. The evidence of his arousal pressed against her belly, and she closed her eyes with a sigh. "It's not important."

"You'll go to Elspeth's?"

"Yes." She leaned into him, running her fingertips

along his corded midsection, inhaling the scent of his skin, filling her senses with him once again. "Anything you want, Lock."

"What I want is to banish your bad dreams forever," he said in a strange, solemn voice. Bending his head, he whispered against her lips. "But what I'll settle for tonight is something to help us both sleep."

It was both annoying and reassuring to have a husband who was invariably right, Constance decided as she crossed Boston Common the next day.

Girls in pigtails and freckled boys in knee britches whooped across the grassy spaces or chased wooden hoops down the white shell pathways. The overhead greenery filtered the sunshine, providing relief for pedestrians from the summer's heat. Babies drowsed in wicker prams while their nurses gossiped, and couples strolled arm in arm through flowery arbors filled with the hum of bees. Constance's feet crunched satisfyingly on the paths, and the lavender ribbons of her chip bonnet floated gaily in the breeze.

Constance couldn't contain a smile of sheer pleasure. Lock was right. It felt wonderful to stretch her muscles and to feel the sunlight on her face. She laughed softly to herself at the sheer joy of being alive on a glorious afternoon.

Constance had bidden Elspeth good-bye not ten minutes earlier at the corner of the Common after a most edifying time together. They'd paid a visit to Mr. Evans, the publisher on Washington Street, and had seen the preliminary proofs of the engravings for *Sandwich Islands Sketchbook*. Constance had dictated the short commentary for each. It was heady to see the book taking form, and daringly, she even contemplated a small profit, something to add to the coffers of the McKin Brothers Shipyard to help Lock build his great ship. To celebrate Constance's

success in advance, Elspeth had treated them both
to cakes and small glasses of sherry in the Tremont
Hotel's dining room.

Elspeth's gossipy wit and easy chatter about the
literati of Boston had been just what Constance had
needed to lift her spirits and help restore her self-
confidence. She hadn't gone vague even once, and
had truthfully been able to tell her kindhearted
friend that her health, as well as her relationship
with Lock, was much improved.

Assuring Elspeth that she'd find her own way
home, Constance lingered a bit along the Common's footpaths, finding in the turn of a child's
chubby cheek or the shape of sunlight through a
stand of willows or the bowlegged gait of a top-
hatted octogenarian the germ of a new painting.
She came to an abrupt halt at the sight of the imposing bulk of Latham House rising across Beacon
Street.

To humor her suddenly weak knees, she sank
down on the edge of a shady bench near the Beacon
Street entrance, wondering what unconscious impulse had brought her to this side of the Common.
For an instant she imagined herself crossing the
street, lifting Latham House's enormous brass
knocker and letting it fall, entering the palatial
foyer, making peace with her grandfather . . .

But he wasn't her grandfather, she reminded herself, wringing the strings of her reticule between her
gloved hands. Not if she was truly Lili Young and
not James Latham's daughter, as the Reverend Tate
avowed. It was just that for a time it had felt as
though she and Alex Latham were family. Even
now the locket that carried James's portrait rested
out of sight beneath her pin-tucked lavender bodice, because despite what Lock had urged, she was
unable to abandon that tie completely. Alex Latham
was undoubtedly a crusty, high-handed individual,
but she'd been on the verge of developing a genu-

ine affection for the old curmudgeon before all hell had broken loose.

But there was nothing she could say to Alex that he might understand, Constance realized. They'd both been at fault, and in spite of Alex's attempted manipulations of her life, she hoped the rumors of his broken health were untrue. Her regretful sigh brought a sickly-sweet odor to her nose. Deep in her brain, a primitive alarm went off, and her heart lurched.

"Woolgathering as usual, Lili?" the Reverend Cyrus Tate asked in a soft voice. "My dear child, that is not a good sign."

Constance pressed a hand to her mouth to stifle a scream and shrank back against the bench. Dressed in his customary white suit and a broad-brimmed straw hat, the minister carried an open umbrella to protect his milk-white skin from the sun. Even out of doors, the overpowering scent of ginger-blossom water clung to him, his excessive use of the perfume due to the fact that his hereditary condition had also robbed him of a normal sense of smell.

At least he can't smell the sherry on my breath! Constance thought wildly.

"Well, child?" Tate's smoked spectacles concealed the expression in his pink irises, but his unctuous tone held a note of impatience that Constance recognized all too well. "What kind of a greeting is this for your old uncle?"

"U-Uncle Cyrus." It was all Constance could manage to say around the cottony dryness in her mouth. Frozen in familiar horror, she watched aghast as he seated himself beside her, then leaned closer in an intimate, almost conspiratorial manner.

"I've been expecting you, Lili. I'm disappointed you took so long to come to me."

"I—what?" Confused, she shook her head. "Here?"

"I saw you trying to gather up your courage from

the parlor window of Latham House. A perfect view of the Common from there, as I'm sure you know."

"Latham House?" she repeated, unable to form any but the most inane of syllables.

"So kind of Mr. Rodger Latham to offer me his hospitality while I preach the Gospel here in Boston, don't you agree? It has proved quite a . . . comfortable venue. You can imagine my concern for you these past weeks after that dreadful courthouse scene. Mr. Latham's nose has been in a plaster—well, never mind that now. I'm just relieved you've come at last."

"I didn't—"

"Don't fret about the delay, child," he soothed. "Forgiveness is the Lord's way and mine. And I will forgive your lies, and even the physical violence you perpetrated on my person in Lahaina, if you'll pray with me, repent of your sins, and agree to return home where you belong."

"What?" The air in her lungs refused to flow. "No, I can't!"

"But of course you can," he replied, laughing indulgently. "How all the plantation children miss their Lili! The songs and stories you told them. It's the Lord's work, Lili, to bring His message to the lost tribes. *Your* work. At my side as always."

What he described made no sense. She'd never been trusted to that extent, never to work with children like that—had she? "I don't know what you're saying."

His smooth, marblelike features took on a pitying expression. "You truly don't remember, do you? But you haven't been well, not for a very long time. All the more reason to return and be among those who really care for you."

Constance jumped to her feet, animated at last by a revulsion that made her nauseous. "I'm not going anywhere. I'm married—"

"A lustful liaison not sanctioned in the proper church, I understand. One has only to see that man McKin to know his animalistic urges. Oh, I fear for you, child, wed to a man like that, savaged by his fearsome coupling. It must rend you in twain each time."

"I love my husband," she protested, backing away desperately. "I have a life here."

Holding the umbrella high, Tate rose as well, his voice taking on the thunderous, accusing tones of a pulpit fire-breather. "Built on the delusions of a sick brain. What kind of life is that for that husband of yours? What guarantee can you give him that you'll not bash *his* head in while he sleeps, as you attempted with me?"

Deep within Constance's mind, a banshee began to wail. "That's not true," she whispered.

"My dear child, you haven't told him, have you?" His tone was sorrowful and pitying all at once. "Yes, it would be unfortunate if these violent tendencies of yours became known."

"You're threatening me," she said with a gasp of realization. "Why? What is it you want?"

"My warnings are made with only the most Christian of intentions, to try to spare your deluded husband more tribulation than is necessary. After all, he is the innocent party in your duplicitous web. You could save him further humiliation by returning to Lahaina, otherwise . . ."

"What?"

"No doubt the scandal would be very hard on your luckless husband's shipbuilding enterprise."

"No." A tightness squeezed her chest. She couldn't stand to be the start of that kind of trouble for Lock again!

"My understanding of business is limited, but I know that Latham and Company will eventually consume McKin Brothers Shipyard. It is the way of large companies. If you could persuade McKin not to fight the inevitable, perhaps no overly malicious rumors about his wife's madness would ever need to surface at all."

"Not fight to save the shipyard? Lock would never give it up voluntarily!"

Tate shrugged. "Then you are fortunate Boston is a civilized city. I'm sure its hospital for the insane is a humane institution."

She was trapped again. Constance pressed her fist against a pain in the center of her chest. Her mouth quivered, and her golden eyes glittered with a desperate hate. "Damn you. Damn you to hell!"

"Blasphemer! You'll pay for this." Tate took an automatic step toward her, the umbrella raised in a threatening way that took Constance back to all the other times.

With a sharp, panicked cry, she picked up her skirts and ran as if all the legions of hell had been loosed, not even noticing that Tate's step into full sunlight left him blinking and cringing and unable to follow. In her head, a dragon breathed fire and demons screamed. Just as in her dreams, all she could do was flee for her life.

When Constance finally reached Devonshire Street again, she was disheveled and trembling, disoriented and unable even to say how she'd gotten there or how long her heedless flight had taken. Sweat stained her armpits, and her bonnet hung down her back on its lavender ribbons. She plunged through the front door and nearly ran into an astounded Mrs. Brack, a spare, competent woman with a nondescript knot of hair and a smocked apron.

"Ma'am, are ye all right? Them apples wasn't so important you had to rush so."

"Apples?" Dazed and dizzy, Constance shook her head. "What apples?"

"Why, the ones for the pie you wanted special. You were so upset that you forgot them when you came in from the market before, you turned right around and went back out for them."

Constance pulled off her bonnet. "I don't have any apples."

"You mean ye forgot them again, even with a special trip?" Surprised, Mrs. Brack pursed her thin lips in confused disapproval.

A deep crease formed between Constance's brows, and a pain like a hot needle pierced one eye. "I didn't go to the market this afternoon."

"But, ma'am, o' course ye did!" The older woman gestured to a duo of string bags on the foyer table filled with produce and packages of sugar and bacon tied in brown paper. "You bought all this. Don't you remember?"

The agony behind Constance's eyes increased. Had she really completely forgotten about this business of apples? Hysteria tickled the back of her throat. Anything was possible after seeing Uncle Cyrus. Dipping her head, she tugged off her gloves while grappling with the remnants of her tattered composure.

"Yes, of course, Mrs. Brack. How silly of me. I met Miss Philpot and ... and I must have gotten sidetracked. Please see that those things are put away."

Leaving Mrs. Brack staring after her in mystification, Constance sought the one familiar place sure to soothe and balance her. But the studio only increased her distress, for it brought back memories of Jerôme, and lessons learned only to be paid for in pain when Uncle Cyrus found out. All the paintings lining the walls seemed flat and inadequate, and the rising chorus of voices in her mind mocked and berated her, scorning her talents, laughing at her feeble attempts to control her world by capturing it in pictures.

Even the portrait of the strong, uplifted crater of Haleakala, the House of the Sun, and the spiky gray tongues of the silverswords seemed to belittle her, for she'd painted several of the rare plants sporting their ever rarer stalks of purple blossoms. But nothing could bloom in the barren wasteland of her life, not with Uncle Cyrus's threats and the proof of a relapse of madness screaming in her ears. If she couldn't get control of these feelings, Cyrus Tate wouldn't have to spread scandalous rumors about her for Rodger to damage Lock's reputation, humiliate him even further, and possibly destroy his business—the mere truth would do the job for him!

With the pain crashing through her brain like a tidal wave, Constance cried out in frustration and rage and helplessness and threw the first thing at the mocking landscape her hands came upon. The bottle bounced off the canvas, losing its cork and spraying solvent over the picture. Pungent fumes filled her nostrils, splitting her aching head into a thousand painful, quivering shards. Colors ran together, blended, and bled. With a tormented sob, Constance grabbed up a brush and slashed at the ruined canvas. Purple-and-black pigments dripped off the easel, staining the wooden floor like blood as the House of the Sun melted under her onslaught.

"What the holy hell!"

Lock's astounded shout rang out over Constance's gasping sobs. He appeared out of nowhere, wringing the brush out of her hand, wrapping his arms around her to control her hysterical struggles. His voice was anguished and discouraged.

"Damnation, woman! Don't start this again. Not now!"

"I told ye, sir, see?" Mrs. Brack shrilled from the doorway. "Quite mad, she is, an' dangerous queer. I won't be staying here, not with a crazy woman shoving a knife in me face!"

That shocked Constance into immobility. She went pasty and her eyes dilated. "I didn't." Desperately, she looked up at her husband's grim face. "Lock, I *didn't!*"

"Then explain this," Mrs. Brack snapped, and extended her left hand, showing a bloody slash across the open palm.

"No!" Constance groaned and sagged in Lock's arms, reality spinning in circles. He eased her into an old rocking chair.

"And ye're a heathen liar!" Mrs. Brack spluttered, wrapping her hand in her apron.

"Get out," Lock ordered curtly. "I'll pay you double what I owe. Just get out!"

"Oh, God," Constance moaned, her teeth chattering. "It's happening again."

"Connie!" Lock knelt and caught her face between his palms. "Calm down. What started this?"

"Uncle Cyrus. I saw him in the Common." Tears glittered on her lashes, and she clasped Lock's wrists with frantic strength. "It was awful. And then I went . . . I don't know where, but Mrs. Brack said . . . I didn't attack her, I swear! At least I think—oh, I don't know anymore!"

"It could have been worse." Lock's mouth was grim, but he found her hands and squeezed them. "What about Tate?"

"He says he'll tell things . . . about me, to make things harder for you and the shipyard if I don't go back to Lahaina." Constance gave a high-pitched, brittle laugh. "As if anything could be worse than this nightmare!"

"Forget it. You aren't going back, and he couldn't do worse than what's already been done."

"What's already . . ." Blinking, she forced herself to focus on her husband's strained features. Something was hurting him, and not just her erratic behavior. It was the one thing that could enable her to shut out the voices, and they began to fade as her concentration increased. "What's happened? Tell me."

"Rodger Latham is offering to sell the *Odyssey* to Tugwell and Kent, our New York clients! They're so anxious to enter the California trade, they're trying to cancel the contract for the ship in the stocks so they can take him up on the offer."

"Can they do it?"

Lock grimaced. "I don't know yet. What they can do is order me to stop construction and hold all of my capital in limbo, starving us slowly into bankruptcy. Rodger's moving his chess pieces around with the skill of a Machiavelli. And Cyrus Tate is surely just another convenient pawn to use against us by upsetting you. It isn't you they're really after, Connie, it's me. Lathams battling McKins, same as always, only now it's to the death."

Dismay tarnished the golden hue of her eyes. "Is there nothing we can do?"

"Tugwell and Kent can't refuse to pay for a ship completed as contracted. Delivering the vessel now could stop the sale of the *Odyssey* and give us some income to work with."

"But it's only half finished. How—?" She broke off with a horrified gasp. "No, Lock, you can't mean . . ."

"It's the only way, Connie. I have to abandon the *Argonaut*."

Her heart twisted with a pang of bitter disappointment and guilt. "But it's your dream!"

"Which will just have to wait, dammit!" His jaw worked. "I'm putting every man I have on the New York commission, every bucket of pitch, every thread of oakum, every timber in the yard. I'll even have Jedediah lathing treenails if that's what it takes. We're going to turn out a ship faster than any yard in the nation and beat Rodger at this filthy game."

"And you need to concentrate on more important things than Crazy Lili's antics," Constance said painfully. "Send me away, Lauchlan. Send me to

Paris or let me stay at Skye, but just help me find a way not to make things harder on you!"

"Now you are talking crazy," Lock replied, his mouth a harsh line. "Seeing Tate upset you, but I'm not letting you run away again."

A tremor rippled down her spine. "I can't seem to remember parts of it, and Mrs. Brack . . . I don't want to hurt anyone, Lock." *Especially you.*

"You're staying and you'll get better again. Is that clear?"

"Sure." The word wobbled dangerously.

With a muffled oath, Lock dragged her into his arms, burying his nose in her hair.

"We'll show them, by God," he said, holding her fiercely. "We'll show them all!"

Constance clung to him, and in her head the banshees were silent just long enough for her to hear the doubt and desperation in Lock's troubled voice.

Chapter 15

The saddest thing in the world, Constance decided, was a discarded dream.

Everywhere she looked, the McKin Brothers Shipyard swarmed with laborers, borers, caulkers, and carpenters. The air reeked of burning pitch and the coal smoke pouring from the deafening steam-driven machinery. Teams of dray horses dragged massive timbers toward the loading ramps, and foremen's shouts and joiners' curses punctuated the incessant hammering. Although it was nearly dusk, the yard was a bustling hive of feverish activity, workers busy everywhere—except for the section where the abandoned hulk of the *Argonaut* stood in silent isolation, stillborn in her cradle.

Work on the *Argonaut* had ended ten days ago, when Lock decided to use every resource to complete Tugwell and Kent's commissioned ship in time to thwart Rodger Latham's scheme. Since the day after Constance's encounter with Cyrus Tate, double crews had worked nearly around the clock, staying as long as the lantern light and their energy allowed each evening and then beginning again at dawn each day. The progress had been truly remarkable, and the launching date, which should have been months away, was now numbered in mere days.

Lock worked the hardest of all, leading the race

to complete the ship informally dubbed "Aunt Tug" for the broad holds and conservative design demanded by the investors. Not that Aunt Tug wouldn't be a fine ship when finished, Constance thought as she watched the scurrying shipyard activity from an out-of-the-way vantage point beside the warehouse office. After all, Aunt Tug was McKin-designed and McKin-built, but her contours looked rather plebeian when compared with what would have been the *Argonaut*'s sleek and aristocratic lines. In contrast to the noisy activity surrounding Aunt Tug, the ramps and work sheds around the *Argonaut* were still and silent and provoked in Constance a sense of desolation that was hard to shake off.

With a dejected sigh, she shifted her empty basket against her hip. She'd had no more of her "lapses," but the fear that any moment something might bring on another one was like trying to walk a tightrope with a case of vertigo. As long as you held yourself carefully and didn't turn your head too fast, you might be all right, but one wrong move and you could end up dizzy and sick again—with disastrous results.

Despite this fear and her husband's misgivings, Constance had insisted she be allowed to do her small part for this grand endeavor by delivering supper each evening to Jedediah and Lock. This evening they'd bolted down their brown bread, baked beans, and fried ham with little time for appreciation, but at least Constance had the satisfaction of seeing them fed. Now on her way to catch the last horsecar home, she let a momentary impulse draw her across the deserted section of the yard, past the piles of timbers and silent scaffolds, for a closer look at the half-finished *Argonaut*.

Though the sun was setting, the temperature and humidity were still sweltering, making even Constance's straight hair curl out of her loose braid. Her

simple summer muslin gown clung to her damp
skin as she picked her way through the litter of
wood chips and sawdust to the secluded side of the
skeleton ship to indulge her morose mood. Though
she understood that finishing Aunt Tug was essential to the shipyard's survival, as well as the means
to keep a roof over their heads, Constance knew in
her heart that the death of Lock's dearest dream
was her fault.

Feeling dwarfed by the immense size of the struc-
ture, she gazed up at the ship's vault of ribs, her
artist's eye scanning the lift and flare of the incom-
plete hull, impressed and pleased by the graceful
and elegant symmetry. There was no doubt about it.
Her husband was an artist and a poet when it came
to clipper ships, and his genius deserved recognition. Somehow, some way, even if it took a miracle,
Lock had to complete his *Argonaut*.

Something rustled and knocked beneath the
shadowy trellis of sholes and stocks and braces.
Frowning, Constance strained to see the cause. No
one was supposed to be working here. "Is anyone
there?"

She hadn't really expected an answer, but all the
same, the silence rattled her. Surely the disturbance
hadn't been in her imagination. That thought shook
her composure even more, and she struggled for
balance. No, this wasn't a mental "lapse." She'd
heard something.

Determined to prove to herself that her mind
wasn't playing tricks again, Constance carefully ne-
gotiated around the supporting timbers and worked
her way down an open work shed running parallel
to the ship. The shed originally housed the manual sawpits, unused since Lock's introduction of
steam-driven saws, and now it stored the most expensive and rare woods—teak, cypress, mahogany—
reserved for the fine interior work. Peering upward
between the ship's half-finished puzzle of stan-

chions and deck beams, Constance saw a shadow
move.

"Who's there?" she demanded again, real alarm
fluttering in her throat.

A movement at the corner of her eye made her
whirl with a startled gasp, to find only emptiness.
Shadows blurred the stacked piles of short, square
timbers under the shed's roof, and an uneasy panic
slipped insidious fingers around her heart.

Rats? she wondered. Perhaps only mischievous
children playing where they shouldn't? Or ... vandals, out to harm Lock's dream! That possibility
made her gasp, and she turned to go to Lock with
the warning.

And stumbled. And felt a pressure. And toppled
with a cry, headfirst over a stack of beams. Her
head smacked sickeningly against something hard,
and she fell, plunging down forever into blackness ...

As black as the inside of an undertaker's hat.

"That sounds like something Alex would say,"
Constance remarked aloud to no one in particular.
Indeed, the bottom of the sawpit was so black she
hadn't been able to tell in the first disconcerting
moments of groggy consciousness whether her eyes
were open or closed. Thankfully, the thick cushion
of composting sawdust she'd landed in had saved
her from worse than a mere knot on the head and
a crushing headache, and reason had won through.

In fact, Constance was quite proud of her calm. A
few minutes' blind exploration discerned the pro-
portions of her surroundings, a trench six by ten
feet square by much higher than she could reach or
even jump, without so much as a handhold or
bos'n's ladder to help her climb out. None of her
cries for help evoked any response, which was not
surprising considering it must be well into the wee
hours and all the laborers were gone.

Chewing on her thumbnail, she realized she was trapped. But she was also philosophical. She wasn't badly hurt. She was in no immediate danger. She wasn't scared of the dark. And sooner or later the sun would come up and somebody would come along to rescue her.

Finding a comfortable corner, she curled up to wait, not really minding the chirrs and squeaks of the insects and other harmless varmints that shared her confinement and her occasional vocal comments. What did worry her was Lock's reaction when she came up missing once again.

Would he be anxious or merely furious? And what explanation for her predicament could she offer him? Constance concentrated on reconstructing the accident in her mind: the shadows, the noises—had they been real or another figment of her imagination? She pondered that question and drowsed until pearly gray light seeped into the top of the pit. The sounds of planks clapping together and irritated mumbling made her scramble up out of the sawdust with a yelp.

"Help! Oh, hello! Is someone there? Please, over here!"

"Jesus, Mary, and Joseph!" A face as wrinkled as a dried apple appeared at the edge of the pit, and Jedediah Shoe's milky eyes strained down into the dimness. "What in heaven's name—is that you, Miss Constance?"

"Yes, Jedediah, yes!" Constance exclaimed in relief.

The old man's hair stood out from his grizzled head like an electrified halo. "What're ye doing down there, child?"

"It was an accident. I fell." *Or someone pushed me.* "Please, Jedediah, find a rope or something. I've been here all night, and Lock must be frantic."

"Right. Hold on." The old man disappeared, then returned almost immediately with a rustic ladder, a pole with crosspieces nailed to it. "Can you manage this?"

"Can I!" Constance hiked up her crumpled skirts and scaled the ladder, falling over the edge of the pit with a gasping laugh just moments later. She let Jedediah help her to her feet, trying to ignore knees that were suddenly wobbly with a delayed reaction. "You see, Jedediah? Just like a monkey up a coconut palm!"

"By Neptune, child!" Thoroughly shaken, Jedediah helped her brush the worst of the wood shavings and sawdust off her skirts. "If I hadn't taken a notion to come after a bit of mahogany this morn, it might have been hours more before you were discovered."

"Lucky for me you're an early riser," Constance said, and dropped a grateful kiss on the old man's cheek. "Nothing else has happened? No harm done to the *Argonaut* or Aunt Tug?"

"No, o' course not. What makes you ask?"

Constance hesitated, unwilling to voice nebulous suspicions that might sound ridiculous or crazy. Since the vandals—if that was what they were— hadn't succeeded in causing any damage, there was no use arousing unnecessary alarm. She could share her misgivings with Lock later.

"Ah—nothing, Jedediah." She pushed her fingers through her tangled hair and winced.

"You're hurt!"

Touching the lump on her head gingerly, Constance found her hair slightly matted with dried blood from her scraped scalp. "Just a bump on the head. I'm all right, but I must find Lock."

"Come on, then."

Jedediah gave Constance his arm, but it was uncertain who was leaning on whom as they picked their way across the shipyard. A few laborers were just beginning to appear like ghosts through the mist rising off the harbor. At Jedediah's insistence,

Constance found herself waiting in the privacy of the empty molding loft with a bracing cup of tea in her hand.

"Lock's likely turning the town upside down looking for ye, but he'll come here sooner or later. It'd be a daft thing to have ye making circles trying to find each other," Jedediah said firmly. "And I'm not so sure that bump of yours doesn't need a doctor."

"I'm fine, really."

"Nevertheless, you'll stay put whilst I send the lads round to find yer husband." With that final admonition, Jedediah hobbled off down the stairs.

The tea did much to restore Constance, as did a trip to the water closet to tidy herself and rebraid her hair. But her concern over Lock prevented her from relaxing completely. As the huge loft brightened, she paced up and down the black-painted floor, now bare of all its colorful markings. On an impulse born of growing agitation, she grabbed a chunk of blue chalk from a box on a drawing board, knelt down, and began to doodle.

At first it was simply a way to fill the minutes of waiting, just an experiment in lines and curves and odd shapes, but then pictures began to take form, and she found herself reaching for the chalk box, choosing different colors, blending and shading and creating on her hands and knees. She was so engrossed she almost didn't hear the heavy tread of boots taking the stairs two at a time.

Constance looked up as Lock burst through the door of the molding loft, and her hand froze over her drawing. His features were controlled, his expression even, but there was a stark look in his blue eyes she'd never seen before. Even as she sat back on her heels in the center of her design, that look was veiled, but she'd seen it, and she knew what it was.

Lock came to a halt on the fringe of her drawing,

still clad in the same stained work clothes from the day before, his jaw shadowed by dark stubble and his voice husky from lack of sleep. "You're the most inappropriate woman I've ever known."

What she'd seen gave her the confidence to answer coolly, with just a trace of a challenge. "Oh?"

"Any other female would be in hysterics after a night spent in a hole. Instead, you're playing like a child."

Her lips tilted slightly. "I like to save my hysterics for more dramatic and memorable occasions."

He scanned the colorful pictures spread out around her, a spangled rainbow of flamboyant birds, lush jungle, rushing water. "Is this your idea of paradise?"

Rising, Constance examined the picture solemnly, then shook her head. "No. You're not in it."

Swifter than thought, Lock stepped into the charmed circle and caught Constance tightly in his arms. "I am now."

And then he kissed her fiercely, so hard he hurt her. She let him, making no demur, knowing he needed the reassurance, more than glad to take it herself.

When he lifted his head, both of them were breathing unsteadily, their bodies throbbing with the hunger that never failed to stir them.

"Jedediah told me what happened," Lock said against her throat. "Are you all right?"

"Yes. Now I am." Constance rubbed her hands over his back, soothing the tightly corded muscles beneath his white cotton shirt, wishing she could sink into his skin.

"I've been everywhere. The police, Elspeth, Maggie . . ."

Her lips nibbled at the angle of his jaw. "I know. I'm sorry."

Lock framed her face with his palms. His hands

trembled. "I was afraid." The admission seemed wrenched from his depths. "God, I thought—"

"That I was doing it again," she finished softly. "But it wasn't that way, Lock. Not this time. Someone was skulking around the *Argonaut*. I was coming to tell you when I was pushed into the sawpit. I don't know if it was intentional or an accident."

A muscle in the corner of his mouth jumped. "You don't have to do this, Connie. You don't have to make things up. I understand."

A chill went through her. "I told you, it wasn't like that. This was real."

Lock released her and dragged his hand through his hair in exasperation and resignation. "All right. Whatever you say."

"You don't believe me." She gave a tiny laugh. "Well, I can't blame you. But I can't even care, because I learned something very important down in that pit."

Lock cast her a suspicious glance. "What was that?"

"That I'm stronger than I thought. I survived a bump on the head and all night in the dark without losing my mind. And I could do it again if necessary. I might even be able to sort through the haze in my head." Her eyes went smoky with stubborn determination. "Even if you don't believe me, Lauchlan McKin. Even if I have to do it alone."

She turned away, but Lock caught her wrist. "Damn you, don't shut me out. I went through hell last night worrying, wondering ..."

Her anger melted away, and she pressed against his chest, murmuring. "Oh, Lock ..."

He pulled her hips against his, letting her feel his arousal, making her gasp, then catching the sound with his own pillaging mouth. His palms cupped her breasts; then he tugged at her skirts, pulling them both down onto the colorful chalk drawings, his intentions plain.

Thrilled, shocked, excited, she exalted in her ability to push the limits of his control even while she protested. "Lock, we can't! Someone will come . . ."

"I gave orders." He groaned against her throat, then began to fumble with his trouser buttons. He gasped as her nimble fingers helped him, brushing that most heated part of him with fleeting and maddening caresses. "No one will disturb us while I'm seeing to your state of . . . mind."

"My mind is quite sound. It's my husband who's totally demented!" Provocatively, she opened her thighs and tugged at Lock's hips, whispering in her throat, "But I'll never reveal it if you'll just come here."

"Damn you, woman," he repeated, capturing her lips again with a hungry mating sound as their bodies moved together.

And Constance laughed in triumph even as she surrendered, for she knew what he really meant by that inarticulate curse. In the stark moment when he'd first seen her, for an instant his feelings had been totally revealed, and she'd known then that he loved her.

The Iron Man was hers, and someday, she vowed as she took him into her body, someday, if life had any meaning and the gods were kind, he'd be able to admit it.

The tiny silver bell over the door of The Attic tinkled merrily when Constance entered the cluttered, busy bookshop two afternoons later.

"My dear, there you are!" Elspeth Philpot bustled around the wide counter, caught Constance's lace-gloved hands in her own, and kissed both her cheeks in welcome. "And looking none the worse for a night in a dreadful hole, thank the good Lord!"

"Your note sounded so disturbed, I hurried right over to show you I'm perfectly fine." Constance pir-

ouetted, making the soft skirts of her yellow promenade gown billow becomingly. Her pert bonnet of
blond straw sported blue ribbons and rosettes.
"See? It was just a minor mishap."

"Even though Mr. McKin let me know you were
safe, the whole city's talking about your adventure,
and it's a relief to see you with my own eyes,"
Elspeth replied warmly.

"It actually may have done me more good than
harm," Constance said with a twinkle of mischief,
and a peachy tide of color washed her cheeks.

Before Elspeth could demand an explanation, a
gentleman customer waiting at the counter cleared
his throat impatiently. She gave Constance's hand a
pat and whispered under her breath, "There's . . .
ah, something I wish you to see in the history section. You go have a look while I tend to this sale."

Constance nodded, then wandered past other
customers through the maze of shoulder-high bookshelves, admiring the latest novels and publications,
inhaling the scent of printer's ink and crisp paper.
Perhaps one day soon her own *Sandwich Islands
Sketchbook* would be numbered among Elspeth's inventory.

At the rear of the shop, she paused before a table
loaded with history books, wondering which of
them Elspeth particularly wanted her to see. A
heavy volume slid off one of Elspeth's more precarious piles to land on the plank flooring with a solid
thud. Constance reached for it.

"Here, let me."

She glanced up at the gruff offer, but her thanks
died on her tongue at the sight of an old man with
a silver ruff of whiskers leaning on an ivory-
handled cane. The sweetness of peppermint tickled
her nose, and surprise made her voice faint.

"Alex."

"Don't go getting the vapors on me, girl," he ordered brusquely, shoving the tome into her unresisting hands. His attitude was a trifle belligerent. "Just come for my reading matter, same as you. A man in retirement has a lot of time to fill."

"Oh." She tried to summon up the feelings of resentment and anger that seeing the old curmudgeon again should have produced, but she found it impossible around a sudden dull ache in her heart. "Yes, of course. I—I hope you've been keeping well?"

It was as close to a question about his health as she could come under the circumstances. Alex gave a snort.

"Other than having a preacher in the house to keep my dyspepsia in an uproar, I'm as hale as ever."

"I'm glad of it," she said with absolute sincerity.

"Heard talk about your accident." Alex's words were so staccato they were nearly a bark. His tobacco-brown eyes raked her from bonnet to instep. "No harm done, I see."

"No. I was lucky." Constance shook her head and swallowed on a foolish lump of emotion. Was it possible Alex had actually been concerned enough to seek out neutral ground to investigate her condition for himself?

Over Alex's shoulder she caught sight of Elspeth watching them from the front counter and sent her meddling friend a "why-didn't-you-warn-me?" look. Sheepish, Elspeth lifted her plump shoulders in a "what-could-I-say?" shrug that denied all responsibility.

"Shipyard's no place for a fool woman, anyway," Alex grumbled, digging invisible pockmarks into the floor with his cane. "Even McKin should know better than that, but Lauchlan's always had more pride than sense."

"It wasn't Lock's fault," Constance protested.

"Someone was trying to damage the *Argonaut*, but I got in the way."

Even as she spoke the words, she reached a sudden conclusion. The inexplicable rash of accidents, the unwarranted difficulties, the unwelcome intruders she'd surprised—all were just continued manifestations of Latham malice. Now anger seemed justified, and she glared at Alex.

"Competition is one thing, but I never thought you and Rodger would carry vengeance so far as to stoop to sabotage!"

"What!" Alex squawked indignantly. "What are you talking about?"

She told him, recounting the problems in the shipyard.

"What drivel! I absolutely deny any involvement in such a scheme," Alex stated emphatically.

"But can you speak for your nephew?" Constance asked.

Alex hesitated. "Rodger is above such pettiness. Besides, you have no proof."

"Do you deny that Latham and Company has offered Tugwell and Kent the *Odyssey* to induce them to renege on their McKin Brothers contract?" Constance asked. "You planned to use the *Odyssey* for the California trade yourself, yet you're sacrificing a huge profit to strike at the heart of Lock's business. Worse than that, he's been forced to lay down his tools on the *Argonaut* in order to deal with the situation. Do not tell me Lathams aren't ruthless!"

Alex scratched at his whiskers, scowling. "I've heard nothing of this."

The fire went out of Constance's wrath, and she gave a mirthless laugh. "You mean that jackdaw Rodger has come up with a scheme like this all on his own? I did not think him capable of it."

Alex chewed his lip and grimaced, muttering to himself. "Nor I. Damn fool! We don't sacrifice the company's profits for mere revenge—ever. If he's done so, he'll have to answer to me."

"Then don't discount that he's had people using petty harassment to hamper work at the shipyard. I believe I ran afoul of one of his nastier attempts, and since I had gone down to look at the *Argonaut* strictly on my own, my 'accident' was certainly none of Lock's fault!"

Alex gave another snort. "Having experienced your penchant for devilment firsthand, I can believe that. He ought to beat you."

Her expression went glacial. "He doesn't."

Slamming the book down on the table, she turned away. Alex cursed under his breath and caught her elbow.

"Dammit, girl! I only meant—" He looked at her stiff, averted features and heaved a sigh. "Does the McKin treat you kindly, then?"

Constance glanced at Alex warily, then spoke the truth. "Most kindly. I love him."

"I see." Alex let go of her elbow. "That's something, then."

"It's everything to me," Constance admitted in a low voice. "And . . . and whether I'm a true Latham or not, I wish this feud with the McKins could end. It's such a waste of goods and talent and emotion. Why, both families could accomplish so much more if it weren't for this eternal quarreling!"

" 'Tis too much to expect," Alex said heavily. "Too much hate and too many years have been invested to ever turn it back."

"That's a terrible thing to believe."

"Yes." Alex's dark-eyed gaze focused on the silver oval hanging around Constance's throat. Involuntarily, she touched the locket, and shivered at the feel of the cool metal between her fingers.

"I—I suppose you'd like this back." Swallowing hard, she reached for the clasp at her nape.

"No!" Alex's sharp bark turned heads in the

bookstore, and he bent closer, lowering his voice to a gravelly murmur. "Keep it. It's been a part of your life too long for me to expect it back now."

"But it once belonged to your wife . . ."

"Keep it, I said."

She covered the locket with her fist, unsure what to make of his generous gesture, yet grateful. The locket was a tie to something intangible, locked behind the wall in her head, but it was still an important symbol, and she would have been loath to give it up. "Thank you."

Alex's jaw worked, and finally a question he could not contain burst from him. "You aren't my son's child, are you?"

Sorrowfully, Constance shrugged. "My memories are . . . uncertain. The only thing I really know is how I feel."

"And how is that?"

She drew a shuddering breath and, blinking hard, turned away with a strangled sound. "I'm sorry, Alex."

He caught her elbow in a firm grip. "Tell me, girl. I must have something."

Constance raised her troubled golden eyes to his, and her voice was a raw whisper. "You always *felt* like my grandfather."

Alex jerked back, turned, and walked stiffly out of the bookstore without a backward glance. But Constance had seen the astonishing sheen of moisture in his brown eyes, and she knew they both wept for lost dreams.

"I tell you, the old fool was seen talking to her like nothing had ever happened!"

"My dear friend, calm yourself," the Reverend Cyrus Tate advised. He folded his slim white hands on his crossed knee and leaned back in a tall, thronelike armchair.

"Mark me. The bitch is trying to get back into

Uncle Alex's good graces." Rodger Latham gritted his teeth and paced back and forth on the imported French rug.

The upstairs sitting room of Latham House was heavily draped against the bright June sunshine, making it a dim but stiflingly hot sanctuary. The closeness was accentuated by the overpowering scents of ginger water and hair pomade, but neither of the two men engaged in earnest conversation noticed.

"Why such foreboding? You're in control of Latham and Company now, aren't you?" Tate asked in his cool, soothing voice.

"For all intents and purposes, though the canny old fox is holding back from signing over the final block of his voting stock. Not enough to tie my hands completely, you understand, but just enough to keep tabs."

"I'd say you have nothing to fear, then."

Rodger made a sound of disgust. "The old man's becoming so soft and senile, he's liable to get a sudden case of sentiment just because Constance—or whoever she really is—got knocked about a bit."

"Lili has always had a knack for turning up at the most inconvenient moments."

"Too bad those clod-fisted hooligans botched the business at the shipyard, eh?" Rodger jammed his fists into his trouser pockets. "Could have eliminated several problems at a single blow if the luck had been better."

"Unfortunate, that." Tate's softly spoken commiseration gave no indication whether his sympathies lay with the injured woman or the spoiled scheme.

Rodger scowled. "And now McKin's posted guards, of all things! Damn his eyes! Who'd have thought he could finish the Tugwell contract so quickly? But he hasn't wiggled out of this tight spot yet. Not if I have anything to do with it, by God!"

A soft tap interrupted his angry tirade, and a

spare female figure carried in a heavy silver coffee tray. The servant wore a smocked apron, and her colorless hair was scraped back in a bun. She filled two cups with competent movements and handed one to each man. Her left hand bore a gauze bandage.

"Thank you, Mrs. Brack," the Reverend Tate said softly.

Gray eyes flicked over the two men. "Of course, sir. Will there be anything else?"

"Leave us." Rodger waved her out with a brusque gesture. The woman nodded and quietly let herself out of the room.

"She's not as comely as our last maid," Rodger remarked after the door had closed behind her, "but she's damned efficient."

"A trustworthy servant is a prize beyond measure," the Reverend Tate agreed evenly. He admired the translucent china cup for a moment, then sipped his coffee with vast sensual appreciation. With a contented sigh, he moved his pink gaze to Rodger, studying him with much the same concentrated appraisal as he had given to the cup.

"So what do you intend to do now?" he asked at last.

Rodger set his cup aside with a careless clatter, and his sulky mouth hardened. "Whatever I have to do. McKin's practically on his knees, and I intend to make him pay a hundredfold for every humiliation he's dealt me. The last thing I need now is Uncle Alex's interference over this woman!"

"Poor Lili is a very unstable person. Your uncle no doubt feels a certain Christian charity toward such an unfortunate soul, but she is no real threat to anyone but herself. After all, her demented state can only get worse."

Rodger looked skeptical. "You think so?"

Tate smiled sadly. "I've seen it over and over."

"That's still no guarantee." Rodger made a fist

and ground it into his palm. "I want to break McKin, drive him into bankruptcy just like Uncle Alex did his father. That will prove to the old man I deserve full control of Latham and Company."

"As your spiritual counselor, Rodger, I advise you to place your trust in the Lord and let Him do the rest."

"But there must be something more—"

"You've done everything humanly possible to make your uncle proud of you." Tate smiled again, and his unnatural eyes held the unsettling gleam of a fanatic. "Believe me. It will take more than a miracle to save any of them now."

Chapter 16

❝It's a gol-danged miracle, that's what it is!"
Jedediah whooped. "Just look at 'er!"

"Good God," Lock breathed.

Down the cobbled length of Long Wharf, stevedores sweated under the bright summer sun, sailors
shouted over the screech of tackle and the flap of
furling sails, and dray horses whinnied against the
traces of wagons loaded to the sky with hogsheads
of goods from every nation. At the distant foot of
the wharf where State Street began, the monolithic
bulk of the Custom House rose in Doric splendor,
the fluted columns of Quincy granite a soaring tes-
tament to Boston's position as a bustling hub of
commercial trade.

But Lock was oblivious of the pandemonium, and
unconsciously gripped Constance's hand tighter. He
strained to see the proud vessel easing toward
the dock through a thicket of ships' masts, tracing
the lines of her hull from bowsprit to gaff, lines that
were as familiar to him as the creases in his own
face.

"By God, Dylan!" he swore again softly, his usual
stoic calm replaced by a growing jubilation. "You
jug-eared son of a mermaid. You did it!"

"It *is* the *West Wind*." Constance's voice trembled
with wonder and something not so easily defined.

"Not even due for another month!" Jedediah

chortled gleefully. Despite his advanced years, he all but danced a jig on the cobbled wharf. "And *ye* didn't want to believe the semaphore signal from Boston Light saying she'd arrived, did you, my fine laddie? Had to be convinced to come meet yer own brother, and him what's set a new record for the China run!"

"I'm a skeptic by trade, you old seadog," Lock admitted as a grin cracked open his face from ear to ear.

"But ye believe yer own eyes now?" Jedediah demanded with a delighted cackle. "Ye know what it means, don't ye?"

Lock's grin grew even wider, and he loosed a totally uncharacteristic shout of joy. "Hell, yes! It means little brother's saved my freckled arse!"

Constance gasped incredulously. "Lock!"

Laughing at her astounded expression, he grabbed her and kissed her hard, nearly knocking her straw bonnet off in his enthusiasm. "Yours, too, beloved, and a lovely one it is, too!" he whispered wickedly.

Constance's expression reflected both shock and delight at her husband's exuberant display. During the week since her night in the sawpit, he'd been grimly absorbed, either working hard on Aunt Tug or ensconced with his ledgers and books until the wee hours. Now his jubilation was infectious, and she blushed and beamed back at him.

The dock shuddered faintly as the *West Wind* came alongside, and seamen leaped to secure the ship with fat ropes the thickness of a man's arm. Lock's heart drummed in his chest, and he felt light-headed, as if he'd drunk too much applejack brandy. He moved before the sailors had finished, eagerness hurrying his steps until he was practically running, dragging Constance in his wake, Jedediah hobbling along after.

By God, it was a damned miracle, and none too

soon, either! There hadn't been two days' worth of wages left in the McKin Brothers account, and no way to beg, borrow, or steal what he needed to finish Aunt Tug, even though she was almost ready to go to the rigging yard. He'd been deadlocked, stymied, and at the bottom of a pit blacker than the one Constance had fallen into, pushed by circumstances and Latham malice to the brink of a failure that would outshine even his dead father's bankruptcy.

But salvation was at hand! Unless he missed his guess, the *West Wind* bore the season's first and finest China tea, and with that lucrative cargo, the means to bail the shipyard out of all its difficulties. Lock hadn't allowed himself even to think about the *West Wind*, knowing that to count on something would only lead to disappointment—but now! With the impatience of a child, he drew up short, waiting for the seamen to lay down the gangway, searching for a familiar face.

"Lock!"

A tall figure in a blue jacket and a captain's billed hat waved broadly from the deck, then strode down the still-vibrating gangplank. Lock met him at the bottom, and the two men clasped hands hard. Dark brown eyes, crinkled at the corners in a seaman's perpetual squint, met Lock's intent blue gaze, and they stared at each other for a silent and solemn assessment.

"Safe and home again, is it?" Lock asked gruffly, searching for changes in the face that was like his own, yet different.

"Yes, praise God." A slash of a dimple creased the bronzed cheek with a cocky grin. "Sorry I'm late."

That absurdity broke the ice, and Lock threw back his head and roared, then caught his brother in a hearty bear hug. There was a great deal of thumping and back-pounding as the manly rituals of greeting were performed.

"Blessed saints, Dylan, but you're a gladsome sight!" Lock said at last, less concerned for the moment about the relief the *West Wind*'s arrival represented. He was filled with simple gratitude for his only living relative's safe return from a hazardous circumnavigation of the globe. His hands on his brother's shoulders, Lock inspected the younger man.

They were of a similar height, though Dylan was a hairbreath narrower in the shoulders than Lock, and they both bore their mother's elegant yet determined jawline. Dylan's mischievous eyes were the color of coffee, and his straight, shaggy hair and luxurious sideburns a tobacco brown, bleached by the tropical sun to a slightly lighter hue on the ends. Clean-shaven and handsome, Dylan had a wide, reckless smile that exuded charm, as well as an openness and warmth that contrasted with Lock's usually cool and reserved manner. In his own way, each man was a force to be reckoned with, and the manner in which Dylan had brought the *West Wind* home bespoke volumes not only about his nautical talents but also about his skill, despite his relative youth, as a captain able to wring the utmost effort from his crew and vessel.

"It's good to be home," Dylan said, his own voice suspiciously husky. He affectionately clouted Lock's shoulder in an awkward and endearing male fashion. "I missed you. But not your eternal lectures!"

Lock feinted as though boxing Dylan's ear. "Quiet, young'un! Have some respect for your elders."

"Never!" Dylan said with a laugh. "Except for this oldster. Still dodging the widow-maker, eh, Jedediah?"

"I'll outlive you, ye claptrap rowdy!" Jedediah returned without heat. They shook hands, Dylan taking care not to squeeze the old man's painfully gnarled knuckles too hard, while Jedediah inspected him astutely. "Ye didn't come a-sailing into Boston Harbor like the Queen of Sheby a full month ahead of schedule without having taken chances that coulda killed ye."

Dylan scratched his temple, his mouth quirking. "Aye, but only a few. Lord, but she's a game ship! You should have seen her fly around the Horn, Lock. The *West Wind's* done you proud, even if I did break nearly every spare spar in that last blow!"

"You feckless hound," Lock said, shaking his head. "I'd wring your neck for risking the *West Wind* if I weren't so glad to see you! Like it or not, this time I'll have to admit your rashness has paid off just when we need it most."

Dylan's eyes narrowed. "There's trouble, then?"

"Nothing we can't handle now, thanks to you." Lock clapped Dylan's shoulder. "I'll explain it all."

"I'm eager to hear any tale that's landed the McKin in hot water," Dylan teased. "There's a few things I need—" He caught sight of Constance hovering uncertainly in the background and broke off with a surprised exclamation. "Jesus! Is it—?"

She squeezed the strings of her reticule in a ferocious grasp, nodding, her golden-brown eyes wide and uncertain. "Yes."

Dylan's face changed, and he brushed past Lock and Jedediah as if in a daze. He stopped in front of Constance, raking her from her smoothly coiffed sable locks beneath the pert bonnet to her lace-trimmed lavender hems in amazement and growing approval. His dark brown regard returned to her strained face, her white teeth tugging nervously at her lower lip, and his expression softened. Dragging off his hat, he opened his arms.

"Don't you know me, *cara?*" he asked gently.

Something painful twisted in Constance's face. With a soft cry she reached for him, shuddering against his chest as he hugged her tightly. Her voice was almost a sob. "Dylan."

Lock stiffened, taken aback by the almost tangible flow of emotion surrounding the two embracing figures, unnerved by the surge of jealousy that writhed in his gut like a serpent—against his own brother! He'd almost forgotten it had been Dylan's mischief that had started them all down this circuitous road. But what kind of bond made Dylan bend his head so solicitously to murmur into Constance's ear? And why did she allow him to hold her so close and protectively as she answered him in equally soft tones?

Though Lock told himself it was curiosity and not jealousy, he stepped forward to put an end to the reunion. "If you're quite finished—"

Dylan raised his gaze and met his brother's icy glower head-on.

"Let me savor this miracle just a bit." He touched Constance's cheek, then grinned. "I had not thought to see this sweet *wahine* so soon, much less looking quite so beautiful."

"I see your charming ways have not deserted you, Captain." Constance eased free of Dylan's arms, but her answering smile was both fond and grateful, and it grated on Lock's nerves.

"I'll remind you," he snapped at Dylan, "that her being here is your doing, and there have been occasions when I swore I'd pound you for all the trouble you started."

"Don't harangue me about feuds and blood wars, Lock. Latham or no, I had no choice but to send her to you, the state she was in."

"What state?" Lock demanded sharply.

Constance's expression flickered, but she squared her shoulders and answered evenly. "The state of my back, not my mind, Lauchlan."

"Tate," he hissed between his teeth, understanding.

"Aye, she was sore distressed when we fished her out of Lahaina Harbor," Dylan agreed gravely.

A look flashed between Dylan and Constance that caught Lock square in the chest with a bolt of unexpected envy. Appalled at himself, he noticed with growing chagrin Jedediah's watchful assessment and ruthlessly clamped down on this shameful wave of roiling irrationality, taking refuge behind a wall of cool sarcasm.

"And you could think of nothing else but to send her here?" he demanded. "With never a thought to what trouble you might be stirring up? Tell me another one, laddie."

Dylan shrugged, his lips lifting in an unrepentant smile. "You live too sheltered a life by far anyway, brother. Besides, with her family in Boston, Captain Jenkins sailing on the next tide, and no way for her to stay in Lahaina for fear of her life, what else could I do? Fair man that you are, I knew you'd do the right thing. And I see she's fared well enough. Is this old man Latham's doing, lass? Have you truly found safe harbor at last?"

Constance flung Lock a mutinous glance, stung at being called "trouble." She shrugged carelessly. "Perhaps."

Firmly, Lock took Constance's elbow, and gave Dylan a baleful, challenging look. "Constance is my wife."

Dylan's jaw dropped; then after a moment he began to laugh. "Snared you with her winsome ways, did she, Iron Man? Hell, that's one damned effective way to end the feud between the Lathams and the McKins!"

"Not exactly."

Puzzled, Dylan looked from face to face.

"She isn't a Latham," Lock explained in a tight voice.

"Or maybe I am," Constance quipped, her flippancy holding a trace of defiance. At a loss, Dylan stared at them both.

"Perhaps you'd better start at the beginning," he said slowly. "It appears I've got some catching up to do."

Constance drew her brush through her hair, then turned from her seat at the dressing table to watch her husband strip off his shirt. She usually enjoyed the opportunity to admire Lock's muscular physique, the quiet touches and bedtime rituals that led to other things, but ever since they'd said good night to Dylan downstairs, Lock had been withdrawn and preoccupied.

"Are you still worried?" she asked.

Seated on the side of the bed, Lock paused with one shoe in his hand. "What?"

"After Dylan's cargo is sold, it won't matter even if Rodger does sell Tugwell the *Odyssey*, will it?"

"No." Lock drew off the other shoe and dropped it on the rug, then slid out of the rest of his clothes and stretched out on the bed with a tired sigh. "If Tugwell fails to live up to our agreement, we'll simply sell Aunt Tug ourselves. We'll have the capital to float it now, and a buyer shouldn't be hard to find, considering the *West Wind*'s run from Canton."

Nodding, Constance set her brush down on the dressing table with a solid thump of satisfaction, and pride shone in her eyes as she smiled at her husband. "A truly remarkable accomplishment for both you and Dylan. Every merchant will now be after you to build them a fleet ship, but the most important thing is that you can finish the *Argonaut*."

"Yes." With his arms crossed behind his head, Lock's expression was distant, even somewhat grim, in the soft glow of the oil lamp.

Rising, Constance tightened the sash of her favored Chinese robe over her muslin nightgown, then sat down beside Lock on the edge of the bed.

"You've won, Lock, you and Dylan. I'm so very glad." When he made no reply, she frowned and lay her palm against his chest, stroking the delineation of his breastbone. "What is it?"

"I've decided to keep the double crews going until the *Argonaut* is in the water. I'm not taking any chances on leaving her unfinished again."

A trill of alarm tickled Constance's spine. "You think there will be more trouble?"

"I don't think Rodger Latham is the type to give up a vendetta just because we've managed to pull the fat out of the fire this time. He's too stubborn—or stupid—to forget a humiliation."

Remembering Alex's reaction when she'd spoken of Rodger's machinations, Constance thought the senior Latham would agree with that assessment. It seemed politic not to mention it to Lock, however, so she made her voice mild.

"Then you'll have to be vigilant, but isn't this what you've always wanted? To build the ship that will prove McKin vessels are the best in the world?"

And for Enoch McKin's son to erase the shame of his father's failure.

But she couldn't say that, so she merely tugged at the springy black curls thatching Lock's chest to emphasize her words. "You told me once the *Argonaut* will make your name."

Lock's lips twisted. "Forget that. It's all just business. And although Dylan's cargo will put things back on an even keel for us financially, the stakes remain high, and there's no leeway for error or ill fortune. Outfitting both the *Argonaut* and the *West Wind* as soon as possible can cushion us against future attacks. I do not relish the prospect of living on the edge of disaster for any longer than is absolutely necessary."

"I can't believe you and Dylan are already planning his next departure," she complained with a sulky pout. "Why, he only just arrived!"

Lock clamped his hand over her wrist, stilling her explorations. "After having me bend his ear all day to bring him up-to-date on you and the Lathams, my brother realizes the precariousness of our situation still, even if you don't."

"I didn't mean that," she protested, giving him a reproachful look. She blamed herself enough for adding to his woes without Lock piling on extra guilt.

"If Dylan takes to the tea route by early July, he'll miss the worst weather around the Horn. That's not long to raise a cargo and prepare for a voyage, so our work is cut out for us. I'm sorry if that interferes with your reunion."

Constance frowned, disliking his insinuating tone. She tugged on her captured wrist, to no avail. "I don't know what you mean."

Lock's blue eyes narrowed, and his voice was low and harsh. "What exactly is my brother to you?"

Constance jumped. "A friend."

"Don't lie about it, Connie. You damned near strangled in your eagerness to invite him to stay here."

"He's your brother, for God's sake!" she exclaimed, exasperated. "Of course I offered him our hospitality."

Using his great strength, Lock dragged her across his chest until they were nose to nose. "I saw the way you looked at each other. Tell me."

Her eyes widened incredulously. "You're jealous? Of Dylan?"

"You're mine, dammit, and there are rules of propriety—"

"You perishing clod!" Constance spluttered indignantly, leaning her elbows against his chest. "It's hard to remember etiquette when you're half drowned, bleeding, and buck naked!"

"Christ Almighty!"

Constance raised her fist and thumped him

soundly in the center of his chest. "Of course there's some feeling between us! He was kind, and he saved my life. I don't tend to forget things like that."

"Well, I saved your life, too!" Lock half shouted, half wheezed. "Damnation! What does that make me?"

"A bullheaded fool!" She jabbed him viciously with her elbow just below his ribs, and was rewarded when he yelped and let her go. Springing to her feet, she shook her dark hair back and glared at him.

"Dylan understands me, as if I'd known him all my life. It's something sweet and uncomplicated and giving, with nothing of romance about it. You're the only man who—" Constance broke off, her face crimson, and shook her head. "I—I can't explain our friendship more than that, but don't make it into something it's not! Better than anyone, you know nothing could possibly have gone on between Dylan and me of a . . . an intimate nature. And it's certainly not now!"

Lock swung his bare feet over the edge of the bed, sitting up and rubbing the sore spots on his chest. "Life's taught me caution, princess, and I won't have you and your damned outrageous shenanigans setting my brother and me against each other."

"How dare you even think such a thing?" she demanded, haughty and commanding in the flame-colored robe. "And what right do you have to dictate to me in such a fashion?"

Lock's mouth fell open in his astonishment, and a dark red color suffused his cheeks. "You're my *wife*, goddammit!"

"But not your possession! And I refuse to be just a convenience for you to use every time a lusty urge strikes."

"I'm not the only one who's found pleasure in our marriage bed," he snapped, rising to his feet.

"Perhaps I can copy a form letter from Mrs. Farrar's etiquette manual to properly express my gratitude," she said nastily. "But don't blame Dylan for something that has nothing to do with him. And don't use propriety or husbandly rights to excuse your own cowardice!"

"Holy saints above!" Lock scrubbed his face in total exasperation. "What the hell are you talking about now?"

"About you, Lock McKin. About a man who's so afraid of his feelings he can't admit he cares for his own wife!"

They stared at each other for an endless moment, chests heaving, mouths clamped in angry lines. Constance waited for some sign that she'd pierced his armor, some tremor, a single word—but there was nothing. With a small, maddened sound, she stormed toward the door.

"I may be crazy, Lock McKin," she flung at him, "but I'm not blind!"

"Where the devil are you going?"

"To paint, since sleep is beyond me at the moment!"

"Constance—"

She paused on the threshold, her back turned and her head bent, her hand showing white knuckles where it rested on the door casing. The angry timbre of her voice dropped to a broken murmur.

"It's wrong of me to ask for what you cannot give. Leave me be a while, Lock. I'll only run as far as the studio this time, I promise."

When he did not answer, she quietly pulled the door shut behind her, then went downstairs through the dark house toward the sanctuary of the back parlor. A single lamp burned low in the front sitting room, and as she passed the opening into the hall, a deep voice from within made her jump.

"From the sound of it, that was quite a row," Dylan said. He rose from the depths of Lock's shabby armchair, his neckcloth dangling from his unbuttoned collar. "Anything I can do?"

"No." Constance hugged her upper arms and shook her head. "It—it wasn't important. Forgive us for disturbing you. I thought I'd work a while to . . . to cool my humors."

"Aye." Dylan nodded in understanding as he joined her in the hall. "Lock is a great one for inducing choler. He's so cool and logical it'll fair make you bust. As a lad, I was accustomed to working off my frustrations splitting firewood. Damned uncomfortable job. Part of the reason I took to the sea so early in life."

Constance couldn't suppress a snort of watery laughter. "A rather drastic solution."

Dylan gestured at the studio door. "Mind if I see what you're doing?"

"Only if you're up to denying a bushel of suspicions if Lock finds us together." She threw open the door, then padded around the room lighting the gas fixtures, the silk of the scarlet Chinese robe whispering about her ankles.

"So that's what it was about." Dylan grinned as the gaslights brightened his countenance. "Me."

"You needn't look so smug, Captain McKin," Constance said severely. "It's insulting as well as damned inconvenient."

With jerky, irritated movements, she fetched brushes and paints, then went to work on the half-finished background of a ship's portrait of Aunt Tug. She felt recovered enough now to follow up on inquiries about such portraits, and creating a career for herself in Boston was still a goal. The first smooth stroke of color across the canvas had an immediate tranquilizing effect, and she began to feel a bit more calm.

"Hadn't you realized younger siblings live to bedevil their older brothers?" Dylan asked, inspecting the paintings lined up along the walls. "Good Lord, Constance—I had no idea you were this talented. Though I must admit some of your subject matter is definitely . . . intriguing."

"Thank you. Madness can be quite inspiring. As can anger." She slapped paint against the canvas. "Sometimes your brother is so damned infuriating!"

"One of his most lovable characteristics," Dylan agreed mildly. "And you are in love with him, aren't you?"

Her brush hovered in midair; then, in a tone so soft Dylan had to strain to hear her, she confessed, "Sometimes I think my heart will burst with it."

"Umm. Thought you might be. Pity. They don't call him the Iron Man for nothing."

Constance's brush slipped heedlessly across the expanse of ocean, spoiling a line of breakers. With a trembling cry, she shoved the palette and brush onto her worktable and dropped her face into her hands.

Alarmed, Dylan hastily set down a painting and turned to her. "Constance?"

She took a deep breath and lifted her face. "I'm all right. I've so much to be thankful for. Lock is kind to me, and tolerant of my . . . eccentricities." She cast a sharp look at Dylan. "He told you?"

"Some of it." Dylan shrugged. "Says you scared him a couple of times, and that's some admission. You're getting better, he says."

"Yes." She took a deep breath and carefully let it out. "I am."

"Do you care that you're not a Latham?"

She shook her head. "Not so much anymore. Lock's all the family I need, yet . . . yet I was becoming fond of Alex."

"Now that's eccentric!" Dylan teased, his dark eyes flashing with humor. "From what I know, the old man's a wag and a half."

"But lonely."

"Like Lock."

She nodded, looking inward. "Yes. Sometimes Lock is very much alone. Oh, Dylan, what am I going to do? Your brother is good to me, and I love him with all my heart, but I want more. I want it all."

Dylan paced, hands jammed in his trouser pockets. He stifled a sigh. "Maybe in time. My father was a hard man, with no warmth for either of his sons, no matter how hard we tried to please him. I always thought Lock somehow blamed himself for Father's death. I was too young to feel the slurs and stares and shame afterward as Lock did. When our world fell apart, he kept us fed and saw to my schooling and his own while he worked as a caulker in what had been our own shipyard. He had to be hard and bury his feelings to survive and prosper as he has. It's going to take time and care to undo all that, Constance."

"There was a time when all I dreamed of was Paris," she murmured. "I could see the chestnut trees all golden on the boulevards and smell the Seine and see myself there, happy and free and safe. I can't see Paris anymore, Dylan. When I dream now, all I see is Lock."

"Then don't give up, *cara*." Dylan squeezed her hand encouragingly. "You're already well under his guard."

"How can you say that?"

Dylan laughed. "I haven't heard him lose his temper and bellow like that since I was nine and drilled holes in the hull of his sloop. If he's a bear, then it must be because something's under his skin." He winked at her. "And, honeybee, that something is you."

It was Constance's turn to laugh. "And you don't mind coming home to find your solid and logical brother impulsively married to an impossible woman who isn't even sure of her own name?"

He made a wry moue. "It seems an ideal match to me."

"And you, you charming scoundrel," she said with a smile and a kiss to his cheek, "always know exactly what to say."

Still holding her hand, Dylan furrowed his brow. "It's odd, isn't it?"

She knew what he meant. Odd how they'd picked up their friendship as if the intervening months didn't exist. Unusual that they could talk with no restraints despite the way they'd met and his knowledge of her secret hurts. Rare and singular that affection flowed freely between them with no sexual spark.

"Odd," she repeated softly. "But very special."

"And my brother's a lucky man. I'd tell him so, but I'm sure he already knows."

Constance grimaced. "He knows what a termagant he married."

Dylan gently chucked her chin and grinned. "The Iron Man deserves a taste of his own medicine now and again. I'll say good night now, but don't worry, *cara*. Something tells me you know exactly how to bring my hardheaded brother around."

Thinking about Dylan's parting remark, Constance conscientiously put away her paints and went back upstairs to the dark and silent bedroom. Lock lay motionless on his side under the thin sheets, but she knew he wasn't asleep. Removing the robe, she climbed into bed beside him, took her courage in hand, and touched his bare back.

Lock stiffened, then rolled wordlessly and took her in his arms, and they found the solace of each other's mouths in the dark. Dizzily, as she gave herself up to the inevitable magic, Constance realized that Dylan had been right. There was a level on which she and Lock had never failed to communi-

cate, where need and passion approached the declaration of love she yearned for. But for now, what
they shared physically had to be enough. Fireworks
sparkled behind her lids, and one thought echoed
in the darkness.

It was close.

Chapter 17

Rainbows blossomed, thunder rumbled, and the earth trembled. Red, blue, and silver spangles exploded into brilliance. A collective sigh of ecstasy rose into the steamy night.

"Oh, Lock, how wonderful!" Constance's voice was dreamy and breathless.

"Wait, there's more."

"How could it get any better?"

He gave a husky chuckle. "You'll see."

Across the Charles River Bridge in Cambridge, another rocket whistled heavenward from the granite base of the monolithic Bunker Hill Monument, screaming shrilly, then exploding with a crack, spewing starbursts that reflected in the dark water. Constance jumped and snuggled even closer on the carriage seat.

"This is the best Independence Day I've ever had!"

"You mean your first and only one, don't you?"

"The best," she repeated with a firm nod that made the rose satin ribbons on her bonnet flutter.

Their landau sat jammed alongside scores of vehicles filled with holiday revelers, all surrounded by the jostling, celebrating, Stars and Stripes-waving crowd lining the quay for the best view of the spectacle. Lock's hands lay easy on the reins to soothe the restive horses.

"Not a bad going-away party, either," Dylan remarked beside them.

"I'm certain the city of Boston had you in mind when they made their Fourth of July preparations, Captain McKin," Elspeth Philpot said humorously. Her sausage curls wagged beneath a lace cap that tied under her plump chin.

"They could do no less for a favorite son, Miss Philpot. After all, I *did* bring the *West Wind* home in record time," Dylan replied with a teasing grin as another cannonade of fireworks split the night sky.

He gallantly sat back so that the portly little woman, who'd been part of their company throughout the day's festivities of parades, picnics, and patriotic orations, had a clear view of the finale taking place across the river. President Zachary Taylor might be lying ill in Washington, and Henry Clay's proposed Southern compromise might be in a shambles in Congress, but Bostonians spared nothing in commemorating the American holiday.

Dylan watched a Roman candle arc overhead with satisfaction. "All in all, quite a send-off for another McKin expedition."

Constance reached across the seat and squeezed his arm. "I still wish you didn't have to leave."

"Pleasant as I've found these past weeks with you and Lock," he replied easily, "I confess I hear my true mistress calling."

But he caught his older brother's eye over Constance's head, and she knew that Dylan's assurances weren't entirely based on his restless need to sail the seas again.

Even though Tugwell and Kent had finally declined Rodger Latham's offer to buy the *Odyssey*, and Aunt Tug had been successfully launched and turned over to her new owners, neither Lock nor Dylan was content to rest on his laurels. In fact, no sooner had the transaction taken place than McKin Brothers crews were working overtime on the *Argo-*

naut. In his determination to complete this ship, Lock had even gone so far as to have her rigged in her cradles, an innovative and controversial decision made possible only by the use of his new, giant steam derrick to seat the massive masts. The critics were still divided regarding her design, piquing public interest, a factor Lock wanted to take advantage of by launching her before the summer was out. The income the *Argonaut* could generate by making a voyage this year couldn't be discounted, either.

Adding fuel to the fire of Lock's obsessive determination was news that Latham and Company had decided to outfit the *Odyssey* for the California trade themselves. Constance had wondered how much influence Alex, even though officially in retirement, had on that decision. Still smarting from the way the Lathams had successfully gained control of that vessel, Lock believed it was a point of honor to see the *West Wind* on her way before the *Odyssey* cleared the rigging yard. The books and balance sheets reflected the high costs of these projects, eating up a goodly portion of the *West Wind*'s and Aunt Tug's considerable profits, but it had always been a gambler's game, and when it came to showing up the Lathams, the McKins considered the price of pride worth any sacrifice.

That was why the *West Wind* lay anchored at Long Wharf with her holds stuffed with goods, everything in readiness for Dylan to take her to California with the morning tide.

"Just don't abandon the *West Wind* in San Francisco Bay and head for the goldfields as so many others have, you young cockerel," Lock said with a mock growl. "We'll make more profits supplying the fortune-seekers than anyone ever did waist-deep in a cold mountain sluice!"

"Have no fear, brother," Dylan said with a laugh. "As tempting as a California adventure sounds, after San Francisco, I'm bound for China. I'll bring home next season's tea crop so quickly we'll command a premium price. Just make certain the *Argonaut*'s finished so I can take her out on the next voyage and see what she's made of."

Lock's mouth twitched. "I'll wager a gold piece you'll see the *Argonaut* in Canton this year, and then she'll beat you and the *West Wind* home!"

"Done!" Dylan said, grinning at the challenge.

Constance suppressed a shiver of apprehension. Lock would never make an idle boast, but his belief in the *Argonaut* was close to a religion these days. His other accomplishments paled in comparison. It was the *Argonaut* that would redeem the McKin name once and for all, and nothing was going to stand in his way. Sometimes she wondered just exactly what he'd be willing to sacrifice to achieve that end, but one look at the ruthless determination lurking behind his icy blue eyes told her it was better not to know.

"Sounds like the makings of a grudge match," Elspeth said impishly just as a new rocket produced another "Ooh!" of appreciation from the crowd. "Wouldn't that make an intriguing plot for one of Mr. Hawthorne's novels, Constance?"

"At least we'd know which of Lock's designs is superior," Constance replied, "but I'm glad that's where the rivalry stops."

She and Lock had reached an unspoken agreement about Dylan the night they'd argued, and there'd been no repetitions of Lock's amazing and in some ways most satisfying flash of possessiveness. Constance wasn't altogether pleased, for the way he set her on fire with wanting yet managed to hold her at arm's length was altogether maddening. But she had promised herself she'd be patient, and it was gratifying to know that the easy and affectionate relationship between the brothers was unaffected.

"Well said, *cara*," Dylan replied now with a wink of approval. "Beautiful, talented, and diplomatic! Brother, I hope you appreciate the prize you have in this fair *wahine*."

"Since you sing her praises so often, I'm not likely to forget," Lock replied dryly. "But Constance will develop an inflated opinion of herself if this keeps up, so it's just as well you depart for the Pacific on the morrow!"

"After the resounding success of the *Sandwich Islands Sketchbook*, Constance is entirely justified in feeling proud," Elspeth stated indignantly.

"I'm glad I was here to share in your moment of triumph, *cara*." Dylan kissed Constance's hand in a flamboyant fashion. "I know I'll treasure my own copy."

"Desist, you rogue!" Constance scolded, laughing. "You're making me blush."

In truth, the debut of her *Sketchbook* at Elspeth's Attic bookshop had been nothing short of overwhelming. All of Elspeth's acquaintances among Boston's literati had turned out to buy copies, and the book had been reviewed kindly and received a quiet acclaim that Constance found heady indeed. She'd even had the temerity to secretly send Alex Latham a copy with a note saying she hoped he enjoyed her depictions of the land where his son had made a life for himself.

As Constance's biggest fan, Elspeth basked in the reflected glory of having found the artist and brought her to publication. Already Elspeth's entrepreneurial mind had latched onto an idea for a second *Sketchbook*, and she was full of questions about the islands. On one level Constance answered these probing inquiries readily enough, yet on another they provoked an anxiety about a life her mind obviously wished to put behind her. Elspeth's persistent questions about a particular character who appeared several times in the *Sketchbook* were most disturbing, for the kindly yet aristocratic face of the older female islander seemed achingly familiar, but try as she might, Constance could not say why. That face had even begun to appear in her dreams. Hating to burden Lock with her anxieties while he was so preoccupied with the shipyard, she hadn't told him about the face, or that her nightmares were increasingly populated with white dragons.

Constance shivered slightly as her thoughts veered away from this inner precipice, and she pressed closer to Lock as the final barrage of fireworks went up on the opposite shore. It still made her giddy to look directly at the open water, so she concentrated on her husband's handsome profile instead.

"Connie?" Lit by the different-colored flares above them, his face was hard to read. He raised a curious eyebrow and murmured in her ear, "Are you cold?"

"No." She gave a shaky laugh. "It's just been a long day, that's all. Wonderful, but exhausting."

"I expect this is the last of it. We'll start back as soon as this crowd thins out a bit."

She turned with him to enjoy the final pyrotechnic display, but the flash and reflections of the rockets bounced off the river and made her brain leap with vertigo. Hastily, she dragged her gaze away, looking back toward downtown Boston. The merrymaking around Quincy Market and the dockside areas surrounding the Custom House was still in full force. Atop Faneuil Hall—called the "Cradle of Liberty" because of the many Revolutionary meetings held there—the copper grasshopper known to true Yankee sailors all over the world looked down on paraders and celebrants prancing under lit flambeaux, while Chinese lanterns bobbed in the distant streets like so many fireflies.

Rocket sparks drifted earthward, leaving the sky empty and sprinkled only with stars again. As a single entity, the crowd drew a deep breath and applauded, then began to disperse in a crush of rattling carriages and chattering pedestrians.

Picking up the reins, Lock turned again to Constance, and found her looking not toward Bunker Hill but back at the city with a strange, startled look on her face.

"What's that?" she demanded, pointing.

They all turned curious stares toward the outline of distant buildings, seeing without comprehending the glow lighting the dark sky—until they heard the tinny clanging of the alarm bells. The wind off the harbor brought the scent of scorched powder and destruction to their noses.

"Holy Moses!" Elspeth exclaimed. "Some drunken fool has set the whole waterfront ablaze!"

It wasn't the entire waterfront. It was worse.

Lock whipped the lathered horses through the crowd of spectators clotting Long Wharf, shouting and cursing to clear a path. White smoke and glowing crimson sparks roiled toward a sky illuminated with an unholy orange light. From the moment of discovery, Lock had known with a sick certainty what they'd find, but nothing could have prepared him for the sight of the *West Wind* with her masts aflame and her sails burning.

When they could force the carriage no closer, he tossed the reins to Constance and gave her curt orders to stay put. Then he and Dylan vaulted down and plowed their way through the throng. Two fire engine companies arrived, and men in heavy gear worked feverishly at the pumpers. Canvas hoses crisscrossed the wharf, some from the engines, some from the hand pumps siphoning water straight out of the harbor and spewing it at the ship in graceful but ineffective arcs. Even a bucket brigade had been formed.

It was not enough.

"Holy Mother, what the hell happened?" Dylan shouted. Frustration, disbelief, and anger twisted his handsome features into an unrecognizable mask. "Where's the watch? I'll have somebody's head!"

Grim-mouthed, Lock nodded, feeling the same murderous rage. This couldn't have happened at a worse moment, with the *West Wind* fully loaded and sluggish, and a large portion of the fate of McKin Brothers riding on her. Cursing destiny and ill fortune, Lock shoved through the chaos until he reached a helmeted individual in an oil slicker shouting orders to the fire brigades through a megaphone.

"We're the owners," he snapped. "How did it start?"

"What am I, a goddammed newspaper reporter?" the frazzled fire chief demanded. "A stray spark, a careless sailor's pipe, a drunk with a torch from the damned parades—who the hell knows? Now get out of my way! We've got to get this hulk away from the wharf before all the warehouses go up! Johnson, are those tugs ready?"

"You're giving up?" Dylan demanded furiously. "The cargo, man! We aren't insured! Give us a chance to salvage the cargo!"

The chief glared at him with smoke-reddened eyes. "I'm having her towed out to deep water. I can't risk the entire city because of one ship." He hesitated, then shrugged and gave a brief apology. "Sorry."

Lock assessed the progress of the flames through the superstructure, then caught Dylan's eye. "Axes."

Dylan took his brother's meaning. "Right."

Sprinting into action, they each ripped a fire axe off the nearest engine, then made for the burning ship. The intense heat wafted in blistering waves across the railings. Plunging past the hose gangs,

Lock and Dylan raced up the smoldering gangway amid shouts of protest.

The deck of the *West Wind* was still relatively free of fire, blazing in only a few places where falling canvas and rope had ignited it. While the aftermast and mainmast sported only minor patches of flame, the foremast was completely engulfed. Lock and Dylan raced to the base of the mainmast, lifted axes; chips of hard white oak flew, the clear *thwang* of the axes biting into the wood ringing out over their labored breathing.

The heat above them singed their eyebrows and the hair on the backs of their hands and arms. Each effort to lift the axe was harder than the last. Choking, coughing, they worked in a superhuman flurry of blows, ignoring the demands made on their bodies.

"They're trying to demast 'er!" one of the firemen shouted. "C'mon, lads, give 'em a dousing!"

One of the hose gangs immediately turned the brunt of its puny spray directly over the two axe-wielders, forming a cooling rain that soaked their clothes and steamed up from the smoking deck. Water mixed with soot ran into Lock's eyes. The danger wasn't any less, for tons of charring spars and smoldering canvas lay above them ready to crash down, but at least they could breathe again. If he and Dylan could drop the mainmast across the bow and take the flaming foremast with it, there just might be a chance . . .

Lock slammed his axe into the hard column again and again, the shock of the blows vibrating all the way up to his straining shoulders. Distantly, he heard the chief shouting orders to cut the ship loose.

"Not yet, dammit!" he roared, and put all of his might into the next blow.

The tortured wood gave an eerie, inhuman

screech. It was getting close. They just might make it . . .

"Lock, look out!"

The mainmast strained toward the bow, then snapped with an explosive clap. Simultaneously, the foremast collapsed, colliding with the mainmast in an impact rivaling a volcano's eruption. Instead of both masts going overboard with relatively little damage, the foremast's unexpected disintegration brought everything down over the deck.

Right on top of the two brothers.

Spars struck the deck like harpoons, smashing the planks with the devastation of cannonballs. Smoke blinded Lock. Burning canvas flailed him with a smoking brand, and he fell. At the same moment, he saw Dylan disappear under a blazing yard.

"Dylan!"

Fear had been controllable until that moment, submerged beneath the greater need to save the *West Wind*. Now Lock's heart jumped into his smoke-clogged throat and stark terror chilled his heated lungs with the scent of death. "Dylan, no!"

The *West Wind* listed suddenly and shuddered as a steamer tug began to pull her from the dockside. Lock struggled up from the litter of destruction surrounding him. Something hit him across the cheek and he fell again, stunned. Wrestling for consciousness, he clawed his way through the debris, flinging aside ruptured timbers and smoking tarry sheets, not even noticing his burned palms in his frantic search for his brother.

"Dylan—" Lock's raspy shout ended in a gurgle. "Oh, Jesus, no!"

Dylan lay beneath a beam that had once been part of the foremast. There was blood on his face, and his arm was twisted at an unnatural angle. He was very still.

In a cold sweat, blinking against the tingling that was rapidly closing one eye, Lock used all of his re-

maining strength to hoist the beam and shove it off
Dylan. An inferno leaped up around them, dancing
walls of flame to trap unwary victims. With only a
split second of regret for the *West Wind*, Lock
dragged Dylan to the railing, then pitched them
both into the murky depths below.

The water was cool enough to be a shock, but
Lock welcomed it to clear the foggy mist clouding
his brain. Holding Dylan's collar, Lock rolled him
faceup, kicking hard to stay on the surface. Dylan
groaned. Alive! Lock would have laughed aloud for
joy if he'd had the breath. Instead, he gritted his
teeth and swam away from the conflagration.

Holding Dylan's dead weight afloat was harder
for him than when he'd rescued Constance from the
surf at Skye. More than once Lock went under,
choking on a mouthful of black harbor water. Sheer
stubbornness kept him kicking. Damned if he'd let
it all end this way for the McKins!

"Easy, mate! We have you!"

Hands reached out. Voices echoed hollowly over
his head. Someone took Dylan. Relieved of his burden, Lock went under. Another set of hands
snagged his coat, and he was dragged over the gun-
nel of a small rowboat to lie gasping like a mackerel
in the malodorous bottom.

By the time the rowboat slipped up against the
wharf again, Lock had recovered enough to roll to
his shaky knees, head throbbing, hands aching, and
peer through his one good eye at Dylan's pasty
face. His utter stillness and blue color made Lock's
heart twist painfully. Their seamen rescuers slung
the unconscious man in a canvas and hoisted him
hand over hand to the top of the dock. Shaking off
help, Lock managed to climb the ladder without assistance. He found Constance and Elspeth bending
over Dylan.

"Damn you, woman," he croaked. "I told you to
stay put!"

"And since when have I ever listened to you?" Constance demanded back, then threw her arms around him. "Thank God," she whispered against his soaking, sooty shirtfront. "I was so afraid."

She drew back to inspect him, her face white but composed and businesslike. "How bad are you? Your eye—your hands! Oh, Lock!"

"I'll be all right." He brushed off her concerns, moving to Dylan's side. Dripping, he knelt beside his brother.

Elspeth had already demanded splinting materials for Dylan's arm, and she and several volunteers were immobilizing the broken bone. Constance knelt down beside Dylan, smoothing back his wet, dark hair. She frowned and bit her lip at the sight of the blood flowing from the massive contusion on the side of his head, the red mingling with the water to form a pink pool on the cobbles. She reached for her handkerchief, but that pitiful bit of linen did little to staunch the flow.

"Parbleu!" she muttered, jumping up.

Oblivious of the crowd of onlookers surrounding them, she hoisted her skirts and stripped off a cotton petticoat, then pressed the pristine, lacy garment to the wound. A part of Lock that watched the scene from a distance laughed wryly. Damned if the infuriating woman never thought twice about showing off her underthings! Another part of him was so frightened he wanted to weep. But the Iron Man couldn't allow himself that luxury.

"How bad is he?" Lock barely recognized the hollow, smoke-roughened voice as his own.

"Bad enough," Elspeth snapped, pulling the last tie tight. Scrambling to her feet, she fired instructions at the gawking spectators, demanding a stretcher, a wagon, willing hands—and getting them.

Lifting one of Dylan's eyelids, then the other, Constance tried to evoke some response, speaking softly, then more forcefully. Dylan didn't move, and his breathing seemed labored and shallow.

"We need a doctor, quickly." Constance shook her head. "I don't know ... oh, Lock, he's badly hurt. This accident—"

"It wasn't an accident." Lock's voice was deadly calm now. "If Dylan dies, it's murder."

Shock made Constance's eyes nearly bulge. "*What?*"

Lock staggered to his feet, fury uncoiling in his chest, hate burning deeper than the blisters on his palms. "That fire was deliberate. It started in the forward hold, but there was *nothing flammable stored there*. And someone tampered with the foremast stays, or it would never have fallen in the direction it did and hit Dylan."

"How can you be sure?" she whispered.

Lock felt something slip inside him, felt the control that had ruled his life disintegrate, releasing a savagery that was totally satisfying.

"Goddammit, I built the *West Wind*! I know my own ship! And I know the bastards who did this." He bared his teeth in a warrior's predatory snarl. Tasting venom and smoke and vengeance, he spit out the name. "*Latham*. I'll make them pay, I swear."

Fresh alarm skipped down Constance's spine, and she jumped to her feet. "But, Lock, you can't prove anything—"

Lock whirled to address the hovering crowd. Across the dark harbor, the flickering light of the burning *West Wind* revealed the Iron Man's archangel countenance, transformed by his injuries and by furious hatred into a gargoyle's demonic mask.

"You heard me! Some bastard did this to us! Ten thousand dollars to the one who tells me who and brings proof."

Avid, excited muttering broke out just as a flatbed wagon appeared to transport Dylan. Elspeth sprang forward to give directions, but Constance stood frozen in horror.

"Don't do this, Lock," she said. "This isn't a witch-hunt! There's a better way."

"No longer. I've taken all I'm going to. They want war. So be it." He smiled, a crooked, grotesque thing that bespoke a man pushed past his limits. Seamen loaded Dylan onto the wagon, and Lock watched grimly, determination and bloodlust gleaming in his one open eye.

"The last one standing wins, princess," he said. "And I'm going to be that man if I have to tear out the Lathams' black hearts with my bare hands!"

President Zachary Taylor died on the ninth of July, 1850, and Vice-President Millard Fillmore became the thirteenth man to hold the highest office in the United States. That same evening, Dylan McKin came to his own crisis.

Constance sat beside the bed in which Dylan had lain unconscious for the five days since the burning of the *West Wind*, watching her brother-in-law's life slip away inch by painful inch. His head was swathed in a white bandage and his broken left arm was heavily splinted, but it was his still, pallid features under a heavy sprouting of black whiskers that made Constance redouble her prayers.

When the doctors said they could do nothing but wait with a head injury like his, Lock had brought Dylan back to Devonshire Street. With Maggie's and Elspeth's help, they'd kept constant vigil, spooning broth and tea down his throat when they could, bathing him with cool compresses when the fever rose, talking to him, praying that the swelling in his brain would subside and he'd wake up. Today, it seemed Dylan was losing the battle, for the fever had peaked again and again, forcing them into frantic applications of ice. He'd muttered and struggled at first, but now weakness overcame him, and he lay too still, hardly seeming to breathe.

Wearily, Constance rose from her chair and wrung out another towel in the basin. She threw back the light sheet covering Dylan's nude form. Intent on saving his life, they had been well past the point of modesty for some time. Bending, she swabbed his broad shoulders and lean legs with the towel, then tenderly wiped his wasted face. A niggling sense of having done this before made her frown, then shake her head at a fancy that could only be the result of anxiety and fatigue.

A soft, sultry night breeze wafted through the open window, fluttering the muslin panels and making the oil lamp's flame waver. Though the moving air helped cool the dampness on his skin, Dylan still felt much too hot when she laid the back of her hand against his brow. Straightening, Constance rubbed the small of her aching back. She'd have to send Lock for more ice if the fever went up again.

As she dried her hands on her apron, Constance's worried thoughts moved to her husband. He'd had the hardest time of them all. The seriousness of his brother's condition made Lock almost as haggard as Dylan, but he'd insisted on taking his turn at the sickbed as well as continuing to oversee operations at the shipyard. The *West Wind* was a total loss, burned to the waterline to finally sink beyond the boundaries of the harbor, leaving McKin Brothers in another financial hole even worse than the last.

But it was Lock's ferocious anger against the Lathams that frightened Constance the most, and she feared that if Dylan should die, Lock might do something rash, something totally illogical and unlike the Iron Man McKin she knew. Once again, she damned the twisted destinies that had drawn the Lathams and the McKins into this accursed feud, the secret hates, jealousies, and loves that had destroyed two families. No lessons had been learned from those old tragedies, and now new catastrophes lurked at every turn. But there was no way to undo the tangle that had come of James Latham's passion for another man's wife, no way to bring back Eliza or Enoch, no possibility of forgiveness between their sons and Alex. If there was only some way to break this deadly cycle before the dark tug of vengeance destroyed them all!

Drawing the sheet up to Dylan's hips, Constance carefully punched up his pillow, then reached for a spoon and a bowl of broth.

"Come on, Dylan," she whispered, touching the spoon to his cracked lips, trying to slip a nourishing drop onto his parched tongue. "You've got to try."

A portion of the fluid dribbled off the corner of his mouth into the forest of dark stubble on his cheek, but he managed a weak swallow. Heartened, Constance tried again, crooning encouragement, with similar mixed results. But then he'd take no more, no matter how hard she tried. Over and over, she repeated the action until the pillowcase was soaked with broth, and frustration and weariness and fear provoked an irritated outburst.

"All right, then, starve!" Near tears, she threw the spoon across the room. "I don't care!"

I don't care ... I don't!

Echoes of another time and place rippled across her memory. A little girl in a tapa skirt. The coconut-shell cup she pressed futilely to the sick man's lips. *Don't drink it, then, Papa! I don't care!*

But he wasn't sick, Constance saw now through the distance of years, only drunk. She'd been too young to understand that, knowing only that the man with the dark beard who lay so still and miserable on the woven palm mats of their hut needed her help.

"Oh, Papa," Constance whispered, afraid to breathe, afraid to blink, so tenuous was her hold on the mental scene. For an instant, she saw things with perfect clarity; then the vision slipped away again behind the hazy wall in her head, and she could have sobbed with frustration. But one thing she knew with a new, unshakable certainty—the man she'd seen was her father, and her father's name was James Latham.

She had no way to prove it, but it didn't matter. For a moment, she'd *remembered*. She knew who she was again, no matter what Cyrus Tate said. At that moment she couldn't even care why he hated her so much that he'd lie about something as basic as her name. She had her identity back, although she was the only one who would rejoice in that. How ironic that her husband's hatred of the Lathams should reach its peak just when she could claim 'hat birthright again!

Constance's sight cleared slowly, the memory of her father's countenance dissolving into the reality of the face before her now. Her eyes grew bigger, and she inhaled sharply. "Dear God!"

Her heart thundering against her rib cage, Constance pulled her silver locket out from under her apron bib and opened it with trembling fingers. Dumbstruck, she stared at the man in the portrait, then looked back at Dylan.

The same prominent profile. Identical heavily marked brows. A broad brow and a sensitive upper lip. The tobacco-brown hair and eyes. With the black thatch of whiskers hiding the distinctive jawline he shared with his brother, the picture Dylan made lying on the bed matched almost feature for feature the image of James Latham.

"Dear God," she repeated, awestruck. "How could I be so blind?"

Unless there had been a totally preposterous genetic coincidence, Dylan McKin could not have been fathered by anyone other than James Latham. James's passion for Eliza had been neither impossi-

ble nor unrequited, the rumors not so farfetched after all.

"Oh, Papa, what did you do?" Constance murmured, gently taking Dylan's hand between her
own.

Questions with no possible answers raced
through her head. Had James's involvement with
Eliza forced Alex to banish him? Had Enoch suspected his wife of betraying him with his partner's
son? Did James know he'd fathered a child before
he left for the Pacific? And poor Eliza. Had she
loved James? Perhaps he had begged her to go with
him, only to find she could not choose between her
lover and her firstborn. Maybe that was why Constance's few memories of her father were all of a
sad and unhappy man.

Yet there was one redeeming fact in this sorrowful tale—Dylan himself. Through a quirk of fate, the
same blood flowed through the veins of both of
them. Emotion churned in Constance's chest as she
gazed at her half brother. They'd felt as close as siblings from the very first. Surely God would not be
so cruel as to let her discover she had a brother,
only to lose him again!

With a tight little sob, Constance threw herself
against Dylan's chest. "Oh, God, please. Don't die,
Dylan. You've got to wake up now. Oh, please . . ."

She cried against his bare chest, imploring the
Creator for mercy, her tears wetting her brother's
skin like a balm of atonement. She'd never known
whether she really believed in the Reverend Tate's
Jehovah, so she prayed to a gentler, loving Lord,
someone who'd raised his own friend Lazarus from
the tomb when his sisters wept. Surely that Jesus
could understand her need now.

A gentle, trembling hand smoothed her wild
mane of hair, and a husky voice said, "Don't cry."

"Dylan!" Constance lifted her tear-streaked countenance, wonder and gratitude swelling her heart. "Dylan, you're awake!"

"Umm." He grimaced wryly, creasing his damp brow. "Hell of a headache."

"I know, I know." She pushed his dark hair back from his forehead, then looked curiously at her fingers. They were wet with sweat. In fact, his whole body was soaked. She'd been too busy bathing him with her tears to notice that his body's natural defense mechanism had broken the fever's hold at last. She laughed quietly, joyfully. "You've given us quite a scare. Are you thirsty?"

"Umm."

She helped him drink from a tumbler of water. "Better?"

He made that inarticulate sound of assent again, too exhausted by the effort to drink for anything else. Constance pressed a kiss to his salty brow.

"Sleep now, my dear one. Everything is going to be fine." She touched his face tenderly. "Oh, Dylan, I have so much to tell you!"

"One thing?"

"Yes?"

His eyelids were heavy with drowsiness, but he slanted her a look that was pure Dylan at his roguish best. "Where the devil are my pants?"

Chapter 18

Seated in his comfortable old armchair, Lock McKin stared at a spot on the parlor wall with an index finger pressed to his upper lip in an attitude of intense concentration. Black stubble spouted from his jaw, and fatigue rimmed his bleary eyes. The faint remnants of bruises shadowed his temples, but the burns on his palms were almost healed.

When Constance entered the room, he roused slowly, reluctantly raising his dark head. Her tear-streaked countenance told him all, and what was left of his heart shriveled in his chest.

"Dylan's dead, isn't he?"

Constance reached his side in an instant and placed her arms around his neck. "No, my love. The fever's down, and he's much better. Truly. He even spoke to me before he fell back to sleep."

Steeled for the worst, Lock couldn't handle the best. Tears smarted at the corners of his eyes. Choking, he dragged Constance onto his lap and buried his face in the tender, flower-scented crook of her neck, shaking uncontrollably.

She stroked the ebony curls at his nape and soothed the tense shoulder muscles under his rumpled white shirt, murmuring words of reassurance and making comforting noises while he dug deep for control. When he found it again, he was embarrassed and rose abruptly, setting her on her feet while he knuckled the telltale moisture away.

"Sorry," he muttered.

"For what?" Her eyebrows arched in surprise. "You've been strong for me so often, it feels good to be the one you lean on, even for a moment." Her hands buried in the apron's deep pockets, Constance gave him a gentle, shy look. "People who care about each other do that, you know."

Her words were like the flick of a whip on Lock's conscience. Damn her, he knew what she was up to, asking indirectly for words of devotion he couldn't pledge, didn't dare speak, not with his insides in a shambles and his emotions shredded by all that had occurred. Couldn't she understand that his world was falling down around his ears? The shadows of his father's failures stalked him. He couldn't let emotion overrule logic, not now, not when everything depended on him. He couldn't be *weak*.

"Is Dylan really out of danger?" he asked, gruffly reverting to their original subject.

Disappointment flickered in Constance's topaz eyes. "I think so, now that the fever's broken. Don't worry. His constitution is strong."

Lock's mouth twisted. "Thank God his head is hard, too."

She smiled at that attempt at lightness; then an unusual excitement lit her expression. "The most amazing thing happened just now with Dylan. I remembered about my father. I just *saw* him, like a miracle. I'm sure he *was* James Latham, and . . . and that's not all."

Lock stared at Constance in utter astonishment and with growing incredulity as she recounted her experience in the sickroom, her words tumbling eagerly out of her mouth like the waters of a fast-rushing stream falling over smooth stones. But Lock felt as though he'd been pitched headfirst into white-water rapids, his panicky soul tossed and twisted and sucked under by images so incredible, so foundation-shattering, that he fought back in sheer self-defense.

"That's absurd!" He cut Constance off, scowling fiercely. "Dylan's no Latham."

"Just look," Constance begged, shoving the open locket into his hands. "How could we have missed the resemblance before? But can't you see it now? Your mother and my father, Lock. It has to be, and it explains so much."

Shocked to his core, Lock stared at her in horror. In one form or another, he'd been working to redeem his family's honor all his life. If that family had no honor, what did that make him? His illusions threatened, Lock exploded. "No, goddammit! My mother—"

"Was only a woman, after all, Lauchlan, and your father was . . . was much like you, a hard man, engrossed in his work. Is it so inconceivable that Eliza might have found the affection she needed in someone more her own age? It doesn't make it right, but it does make them human."

"I'll never believe it!"

"You can't doubt the proof before your own eyes."

"You're dreaming again." He cast a withering look at the locket, then tossed it back to her. "Hallucinating."

"I'm not!" Constance stood her ground, indignant at his dismissal. "I remembered, Lock."

"You're not remembering, you're making up fantasies again to explain a situation that has nothing to do with you." He grabbed her shoulders. "Stop it, Constance! You'll only make yourself ill again. I thought we'd come farther than this."

"Why won't you believe me?" she cried. "Isn't remembering a sign I'm getting well? You wouldn't discourage a cripple from taking a first step, would you?"

He released her abruptly. "Let the dead rest, Constance."

"And their secrets with them, no matter who they continue to hurt?" she demanded in a caustic tone. "Don't you understand? I can't. Until I know what's behind the wall in my head, I'll always be handicapped. I'll never be a whole woman."

She looked up into his stony expression, and her voice caught. "And I want to be whole again, Lock, for you."

Lock heard the silent appeal behind her words, and read it in her tremulous gaze. *So you'll love me.*

And it tempted Lock almost beyond his limits to forget the duties of honor and vengeance and lose himself in the humanity of giving himself totally to Constance. Their physical relationship was all a man could hope for, and he wanted her in ways that defied the imagination, but he feared that loss of control most of all, and the situation was too critical to jeopardize it in any way.

So he steeled himself against that wanting, knowing instinctively that his weakness for this woman could bring him to his knees, might send him careening into the same kind of failure and disaster that had claimed Enoch in the end. Lock couldn't risk the destruction of everything he and Dylan and their father had worked for, couldn't imperil perhaps the last chance to redeem the McKin name, even for Constance. Even for himself.

The Iron Man spoke. "I've accepted you the way you are."

So you must take me as I am. His unspoken demand echoed silently between them.

"You're my wife, aren't you? That's got to be enough."

Constance flinched at the harshness in his voice, but tried again doggedly. "Lock, it's important. I remember—"

"I'm warning you, Constance. Don't push this delusion, and don't involve Dylan in this irresponsible theory. It won't change anything."

"Not change anything?" Her angry words bounced off the faded paper roses on the parlor walls. "Oh, you blind, stubborn ... McKin! Of course it does! It could put an end to this perishing feud, if only you'd see—"

"So that's what this is all about." A pulse leaped in Lock's jaw. "You think a wild story like this is going to make me stop fighting the Lathams?"

Constance shook her head in frustration. "Fight how? You can't prove anything."

"Tip Maddock's poking around the waterfront. With the reward I offered, we're certain to find out who actually set the fire aboard the *West Wind*."

"You'll go to the authorities then?"

"That depends." Lock frowned and shrugged. "Even more important than bringing the actual arsonist to justice is proving who hired him. That kind of leverage might even be used to restore some of what the Lathams have taken from us."

"Blackmail now? Lock, listen to yourself!" she pleaded. "That is no honorable path! And since you're already convinced the Lathams were behind everything, you're throwing away money you can't spare and further jeopardizing the shipyard. This vendetta is blinding you to what's sensible, and that isn't like you at all."

Stung by her accusations, Lock glared down at her, his mouth tight with fury. "It isn't your place to worry about the shipyard. I'm well able to drum up more commissions like Aunt Tug. We'll survive."

"But there's got to be more to life than just revenge and survival," Constance argued. "What about the *Argonaut*? What about all the other great ships you've yet to dream into existence? What about *us*? Will you sacrifice all that?"

"Our success will prove the best revenge," Lock stated flatly. "I won't deny the *Argonaut*'s my first hope for salvaging both finances and reputation. I'm going to launch her as soon as she's rigged. Meanwhile, there are others who deplore the Latham methods. Rodger's stewardship of Latham and Company is shaky at best, and together we can make an assault on it. I may not be able to regain control of the *Odyssey* before she sails, but I can make it damned hard for Latham-owned enterprises to find laborers and seamen, spare parts and repairs, and even cargo in this town."

Frustration etched worried creases at the sides of Constance's soft mouth. "But at what cost, Lock? This 'eye for an eye' mentality will only bring further tragedy!"

"Damnation, woman! They took the *West Wind* and the *Odyssey*, and nearly cost me my brother as well! You think I can forgive that?"

Constance lifted her chin, but her voice was quiet. "Dylan is *my* brother, too."

He threw up his hands with an angry growl, cursing under his breath. "Nothing will convince me there's a grain of truth in any of that, and I haven't got the time or the energy to waste discussing it. If you value anything we share, you'll forget this wild dream."

Constance went pale at the implied threat. "I see. You'd rather live with Crazy Lili and hate the Lathams than know the truth."

"Stow it, I said!" he roared.

Stricken, she stared at him for a long, tense moment, and her expression was so hurt, so full of betrayal, Lock couldn't stand it. Reaching for her, he pressed her to his chest, soaking in the nuances that were uniquely Constance, and lowered his mouth to hers, asking for . . . atonement, reassurance, understanding? He couldn't say. He brushed her skin with his mouth, touched the tip of his tongue to the seam of her lips, and shivered with the instantaneous ache that flamed in his loins. But for the first time in their precarious, shuttlecock relationship, there was no answering response from her.

"Connie. Princess." He threaded his fingers through the shining richness of her sable hair. "Don't you understand I'm drowning here? I need you . . ."

Her fist lay over his pounding heart, the damning locket clenched within her palm, and her eyes were clear, yet fathomless as the deepest ocean crevice. "The Iron Man doesn't need anyone."

His thumb brushed her lower lip, teasing, inviting, cajoling. "We both need this."

"I thought it would be enough." Her breath shuddered. "It's not."

His hands tightened on her. "You're my wife."

"Compelled by duty, if not by feeling?" She laughed without humor. "No doubt Eliza understood that, too. But tell me, Lock, was she happier as Enoch's wife or James's mistress?"

"Damn you." Pricked by her sharp question, Lock thrust her away. "Leave that notion alone, or to hell with you!"

The parlor rang with silence.

With jerky little movements, as if she might fly to pieces at the barest touch, Constance tucked the locket away in her apron pocket. "Excuse me. I must prepare more broth for Dylan. No doubt he'll be ravenous when next he wakes."

She headed for the door, her skirts swishing rhythmically, her spine stiff.

"Constance—"

The final look she turned on him burned with hurt, with rebellion, with a golden determination. "Hear me, Lock McKin. The walls of Jericho are crumbling in my head, and no one—not you, not even Jehovah Himself—is going to stop me from climbing over them!"

* * *

"I didn't think you'd come," Constance said in a tone that matched the reverential hush of the Boston Athenaeum library. She swallowed hard, but dared not take her eyes from the portrait of a long-dead Yankee hanging in the picture gallery.

"I almost didn't." Dignified and very Bostonian in his dark frock coat, Alex Latham leaned on his ivory-handled cane to inspect the dour visage in the gilt frame.

The mid-July heat did not penetrate the dark brown Paterson sandstone facade of the Athenaeum. The interior of the Italianate-style building was a cool oasis of quiet and culture, as befitted an institution that housed some of Boston's most prized literary treasures, including the recently acquired library of President George Washington himself.

Despite the coolness of the gallery, nervous moisture prickled beneath the bodice of Constance's muslin promenade gown. She gave Alex a guarded look from under the brim of her blond straw bonnet. The faint scents of bay rum and peppermint tickled her nose, and she had to restrain the urge to throw her arms around him and bawl. Misunderstandings and mistakes aside, she was willing to love this man as her grandfather simply for the sake of shared blood and mutual hardheadedness. Convincing Alex of that fact was a different matter, however, and while emotion ran high within her, prudence cautioned that she move carefully.

"Why did you come, then?" she asked in a small voice.

"Idle curiosity. And to thank you for the book. Not a bad piece of work, that."

She smiled, grateful for both his grudging admiration and a neutral topic. "I'm glad you enjoyed my *Sketchbook*."

"It's an accurate representation of life in the Sandwich Islands?"

"Yes. Your son knew it well—the fishing canoes,

the luaus, the simple ways of a simple, happy people at work and at play."

Alex cast her a sly glance. "The Reverend Tate did not agree. In fact, I'd never seen that cold fish so agitated over anything before, much less a bunch of native faces. Called such heathen pictures the devil's work and advised me to burn it."

Constance had gone pale at the mention of the minister's name. "D-did you?"

Alex snorted. "Of course not, girl. I've had my fill of priggish clergymen, and only wish that tiresome, whey-faced creature would decide to go when the *Odyssey* debarks next week for the Pacific."

"He's leaving?" Constance's eyes widened with the happy possibility.

"Well, there's talk of the reverend returning to his mission. His flock at the sugar colony needs him, or some such drivel, though he seems to enjoy the comforts of the material world so much, I'd wager he has interests other than God's," Alex grumbled. "I wouldn't be sorry to see the back of Tate, though I suppose Rodger felt some sort of obligation to be hospitable after he testified—"

Alex broke off, flushing from his ruff of silver whiskers to the point of his peaked eyebrows.

"He lied about me," Constance said quietly. "I don't know why he hates me so much, but he lied."

"It's worthless to rehash the past, girl," Alex began, his craggy features drooping in weary lines.

"No. I can't believe that." Constance's chin firmed stubbornly. "That's why I asked you to meet me. You're the only one who might really know the truth."

Alex gave her a wary look. "About what? If this has to do with what happened to the *West Wind*—"

"Not really, but Lock does blame the Lathams, you know. We were lucky Dylan wasn't killed."

"Blast it all! Accidents happen to everyone, girl." Alex's strident bellow drew the eyes of several other visitors in the gallery. He took Constance's elbow and steered her toward the entrance, continuing in a low, irritated hiss. "Why must every misfortune that befalls a McKin be laid at my feet?"

They passed under the arched entryway of the Athenaeum and paused in the sunshine on the sidewalk. Constance took a deep breath and met Alex's stormy brown gaze.

"It was no accident, Alex. That fire was deliberate. Considering the earlier harassments McKin Brothers has suffered at Latham hands, the obvious conclusion is that you or Rodger ordered it to finish the McKins off for good."

"What preposterous slander!" Indignant, Alex glared at her through a thin haze of dust stirred up by the carriages and hacks moving up and down Beacon Street. "No Latham need use underhanded methods to best a competitor! The McKins are seeking a scapegoat for their own inadequacies—as usual!"

"You don't understand, Alex," Constance said. "In a way, I'm glad it happened."

That shocked him into silence. Then his jaw clenched, and he jammed his high-topped beaver on his head. "You, miss, must be deranged to show such an utter lack of loyalty. Whatever your purpose, I'll not be your dupe. Good day."

He stamped up the sidewalk in the direction of Latham House, but Constance kept pace with him, frantically digging into her reticule. "Listen, please! What happened helped me to remember things about myself and about your son."

"I'll have no part in your schemes, my girl!" Alex stalked across an intersection, then plunged down the sidewalk opposite the Common, dodging other pedestrians, muttering under his breath. "Damned old fool that I am, I should have paid Rodger more heed. Get out of my way!"

They'd almost reached Latham House, and the

fear of meeting the Reverend Tate or Rodger made Constance throw herself directly across Alex's headlong path, so that he had either to stop or to plow over her. He drew up short, huffing and puffing his ire, but Constance had come too far to be intimidated now.

"Please, Alex!" She shoved a book-sized portrait into his hands. "Look."

One glance at the man in the picture, and Alex's truculent expression changed to one of wonder. "Why, that's James."

"No, Grandpa." Constance felt her throat grow thick with emotion. "That's Dylan McKin. Your other grandchild. My half brother."

"No!" Alex's denial was automatic. "That's ridiculous! I'd know my own son."

"You've never met Dylan, have you? I painted that not two days ago, with Dylan chafing constantly to be up and about, even with his arm in a splint. With his new whiskers, the likeness is uncanny, is it not?" Constance's mouth quivered suddenly, and her voice shook. "When I saw it, I remembered another time in Lahaina, Alex. No matter what Uncle Cyrus says, I know James Latham was my father, just as surely as you can see that Dylan bears Latham blood."

"Impossible," he choked, though the uneven timbre of his voice betrayed his wavering conviction. Then he shook off the moment of doubt and rapped the face in the portrait with his knuckles. "This is just another ploy by the damn McKins to destroy me for what happened to Enoch."

Constance's lips trembled. "You're wrong. I haven't even told Dylan anything yet, and Lock is no more willing to accept this than you are."

"Then what do you want, girl?"

"Nothing but truth and peace between the families, I swear. But I can't have it without your help," Constance pleaded, tugging urgently at Alex's sleeve. "I need to remember about myself. I need to know what my father was like. Start by telling me the truth about James Latham and Eliza McKin."

"I—" Alex opened his mouth to speak, then snapped it shut again, shaking his head as though it ached. "There's nothing to tell, so cease these fantasies and let the dead rest in peace. Now, let me alone!"

Alex wrenched his arm from her grasp and turned toward the steps of Latham House. Above him, a curtain twitched at a window frame.

"Hiding secrets hurts more than acknowledging the truth, Grandpa," Constance cried after him.

She felt the tenuous thread that remained between Alex and her unraveling amid his disbelief and denial, but she knew of no way to make him see a truth she could prove only in her own heart. Her words grew more and more frantic.

"Lock's planning every obstacle he can to delay the *Odyssey*, and who knows what nefarious scheme Rodger will concoct? Will the *Argonaut* be the next target? Will someone be killed then? Twenty-five years of suffering is long enough, Grandpa! We could end this feud, you and I."

Alex hesitated on the steps of Latham House, his expression beleaguered, so agitated he didn't even realize he still clutched Dylan's picture. "You're blathering. Leave me be!"

"The truth, Grandpa! Whether we want it or not, it's coming for both the Lathams and the McKins." Recklessly, she followed him to the foot of the steps. "What have you got to lose? Ask Rodger about the *West Wind*. Ask Uncle Cyrus about *me!*"

The door of Latham House slammed behind Alex, and futility filled Constance to the brim of her straw bonnet. Swallowing back tears of helpless despair, she turned and fled down Beacon Street. From the window above, a slight figure in a smocked apron watched and slowly smiled.

* * *

"I thought you said she couldn't cause any more trouble."

"Calm yourself, my son. You have nothing to fear."

"Cork it, Cyrus!" Rodger Latham snapped rudely. He stirred the remnants of his luncheon, then dropped his fork against the blue-and-white willowware plate in disgust. The strident clatter disturbed the cool, serene elegance of the Latham House dining room, its draperies drawn against the light of the outside world in deference to the infirmity of the other diner. "And spare me your pious platitudes, for God's sake!"

"Your ill temper indicates you share your uncle's predisposition toward stomach upsets," the Reverend Cyrus Tate returned in a mild tone. Peering kindly through his smoked glasses, he lifted the heavy silver pepper mill in his milk-white hands and added a generous grinding to his plate. "A pity. Eloise's poached scrod is delightful today."

"I can't eat knowing that lying bitch Constance has the old man stirred up enough to be asking some damned uncomfortable questions!"

With delicate efficiency, Tate wiped his pallid lips with a linen napkin. "The Lord will provide—"

"I didn't pay the Lord, I paid you, and very well, I might add," Rodger ground out. "We had an agreement: you to testify unequivocally that Constance is no Latham—"

"Merely the truth," Tate interjected smoothly.

"—and I to finance the expansion of your sugar kingdom."

"I'd prefer you refer to my little enterprise as Holy Sanctuary Mission School. It makes you quite the philanthropist, and my title to the property's three thousand acres of cane fields is immaterial."

"As is the fact that your labor force is mostly mission *students*." Rodger took his last swallow of coffee in an irritable gulp. "Not that it matters to me as long as you use Latham ships to transport the sugar harvest, but how did you get your hands on so much native land?"

Tate's alabaster features stiffened, and his eyes gleamed red behind his smoked spectacles. "As Lili's guardian, I'm entitled to certain compensation from her people. And you have nothing to complain about, Rodger. It may be taking a bit more time than I originally thought to return Lili to her rightful place and homeland—"

"I'll say." Rodger snorted and used his little finger to rearrange a pomaded yellow curl on his forehead. "A night in a sawpit, Mrs. Brack's tall tales—your methods are too subtle for my tastes."

"Not everyone's style is as ham-fisted as yours, my dear friend, but the effect will inevitably be the same." Tate's tongue flicked across his pale lips. "I only have Lili's welfare at heart, after all. You destroy that bestial whoreson who debauched my poor demented child, and I'll prove again that Lili is too unstable to be left to her own devices. I must take my dear daughter home again with me, where she truly belongs."

"Well, this campaign has taken too long already, and if Constance is as unbalanced as you say, why does Uncle Alex tell me she's remembering things?"

Tate's fork paused halfway to his mouth, and his voice became sharp. "What things?"

Rodger shrugged. "What difference does it make? But if Uncle Alex finds out—"

"Finds out what, nephew?" Alex Latham demanded coldly from the dining room door.

"Uncle!" Rodger leaped to his feet in obsequious welcome. "We missed you at luncheon. Come, take your chair, and I'll have Mrs. Brack tell Eloise to prepare your plate."

"I think not." Alex slammed the heavy door behind him and glared at his nephew. "I'd be afraid

I'd find a dinner knife in my spine by meal's end, you backstabbing, ungrateful imbecile! How could you be so utterly stupid?"

Rodger's eyes widened owlishly in bafflement. "Really, Uncle Alex, I have no idea what you mean."

Alex stalked to the table, his face flushed to a ruddy hue with choler, his white-knuckled fists clenched. "Tell me you don't know a ruffian by the name of Sagwin who has a particular fondness for whale oil fires!"

"Sagwin?" Bewildered, Rodger shook his head.

"Don't lie to me, you jackass!" Alex roared. "You think I couldn't find him? Greased a few palms in my time, you young fool, and I still know how. If you were going to hire someone to torch the *West Wind*, you should at least have made certain he left the goddamned city afterward!"

"Burn the—?" Rodger touched his fingertips to his pristine shirtfront. "Me? You think that I—?"

Furious, Alex struck Rodger full across the face, spinning the younger man back against a chair.

"When I waved enough greenbacks in his drunken face," Alex raged, "Sagwin told me himself he took his instructions from the man at Latham House!"

Hanging onto the carved mahogany chair, Rodger stared as the Reverend Cyrus Tate rose calmly from his seat. Beads of sweat popped out on Rodger's brow.

"You!" he breathed. "Cyrus, you fool!"

"And just a moment ago you were complaining I moved too slowly," Tate mocked softly.

Rodger turned frantically to his uncle. "Uncle Alex, I had nothing to do with it!"

"You expect me to believe that, do you?" Alex barked. "If word gets out, we're ruined. And if I could track Sagwin down, what makes you think someone else won't? Do you think we can buy the *McKins'* silence?"

"But, Uncle—"

"We're ruined in this city, I tell you! No one will do business with arsonists!" Alex's face contorted, and he made a sharp, dismissive motion. "I want you out of this house, now! And take this unnatural piece of filth with you!"

With a final contemptuous grimace, Alex turned for the door.

"Stop him." Cyrus Tate's quiet calmness was a sharp contrast to Alex's fury and Rodger's panic. He shoved something heavy into Rodger's numb hands. "Stop him."

The silver pepper mill caught Alex on the back of the head, and he dropped like a felled timber, sprawling on the colorful Turkey carpet. He groaned softly, then lay still. Rodger looked in horror at the blood-spattered object in his hands, then back at Tate in shocked disbelief.

"He'll take everything from you now, my son," Tate said softly. "Everything you've worked so hard for. He is a threat to you, just as Lili's memory is to me. We can't allow such threats to spoil the Lord's plan for us."

"I—I can't murder my own uncle!" Rodger gobbled like a turkey, his Adam's apple bobbing uncontrollably.

"There are better ways, for both of us." Tate smiled, showing teeth like pearls. "Let me help you."

Chapter 19

"What the devil are you trying to do to me?"
Constance jumped, startled from a pensive, thumbnail-chewing contemplation of her unfinished canvas by Lock's deadly quiet question. A bubble of resentment surfaced at his intrusion into her studio, especially at this moment when the portrait under her brush was coming to life and the sensation of discovery was imminent and increasingly urgent. The face belonged to the same matriarch who'd held such a place of importance in the *Sketchbook*, tantalizing and mysterious, yet so familiar. In another moment Constance was certain she could sweep aside the curtain that kept her memory veiled . . .

Even as she formed the thought, the certainty faded and reality intruded: the ache in her shoulders, the sticky perspiration beneath her paint-smeared smock, her braid lying heavily against her nape, the emptiness in her belly that said she'd worked through the luncheon hour well into the middle of this sultry July afternoon. With an exasperated sigh, Constance plunged her sable-hair brush into a jar of pungent linseed oil, wiping irritably at her hands with a rag as she turned to her husband.

Her regard was cool and wary, just as their relationship had been since their last argument, but as always, Lock's fierce masculine beauty took her breath and made her yearn to touch the angles of his proud archangel's face and feel the lithe strength of his body against her own. Only this morning, he'd loved her back to sleep after another recurrence of that old, terrifying dream, and though he'd left their bed silently, going off to work at the shipyard with Dylan before dawn, she'd hoped the estrangement over the matter of his brother's parentage and her own memory was, if not fully resolved, at least easing. But now, as Lock met her gaze, the fiery blue light behind his eyes held even more dissatisfaction than usual.

Constance lifted her chin a fraction. "Was I doing something wrong, Lauchlan?"

"Don't play the innocent with me, princess! You know damn well you saw Alex Latham behind my back after I ordered you to stay away from him!"

She shrugged, making a production of erasing a smear of red ocher from her knuckle. "What of it?"

An angry muscle twitched in his jaw, and a dull flush rolled over his cheekbones. "Whatever you said to him made him move to cover Latham tracks. Tip located a sailor by the name of Sagwin, well known for his handiness with a torch, but he shipped out for the Orient not an hour after being seen with old Alex."

"What?" Constance's head jerked up and her mind worked furiously. She had believed her grandfather when he'd said he personally had nothing to do with the *West Wind*'s destruction. That he appeared to be investigating her assertions of Latham involvement made her voice shake with growing hope and elation. "He believes me. Dear God, he believes me!"

"Believes you, hell! Is that all that's important to you?" Lock dragged his hand through his hair in a gesture of maddened frustration. "Your meddling spoiled a chance for us to repay the Lathams. This Sagwin could have been our trump card."

She jerked off her stained smock and threw it across a rocking chair. "I'm sick of this infernal tit for tat! It's disgusting, perverted, and it's got to stop somewhere!"

"God's teeth, woman," Lock thundered, "just whose side are you on?"

"Why does it always have to come down to sides?" she shot back.

"Because it can't be any other way. I won't have my own wife undermining me at every turn!" His hard fingers dug into her shoulders, and his expression was dark and imperious. "Choose, Constance. I must have your complete loyalty, or we have no future together."

The blood drained out of her face. "I've said I love you, Lock McKin, and I'd never do anything to bring you harm—"

He shook her, snapping her head back. "*Choose.*"

Tears welled up in her eyes and hung suspended on her dark lashes. "Between finding my sanity or the man I love?"

"Between the Lathams and the McKins."

"But we're all connected, don't you see?" she cried. "How can I make such a choice? It's impossible."

"You either stand with me or stand against me," he said in a stony voice. "It's as simple as that."

Helplessly, she shook her head. "I can't—I *won't*—fight this fight with you. I don't want a future that's filled only with bitterness and contention."

"That's it, then." He released her so abruptly that she staggered, and his face was as rigid and unmoving as iron.

"No!" Desperately, she grabbed his shirtfront. "Don't you dare think you can be rid of me so easily, Lock McKin! This is no black-and-white question, no mathematical equation that you and your damnable logic can solve! For God's sake—for *my* sake—you've got to bend a little, Iron Man!"

Lock's hand closed over her wrist, but she wouldn't release his shirt, and he would have been forced to hurt her to free himself from her grasp. Instead, they glared at each other, their breaths sawing in and out, stalemated.

"You see, Lock," she said softly, "it doesn't make you a failure to admit there aren't any clear answers. It was Enoch's fight, and his and James's and Eliza's tragedy, but it doesn't have to be *ours*."

His lip curled in a sneer. "You want me to forget it all? Roll over and lick the Latham hand like a cowering dog? I'd die first!"

"It doesn't make you weak to show compassion and to forgive your parents, and Alex, and me. It isn't dishonorable to abandon ideals that have lost their meaning!" Her voice was husky with tears and earnestness. "Those iron bands of pride bind *you*, not them. Hurt *you*, no one else. They keep you from accepting that wonderful, giving part of yourself I love so well, and they make you afraid to *feel*, because then you might have to admit you're just like me—a fraud."

He jerked, scowling down into her upraised face. "What nonsense is this?"

"Admit it, Lock," she murmured, twining her hands around his neck and pulling him closer. "You aren't really the Iron Man, you're only a man who hurts and needs and loves . . ." Her lips brushed his, beseeching, entreating. ". . . just like everyone else."

Constance felt Lock's hesitation and his tension, and pressed her mouth to his, pouring all her love and emotion into that kiss, praying somehow he would understand and believe. In the next instant, he thrust her away, and disappointment washed through her in a scalding tide.

"Damn you!" Growling, enraged, tempted, and furious at his own weakness, Lock exploded. Slamming his fist into the unfinished canvas, he sent it toppling to the floor.

"You think you can seduce me away from what I know is my duty? By God, I won't be swayed or lectured to regarding my own honor by a deceitful, conniving madwoman!"

The thrust struck home, and Constance gasped, stabbed at her most vulnerable point by his caustic denunciation. Every fear about herself raised its fusty head. Every inadequacy and insecurity returned a hundredfold as all the doubts she'd held at bay with Lock's help flooded her being again, transforming her back into that quaking, puking, fearful girl who'd stepped off the *Eliza* all those months ago. Nothing had changed. Crazy Lili hadn't gone anywhere. She'd only been in hiding.

Lock glared at her for another wrathful second; then with a rough sound he turned and stalked from the studio. When the front door slammed, the dam burst in Constance's soul and the tears came. Sobbing, crushed, she fled to their bedroom, swept along by the old need to run and hide from a life she found too painful.

Tears streaming, she raged about the bedchamber, ripping open drawers, throwing lacy garments into haphazard piles, searching out an old carpetbag and stuffing her petticoats and gowns into it until it bulged.

Madwoman, was she? Ha! Not mad enough to stay with a coldhearted bastard like Lock McKin! She had a bit of household money, enough to get out of Boston, anyway. Wretched, hateful city! What had she been thinking, trying to live in this snobbish, puritanical town with a man whose head was so full of science and ships he couldn't see that there were more important things in the world than misguided duty and outdated vengeance? She *had* been mad to hope to change him with her puny love! Well, there was always Paris!

Paris, indeed.

Constance sank down on the side of the bed, buried her face in the hem of Lock's Chinese robe, and gave in to a storm of weeping. There was no place in the world where she could run to escape what Lock had done to her heart. And running was the coward's way. Lock had once said it only prolonged the problem. How could she leave the man she loved and the only chance of happiness she was likely to find in this lifetime? Stiffening her resolve, Constance raised her head, sniffling, and dabbed her eyes with the robe.

"I won't make it so easy for him," she muttered fervently. "He loves me. I know he does. Even if he threatens to throw me down Haleakala's smoking throat, this time I *won't* run away."

Wiping her face dry, she smoothed back her hair into its braid and found a semblance of composure just as someone knocked on the entrance door below. With a little jolt of panic, she jumped to her feet, clutching the carpetbag guiltily, then shoved it under the bed. She was halfway down the stairs before she realized Lock wouldn't trouble to knock at his own front door. Feeling foolish, she opened the door to find a long-nosed hack driver removing his floppy hat.

"Message for Missus McKin," he said, holding out an envelope made of heavy, expensive paper. "I was told to wait for an answer."

Constance accepted the envelope and ripped it open, scanning the short missive with a horrified murmur. "Dear God, Grandpa's been hurt! Of course I'll come. Can you take me to Latham House, driver?"

She turned away as she spoke, dropping the note on the hall table and reaching for her bonnet and reticule in one swift movement.

"O' course, missus. Right this way."

Tying on her bonnet, Constance rushed after the man, down the steps to the street, where a rather decrepit but heavily curtained carriage waited. He attended to the niceties more politely than his appearance would have suggested, pausing with a hand on the door handle as she approached.

"Please hurry," Constance said, placing one foot on the step as he tugged the door open. "I fear something dreadful—"

The heavy perfume of ginger blossoms was like a solid wall, and she came up short, one foot on the threshold of the dim coach. The driver shoved her from behind, and a slim white hand grasped her wrist and forcibly propelled her into the stiflingly hot interior. The door slammed, and she landed hard on the slick leather seat.

In the flicker of an eyelid Constance took in her cousin Rodger's blank, shocked expression from the opposite bench, and the too-still form in the corner whose silver ruff of identifying whiskers was visible despite the turned-up collar and tipped-down hat. But it was the man on the seat beside her who made her recoil in terror.

"Welcome, my dear," Cyrus Tate said softly, his red eyes gleaming in the dimness. "I've missed you, Lili."

Constance took a breath to scream, but a fist out of nowhere landed on her chin, spangles exploded behind her eyes, and she plunged into nothingness . . .

Lock knew Constance was gone the moment he stepped inside the quiet house that evening. It was still and lifeless without her presence, as if her going had deprived the air itself of some essential life-giving element. It was no more than he expected or deserved after the hurtful things he'd said, but he hadn't anticipated that the loss of a dream would hurt so badly, or that his usual stoic acceptance would fail him so utterly.

"What do you mean she's gone?" Dylan demanded hotly. After a long day helping Lock supervise the *Argonaut*'s half-finished rigging, he favored his splinted left arm in its sling, but his fatigued expression under its short new crop of sable-brown whiskers changed to instant consternation. "Gone where?"

"It doesn't matter, does it?" Lock returned bitterly. "She's left me."

Dylan's eyes reflected his shock; then, shouting Constance's name, he searched the house, poking his nose into the disastrous mess of her studio and mounting the stairs at a run. When he returned moments later, his features were stiff and grim.

"She's packed her things, all right. Dammit, Lock! What did you do to her?"

At the hall table, Lock looked up from a perusal of the discarded summons. Jaw clenched, he flapped the letter. "Only told her she had to decide between me and the Lathams. You can see for yourself the choice she made."

Dylan snatched the paper, read it, then crumpled it in his good fist with an oath. "You arrogant son of a . . . That's the most monumentally selfish thing I've ever heard! Choose me and no one else? Constance is capable of depths of emotion you can't even imagine. She loves you, you damn fool, but how could she live with such an ultimatum!"

"Let it go, Dylan," Lock interrupted wearily. His chest felt tight, and his throat was hot with the pressure of tears that hurt too much to shed. "It's better this way."

"That lady's the best thing that's ever happened to you," Dylan replied angrily. "Are you just going to let her go?"

"I've got no choice."

"I suppose not if you're trying to walk in Father's

footsteps." Dylan's tone turned scathing. "Well, congratulations, Lock. You've succeeded in making yourself as hard and unforgiving a bastard as Enoch McKin ever was. Maybe Constance is right to clear out while she can. God knows Mother never could, and living with a man who never gave her an ounce of feeling made her so unhappy it killed her."

Startled, Lock scowled at his brother. "How can you say that?"

"Don't think I was too young to know. Mother wasn't strong to start with, but Father was so cold to her she withered like a rose struck by hoarfrost. When she got sick that last time, she simply didn't want to live." Dylan swallowed, and his brown eyes were murky with old sorrow and hurt. "Two small boys who loved her weren't enough."

Lock's throat constricted, and he laid his hand on his brother's shoulder. "Dylan—"

Dylan shook off Lock's comforting hand. "I only wish she'd had Constance's courage to leave a coldhearted man. Then Mother might have found some happiness."

A muscle twitched beside Lock's mouth. Until this moment, though he'd shared the loss, he hadn't really understood the depths of Dylan's bitterness and pain over Eliza's death. Perhaps there was something he could give his brother that would help ease it a bit—understanding. But that would entail embracing an idea he'd fought hard to deny, and an acceptance that would forever shatter assumptions about himself and his family that had forged him into what he was. To sustain his pride, Lock could let Dylan remain ignorant and go on hurting, but if brotherly love meant anything, Dylan deserved a chance to decide for himself which version of the truth he'd make his own.

"Maybe she did find it, for a time," Lock said. His voice was quiet, but strange and uncertain as he struggled like a blind man to feel his way through a thicket of conflicting emotions. He only knew his affection for his brother demanded no less.

Now it was Dylan's turn to look startled. "You'd better explain that."

"It's Constance's idea. You may not like what you hear."

"Try me."

Haltingly, Lock told Dylan about the locket, about a liaison between Eliza McKin and James Latham, and about conclusions regarding Dylan's parentage that could well be true, considering the physical resemblance between Dylan, the portrait, and Constance's memory of her father.

"My God." Dylan scrubbed his fingers through his unfamiliar beard, shaking his head in amazement. "Jesus, what a god-awful tangle!"

"Perhaps you'd rather not have known. And it may not even be true . . ."

"Can you look at me and deny it, Lock? What an irony!" Dylan laughed harshly. "Imagine, me—a Latham. It puts rather a new light on things, doesn't it?"

"You're still my brother."

"Good God, and it makes Constance my sister, doesn't it?" Dylan grinned wryly. "That's some consolation."

"Look, Dylan, I know this is a shocking possibility—"

"No, it's got to be the truth. It makes too much sense, don't you see?" Pacing restlessly, Dylan chewed his lip. "But if Father suspected I wasn't truly his, he never let on to me."

"Enoch was equally aloof to all," Lock agreed heavily. "But was he cold and hard because his wife had betrayed him with another, or did she look for the love she needed elsewhere because he was cold and hard?"

"That's a riddle we'll never solve. All I know is he was dead long before he took his life, every scrap of humanity and compassion squeezed from him so there was nothing left but a wasteland. Small wonder he chose not to live."

"Maybe he missed Mother too much," Lock murmured.

An upswelling of sorrow and loss made his chest tighten and his eyes sting. He'd tried to emulate Enoch all his life, tried to live out the drive for vengeance against the Lathams, tried to build a career that would make his father proud. All he'd succeeded in doing was to bring the tragedy full circle, ending as his father had, without the woman he needed beyond anything, alone and empty. He could understand Enoch's despair, for his own future stretched out before him bleak and arid as a desert.

Sinking down on the stairs, Lock covered his eyes, overcome with pity for Enoch. And for himself. "What a waste. What a goddamned bloody awful waste."

"You're not like him," Dylan said softly. He leaned on the newel-post, both fascinated and appalled at Lock's amazing display of defeat and resignation. "You may carry the only McKin blood in this family, but you aren't like Enoch."

Lock gave a self-derisive snort. "Not much. I'm better. Iron Man McKin, that's me. Can't even keep a wife."

"Go after her, man!"

Lock heaved a ragged sigh, and his face worked. "You said it. She'll be better off without me."

"But you won't. That woman's given you your humanity and a chance to care about something more than charts and ships' plans. Don't let that slip away."

Lock laced his fingers behind his neck and hung his head, staring at the patch of floor between his boots. "I said some things . . . she'll never forgive."

Dylan spit a crude expletive to show his contempt for that remark. "So tell her you were wrong. She loves you, you idiot! Don't you care about her at all?"

Lock continued to ponder the floor, and his voice was muffled with pain. "I love her more than my own life."

"Did you ever tell her that?"

Slowly, Lock lifted his head. A dusky flush heated his cheekbones as he admitted his failure, his cowardice. "No."

"So tell her! Good God, man, are you going to let your damned pride stand in the way?"

"It has nothing to do with pride."

Dylan's eyes narrowed a fraction. "Hasn't it? I imagine that's what Enoch thought, too. But who'll be the greater failure if you let Constance go now?"

Breathing hard against a weight in his chest, Lock struggled inwardly. Dylan was right. He'd been afraid of failing his father for so long, it was difficult to see another path. But he needed Constance—her love, her laughter, her impulsive liveliness—so badly, he'd crawl on his belly to get her back. And he'd have to. He'd have to swallow his pride, humble himself to make peace with the Lathams, and give up forever his obsession with revenge if he had a chance in hell of convincing Constance they could make a future together.

It was hard. It was damned terrifying. She might not even believe him, and he couldn't blame her if she didn't. It was the most difficult thing he'd ever demanded of himself, but it was a small price to pay if he could redeem himself in the eyes of the woman he loved. Whether she was Crazy Lili or Constance Latham or simply his own beautiful pagan princess, she was the most precious gift ever to come into his solitary life. If she'd have him, he'd spend the rest of it showing her and telling her just how much she meant to him.

Lock stood up. "I'm going to fetch my wife. Coming?"

"To see the Iron Man brought to his knees before a mere slip of a female?" Dylan grinned, and for a brief flash, the sudden mischief that danced in his brown eyes made him look uncannily like his sister. "I wouldn't miss it!"

It had to be the dream again. Constance moaned and screwed her eyes tight against another wave of dizzying terror. In a moment she'd wake up in Lock's arms and he'd kiss away her fears . . . but no, that wasn't possible. They'd quarreled most bitterly, hadn't they? Her brow pleated as she tried to follow the thread of that painful thought.

Fighting her way up through a black mist, she became conscious of other discomforts: her awkward reclining position, a constriction about her wrists that held her immobile, the cottony taste of a linen handkerchief reeking of ginger water tied against her lips. But it was the familiar tilt and dip of movement and the rushing, sibilant sounds on all sides that filled her with horror. Her eyes popped open, and she knew the worst.

Dear God, she was in a cabin aboard a ship plying the open waters!

Shivering, retching dryly, Constance struggled upright, only to be forestalled by the short hemp cord that bound her hands to a carved dowel adorning the side of the narrow bunk. Desperately, she used her fingers to scrape aside the muffling gag, drinking in great draughts of air to battle the vertigo that was making her head swim. Her jaw ached abominably, but she clenched it to stifle a wave of nausea as her eyes adjusted to the cabin's enveloping darkness.

A gruff voice called out, "Constance?"

"Alex!" She lunged toward the shadowy figure in the opposite bunk, only to be drawn up short by her bonds. Sitting on the edge of the bed, she cursed in frustration and fear. *"Parbleu!* Alex, are you all right?"

"Head aches. Damned craven ruffians walloped me when my back was turned." Alex, too, was bound by ropes to the bunk, and he gave them a futile, defiant shake, but his voice wavered revealingly. "Thank God you're unhurt. Was beginning to think you weren't going to wake up, my girl."

"What's happening?" she asked, bewilderment causing her to tremble violently. "Why are we here?"

Alex's craggy features twisted. "Rodger. That greedy mongrel! You were right, Constance. He and Tate burned the *West Wind.* When I found out, he panicked, and here we are, safely out of the way, bound for who the devil knows where!"

"Oh, God, this isn't possible." She moaned softly. "Lock will think ... we've got to get out of here! Yell, Alex! Someone must hear us."

"I've already tried. We must be the only passengers. No telling what story Rodger concocted— maybe they think we're carrying a contagion or madmen or convicts."

"In truth, I *will* go insane if I'm forced to stay here," Constance murmured, gulping for breath. "Oh, God, oh, God ..."

A key rattled, and the cabin door swung inward. "I'm glad to hear you have not abandoned your faith, my daughter."

Constance gasped and cringed into the corner. The Reverend Cyrus Tate carried a small shuttered lantern, and the light threw his milky features into the stark black-and-white relief of a death's-head. Her fear of the water paled to insignificance beside the terror she now experienced.

"Well, it's about time!" Alex snapped, struggling into a sitting position similar to Constance's.

"What's the meaning of this outrage, you leprous hypocrite? I demand you release us immediately!"

"Quiet, old man," Tate chided gently, hanging the lamp on a hook. "I have not Job's patience with those who chafe me. And unfortunately, you've become more than a simple inconvenience. Irritate me, and you may find yourself joining Jonah in the belly of the whale."

"You dare not!" Alex scoffed. "I'll not cow to a bleating braggart's empty threats."

Tate chuckled, a sound like papers rattling in the wind. "You'll have plenty of time over the next months to learn differently."

"Months?" Constance repeated, her voice so faint she was surprised Tate heard her.

"Yes, my dear one. Even so swift a ship as the *Odyssey* cannot carry us home overnight."

Constance jumped on hearing the *Odyssey*'s name. Lock's ship! Somehow that was comforting to her, but it only incensed Alex all the more.

"You villain! I own this ship! Someone aboard will figure out what you're trying to do and put a stop to it!"

Tate carefully removed and pocketed his smoked spectacles, and his bloodless lips made a moue of regret.

"Hardly likely when Rodger's instructions to the captain put me completely in charge. And don't get any wild ideas, my dear Alexander. The crew understands the passengers suffer from an unfortunate nervous condition that demands complete solitude and rest for the duration of the voyage home. Pity we had to sail without a full cargo, of course, but it matters little, and once we skirt the coast and pass New York Light, we'll set a fair course for Lahaina."

"No," Constance whispered, horror-stricken. "Not back to Lahaina."

"But of course." Tate stepped nearer and ran his fingers across her cheek. His skin was dry as a serpent's, and she was just as repulsed, yet sat placidly beneath his touch, mesmerized like a sparrow confronted by a cobra.

"Your place has always been there with me, seeing to God's work together," he crooned, stroking her throat. "Where others may try to use you and your legacy for their own selfishness, I have only your best interests at heart, my sweet Lili, my precious Lilio. Did not James give you into my safekeeping for that very reason?"

"James!" Alex exclaimed. "But you said—"

The Reverend Tate released Constance and gave the old man a pearly smile. "The Lord forgives small untruths for a greater good, my friend. I could not tell you then that James Latham sired his daughter off a princess of the ancient and royal Hawaiian blood. Who knew what that unscrupulous whoreson McKin would do if he found himself in possession of his wife's vast sugar estates? I had to protect her."

"You mean protect your own interests, don't you, you lying bastard!" Alex shouted, indignation and fury reddening his face as he struggled unsuccessfully to stand. "You're the one who's reaped the benefits that are rightfully hers, haven't you? And lied about her birthright! Constance, I'm sorry I didn't believe you. Forgive me, girl."

"I wasn't wrong," she muttered, and a perplexed frown knitted her brow. Surely with this knowledge she'd remember, and Crazy Lili would disappear for good. But there was nothing, only that hazy wall in her head hiding the past as always.

"It was the working of the Evil One that made you run away from me," Tate said softly. He touched Constance's hair as though unable to stop himself. "But I forgive you. All will be well, Lili, I promise."

She drew back, shuddering, turning her face

aside so she didn't have to look into his unnatural eyes. "No. Uncle Cyrus, please . . ."

"Repentance is all the sweeter when the prodigal returns." He bent closer so that the cloying fragrance of ginger sickened her, and ran his hand over the curve of her shoulder down to the swell of her breast. His breath came faster. "There will be ample time during our voyage for you to learn to please me."

Constance's eyes dilated in revulsion and terror. She had repented for past sins under her foster uncle's violent hand too many times to forget what that meant now, but her fear was compounded by confusion over his suggestive touches, his talk of pleasing him. He couldn't mean . . . but it seemed he did.

Her gorge rose. "I won't!"

Tate opened his white coat, revealing the horn grip of an ugly Paterson Colt protruding from his waistband. He smiled, serene and unperturbed as a marble bust. "You wouldn't want anything to happen to your grandfather, would you, Lili?"

At that mild threat, something hidden and deeply primitive snapped inside Constance. Shrieking, she twisted her shoulders to throw off Tate's loathsome touch and kicked out with both heels. The blow caught him on the thighs and sent him thudding against the opposite bulkhead. He righted himself easily, a barely audible growl emanating from his throat.

"Leave her be, you slimy bastard!" Alex thundered, tugging viciously at his bindings. "Help, someone! Rape! Murder! Anyone—"

Spinning on his heel, Tate whipped the revolver out of his waistband and slammed it into Alex's face. The old man reeled backward onto the bunk, blood from his smashed nose staining his silver whiskers. Snarling, Tate crouched over him, hitting him again and again . . .

Time shuttered down to a single pinpoint and hung suspended. Images spiraled through Constance, flashes of another time, another violent act. The pictures in her head blinked in and out, becoming one with the brutal pummeling happening before her eyes. In a white-hot flash, the hazy wall in her head burned away forever.

She screamed.

Tate whirled around, and Constance stared into his red, lust-filled eyes. She was ten years old again. *And she remembered everything.*

Chapter 20

"I tell you, she ain't here, and neither is old Mr. Latham!"

"You damned bitch." Lock grabbed Mrs. Brack by her smocked apron bib as comprehension smacked him between the eyes.

Finding this woman at Latham House this evening made him savage. She and Tate and Rodger had played a cunning, insidious game with Constance, and Lock's own doubts and misplaced advice had even helped them! With a snarl, he roughly thrust the colorless she-snake out of his way and stalked across the checkered marble foyer toward the parlor. Dylan followed close behind.

"You can't go in there!" Mrs. Brack spluttered.

"Watch me."

Lock splintered the double paneled doors with one violent kick. Mrs. Brack gave a terrified screech and scuttled away. To hell, Lock sincerely hoped. A natty figure slumped in an armchair before the cold fireplace, a cut-glass liquor decanter dangling from his elegant fingers. Lock halted before the chair, his feet spread belligerently, the fire of battle in his blue eyes.

"Where are they, Rodger?"

Rodger lifted his thinning pate and glared blearily at Lock. "Damned mannerless dog, barging in

377

on my—" He belched delicately. "—celebrations. Go
'way, McKin."

"I want my wife. Where is she?"

"And where's old Alex?" Dylan demanded. "The
note said he'd been hurt."

"No, no." Discarding the empty bottle, Rodger
waved a negligent hand, his words slurring drunk-
enly. "Just a li'l bump, is all. Nothing to worry
about."

Grabbing Rodger's lapels, Lock hauled him to his
feet. "Damnation, you sotted prig! Where's Constance?"

Rodger's expression turned mulish and resentful.
"Wa's the matter, McKin? Wife sick of you? Can't
say I blame her for going home. She got a bellyful,
I'll bet."

"Home?" Lock's stomach lurched. Good God,
had his stubbornness pushed her that far? How
could he bear it if Constance had run so far from
him this time that he'd lost her forever? His grip
tightened on Rodger's jacket. "Tell me, damn you!
What do you know?"

Rodger's shifty glance slid uneasily away from
Lock's. "Nothing, I swear."

"He's lying," Dylan said flatly. "Probably about a
lot of things."

"Don't think you can blame me for all your troubles!" Rodger shrilled. Moisture dotted his forehead. "It wasn't me who burned the *West Wind*."

Dylan's dark eyes narrowed dangerously. "But I'll
bet you know who did."

"I broke your nose for you once before, Rodger,"
Lock said tightly. "It'll give me great pleasure to do
it again if you don't start talking. *Now.*"

Rodger's face crumpled. Cringing, whining, he
babbled excuses.

"It wasn't my doing. It was like being under a
spell. Cyrus said to stop him, but I didn't mean to
strike Uncle Alex with the pepper mill, and then I

didn't know what else to do . . ." Weak tears streamed down Rodger's flushed face. "I'd be ruined, no matter what I did, don't you understand? My place, my position. I've worked so hard. I couldn't bear to lose it all for one mistake!"

"Where . . . are . . . they?" Lock shook Rodger with each gritted-out word.

"Gone," he gasped. "All of them, aboard the *Odyssey*, bound for the Pacific this evening. Cyrus promised to take care of everything, and what else could I do?"

"Take care of them how?" Dylan demanded. "Pitch them overboard at the first sign of blue water?"

Rodger blanched. "No, no, of course not. Just a long trip. See the world and such."

"While you run Latham and Company and live the high life?" Dylan sneered. "And how do you expect to explain yourself to old Alex if and when he returns?"

"I—I'll think of something," Rodger muttered sullenly. Then his tone turned pleading again. "I didn't plan it this way, but I had no other choice! Doesn't that satisfy you?"

"Not by a damned long shot!" Contemptuously, Lock shoved Rodger back into the chair, but his insides congealed with fear, and the look he shot Dylan was haggard. "Constance would never go anywhere willingly with Tate! He's the one—"

"Yes, I know," Dylan said, his face as grim as his brother's. "We've got to stop them somehow."

Rodger's drunken, derisive laughter rang out. "Good luck to you with that! Didn't the famous McKin brothers brag the *Odyssey* was the fastest ship afloat? There's nothing you can do. You'll never catch them!"

Something snapped inside Lock. He caught Rodger by the throat and raised a fist to wipe away his gloating smile. Owl-eyed, Rodger choked and whimpered, scraping ineffectually at Lock's viselike grip on his jugular. Wrath burned Lock's blood, but taking his revenge on this sniveling, greedy weakling suddenly held no appeal.

"If you're still in Boston when I return," Lock said in a deadly voice, "you'll answer to the Iron Man. Understand?"

Rodger nodded vigorously, and with a growl of disgust, Lock released him to flop like a slaughtered goose on the ornate rug.

With a sharp gesture to his brother, he turned on his heel. "Come on, Dylan."

"Rodger's right about the *Odyssey*'s speed," Dylan said when they reached the street. "We can telegraph New York for assistance, and if they can signal her before she heads for the open water ..." He shrugged his frustration at the poor possibility for success. "Any other ideas?"

Lock stopped short beside their hired carriage. "We have to go after them."

"What? How? Lock, it's impossible!"

"I've got no choice." Lock's eyes were haunted. For once in his life, he trusted wholeheartedly to the *feeling* rising from his gut. "Tate will kill Constance this time. Or worse."

"You'll have to kill me now," Constance said softly. "You tried before, but now you'll have to do it."

She saw understanding dawn behind Cyrus Tate's crazed eyes, and he slowly lowered the blood-glazed revolver. Alex moaned in the bunk behind him, but her concern for her grandfather would have to wait. Never taking her eyes from Tate's, she parted her lips in a smile of hatred and pure defiance that burned away her fear.

"You've been dreading this moment for over ten years, haven't you, Uncle? For when I could call you by your true name." She spit the word. *"Murderer."*

He took a step toward her, his face working strangely. "My child . . ."

"It wasn't a fever that killed my father, it was you! You hit him when he was drunk and defenseless, smashed his skull from behind like the despicable coward you are. And when I saw that, you came after me and held me under the surf until I was nearly dead."

She shuddered, reliving the suffocating terror, seeing the silver bubbles rising from her own tortured lungs, and knowing she was going to die like her papa. Small wonder the water terrorized her! With her golden gaze blazing, Constance's tone became mocking, taunting.

"But someone came along, and you had to pretend you'd rescued me instead, didn't you, Uncle? Did you pray for me to live or die then? A dead girl would be of no use, for my inheritance would be reclaimed by my mother's people, but what would the poor distraught child say when she awoke? Perhaps you are one of the Lord's favored, for He answered your prayers by taking my memory—until now."

"Quiet, Lili—"

"Don't call me that, *haole!*" she hissed, tugging at her bound hands. "You have no right! Only my grandmother Kanai called me Lili. My mother was her own half-white daughter, so she understood when Namaka fell in love with James Latham. Kanai's blood made me a princess of the royal house, and when at her passing I became heir to her lands, it was then your attention fell on my father and me."

"Poor, demented child. You're surely out of your head again," Tate said coldly, shoving the ugly revolver back into his waistband. "You've been ill so long . . ."

"No more!" Constance refused to let those old threats silence her now, and her voice dripped with scorn. "How you must have feared this day! All these years, keeping my memories at bay with your cruelty, calling me Crazy Lili, trying to convince me and everyone else I was mad. But my eyes are open, and *I know the truth.*"

Remembrance flowed in welcome torrents through Constance's head. The happy, loving life as Princess Kanai's favorite and only grandchild. Her father's gentleness, his sadness over Namaka's death, and the solace he sought in drink and a misguided search for peace at Holy Sanctuary Mission. She understood now how losing his first love, Eliza, and then his young native wife had been a burden too heavy for James Latham to bear. And she remembered clearly that awful day when Tate's temper had exploded in violence.

"Papa wouldn't do as you wanted," Constance murmured. "Even drunk and sick, he respected and loved my mother's people and wanted to protect the royal sugar holdings from your greed. Instead, you murdered him, then pillaged my birthright."

"They are an ignorant, slothful people in need of my guidance. I've made the plantation what it is. Without me, it would be nothing. Jehovah deprived me of so much, why should I not be rewarded for my enterprise?"

"You played the king at my people's expense!" Constance's lip curled. "You pitiful defect! You aberrant slug! As if any amount of earthy pomp could disguise your vileness!"

"Shut up!" Tate's slim white hand closed around her throat.

"You'll have to kill me," she said once more, forcing the words past her constricted vocal cords. "I'm not afraid of you anymore."

"You're more useful to me alive." His breath whispered across her face, mingling foully with the scent of blood and blossoms. "And there are more pleasurable ways for me to ensure your cooperation."

She laughed at him. "Does talk of rape make you feel more the man? I'm not a child you can terrorize any longer! That puny cock rises only in the presence of another's pain. We both know you couldn't mount a flea, much less a real woman!"

"Whore of Babylon!" Tate slapped her. "Silence!"

With the coppery taste of blood in her mouth, Constance laughed again. No matter how dire her circumstances, she knew she would never again feel totally powerless. "Go to hell."

Tate raised his hand again, but the sound of trampling feet and shouted orders as the watch changed above decks made him hesitate. Pushing Constance backward onto the bunk, he glared at her with his red eyes, breathing hard from impotent rage.

"I'll deal with you at my leisure, Lili. You have much to learn."

Constance licked at the trickle of blood on her lip. "And you have much to answer for. Hell burns hot for hypocrites who pursue their evil in the Lord's name."

Tate's colorless eyebrows lifted slightly, and he showed his perfect teeth. "I shall enjoy a battle of wills. Until then, I suggest you reflect on the meaning of repentance and what value you place on the old man's life."

The cabin door closed behind him, and the lock clicked. Constance sat tensed for a long second, then slumped, raising her bound hands to her stinging cheek.

"By gum, girl," Alex croaked, "you do the name Latham proud."

"Grandpa?" Her voice shook now. "He hurt you."

"Easy, Constance. It looks worse than it is."

His features were swollen and bloody, and she

heard the pain behind his bravado. An old man couldn't take much punishment, no matter how valiant his heart. "You heard?"

"Most of it." Alex grunted. "The truth at last, out of the devil's own mouth. Hope your teeth are as sharp as your tongue, my girl."

A gurgle of laughter surprised her. "What?"

"To chew through these ropes. We aren't going to let him get away with this, are we?"

Constance sobered again. "No."

"Then we've got to be ready when he comes back." Alex's voice was strained. "I won't allow him to use me to bend you to his perverted will. There must be someone aboard who will listen to reason, if only we can free ourselves. He's mad, isn't he?"

She shuddered. "Yes." A relieved, wondering smile touched her lips. "But I'm not. I never was, really."

"No, the Lord gave you enough grit to endure even that, and I'm damned proud of you. But hurry, girl. We haven't much time."

From the weakness in her grandfather's voice, Constance knew he was right. She tore at the hemp ropes with her teeth, pushing aside all thoughts of Lock. He'd believe she'd run away again without a word, and that was even more painful than the bloody welts that were on her wrists when she finally tore free of her bonds.

As the first rays of dawn peeked through the porthole, she untied Alex and bathed his swollen face in water from a tin jug she found beneath an attached cabinet. He was conscious but weak, and she racked her brain desperately for a way the two of them could overcome a madman armed with a pistol. It was only a matter of time before Tate came back to resume his torment. If somehow they could escape, surely they could appeal to the captain. Grimly, Constance examined the door, then worked

at the keyhole with a hairpin. The futility of that effort was soon apparent, and she'd just turned her
attention to the iron hinges that held the cabin door
when Alex spoke from the bunk.

"We've changed course."

She went immediately to his side, laying her
hand on his brow. At least he wasn't feverish.
"What does it mean, do you think?"

"Probably that we've left the coastline and are
headed for the open water," Alex said heavily.

Constance's heart fell. She pried open the tiny
square porthole, standing on tiptoe to gaze out, and
was surprised by the number of vessels within
sight. Ketches and sloops, fishing boats and trawl-
ers, steam tugs and coal carriers paralleled their
path in the distance, then were left behind by the
Odyssey's superior speed.

Constance turned to her grandfather eagerly.
"There's so much activity, we can't be far from
shore. Perhaps we can signal one of these boats!"

From the deck overhead, shouted orders, the
harsh clapping thunder of sails unfurling, and the
whine of ropes through a windlass made a raucous
disturbance. The *Odyssey* heeled over, changing
course yet again, and Constance grabbed the edge
of the bunk for support.

"What the devil?" Alex rose and struggled to the
porthole. His lip was puffy, and one eye was black-
ened and swollen shut, but his chin jutted as pugnaciously as ever. "Something's amiss, girl. You'd
think we were under attack . . ."

As the *Odyssey* came about, the scene visible from
the porthole shifted, revealing a ship with her sails
straining full, silhouetted against the plum-and-
saffron streaks of the dawn sky.

"There's the culprit," Alex grunted. "A rare
beauty, that. Looks like she's trying to outpace us,
too."

Constance frowned, perplexed and tantalized by

something unexpected and yet so familiar her eyes grew wide.

"You great, lovely, perishing dreamer," she whispered, dazed and awestruck. "You did it."

"What is it?"

"Our deliverance, Grandpa!" Constance's face shone radiant with joy at the miracle before her eyes and the swelling love within her heart. "It's the *Argonaut!* The Iron Man's come for us!"

"He's too late."

Constance and Alex jumped at the harsh statement and turned to find Cyrus Tate glaring at them from the companionway door. His hair stood out in stark white patches, and his face twitched, but the girlish hand holding the ugly revolver didn't tremble. Fast as a striking rattlesnake, he grabbed Constance's wrist and twisted it up behind her back. She cried out from the pain.

"Give it up, Tate," Alex growled. "The game's over. Free us, and you may go on your way gladly—to hell, for all I care!"

Tate pressed the barrel of the gun to the curve of Constance's jaw. "Not just yet, Alex. Come ahead of us, and be careful what you do if you value Lili's life."

Ruddy with impotent rage, Alex had no choice but to comply, moving carefully into the companionway as instructed. Tate pushed Constance after her grandfather, and she swallowed hard, holding herself tense against the agony in her arm and the cold caress of the steel against her jawbone.

"What are you going to do with us?" Alex demanded over his shoulder.

"Captain Isaacs requires incentive to outrun our pursuit." Tate smiled tightly. "He'll make the correct choice, or see Lili's brains splattered all over his quarterdeck. Now, march!"

* * *

"Still no response to our signals, sir!" The look-out's call drifted down over the heaving deck of the *Argonaut*.

"Damn! For a minute I'd thought she'd eased up," Captain Dylan McKin muttered. "Signal her again!"

Standing at his brother's side at the helm, Lock McKin cast a weather eye at the clouds of white sails stretched out above them. The freshening wind was abeam, every scrap of canvas was aloft, and all studding sails were set. The *Argonaut* cut through the green Atlantic chop, sending arcs of white spray high on both sides of her sharp, elegant prow, fly-ing at a remarkable clip for a ship only half rigged, with only a third of the proper ballast aboard and a skeleton crew.

Grimly, Lock judged the diminishing distance to the *Odyssey*. Dylan had ordered a course that would bring them alongside the other ship's port quarter in an effort to crowd the vessel toward shore and away from the open sea-lanes. Dylan squeezed every extra knot of velocity out of this ship, demanding as much or even more than the overstressed sheets and full, iron-hard sails could stand. It was a dangerous and desperate gamble, but they had no choice.

"We'll make it," Lock said. *We must.*

"Unless our jerry rigging collapses or the wind shifts." The partially fitted topgallant masts creaked alarmingly in a sudden gust, but Dylan ignored the sound of impending disaster with an air of reckless equanimity. "Hell, Lock, who'd have thought the Iron Man would take such a chance? You've set all of Boston on its ear! Nay, even all of the eastern sea-board, judging by the number of escorts we've picked since we dropped the dog shoes on the *Ar-gonaut*."

"The devil take Boston," Lock growled, for once caring nothing for his own repute or public opinion.

But there was certainly no doubt the McKin

brothers' surprising actions had stirred the water-front's curiosity and caught a city's imagination. A kidnapping and a desperate rescue effort—the word spread like wildfire into the markets and homes, across the front pages of the evening newspapers, and onto every seaworthy vessel south of Boston Light.

In the space of just hours, telegrams went out to the port authorities all along the coast, Tip and Jedediah rousted out crews, and a major vessel was launched in a manner totally unprecedented in the annals of marine history, changing a quiet Boston summer evening into the event of the decade. Word of mouth produced a crowd to cheer on the *Argonaut* as she slid off her cradles into Boston Harbor. Before she'd stopped bobbing, tugs towed her to the bay's entrance. Under Dylan's expert guidance, even the deficiencies of her unfinished rigging didn't slow her as she disappeared into the night to take up the chase.

And they'd done it. Miraculously, off the New York coast, first light had shown they were closing on the *Odyssey*. Within Lock's heart, fear for Constance's safety mingled with pride for the performance of his great ship. The *Odyssey* was no slacker, either, as well he knew, but the *Argonaut*'s swiftness was a vindication of his vision as a naval architect and shipbuilder. Only he'd never imagined that he'd have to depend so completely on his own handiwork to save the woman who'd become more important to him than any renown or worldly accomplishment. And it wasn't over yet.

"The only ship in the world capable of catching the *Odyssey* is this one," Lock said to Dylan. "I designed the *Argonaut* for speed and hard usage, and, by God, I intend for her to do her duty!"

"They've got a complete rig and more sail," Dylan warned.

"But we've got Captain Dylan McKin, the fastest

driver this side of Canton," Lock rejoined. "Spare nothing, do you hear?"

"Aye, I hear." Dylan grinned. "Miss Philpot gets her grudge match at last. God, what a race!"

"My only concern is stopping that ship before Tate—" Lock broke off, his jaw working under its layer of black stubble. "What I'd give for a couple of hundred-and-ten-pounders right now."

"Don't worry. You're not the only one who learned a bit about pirating in the China Sea. We'll cut across the *Odyssey*'s quarter until she's either hauled in or run aground, I promise you."

Dylan raised the ship's glass to his eye to inspect their quarry, then gave a grunt of surprise. "Look there, Lock! A woman—"

Lock grabbed the glass, focusing on a group of figures standing beside the *Odyssey*'s wheelhouse. Tate's stark white hair was like a beacon, but the dark head beside his . . .

"Connie." The vise that had squeezed Lock's heart since she'd gone missing eased a trifle. "Thank God. She's alive."

"What's Isaacs about?" Dylan muttered to himself, scowling. "Can't he see—damnation, they're putting out the royals!"

"Don't let her escape!" Lock shouted. "String up everything we have!"

Dylan cursed roundly. "Dammit, all we've got left is our nightshirts! I'm not sure I can—oh, *hell!*"

With a sharp "crack" like a cannon shot, a topgallant mast split under the strain. Tortured wood shrieked and splintered with the force of an explosion. The topgallant collapsed in a tangle of suddenly free-swinging spars, lashing ropes, and shredded rigging, falling and flapping like a wounded bird toward the deck below. Commotion broke out among the harried crew, who dodged the lethal debris with the nimbleness of monkeys and a flurry of curses that would have made even the crustiest old salt blush for shame. Dylan shouted commands through a brass mouth trumpet, restoring order immediately, but the damage was done and irrevocable.

With absolute clarity and cold-blooded calculation, Lock assessed the disaster. In another moment, the *Odyssey* would pull out of their reach. They wouldn't get another chance. He estimated stresses, velocities, and hull strengths, compared weaknesses, burdens, and maneuverability. In a split second, Lock used the training of a lifetime to come to a decision.

"Steer across her bow, helmsman!" he ordered.

The sailor hesitated, looking at his captain for confirmation.

"If the *Odyssey* won't head up into the wind," Dylan said, "we'll ram."

"Yes." Lock's features were as carved and determined as a figurehead as he coolly accepted the risks, the sacrifice, the danger. "Do it."

"Keep going, I tell you!" Cyrus Tate jabbed the barrel of the revolver against Constance's chin. "I'll kill her, I swear!"

Captain Isaacs, a dour, bearded Down Easterner, clamped his teeth together in fury. "They're cutting across our bow, you damn fool! If we collide, we'll all die!"

Wind whipping her hair about her face, Constance bit her lip against the throb in her abused shoulder socket. Alex staggered at the railing, and panicked disbelief scored Captain Isaacs's expression as the magnificent flying marvel that was the *Argonaut* bore down upon them. Cries of alarm ricocheted from every portion of the *Odyssey*, but Tate held adamant.

"They won't do it, you'll see," he promised. "The whoreson McKin won't risk his slut's life."

Constance groaned, more in anguish than in fear. What was Lock doing? She couldn't let this happen!

"When Mr. Latham instructed me to follow your orders, he never meant I should give over my common sense!" Captain Isaacs ground out, taking a belligerent step toward Tate.

Seizing Tate's split second of inattention, Constance brought all her weight down on the cleric's instep, then flung herself away to sprawl at Alex's feet in a coil of rope. Tate lunged after her at the same instant Isaacs snapped an order to his helmsman to come about. With an infuriated howl, Tate fired and Isaacs fell, clutching his wounded leg.

The helmsman darted to help the captain, and the ship's wheel spun furiously. Sailors stampeded from every direction. The mate shrieked orders to reef the topsails, but his words were lost in the tumult. The *Argonaut*'s billowing white sails filled the sky. Snarling like a jackal, Tate pointed the pistol at Constance. Alex slung the rope at him. Ducking, Tate fought off the tangles with a blasphemous curse.

The *Argonaut* thundered straight at them. Oblivious in his rage, Tate raised the gun again.

Time stood still. It was as if for Constance the world had stopped at that instant. She saw Tate's finger squeezing the trigger. She examined the distance between the two ships. She studied the oaken railing that separated them from the frothy-topped waves of the green ocean swirling below. With all the time in the universe telescoped in that split second, Constance had sufficient time to weigh a course of action. She didn't think twice.

Grabbing Alex's hand, she shoved him toward the railing, tumbling him over the waist-high bar with an excess of desperate strength. "Jump, Grandpa!"

The old man pitched headfirst over the side, disappearing into a whitecapped comber. In that in-

stant, Constance heard the hammer of Tate's pistol
fall, sensed the pressure of the explosion, and felt
herself tumble over the side after her grandfather.

"Brace yourselves!"

Dylan's shouted warning hardly registered before
the *Argonaut* slammed into the *Odyssey*'s stern port
quarter. The collision shattered the *Argonaut*'s bowsprit and threw everyone to the decks.

Lock clawed himself to his feet as the *Argonaut*
tore off the *Odyssey*'s rudder and swept on past.
Dylan and his mate barked orders: come about; reef
the mainsails; strike the studding sails; check for injuries, damage control!

The *Odyssey* listed to port and immediately began
taking on water from the huge tear in her keel. Seamen poured out of the holds like ants, and mates
tore frantically at the gig and lifeboats strapped to
the cabin roofs. Others bypassed that altogether and
dove off the canted railings into the teeming ocean.
Watching the *Odyssey* tilt at an increasingly ominous angle, Lock felt as if he had murdered his own
child.

Then a new fear clogged his throat. Choking on
his own bile, he managed a shout: "Man the lifeboats!"

Now that he'd committed this desperate act on
his own creation, *where was Constance?*

The water was surprisingly warm.

A portion of Constance's mind suggested this
was merely a finger of the Gulf Stream, but the sensation recalled a childhood memory of swimming in
the warm blue Pacific waters. She hadn't been
afraid then. As the weight of her skirts dragged her
deeper and deeper, she made another startling discovery.

She wasn't afraid now, either.

With that thought came power and calm. By not

fighting, by letting the water's buoyancy help, she stripped down to her chemise and pantalettes. Released of the constrictions of clothes, she glided easily to the surface. Bobbing to the top, she saw Alex not six feet away, splatting the foamy waves desperately with his open hands in an effort to stay afloat. Diving like a porpoise, she came up beside him.

"Grandpa, I've got you." She urged him out of his jacket and shoes while kicking off her own and, helping him float on his back, began towing him well away from the doomed *Odyssey*. "We'll be fine."

"Look, girl," Alex gasped, pointing over the crests behind them. "She's going down."

Constance managed a quick glance over her shoulder just as another wave tossed them to its peak. "My God, it's Uncle Cyrus!"

The pale figure stood at the railing, hands upraised to Heaven, exhorting the sky in a pantomime of prayer. He made no move to join the crew now safely in lifeboats, and in the next moment the *Odyssey* gave a mighty groan, rolled, and capsized, and the Reverend Cyrus Tate disappeared from sight, a victim of the element he'd tried to use to end Constance's life so many years before.

Huge bubbles roiled and boiled to the surface, along with boxes of cargo, marine equipment, pots and pans and tools and clothes and flotsam of all kinds, a legacy that would be salvaged by the flotilla of small boats and dinghies hurrying toward them from shore. But there was nothing else left of the *Odyssey* save the men in the lifeboats.

Constance found she couldn't feel anything for the demise of Cyrus Tate, not sorrow, not joy, not even relief. But the loss of the *Odyssey* pierced her with pain for Lock. Treading desperately, struggling with her rapidly tiring grandfather, Constance looked around for the *Argonaut*.

What she saw was a white-painted lifeboat cut-

ting through the waves toward them. A dark archangel stood in the prow, and as he lifted her from
the ocean's covetous embrace, the love in his eyes
proved she was not the only one who was saved.

Much later, waiting barefoot on a sandy strip of
beach dotted with flotsam, wrapped in a scratchy
blanket, and holding one of the steaming tin mugs
of tea pressed upon her and Alex by a helpful matron, Constance watched her husband walk at the
water's edge. Sailors and boats and dinghies spread
up and down the beach, and groups of kindly in-
habitants of this stretch of New York coastline min-
istered to the survivors. Luckily, there had been
only one fatality of the Great Race.

They'd already begun calling it that, this contest
that was the stuff of which sailing legends were
made. A great romance of the sea, with villains and
heroes and feuds and mythic accomplishments and
fabled tragedies. With a murmur, Constance passed
her cup to her grandfather and stumbled down the
incline to stand at Lock's elbow. He pressed his index finger to his upper lip in that familiar gesture of
deep contemplation. She followed his gaze out
across the ocean, oblivious of her lack of vertigo because the painful sight before her crowded out everything else.

"Oh, Lock, I can't bear it," she whispered.

"Princess." Lock caught her close to his side. Her
arms went around his waist and her cheek pressed
against his chest, so that she felt as much as heard
the low rumble of his chuckle. "You are the
damnedest woman I ever saw for going about in
your underwear. Couldn't they find you a bigger
blanket?"

"Don't joke. She's not going to make it, is she?"

"No. Her hull's sprung."

Constance raised her head, and tears glittered on
her lashes. "Your beautiful *Argonaut*."

A mile or better from shore, only half of the highest royal masts were still visible over the horizon as the *Argonaut* settled to her watery grave. The last of the lifeboats rowed toward the beach, oars glinting in the sunshine. Lock's voice was emotionless as he ruminated out loud.

"I must try to calculate the force it took to do that. I wonder how many knots we were making when we collided with the *Odyssey*. The naval archives might find the lesson salutary. I'll have to prepare a paper . . ."

Constance trembled with the force of her regret and her sorrow. "They're both gone, because of me. All your work ruined, and the business . . . I'm so sorry. I—"

"Connie, don't." He smoothed back the wild mass of her salt-dried hair and kissed her tenderly. "You're safe, and by the grace of God you have your memory again. If you're searching for someone to blame, blame me for being too stubborn to give up a feud that helped no one, and for not having enough faith to believe in your feelings or my own."

"I don't want to blame anyone," she murmured, her lower lip trembling, "but with three McKin Brothers ships lost, it's hard not to feel responsible."

"Listen to me." He turned her, holding her shoulders firmly between his big, skillful hands while waves lapped about their ankles. "I was always afraid of ending up like my father—a laughingstock, ridiculed as a failure, a bankrupt. Well, I suppose they can say all that about me now, so the worst has finally happened. And do you know what?"

She shook her head, swallowing a thickening in her throat that threatened to choke her.

His mouth tilted wryly. "It's not so bad. I'm not saying things will be easy from now on, but we'll make it, because the only thing I couldn't have borne was losing you. I love you, princess."

She blinked back tears as a soul-deep happiness spread its warmth through her. "Lauchlan . . ."

"The Iron Man hadn't an inkling about what's really worth fighting for until you came to melt the ice in his soul with your spirit and fire and love." Lock touched her cheek, and his expression was open with honest emotion. "I'm no good at saying how I feel, Constance, but I need you so damned much."

Her lips quivered, and she threw her arms around his neck, enveloping them both in the scratchy blanket. Her voice was husky from the overflowing fullness in her heart. "You say it just fine. And I need you just as badly."

"You've endured so much," he murmured, pressing her close, nuzzling her temple as if he could never get enough of her. "When I think of what Tate did—"

"Shh." She pressed her fingertips to his lips, relishing the freedom his love gave her to take that liberty. "It's over. I won't feel helpless ever again, because you made me see I wasn't to blame for his cruelty. You gave me your strength when I had none of my own and made me whole again, and I love you best for that."

Lock's mouth covered hers and sealed the covenant of love and caring, two hearts sharing the promise of eternal passion with a commitment forged by fire. When Lock lifted his head again, he tucked Constance next to his heart, and they turned as one to watch the lifeboats come ashore.

One of the first men to splash through the surf bore his arm in a sling.

"God, I'm sorry, Lock." Dylan's dark hair fell over his forehead, and his expression was defeated. "We couldn't save her. The *Argonaut* was one in a million, and it killed me to order us to abandon ship."

"Not your fault. It was my choice." Lock pulled Constance tighter against his side. "And the prize was well worth it."

Dylan gave a lopsided grin and took Constance's hand. "Indeed, a sister is a most precious gift from the sea."

"You know?" Constance asked softly.

"Lock told me."

Constance gave her husband a loving glance, then squeezed Dylan's fingers. "Can you believe it?"

"How could he not?" Swathed in his own blanket, Alex Latham shuffled up beside the trio. His sharp brown eyes inspected Dylan from head to toe. "Aye, you've the look of my James, God rest him, if saying so doesn't displease you."

"It may take some getting used to," Dylan answered dryly.

"Grandpa—" Uncertain, Constance glanced between Lock and Dylan.

"I hope—" Alex began, then broke off as emotion made his voice overly gruff. Clearing his throat, he tried again. "I've a debt of gratitude to both you men this day. You saved my life and my Constance, at a great price. Let an old, foolish man be the first to say it's time to put the mistakes of the past behind us. We've all taken losses, but perhaps the Lathams and the McKins can salvage something more important this day than mere vengeance."

"I'd like nothing better," Lock said simply and gave Alex his hand. "Constance's happiness means as much to me as my own, and I've learned well how important her family is to her."

Alex turned to Dylan with a diffident air. "It would give me great pleasure to know a grandson as well as a granddaughter."

Dylan nodded slowly, the fatigue leaving his face

as a roguish smile creased his cheeks. "Aye, sir. I daresay you're in for a rare treat at that."

"Dylan!" Constance admonished, then laughed softly as she saw an answering twitch on Alex's lips. Standing in the safe harbor of Lock's embrace, Constance gravely took Alex's hand and joined it with Dylan's, holding them both between her own.

Solemnly, but at peace at last, a family watched the last of the *Argonaut* disappear beneath the silent waves.

Epilogue

〜〜〜〜〜

"**C**ome back here this minute, young man!"

The brown-eyed toddler wearing a perky straw boater and knee britches sent his harried mother a dazzling smile, then dashed through the well-dressed spectators crowding Long Wharf as fast as his chubby legs could carry him.

"Lock!" Exasperated with her firstborn, Constance Latham McKin appealed to his father for aid.

The tall shipbuilder, conversing with a group of investors attending the send-off of the latest Latham, McKin and Company's creation on her maiden voyage, looked up at his wife's call, and his lips twitched at her predicament. With a quick word to his companions, he set out in hot pursuit, chasing the lad down with absolutely no thought to dignity.

Within a few strides, Lock caught up with the runaway, grabbing the boy under the arms with a roar, then tossing him high into the cloudless sky. Legs still churning madly, the toddler shrieked with delight, well pleased with his favorite game. Grinning, Lock sat the lad, whose black hair exactly matched his own, onto his shoulder and marched back to Constance.

She couldn't suppress a smile. The Iron Man had changed enormously in the three years since the loss of the *Odyssey* and the *Argonaut*. Before, he would never have thought of tussling with his son in public, nor would he have dreamed of showing his obvious pride, delight, and love in such an open fashion.

She'd done that for him, Constance thought with satisfaction. She held onto her stylish bonnet as the balmy breeze made the shrouds and sails of the many ships lined up along the wharf sing and vibrate with their own peculiar melody. Though Lock was still the same determined, ambitious visionary when it came to clipper ships, he was the fondest of fathers and the most loving of husbands, a man courageous enough to share his deepest feelings with the ones he loved.

Not that it hadn't been a struggle. Even with Alex's financial support and the resurrection of the Latham and McKin partnership, the shipyard had been through austere times. But there were still plenty of merchants eager to add the world's fastest ships to their fleets, and Lock's innate genius for design and the almost mythical stories making the rounds about the Great Race had proved a potent combination for attracting commissions. So much so, in fact, that Lock had finally felt secure enough this past year to build another "perfect ship," a vessel he'd dreamed into life incorporating what he'd learned from the Great Race, thus transforming a moment of defeat into a victory in inimitable McKin fashion.

"Whew!" Lock joined Constance, bouncing the giggling child on his shoulder. "What a little hooligan you are, my lad! Tell your mother you're sorry for running away."

Chewing on one plump finger, the boy gave his long-suffering mother a totally charming cherub's smile. Removing the soggy finger, he pointed at the majestic, tall ship gleaming with black paint and new varnish moving slowly out to sea. "Dee!"

"Yes, dear," Constance said. "Wave good-bye to Uncle Dylan."

Insistent, he pointed at the sleekly elegant vessel again, his McKin jaw jutting in the determined manner of his father. "Go . . . Dee!"

Lock laughed indulgently. "Not this trip, sailor. Someday soon."

The boy's expression promptly clouded, and his lower lip trembled threateningly.

"Lock, don't give him ideas! He's got plenty of his own," Constance scolded, reaching for her son. She cuddled him close, adjusting his boater hat with its floating navy ribbons. It was just like the one Lock himself had worn the day of the *Silver Crest's* launching so many years earlier. "Besides, he's just a baby!"

"And no mother relishes the thought of seeing her fledgling striking out into the world on his own," he guessed. Smiling, he chucked her under the chin. "Make no mistake about it, my love, he's got ships in his blood already. One day he'll take to the sea despite you."

"You're a brute, Lock McKin, to make it so clear, especially today when I'm missing Dylan already!"

"You'd trust no one else to see to your wishes for Lahaina."

She sighed. "You're right. As a regent, he has no parallel."

"You know, it's still a bit of a shock to me when I realize I've married royalty, and a sugar heiress at that."

"I'm simply grateful that between Grandpa's business acumen and Latham, McKin and Company's transport, my people can at last enjoy the fruits of their labors. The villagers' lives have improved so much."

"It's very generous of you to return the profits of the sugar harvest to your subjects."

"I was not the only one who suffered under Cyrus Tate's heavy hand," she returned softly. "And democracy is the way of my new homeland. I know

Dylan will see that everyone receives an equitable share, but I do miss him dearly when he's gone."

Lock followed her gaze to the departing clipper. "Aye, but you've never seen him happier, have you?"

She shook her head ruefully. "Eager to test the mettle of a spanking new ship? No, I daresay Dylan thinks this is better than Christmas!"

"Go Dee!" came another tearful demand.

"Here, sweetheart." Constance plucked an intricately carved model ship from her reticule. "Look what Jedediah's made for you."

That diverted him for a moment, and he took the toy and studied it with one finger in his mouth, in a pose so like his father's habitual stance that Constance's heart melted with love for both of them. Then he saw something even more interesting, wiggled out of her arms, and flung himself at the old gentleman approaching them with a glad shout of recognition.

"Hello, my boy! Come talk to your grandpa."

Alex Latham, vigorous and hale in semiretirement, paused to lean on his ivory-headed cane and have a discussion about peppermints and pockets with his great-grandson. Never had there been such a case of instant adoration between young and old as with these two.

Transactions complete, Alex took the toddler's hand and winked at Constance. "We'll go have a chat with your papa's new foreman and give Mama a rest."

"Thank you, Grandpa," Constance said in relief, and waved down the dock at Maggie Maddock. Maggie returned the wave, beaming proudly at her newly promoted husband's side while Tip tugged at his unaccustomed neckcloth and tried not to look too uncomfortable.

Lock tucked Constance's hand into the crook of his arm and gazed fondly after the small boy and the old man. "That little rapscallion becomes more like you every day, princess. Willful and contrary—"

Strolling down the dock at his side, she took instant affront. "Thank you very much, I'm sure!"

"—and utterly lovable," Lock hastened to add, chuckling.

Constance's lips twitched. "Thank heaven our son is generally a sweet-tempered child, despite that streak of McKin stubbornness you gave him."

"It's a combination that should make life quite interesting for some time to come," Lock predicted. "I'll take him up to Skye for a few days so you may finish your latest commission in peace."

"You're not the only one who's completed a piece of work this day, Lock McKin," she said with a laugh. "My ship's portraits have kept me so engaged these past months, I'm determined to refuse the next one so that I may sail to Skye with you and paint wildflowers for a change!"

"A fine plan. I'm proud of your artistic success, but I would not be adverse to a few days of your undivided attention."

Constance smiled coyly at her husband from beneath her lashes, and a delicate, peachy tide washed her cheeks. "Then perhaps we'd best leave the lad at home."

Lock's gaze heated with the promise behind that smile. "Perhaps we should. The boy can wreak more havoc on his parents' plans than a typhoon. Sure you want another?"

"Actually," she said in a careful voice, "it's a bit late to worry about that now."

For a moment the Iron Man looked totally disconcerted. "You mean—? Again? Connie!"

He swept her into his arms and kissed her thoroughly right there on the wharf in full sight of everyone. When he raised his head again, his smile stretched from ear to ear. "God, I love you."

Trembling just a little with joy, she tenderly touched his cheek. "It shows." Then she laughed. "Just as I will before long."

Lock ran his hands over her shoulders as though he could not believe his good fortune. "Now I really wish you'd let me call the ship *Princess Lili*."

Constance's glance darted again to the departing vessel. The brightly painted legend on the stern shone in the sun: *James Latham*. She shook her head, secure in their choice. "No, it's perfect the way it is."

"Jamie will think we named this ship after him and not his grandfather," Lock warned. "Especially when Dylan breaks every speed record on the books."

"Jamie McKin will simply have to learn a proper modesty—as will his father," she said with a proud twinkle. "However, when a man dreams the perfect ship into being, and earns a lasting name for himself, I suppose one can make allowances."

Lock placed his arm around her shoulder and held her next to his heart, the place where she would always belong. "No more bad dreams, my love."

"No." Lifting her face for his kiss, she knew it was true. "Only good ones, now and forever."

Avon Romantic Treasures

*Unforgettable, enthralling love stories,
sparkling with passion and adventure
from Romance's bestselling authors*

ONLY IN YOUR ARMS *by Lisa Kleypas*
76150-5/$4.50 US/$5.50 Can

LADY LEGEND *by Deborah Camp*
76735-X/$4.50 US/$5.50 Can

RAINBOWS AND RAPTURE *by Rebecca Paisley*
76565-9/$4.50 US/$5.50 Can

AWAKEN MY FIRE *by Jennifer Horsman*
76701-5/$4.50 US/$5.50 Can

ONLY BY YOUR TOUCH *by Stella Cameron*
76606-X/$4.50 US/$5.50 Can

FIRE AT MIDNIGHT *by Barbara Dawson Smith*
76275-7/$4.50 US/$5.50 Can

ONLY WITH YOUR LOVE *by Lisa Kleypas*
76151-3/$4.50 US/$5.50 Can

MY WILD ROSE *by Deborah Camp*
76738-4/$4.50 US/$5.50 Can

Avon Romances—
the best in exceptional authors and unforgettable novels!

America Loves Lindsey!

The Timeless Romances
of #1 Bestselling Author

Johanna Lindsey

PRISONER OF MY DESIRE   75627-7/$5.99 US/$6.99 Can
Spirited Rowena Belleme *must* produce an heir, and the magnificent Warrick deChaville is the perfect choice to sire her child—though it means imprisoning the handsome knight.

ONCE A PRINCESS   75625-0/$5.95 US/$6.95 Can
From a far off land, a bold and brazen prince came to America to claim his promised bride. But the spirited vixen spurned his affections while inflaming his royal blood with passion's fire.

GENTLE ROGUE   75302-2/$5.50 US/$6.50 Can
On the high seas, the irrepressible rake Captain James Malory is bested by a high-spirited beauty whose love of freedom and adventure rivaled his own.

WARRIOR'S WOMAN   75301-4/$4.95 US/$5.95 Can

MAN OF MY DREAMS   75626-9/$5.00 US/$6.99 Can

Coming Soon

ANGEL   75628-5/$5.99 US/$6.99 Can

America Loves Lindsey!

The Timeless Romances
of #1 Bestselling Author

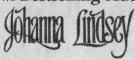

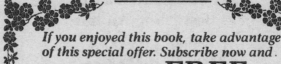